MOONLIGHT BETWEEN THE CROSSFIRE

BEING THE SECOND PART OF

THE MIDDLETON SAGA

BY
RICHARD BROOK

Cover Photo by Grant Hyatt
Instagram: @grant_hyatt

ISBN: 978-1-9997381-3-6

First Edition 2024

To my late Father, David.

I cannot express the depth of sadness I feel that we did not have a little more time together. Yet I am glad that after what I can only imagine was twelve years of torment, trapped in a body with an active mind but robbed of the ability to vocalise your thoughts, you were finally granted peace.

I will always be grateful for you unwavering support, guidance and zest for life.

I had hoped you would still be here to enjoy the second instalment as much as you did the first, alas that was not to be.

Take care Old Boy, we will meet again.

Contents

ACKNOWLEDGEMENTS

Many thanks to family and friends for their continued support and input.

Special thanks to Joe Barnes for his non-stop enthusiasm for the series and to Josh MacNab for lending me his ear from time to time over the final eighteen months before publication.

I can honestly say that without them this book wouldn't even exist, such is the depth of emotion and connection the whole series holds for me to my late Father. Upon his death I almost threw it out, along with any prospects for the books still to come. And it was really because of Joe, Josh and a few others that my hand was stayed.

I began writing this series for my Father as a way of maintaining a deeper connection with him than the one I found myself faced with after he suffered a series of catastrophic strokes and also as a way to process my own personal feelings on those events.

This is the second in the series and was finished apart from a bit of proofing and editing, while he was still alive. So when he suddenly passed away there was a moment when I considered just discarding it; such was the void and oblivion at the time I felt surrounded by.

So all I can say to all those that helped to keep me on track is thank you. It will of course always be a far better tribute to his memory for this work to be and I truly hope you will all enjoy it.

MOONLIGHT BETWEEN THE CROSSFIRE

BEING THE SECOND PART OF

THE MIDDLETON SAGA

Chapter One: Final Acts

The xenon headlights of the car fast approaching the gate almost blinded the guards at their posts. They straightened and steeled themselves for whatever was coming. The last six weeks at Glympton had been tumultuous; Lord Norwood had left, with Chamberlain and a few others, in such a turbulent rage without so much as a word to anybody else as to where they were going or when they expected to be back that everybody had been on edge ever since. It was very uncharacteristic of his lordship to leave for such a long period of time without so much as a bye or leave. Whatever it had been to not only cause such great indignation but also to detain him for such a period must have been something very grave indeed.

The car came to an abrupt halt ten meters short of their position, and as difficult as it was to see past the dazzling beams, the guards could just make out the silhouettes of two men exiting the vehicle. Their sweaty grips tightened around their flashlights, furtively glancing at one another as the two shadowy figures began to approach the gatehouse.

'H-halt, identification, please.' One of the pair stammered, his apprehension catching the flow of words in the back of his throat.

'Don't be absurd, open the ruddy gate. Now!' The familiar commanding voice of Lord Norwood bellowed, shattering the tension.

'O-of course, S-sir. Sorry Sir. Didn't recognise you.' The apologetic guard submissively replied.

'Just get on with it. And fetch me the keys for the Jeep.' Lord Norwood demanded, referring to the four by four stationed at the gatehouse for the security teams to patrol the estate's extensive grounds surrounding the main house.

'Home at last, nice to have both feet on dry land again.' Norwood commented as he jumped into the passenger seat. 'Don't think I'll be travelling by trawler again anytime soon if I can help it.'

'When needs must, my lord.' Chamberlain replied.

'Yes, well I suppose the boat captain was a good as his word getting us back to the mainland. I trust you rewarded him for his efforts.'

'He won't need to clean the decks anymore.' Chamberlain replied coldly. Remembering how he'd leapt upon the unsuspecting fisherman with the speed and force of a spider springing its trap on some ill fated insect; the man had writhed, kicking and flailing his limbs, attempting to free himself from those powerful vice like arms clamped tight about him crushing his very being before his head was ducked deep into the icy salt water of the lobster holding tank until the last bubble of his breath had long since broken the surface.

'What did you do with the boat?'

'After I'd tipped half a bottle of scotch down his wasted throat, I set the boat's auto pilot and sent it back out to sea. If they do find the vessel, they will discover his leg caught in the pot lines, they'll just assume he'd had a few too many, got tangled up while he was setting his pots and got dragged over the side. Nothing to point to any foul play. With any luck the storm coming up from the south west will smash it to pieces long before it's discovered.'

'Good. We can't afford any loose ends at this point.' Norwood replied as Chamberlain pulled the jeep up outside the main house and headed straight for the study. Norwood wanted to make sure that his most recent acquisitions were safely under lock and key as soon as possible. Upon entering the study his lordship immediately sensed that the room felt different, not significantly, but there was just something about it that didn't seem to be as he'd left it.

'Jacobs!' Lord Norwood bellowed, his deep voice booming throughout the house. 'Where is that blasted man?' He added as he impatiently waited for his butler to arrive.

After what seemed like an age, his pristinely dressed valet entered mopping his creased brow. Mr Jacobs knew that for his lordship to summon him so abruptly something had displeased him greatly, he just hoped that whatever it was could be easily rectified.

'You called, my lord?'

'Has someone been in here during my absence?'

'Apart from the maids to clean, I'm not aware that anyone has been in here, my lord.'

'Then please explain to me why this draw in my desk is not fully closed, and for that matter why the picture over there is crooked?'

'I'm at a loss, my lord. Unless the maids disturbed them whilst dusting and failed to leave the room as they found it. I do not know, my lord. I can only apologise on their behalf and ensure that it does not happen in the future.'

'See that you do.'

'Is there anything else, my lord?'

'Yes, would you be so kind as to fetch some food, nothing special. We've both had a rather long day and are in need of some sustenance.'

'Certainly, my lord. Would one also like some tea?'

'Tea? Really, don't be absurd! What do you think this place is; we're not in wonderland. No, go fetch a bottle of the '52. And be quick about it, these spirits aren't going to revive themselves. Why are you still here? That's all, go.'

'Maids my arse.' Lord Norwood stated after Jacobs had left the room. 'They know better than to leave things out of place; someone else has been in here.' He added as he removed the picture in question concealing a small wall safe.

His suspicions were confirmed as soon as he opened the safe. Along with all the documents and bundles of cash, there was a small hand written note lying in wait for him.

'You are no longer in the shadows, I know all your secrets. Once I have dealt with Michael's reptilian treachery, you are next.'

Norwood smiled as he read the note. 'I don't think we'll have to worry about that anymore. Such a foolish man.'

'Who, my lord?' Chamberlain asked.

'That fool Middleton's been here. He must have decided to drop by before pursuing Michael Collins. Well he can take my secrets with him to the grave. He's gone, nothing can stand in our way now. Nevertheless, if he can get into the safe others may try to do the same. I think these parts of the *Liber Veritatis* will better off secured in the vault. We can't afford to lose them now.'

'As you wish, I can leave directly, my lord.'

'I think that would be best. Oh, and take that map with you. I would rather it was locked away until I have need of it.'

'Certainly. I'll return as quickly as I can, my lord.' Chamberlain replied as he snatched up the objects in his massive hands and left.

'Your supper, my lord.' Mr Jacobs said as he returned to the study carrying a tray of food and the bottle.

'Thank you, Jacobs. I'm afraid Chamberlain has had to depart on an errand so only one plate is required.'

'Very good, my lord.' Mr Jacobs replied. He was quite used to that sort of occurrence, so wasn't put out in the least that half of what he had just prepared would now go to waste.

'Is there anything else your lordship will require this evening?'

'No, thank you, Jacobs. Take the rest of the night off.'

'Thank you, my lord. I'll bid you good night, Sir.' Mr Jacobs said as he departed for his quarters.

'Good night, Jacobs.' Norwood replied as his valet left.

Having spent the last few weeks living rough with Chamberlain on Jersey trying to avoid the police until such time that they could make their way back to the mainland, a hot meal felt like a luxury to Norwood compared to the scraps they had been living off. He was more than pleased that they had achieved what they had set out to do. And that in the process two of their greatest thorns had been put out of action. It was a slight blow that Michael Collins had been killed when he was just starting to become useful. Needless to say, it was more than ample compensation to know that James Middleton had died in the same instant. He smiled to himself as he finished the last of his meal, leaving the tray on the desk for Jacobs to clear at a later date, he decided to wake Miss Adams. A triumphant return deserved celebrating.

Chapter Two: The Man of The Sea

Stepping out from his terraced house into the freshening winter's night breeze onto the damp pavement at the top of Belgravia Street, DI Glen Harris headed off down the road. This had become part of his new routine every Tuesday since his big case had gone sideways so quickly. He'd felt robbed at the time that the case had been closed without ever really having all the answers or for that matter being able to bring the prime suspect to justice, as James Middleton had been killed in a river accident, a few days after Glen had almost caught up with the man on the isle of Jersey. It had been such an anti-climax, so he'd sought solace in the one thing that he'd always had a passion for and that he found helped him think, music. Like so many, his parents had insisted that he learnt a musical instrument whilst he was growing up and after toying with scores of different shapes and sizes, he settled on the guitar. He was by no means the best player in the world, but he was a lot better than average. He had a pretty strong voice as well, on occasion people had commented that he had a similar style to Sammy Davies Junior.

So guitar case in hand he made the short walk down to Bread Street, where there was a great little bar nestled between the old shops and warehouses of Penzance which held a regular open mic night.

'Hey guys, how's it going? Good to see you.' Glen said to a couple of musicians, he'd got to know over the last few weeks, standing just outside the small venue having a quick drag on a cigarette before they headed into the bar.

'Not bad, how's you?' One of them replied.

'Yeah, doin' okay. You ready for some rocking music tonight? I've got a new song I've been working on. So hopefully will be good, we'll see how it goes down.' Glen commented hoping that his new piece would be warmly received.

'Nice man, looking forward to it.' The other musician replied.

'Cool, catch you guys inside, I gotta go setup.' Glen replied.

'See you in a bit.' Said the other as he took a long drag of his cigarette.

'Yeah man, see you inside.'

Glen left the two at the door and wandered in to find Soph, the local singer-songwriter who ran the night.

'Hey Soph, how's you?' Glen said catching up with her at the bar.

'Ah Glen, you came. Awesome, wasn't sure if you were going to make it this evening.' She said turning to catch his eye.

'Wouldn't miss it for the world. What's new, tell me all your secrets.' Glen said in his usual friendly manner.

'Ah not a lot, same old. Giggin', partying and then more giggin' and now here. Nice to sort of have a night off where I don't have to play to be honest and at the same time still get to feel the vibe.' She replied.

'Yeah, I can imagine, it's pretty hectic. It's busy in here tonight.' He said.

'Looks like it's gonna be a good one I think. Much better than last week. Last week was a bit too quiet really, always the same, the week that one band's busy, everybody else seems to be busy too.' She remarked.

'Yeah, was still good though, well I enjoyed it at least. Had kinda hoped that tonight would be less of a crowd, got a new tune so now the pressure's really gonna be on.' He said.

'Oh you'll be fine. If you ever decided to hang up the blue hat, you know you'd make it as a musician.' Sophie replied smiling.

'Maybe, but I think for now I'm happy to dabble. You know best of both worlds and besides I got the family as well. Not sure how much they'd appreciate all the late nights and long days. Would be hard.' He said, thinking his wife would have a few choice words for him if he suddenly announced that he was leaving the force to try and make it as a musician.

'True, is much harder than most people realise. Most only see the party side of it, they never think about the logistics, the miles and miles travelled between gigs, the endless emails and enquires, and somewhere one has to fit in learning new material. Could you imagine what would happen if you turned up to a wedding and hadn't had time to learn the first dance, nightmare. Speaking of which, you've been working on some new material haven't you?'

'Ah, you'll have to wait and see. I'm not giving away all my secrets.' He replied with a friendly laugh.

'Such a tease. When do you fancy going on?' She asked.

'Oh whenever, really. I'm easy, just go with the flow, you know. Maybe I'll grab a beer, listen to a couple, and then go from there. Sound okay?' He replied.

'Yeah, man. That's fine, you know it's pretty chilled here.' She said.

'For sure, wouldn't be the same if it wasn't. All about the music, good vibes, relaxed chat and chill, just what I like. You wanna drink?' He asked.

'Sure a coffee, would be great.' She replied

'Drivin' huh.' He remarked.

'Yeah, unfortunately got all this gear to cart around. Haven't quite made it to the point where other people do that for me.' She laughed. 'One day.'

'Like it, good attitude. Any particular coffee?' Glen replied with a smile

'An espresso would be great. Thanks.'

'Hey, no worries. Can I get two espressos please?' Glen said turning to the guy behind the bar.

'Sugar?' The barman asked.

'Yeah, please. Thanks man.' Glen replied.

'I though you said you were gonna have a beer?' Sophie said.

'Well, I will later. But when you mentioned espresso I changed my mind. They do a really good one here.' Glen replied as he dropped a lump of brown into the rich darkness.

'I just gotta go set this guy up and then I'll be back.' Soph said as the first act of the evening sauntered up to them.

'Sure, you go do your thing. I'm not going anywhere.' He replied settling onto a high stool at the bar.

Glen had almost finished his espresso by the time Soph returned.

'I hope there are some better acts than this one tonight. Otherwise everybody's gonna leave.' Soph said as she necked the hot shot. 'He's got such bad rhythm.'

'He just needs more practice, he'll get there.' Glen replied.

'Not sure about that, he's been like this for weeks. I just can't say no, it's open mic after all, so anybody can play.' She said.

'Well you gotta give him credit for giving it a go. It's hard when you know there are better people out there, and you stand up in front of a room full of people and play.' Glen replied remembering all those mixed thoughts of self doubt, excitement and nervous trepidation the first time he stood up on stage.

'Yeah, I suppose, still I wish he'd go do it somewhere else.' She said with a sigh.

'It'll be fine, look Stevie's turned up and she's rockin'. Hell of a good musician.' Glen replied, nodding to the girl who'd just walked through the door.

'Ah sweet, for sure. People'll hang around for her. Right, gotta go introduce the next act.' She said walking back to the mixing desk. 'Let's give it up for Shaun everybody.' She said over the mic. 'Okay, so next up we've got Jake, lets give it up for Jake, everybody.' She said. As the applause died down and another guitarist picked up, firing out some generic pop with the aid of a looper.

'He's not bad.' Glen said as Soph returned.

'Who, Jake. Yeah, he's great, bit of a one man band type. But, yeah. Got a good voice and he plays the new stuff that people like to listen to.'

'Can I get a beer, man? Thanks.' Glen asked the barman briefly turning his attention away from Soph and the music. 'You want one?'

'I'm okay for a bit, thanks. I might sneak one a bit later. You happy to go next?' She asked.

'Oh go on, you've twisted my arm.' He replied. 'If I get it over early people will've forgotten how bad it was by the end.' He joked.

'Yeah right, like it's gonna be bad.' She replied with a smile as Jake started his final track.

'You got your cajon here?' Glen asked.

'Course, you want someone to give you a beat? I can ask Stevie, she's pretty bitchin' on the box.'

'That would be sweet.' Glen replied, taking a sip of his beer. 'Right better get my guitar set up. Sure people don't wanna wait for me to tune it.' He added, plucking his guitar from its sleek black case and began to twist the knobs, watching the tuner gradually turn from orange to green as he strummed his thumb against each string.

'Okay, think Jake is about to finish.' Soph said as she went back to the desk. 'Give it up for Jake everybody. Okay Glen's gonna give us a few tunes.' She added as Glen took to the stage.

'Hey guys, how's everybody doing tonight? Okay so I'm gonna play a bit of as mix this evening. Hope you enjoy it.' Glen said just before he started to play his version of *'Happy'*. And for the first time in a week he left his worries behind.

Part way through his set Glen felt his phone begin to vibrate in his pocket, but he couldn't stop playing so whoever was calling would just have to wait. Stevie joined him for his second song, a lively rendition of *'I got a woman'*, and again his phone began to vibrate in his pocket, deciding that it might be his wife calling Glen waved Soph over. 'Sorry, Soph can you take over for a bit, I think the better half is trying to call me.'

'Sure, no worries.' She replied. 'As long as your coming back, right?' She replied.

'I'll do my best.' He said as he left the stage, pulling out his phone to see who had been trying to contact him. It wasn't his wife, in fact he didn't recognise the number. Now wondering who would be trying to get hold of him at that time of night he hit the call back button and waited for someone to answer.

'Hello, Carline speaking.' The voice at the other end of the phone said. For a second Glen tried to rack his brains, the name sounded vaguely familiar but just at that moment he couldn't place it.

'Hi, it's Glen Harris. You just tried to call me.' Glen replied hoping that things would become clearer.

'Ah great, hi Glen. It's DCI Carline. Sorry for the late call, but I have some information that I didn't think could wait.' The man said, as the penny finally dropped in Glen's mind.

'Oh hey, no worries at all.' Glen replied as his heart began to race as a torrent of questions and hopes began to crash through his mind. 'What's up?'

'There's been a development, which might be nothing but I felt you should know. A fishing trawler, that was registered in Jersey, has been picked up by a lifeboat crew in the channel. The captain appears to have drowned accidentally, but there are certain aspects that don't seem to correspond to information we have.' Carline explained.

'Okay, I'm intrigued, but how does this fit in with a case that was closed weeks ago?' Glen asked, as he tried to keep his flood of questions under control.

'Only your part of the case revolving around the murder of Jack St Aubyn was closed, the connected robbery at our end is still very much open as we have not caught the perpetrators yet. And this could still turn into a murder investigation depending on whether Professor Middleton pulls through his coma or not. So, as I currently understand the incident, the captain appears to have been intoxicated while he was laying some lobster pots, it seems as though he got caught up in the lines and was dragged over the side with the pots and failed to pull himself back on board, and as the boat was under power he was dragged by the boat and drowned. The problem I have is that he was a renowned teetotal and would never have touched a drop of alcohol. Also from the reports I have from speaking to people down at the harbour he was accompanied by two men when he set out from St. Helier. Yet when the boat was found, there was no trace of either men on board. To me the whole thing looks staged.'

'What course was the boat on when it was discovered?' Glen asked interrupting the DCI.

'Well that's the strange thing. The auto pilot had been set on a course which would have taken the boat straight out into the channel and into the path of a storm. It was only by chance that the storm had veered away from the vessel, otherwise it is highly likely that it would have been totally destroyed and most likely never found. But taking a back bearing of the course and allowing for a bit of tidal drift, the reverse course would take you straight into Weymouth and Portland which is way out of his normal operating area. But would be perfect to drop people off onto the mainland. It's early days so I'll have to wait for the Marine Accident Investigation Branch (MAIB), to finish their report, but I'm of the opinion that the two men were dropped off on the mainland. My suspicion is that these may have been the perpetrators of the attempted armed robbery at Noirmont, and that having evaded capture on Jersey they commandeered the vessel and used it to return to the mainland before killing the captain and staging the accident, programming the autopilot to take the vessel into the predicted path of the storm in order to destroy the evidence. Obviously it's only a theory at this point but it would fit the facts as they currently stand. What do you think?'

'Hmmm, it's a bit of a long shot. But I can see what you are saying. How can I help? Weymouth isn't part of my jurisdiction.'

'Let me sort that out, I have a few strings I can pull. I'm going to get MAIB to pull prints and then I'll compare them to all the one's I have from Noirmont, if they match then we have a starting point. I've got to work the case from the island, but could really do with someone I trust that's familiar with the case and the mainland, hence why you were my first point of call.' Carline said.

'Count me in, send me what you've got so far.' Glen said as his heart leapt at the chance to reopen the biggest case he'd ever worked on. 'And thanks, Carline. I knew there was more to this case.'

'Don't mention it, more than welcome. I'll be in touch.' Carline replied before hanging up.

Glen's head was spinning as he re-entered the bar, there were so many new avenues suddenly lying in from of him not to mention a host of fresh questions to explore. One thing was certain, the music was going to have to be put on pause.

'Soph, I'm really sorry but I'm going to have to bail, something's come up.' Glen said to her as she looked up from behind the mixing desk.

'Ah shame, you never got to play that new song you've been working on.' She replied with a sigh.

'Yeah, I know. Sorry. Maybe next time.' Glen said.

'For sure, take care, Hun. Hope you're not going into work now.'

'Unfortunately, duty calls. No rest for the wicked.' He replied picking up his guitar case and hastily making his way back home.

'Hey Hun.' He called up the stairs as he entered.

'Oh hi Sweetie, your home early. I hadn't expected you to finish playing yet.' His wife replied as he dropped his guitar in the hallway.

'I know, something's come up. I'm going to have to go into the station.'

'Really, at this time of night. You promised you were gonna stay in after your set.'

'I know, sorry. This can't wait. There's been a development in that Marazion case I'd been working on.' He replied.

'I thought that case had been closed?' His wife remarked.

'It had, there's been a development in Jersey.'

'Oh Honey, that's not even in your jurisdiction. Why are you getting involved? I know you put a lot of time and effort into it, but if you get sucked back in, you'll have to go through all that all over again. And what about us, don't forget about your family. This has an effect on us as well, you know. It was hard enough the last time when you spent almost every waking hour away from home. You missed your son's first steps, what will you miss this time? His birthday? I know what you're like. Can't you just let someone else handle it?' The frustration of her tone cutting through the room.

'I'm sorry, I just can't. I have questions and I need answers.' He replied.

'Can we at least discus this before you go galavanting off across the country. You hardly see your son as it is. If you reopen this investigation you'll never see him.' She fired back.

'I'm sorry Hun, I gotta go, we'll talk about this later.' He said grabbing his overcoat and leaving his wife to stew, knowing full well that when he did finally returned he'd get both barrels full in the face.

Chapter Three: Reading between The Lines

The storm clouds were as black as the wrought iron gates of Noirmont when the recovery truck arrived conveying the driverless AC Cobra back to its home. The rough growl of the lorry's heavy diesel engine cutting through the roaring wind as it pulled up in front of the house caused Chris to leave the pile of papers in the study and step out into the miserable weather to investigate the new arrival.

He had been expecting this day to come, and yet he was still unprepared for the surge of raw emotion that welled up as he saw the unoccupied lifeless carcass lying atop the steel flatbed. Helping the driver to offload the car into the garage, and slowly dragging the tarp across the sleek lines, he began to feel a sense of closure over the recent events, leaving it in the peaceful stillness of its customary resting place. Deep down in his heart there was still the faintest glimmer of hope that he may yet see his old friend again. Only Michael's battered body had been pulled from the wild river, and although even he knew the likelihood that anybody had managed to survive those treacherous currents were very long odds indeed. He hoped that James might have somehow defied the spread.

The rescue teams had called off the search for James after two weeks and the inquest that followed a few weeks later into the accident had concluded that both men had died due to misadventure.

Certainly questions had been raised about Michael's broken neck, however the raging river had been so vicious that there wasn't any evidence to suggest that it had not been caused by the snake like currents smashing the body into the boulders and bedrock as it raced through the countryside.

Legally without a body the inquest could not actually declare James dead, nevertheless in the minds of all those present it was the most realistic scenario.

All at Noirmont had been deeply saddened when they had first heard the news, but in retrospect they weren't really surprised. They had known full well when James had left that he would ensure he took his vengeance; no matter what that would entail and regardless of what the outcome or cost would be.

It was an unfortunate setback for the *Order of Pepin*, at such an important juncture when they really need to regroup. Faced not only with having to recover two parts of the *Liber Veritatis* from the clutches of Lord Norwood, they also had to tackle the cryptic passage written by the now comatose Professor Middleton, containing a clue to the next piece of the codex. The absolute last thing they had needed was to have lost their playmaker.

Chris knew that James would have wanted him to step up and continue along the path that they had all embarked upon. His greatest worry was that he would not be able to fill the void. Chris saw James as the talisman; the glue that held the group together and without him there was a real danger that it would fracture and fall apart. He would have to put everything behind him and dig deep to keep moving forward.

The one and seemingly only consolation to arise out of the tragedy was that the police, and in particular DI Harris, had lost interest in their affairs. With the sudden demise of James, DI Harris had lost his lone suspect in regards to the death of Jack St Aubyn and with much reluctance, the young detective had been forced to shelve the unsolved case for the foreseeable future. Thus leaving *The Order* free to operate without constantly having to outmanoeuvre the enterprising sleuth.

Returning to the main house Chris blocked out the turmoil of thoughts running through his head and putting on a brave face; closed the door on the past. Stepping into the warmth of Professor Middleton's study to find Devan deep in contemplation surrounded by the now customary sea of books.

'You're not still working on that note are you?' He asked.

'I'm sure there's something to it. I just can't see the wood for the trees at the moment. You know when there's something as plain as the nose on your face but at the same time just out of sight. It's like that.' Devan replied, as she flicked over a page.

'If you say so, I can't help but think it's just the ramblings of a man delirious from blood loss.' Chris remarked.

'Oh no, I don't think so. There's definitely something here. It's far too meticulous to have been mere ramblings. I think the professor knew exactly what he was doing when he wrote this.

Unfortunately at the moment his thought process is eluding me, hence all the notebooks. I'm hoping that by reading these I might get a glimpse of his intricacies. Then I may have a chance of figuring out what he was trying to tell us. I just need time.' She replied, vainly trying to convince herself that she was on the right track.

'Good luck with that. You've got a far better chance than me. I remember playing Go with him. Never could work out his tactics until it was too late to do anything about it. He always played the long game, kept you guessing right until the very last move. A true master in subterfuge and misdirection.' He replied before adding, 'But I'm sure if anybody can work it out, you can.'

'Thanks, first thing is to work out his notes. He does seem to like using cyphers, at least half of these notes seem to be written in a variety of different codes. He's even done one like Da Vinci, in mirror script. How he managed to keep track of it all is truly astonishing. Definitely going to be an uphill battle.' She said, turning over another page.

'Ha, that's so typical of him. Have fun, I don't envy you in the slightest.' He replied.

'Have you had any thoughts on how to retrieve the books from Lord Norwood?' Devan asked as she looked up from the notebook.

'Not yet, going to have to consult Gaz and Ollie. I'm sure by now Glympton will be an absolute fortress, if the books are even there. Norwood may have decided it would be prudent to house them elsewhere. I know that's what I would do. May have to reach out and wake up some of the more covert members of *The Order*, so you may well see a few unfamiliar faces around here quite soon. Speaking of Gaz and Ollie, where are the troublesome duo at the moment?' He asked wondering where the two had got to.

'Last time I saw them they were out the back concocting something or other.' She replied.

'That doesn't sound good, knowing them. Always was the problem when they've been sitting around for too long. They tend to start messing around with past projects that never quite worked the way they had intended. I better go check on them before they blow the house up. It's not a laughing matter.' He added as he glimpsed a bemused smile spread across Devan's face. 'I'm not joking; it's happened before. And I would prefer to keep this particular property intact for when the professor recovers.' He said.

'Aren't you being a bit optimistic? From what I understand his condition seems to be pretty permanent.' Devan replied.

'I have faith, I think he might surprise you. He's always been a fighter. Either way, I'd prefer to still have a roof to keep me dry. That reminds me, have you seen Rachel today?' Chris asked, with an inkling of what the answer might be.

'No she hasn't come down yet...did you notice if her car was outside?' Devan asked.

'I was a bit distracted but now that you come to mention it I don't think it was. In which case she may well have stayed overnight at the hospital. I have noticed she's been doing that a lot lately. Suppose it's nice to know that the professor has someone there but I do find it a little concerning. She does seem to be spending a lot of time over there.' He replied, thinking that at some point he might have to address that.

'I wouldn't be too concerned if I were you. I think it's only natural to try to hold onto whatever is left of someone you were in love with. I think she probably sees it as her duty to look after James' father.' Devan replied.

'Sorry...what... *in love with*?' Chris replied somewhat taken by surprise.

'Yes, I'm not sure exactly how deeply it was, or whether or not he felt the same way, but I thought it was pretty obvious by the way they were around each other, there was a definite spark. But then I have noticed you aren't always very good at reading these things.' Devan replied. 'I think the best thing to do would be to let her grieve in her own way and if that includes taking time to visit the professor, so be it. Besides at least you can have the peace of mind that there is someone around that can protect him if Lord Norwood or *The Glove* decide to finish the job.' She said.

'True, I really hope she didn't have to fall too far. I did warn her not to get attached to him. It always has a way of ending badly.' Chris remarked with a heavy sigh as he left Devan and wandered through the hall towards the back of the house. His heart was in his mouth as he read the messy sign that had been hurriedly written and pinned to the utility room door 'DANGER EXPLOSIVES ENTER AT OWN RISK'. His only though was: *Please God, not again!*

'Boys, where the hell did you get explosives from?' Chris enquired as he entered the dimly lit room.

'Ah hi boss, we made them.' Gaz calmly replied.

'From what?' Chris asked, not really wanting to know the answer.

'Oh, we found some fertiliser and weed killer in the garden shed. A bit of bleach and presto 'homemade TNT a la Ollie'.' He buoyantly replied.

'Honestly you two are complete liabilities. Clear it up, we've got work to do. Oh, and boys make it safe.' Chris growled at the pair.

'Someone got out of bed the wrong side this morning.' The glaring look that Gaz received suggested that he better change course very quickly. 'Oh alright, sure we can find something to neutralise it with. How you ever expect us to keep our talents up to scratch is beyond me.'

'You got ten, see you in the drawing room.' Chris replied as he left the room.

'Ten, he's having a laugh.' Ollie remarked.

'Make that five.' Chris called out from the hall as if he knew exactly what Ollie had just said. 'That'll keep you boys up to speed.' He added, with an inward smile that those two still managed to keep him entertained with their misguided mischief, not that he would ever admit that to them. They certainly didn't need any additional encouragement from him to wreak havoc.

'Oh for Christ's sake. You had to say that didn't you.' Gaz exclaimed. 'Couldn't resist poking the bear, could you? You know he's been in a foul mood ever since James left.'

'But that's hardly reason enough to be a complete killjoy.' Ollie replied.

'Mate, he's been bubbling for a while, think he needs a mission to clear the air properly. He just needs to let off some steam, we all do. I'd just rather not make for an easy target.' Gaz said.

'Yeah, I suppose you are right.' Ollie said as he started wiping down the worktop.

'So, how do you suggest we are going to dispose of this *safely*?'

'Oh, I'm not. Give us that cardboard poster tube.' Ollie replied with a grin.

'Are you gonna do, what I think?' Gaz asked raising an eyebrow.

'Yeah, why not? He did say we only have five minutes; you got any better ideas of how to dispose of an explosive in less than five? I know it's not New Year's anymore but I'm sure one firework won't hurt, well actually make that two.' Ollie replied as he split the cardboard tube in two, taped the bottoms up, poured in the incendiary powder, attached a couple of stakes and swaggered off with his new toys out into the garden.

'Great, and I thought we'd just agreed not to poke the bear anymore.' Gaz muttered under his breath as he followed his co-conspirator outside.

'What was that?' Ollie asked catching the tone of protest in Gaz's voice.

'Oh nothing, just waving goodbye to my freedom.' Gaz sarcastically replied.

'Yeah, I know. Told you he's become a killjoy.' Ollie replied, totally oblivious to the sarcasm of Gaz's statement, as he pushed the rockets' stakes deep into the soft soil before igniting the short fuses, taking a few paces backwards just in case they didn't go off quite as he expected. They watched with an air of excited anticipation as the fuses slowly burnt down before the rockets spiralled off into the sky, leaving the ground far behind in a matter of seconds, before erupting with bursts of green and gold.

'Hmmm must have been some copper in there, wasn't expecting the green.' Ollie mused as he admired his work. A loud tap on the window behind them signalled the end of their jubilations. Turning Ollie caught sight of the menacing glare of Chris through the window combined with a hard four fingered point that transformed into a beckoning, *you two. Here, now!* Kind of gesture.

'Oh shit, the full four fingers, that's never a good sign. I told you not to poke the bear, but would you listen? Oh, no. Now we're for it. I'm sure you must have been dropped on your head as a child. There's no other way to explain how incredibly stupid you can be.' Gaz complained as he steeled himself for the bollocking they were no doubt about to receive.

'Ha, like you can talk. Sure he'll get over it. I suppose we better go and receive punishment. After you.' Ollie replied

'Typical, always sending someone else in front of you to take the brunt.' Gaz replied.

'Matter of self preservation, dear boy.' Ollie retorted as they stepped through the French windows into the drawing room.

'Six minutes, boys' Chris said looking up from his watch. 'You're slipping.' The thought had crossed his mind, as he heard the explosions, that he was pretty sure he had told them to dispose of the explosives safely and that right about now he should be tearing them both apart, but he decided to take the unexpected and novel path of not mentioning it. He wanted to see them squirm. They no doubt knew they hadn't quite done what he had requested and they would be expecting some sort of recrimination. So would feel particularly uneasy when nothing happened.

Unfortunately Chris had forgotten that the pair were so nonchalant about such things that not doing anything would send the message that they could push the boundaries a little bit further.

'Well we didn't have a lot to work with.' Gaz replied. 'We can always try it again. We've still got enough ingredients for a second run, haven't we?' He said turning to Ollie.

'Oh, yeah. Defi..' His co-conspirator started to say, but was cut short.

'No, once was quite enough for today, I think.' Chris said raising his hand and cutting Ollie off in mid sentence. 'I have a task for you boys, one that should keep you out of mischief for a while, at least. And no, before you ask you can't blow anything up, not yet anyway.'

'Oh okay, what's the plan, boss?' Gaz asked in a rather more eager tone than even he had intended. A sign that they had been going a bit stir crazy at Noirmont, and that at this point any excursion was better than remaining cooped up at the estate.

'We desperately need to get Intel and unfortunately as you two are both now known to Norwood by sight we are forced to reach out to a few other members of *The Order*, that have yet to play their parts.'

'I'm presuming you know how to contact these people, as we only ever knew you, James and the Prof.' Ollie remarked.

'Yes, I have the Professor's contact list. Luckily, one of the only things he didn't put into some infuriating code. A few I already know, others even I haven't met. But I have ways to reach them. So you boys better get your kit together, you're off to London.' Chris stated.

'Sweet, I know some great roof-top bars and clubs we can visit. Off to party central, come on.' Ollie excitedly remarked.

'Umm Ol, concentrate this isn't going to be one of your all night party affairs. You are gonna have to do some work. I've written down your instructions and a few names that you should expect to come across. These people are the best and some have been operating in the shadows for an awfully long time, so don't piss them off.' Chris said directing his final comment mainly at Ollie, as he knew that he was the most likely out of the duo to go careering off course. 'You can use the usual channels to get in contact if you need to, but try to keep comms to a min. Oh and boys, try and stay out of trouble for once.' He added.

'Us, cause trouble. We never cause trouble, it just seems to turn up.' Ollie said.

'That's what I'm afraid of.' Chris replied with a headmasterly look.

'Come on Ol, we better get our gear together, when are we leaving?'

'You're booked on the next ferry. Leaves in about three hours.'

'Wouldn't it be quicker to fly?'

'It would, but you are going to need transport to get around once you are on the mainland and funnily enough a car just won't fit in that sardine tin, they keep trying to pass off as a plane. Even you two have made paper planes with better aerodynamics than that heap of junk. No, boat's a far better option.'

'Dude.' Gaz said kicking Ollie in the leg.

'Dude, what the fuck you kick me for?' Ollie indignantly said rubbing his shin.

'Dude, shut the fuck up, he said car. There is only one car here.' Gaz said waiting for the lights to come on.

'Oh, oh yeah, sweet. We get to play with the Cobra.' Ollie's mischievous grin exploding across his face as it finally sunk in.

'Just don't break it or I can promise you it won't be the only thing in pieces.' Chris interjected before the mixologists got too carried away.

'Come on Ol, let's go before he changes his mind.' Gaz urged as he started to make his way out of the room.

With a slight air of uneasiness about his plan for the boys Chris wandered off to rejoin Devan in the study.

'Having any joy?' He asked as he lent over the desk.

'A little, I think. I may have discovered something. Or rather it appears as though there may be something out of place in the text.'

'Oh really, sounds promising. If there were something out of place I would say that it is intended as a starting point. What is it?'

'Well, bearing in mind that this poem was originally written thousands of years ago, there should be no mention of sunflower seeds.'

'But I thought sunflower seeds were a popular snack in China?'

'Very much so, but they are not native to the country, the first record of *Sunflower* in China was in 1621 AD. Therefore the reference in this text shouldn't exist as it predates that by several centuries.'

'Interesting, have you found anything in Professor Middleton's notes that may shed some light on it?'

'Not yet, but I've still got his journals to go through. Hopefully there might be something that creates a tangible link.'

'Would you like an extra set of eyes? I'm by no means the best reader in the world, still might help to speed up the process a bit.'

'Thanks that would be great. Although I'm not sure you appreciate just what you are letting yourself into.'

'Why do you say that?'

Devan didn't voice her reply. She simply smiled at him with a knowing look and casually flicked a glance towards a bookcase on the far side of the room, jam packed full of journals and other notebooks.

'Ha, I see what you mean. Well, in that case I best get started. I can see the candles will be burning well into the night with this lot.' Chris replied, without the hint of any regret in his tone. He genuinely wanted to help. He knew that this had to be done and the sooner they identified the next piece of the puzzle, the sooner they would be one step closer to finding the next part of the *Liber Veritatis*. 'Guess we may as well start at the top and work our way down.' He added as he reached up and plucked the first journal from the shelf.

It was late afternoon by the time Gaz and Ollie were ready to trade the fresh salty island air for the noxiousness of the capital.

'We'll drop you a text as soon as we get there. Oh, you forgot to mention where we are staying.' Gaz said to Chris as he reversed the Cobra out of the garage.

'It's all in the notes I gave you. Good luck guys and remember what I said.'

'Don't worry, we'll try and find as much trouble as possible.' Ollie shouted out over the rear of the car as it shot off down the drive.

I very much hope not. Chris thought to himself as he watched the car cross the gates and disappear into the distance.

Chapter Four: Spy Craft

It was close to midnight as the AC Cobra reached the outskirts of the capital. Pulling off the main carriageway into a narrow side street, Gaz switched off the engine and took out the envelope Chris had supplied with all the details that they needed.

'Let's have a look and see what budget accommodation he's set us up with. Knowing him it'll be the most drab and dreary place available.' He remarked as he peeled back the seal. 'Ha, I think he must be having a laugh. He cannot be serious.' He said in surprise as he skimmed the notes.

'Why, where is it?' Ollie asked.

'Take a look for yourself.' Gaz said passing the paper over to his companion.

'Love it. Seems he has a sense of humour after all.' Ollie remarked.

'You got any 'G' on your phone? Better pay the congestion charge before we continue.' Gaz said as he remembered what part of the city their final port of call was in..

'Yeah got a couple of bars. Hold on, let me just get the reg.' Ollie replied as he stepped out of the car, walking round to make a mental note of the registration before he Googled the congestion zone and paid for the week. 'Probably won't need all that, but better play safe. Plus I'll probably forget, if we go day by day. All sorted, let's make like a leaf.'

'I think you mean tree.' Gaz remarked.

'Same thing.' Ollie replied jumping back into the sportster, as the engine roared back into life and they sped off towards their final destination in the centre of the metropolis.

The four brilliant white cooling towers of the now silent turbines at Battersea Power station, rose up like giant unlit cigarettes piercing the dark skyline of the city as Ollie and Gaz crossed over the Chelsea Bridge and arrived at their temporary digs just off Chichester Street.

The building Ollie and Gaz found themselves standing in front of was warmly illuminated by uplighters and yet both of them felt that it gave off a cold, sinister and foreboding aura. It was the first time either of them had set eyes on the infamous apartment block of Dolphin Square, as impressive as it was, there seemed to be a sense in the air that something wasn't quite right. This could have been because of its rather chequered and colourful past, steeped in the controversies of Cold War espionage and tainted with the allegations of flats being used by a paedophile ring, Dolphin Square's once illustrious story would now always be tarnished with an indelible stain. Or maybe it was just that the biting snap of the deep February wind highlighted the chilling atmosphere around the block.

Crossing under the central of the three arches, the two sought out the most notorious of all the apartments, No. 807 of Hood House. It had been from that very room on a wet grizzly September afternoon in 1962 that the metropolitan police had stormed into the building and dragged out William John Vassall on charges of spying for the Soviet Union. To which he later confessed and was sentenced to 18 years in prison.

'I can just imagine the chaotic scene around this room as they smashed in the door.' Gaz said as he fiddled with the key in the lock.

'Yeah, I bet he must have been as white as a sheet as they burst in and he realised that the game was up. Think he must have pictured the ominous scene of the gallows fast approaching as they dragged him down the stairs. In a way he was lucky they didn't execute him. Let's hope we fair better. Doesn't bode well for one's sleep patterns, think it's gonna be a long night.' Ollie said as he surveyed the boxy apartment.

'For you maybe, I've been driving for eight hours. Once my head hits that pillow I'm gonna be out for the count, I can assure you.' Gaz replied as he dumped his travel case down in a corner of the living room and disappeared into the bedroom.

'Guess, I've got the couch then.' Ollie muttered to the closing bedroom door.

Pulling out a spare duvet from the airing cupboard near the bathroom, Ollie resigned himself to a less than congenial night on a couch that disappointingly in his eyes was verging on being classed as nothing short of an oversized armchair.

Ollie was awoken much earlier than he would have liked by a thin shard of light sneaking through the one and only gap in the curtains. He'd slept poorly, tossing and turning. Try as he might, he just hadn't managed to find any comfort on the tiny couch. In the end he'd given up and slept on the floor, but again that hadn't been the comfort he'd really been hoping for. Wiping the sleep from the corners of his eyes, he let out a tired sigh. Today was going to be a long day he told himself as he stretched his aching muscles, arching his back, to such an extent that they almost cramped up. There was only one solution; coffee. The darkest, strongest, almost treacle like kind of brew he could possibly make. And if he was up, he was going to make sure that Gaz was too.

'Wakey, wakey. Sleepy head.' He loudly announced as he burst into the bedroom. Tossing a pillow in Gaz's general direction.

'What, huh. Have you any idea what time it is?' Gaz rather groggily replied. 'I need at least another hour.'

'Time you were up, count yourself lucky. At least you had a bed. Come on, we've got work to do. And that includes ordering me a bed, I'll be dammed if I'm spending another night on the floor.'

'I thought you were on the sofa?'

'Ha, maybe if I was three feet tall. Come on get up.'

'Okay, okay. I'm getting up. Is that coffee I can smell?' Gaz asked as his senses gradually kicked in and the distinctive waft of freshly made coffee seeped through the tiredness.

'Yeah, only that instant crap, but better than nothing I suppose. See another thing we need to do, get some decent supplies in.'

'Alright give us a min, unlike you, I need a shower in the morning. Tell you what, while I'm in the process of waking up, why don't you get on the net and order yourself a bed?'

'I would, if I knew where you'd put the laptop.'

'Still in the car.'

'I'm not walking all the way down there, have you any idea how many stairs we climbed last night?'

'Then use the lift. Stop being lazy, and man up.'

'Fine. Could have bloody mentioned there was a lift last night.' Ollie begrudgingly replied, he knew Gaz had a point but he didn't like to admit defeat. And with that he trudged off leaving Gaz to sort himself out.

Ollie had to admit that in the fresh morning light the apartment block didn't appear to be as menacing as it had the night before. In fact the enclosed garden with a playfully sculpted dolphin fountain made the place feel rather charming. Nevertheless, it was now very apparent that they were in the city; as there was now a steady flow of early risers heading off to their various busy offices. Many of whom were far too one tracked to give anybody else the time of day, such was the nature of the high-pressure hustle and bustled of urban living. He was glad that he had never stepped into that world, it would have driven him stir crazy, not to mention that he much preferred to breath air rather than cough and splutter like some sort of archaic motor vehicle. Dodging a couple of preoccupied civil servant types making their way to work he retrieved the laptop and weaved his way back to the flat.

'Found it, then.' Gaz said, raising his head as Ollie re-entered the flat.

'Yeah, you're gonna have to order the bed. I'd forgotten how dirty this place makes me feel. Seriously, this is the only place where being outside makes me feel like I've just crawled up a chimney. There better be some hot water left.' Ollie remarked.

'Yeah I know, not a great fan of this place, either. Even worse after being on the tube for a bit. How this country will cope once it's expanded across what little remains of this green and pleasant land is something I'm glad I will not be around to see. Any particular type of bed or will anything do?' Gaz asked as he turned on the laptop.

'As long as I can fit on it. Can be a camp bed for all I care as long as it's not the floor or that poor excuse for a sofa, I'll be happy.' Ollie called out.

'I think we can do better than a camp bed, but I'm not going to spend a fortune on it. After all we're not going to be here for all that long.' Gaz replied.

'Yeah, whatever you think. I gotta wash this city off.' Ollie hastily replied as he rubbed his fingers and thumbs together, trying to work out exactly what the exact word was that he wanted to use to describe the unclean feeling on his skin.

'No worries, I'll sort it out. Once I've found that damned router.' Gaz said.

'Tidy.' Ollie shouted back over the heavy down pour of water now gushing down from the shower head.

Gaz settled on the cheapest futon type bed he could find that included delivery, there was no chance in hell he was going to waste the rest of the day traipsing around those expansive streets searching for a bed. He'd almost rather let Ollie have his and sleep on the floor himself than spend hours scouring the city streets.

'Ah that's so much better. I feel less like an oily smoked kipper.' Ollie exclaimed as he vigorously rubbed the last of the dampness from his hair.

'Surprising really, considering that water's been through the best part of a football team before you washed in it.' Gaz smirked. 'Anyway bed's sorted, arriving between four and six this evening, so I suggest we crack on. There's a lot of ground to cover today. And unfortunately for you you're about to feel a bit like a sardine.'

'Ah, no way not that infernal tin can of a tube system.'

'If you've got a better, more efficient way of getting around this place, I'm all ears. No, I didn't think so, credit where it's due the tube is pretty good when it comes to getting around.'

'Fine, but I'm calling shotgun on the shower for later.'

'Haha, for someone that's spent days covered head to toe in mud and all other manner of shit, you can be such a clean freak.'

'It's different, that's natural. This place just covers you in all sorts of synthesised shit. Don't worry I can handle it. Where we off to first?'

'Need to catch the Victoria Line, I think. We need to get to Bunhill Fields.'

'Pimlico's not far from here. Change onto the Northern Line at King's Cross and get off at Old Street.'

'Nice, didn't know you had such an encyclopaedic knowledge of the underground.'

'I don't, but my app does.' Ollie replied with a cheeky grin.

'Such a tool. But I suppose I shouldn't really be surprised. Oh and we need to find a corner shop or stationers en-route. I need a pen.'

'I got one here.'

'No, I want a specific type.'

'Alright, *Mr Picky*, probably be one near the station. Generally seems to be a popular sort of spot to setup a newsagent. Anything else?'

'That's it, the rest we will have to work out on the way. And talking about that I think it's time we made tracks.' Gaz said as he swooped up the flat keys from the kitchen counter.

'Ugh, time to go brave the toxicity again. I better get some sort of compensation for the years I'm knocking off my life expectancy.' Ollie muttered as he followed Gaz out of the flat.

The mid morning sun had begun to make its presence felt and although it was by no means warm, the chill of the previous night had been temporarily chased away. They had to battle their way through the crowd of commuters on the platform, all trying to catch the next service.

'Reminds me of playing sardines when I was a child.' Gaz said as they just managed to squeeze into a carriage.

'This train is ready to leave. Please mind the doors.' Announced the automated voice through the carriage. Followed by the well-known triple beep and swooshing sound of the doors beginning to close. But they didn't manage to fully shut as a part of Ollie was blocking the beam. And the doors sprang open again.

'Come on fatty, get your arse out the way.'

'Hey, I doubt it can get any smaller' Ollie replied as he squirmed his way a little further into the confined space. This time the doors did just manage to close, and once they had he was able to reposition himself up against the edge of the door so he had just that little bit more comfort. 'I hope some of this lot get off quite soon. Not sure I can put up with this all the way to Old Street.' Ollie complain as he tried to find a bit of comfort.

'Nothing like a packed tube in the morning.' Gaz replied trying hard not to laugh at Ollie's discomfort. Gaz had spent part of his childhood in the city and although it had been a while since he'd been in quite such a jam-packed service, he'd grown accustomed to it and just took it as par for the course when flitting around the ever-moving city.

They joined the almost robotic like collective making their way out of the tunnels towards the light. Every now and again the automaton like flow broke down as single unit tried to assert its uniqueness and break free from the collective programming, by stopping. Resulting in momentary chaos within the steady flow of people, before the collective reasserted its dominance and order was restored.

'Ah, I hadn't realised there were four subways out of this station. Ol, can you see which one we need to use to get to Bunhill Fields Burial Ground?' Gaz asked.

'Hold on just a minute, I thought we were going to meet a living person not try and revive one from the other side. That's definitely not what I signed up for, I've seen what happens when you start messing around with the undead.' Ollie replied.

'You've watched far too may apocalyptic series. We are not going to do anything like that. We just need to leave a message. Ah that's the one I want, Subway 3.' Gaz added as he spied the sign overhead clearly indicating Bunhill Fields Burial Ground listed under the exit.

They both blinked as they ascended the last flight of steps emerging into the bright daylight, finally breaking free from the rest of the tunnel travellers at street level. Strolling straight on down City Road, passing the bluish grey pub *The Angel* which proudly stated above its entrance in golden lettering that it was: *The Heart of City Road*, and they continued along the pavement reaching a banner flag welcoming passers by to

Islington. Even the black bins trimmed with a touch of gold paint now had Islington ostentatiously stamped onto their sides. As Gaz approach the next bin under the banner he took out the white chalk marker he had purchased and casually stroked a small 'X' onto it without even breaking his stride. Ollie gave Gaz a slight nudge and a subtle nod; up in front of them a section of the pavement had been blocked off by the blue flashing vehicles of both the police and fire brigade.

'Best cross to the other side, before we get too close. Wonder what's going on?' He said.

'I don't know but I'm not going to stop and start asking questions. Especially as it's exactly opposite where we're going.' Gaz replied as he caught sight of the entrance to the Burial Ground.

'Oh they're green, such a dark shade, I thought from a distance they were black and gold.' Ollie remarked as they passed through the gates and on to one of the two paths that split the cemetery into quadrants. 'What exactly are we doing in a cemetery?' He asked.

'Well according to Chris's notes, had you bothered to read them, to arrange the initial contact with this particular member of *The Order* we have to leave a specifically worded note at the monument to Daniel Defoe.' Gaz replied as they reached the intersection where the two paths crossed. 'I just need to write the note.' He added sitting down on one of the wooden benches next to a large rectangular flowerpot embossed with the City of London's coat of arms. Scribbling down what to him felt to be a rather ironic cryptic message Gaz got up and casually strode over to the obelisk at the far end of the path, before laying the message on the corner of the step behind the black metal railing.

'That's it.' Ollie scoffed.

'Yep.' Gaz replied.

'Ha, there's nothing to this espionage malarkey. Now what do we do?' Ollie asked.

'Get on with contacting the rest of the people on the list. This one will be in touch shortly, they have all the info they need in the message.' Gaz replied.

Robinson,

The Greatest, the Longest in Duration, the widest in Extent, of all the Tempests and Storms that History gives any Account of since the Beginning of Time is about to consume us all. Time to break free from the wolf pack before the lightning breaks us, and find a friendly dolphin to cross the battered sea to return to the safety of the fold.

Yours Friday.

Throughout the rest of the day, had they lingered, they would have seen a great variety of characters from snap happy tourists to stressed businessmen searching for a moment's peace gaze up at the obelisk and many a bemused comment by the few that happened to stumble upon the seemingly random note Gaz had left out for all to see. Whether or not they would have been able to spot the individual for whom the note actually held meaning, they would never know. There was no time to indulge in *Guess Who*, having several more cryptic notes to leave in random spots across the sprawling metropolis. Gaz and Ollie rejoined the subterranean world of the tunnellers and headed off in search of their next drop point.

Chapter Five: The Sunflower's Enigma

The soft swishing of pages being turned was momentarily broken by the vibrating buzz of Chris's phone on the study desk.

Glancing at the screen to see a notification of a new message from Gaz, Chris carefully marked the page he was currently on, set the book aside and opened the message.

'One bun in the oven, another two awaiting consummation.'

He smiled to himself as he read the randomly worded message. Gaz always did have an amusing and yet simple way of relaying important information.

'Secret admirer?' Devan asked catching a glimpse of his brief moment of personal amusement.

'No.' He laughingly replied. 'Only Gaz letting me know that they've made their first drop at Bunhill Fields and are setting out to the other drop points. I just found his choice of words amusing. He could have just said; 'One down, two to go.'

'I see what you mean. What is it with men? Why do you more often than not have to put a sexual spin onto the most mundane of things?' She said with a slight sigh as she read the message over his shoulder.

Chris thought about replying to her rhetoric but kept his jaw firmly locked. Experience had taught him that there wasn't an answer, any answer that would even remotely be satisfactory and would more likely than not spark a debate, where the question of requiring a bigger shovel might be an apt one. So instead he elected to change the subject.

'How's the journal skimming going?' He asked.

Devan wasn't oblivious to his change of subject, nevertheless she wasn't surprised that he'd dodged the question.

'About as well as yours, I suspect. It's not possible to skim this stuff. Reading short hand is one thing but all these different codes are sapping the will to live. How the hell anybody could work like this on a daily basis is just astounding and possibly suffering from a severe case of paranoia.' She replied.

'Ha, I'd love to see the Prof's face if you suggested that he was paranoid. I did ask him once why he kept all his notes and journals in code. To which he replied that it first started as a bit of fun and now it keeps the mind active.'

'You're right, he's not paranoid; he's just nuts.' She joked.

'Nah, maybe just a tad eccentric.' He replied smiling.

'Oh come on, just look at this.' She exclaimed, picking up a random journal from the bookcase and flicking about halfway through the pages. 'See, it's just incomprehensible gibberish, a string of seemingly endless numbers. Oh no; correction it has four actual words in it. Taisha, Inoue, Phyllotaxis and Turing. Whatever the hell that's supposed to mean.' She finished, flinging the book in Chris's general direction as her irritation with the entire situation got the better of her.

Chris didn't reply, he just stared at the open book for a few seconds and then burst out laughing, which did nothing to quell Devan's demeanour.

'Just exactly what is so funny?' She snapped.

Wiping the joy from his eyes. 'You're fantastic, I could almost kiss you right about now.' He replied.

'What are you talking about?' She asked in a softer tone.

'When it comes to ancient history you are second to none, but I think your modern must be a bit rusty. I think you might have just found what we've been looking for. I'll try and explain.' Chris said catching the quizzical expression on her face. 'You've heard of Alan Turing, I'm sure. And no doubt familiar with his code breaking and work with computers.' Chris began to explain.

'Yeah, who isn't? I still don't get the connection.' She replied.

'Okay, so his final; and unfinished project was to do with Phyllotaxis. It's the study of growth patterns in plants. In a seminal work in 1952, shortly before his death, Turing claimed to have found the explanation for Fibonacci Phyllotaxis.' He continued.

'As in the Fibonacci Sequence?' She asked.

'The very same, the reason why flowers seem to have petal patterns that follow the sequence.' He replied.

'But why is that important here?' She asked, not making the connection.

'Because Turing's last work was centred around Sunflowers.

I think it's the Prof's way of indicating that this particular number sequence is relevant to the clue in the poem.' He replied.

'Okay, if that's the case. What do the other words refer to?' She asked intrigued by where Chris was taking this.

'Remember I mentioned playing Go with the Professor?' He asked.

'I vaguely recall you saying that he was rather good at misdirection.' She replied.

'Well, Taisha and Inoue are words related to the game. The Inoue House was one of the great schools of the game in Japan and they developed a secret move called the 'Taisha Joseki', most famously used during a game in the Edo Period. It utilised, what in Go term's are known as 'Ghosts'.' He said.

'And this is relevant why?' She asked losing the tenuous thread.

'Because it tells us which cypher he is using. There's only one problem.' He replied.

'Go on.' Devan apprehensively replied.

'I only know two people that know how to decode it.' Chris replied.

'Let me guess; James and his father. One who's dead and the other's in a bloody coma.' She said having a fair idea what the reply would be.

'That's about the gist of it.' He replied.

'But surely with your background, you must know somebody who can run it through a computer algorithm to work it out.' She replied.

'There may be one, possibly two, but I think they will struggle, James only mentioned it once and I seem to recall that he referred to it as 'Fibonacci's Ghost Cypher' and had hinted that without the code book or knowing how to write out the grid, it was almost impossible to crack, even for a computer.' Chris replied wracking his brains for another solution.

'Surely that isn't possible, if it uses a sequence. A computer would find the patterns.' Devan replied.

'That's the problem. From what I understood, Every letter could be represented by a huge amount of different numbers to such an extent that you could write a short message without repeating a single number. On top of which, because of the way the grid was structured some numbers could actually represent more than one letter, so even if a number was repeated it didn't actually mean it had the same meaning. Unfortunately he never showed me how to create the grid, the only thing I know was that it was based on part of the Fibonacci sequence.' He replied dejectedly.

'But isn't that like, infinite? God, I hate these people.' Devan remarked.

'Ha, don't worry. I have an idea. It's a bit of a long shot but right now, it's better than nothing.' Chris replied as he suddenly thought of someone that might be able to help.

'I'm hoping you are going to elaborate, you're not keeping me in the dark this time.' She replied determined that unlike previous occasions she would be kept informed.

'From experience, it seems to prove rather difficult to keep you out of the loop, not to mention unwise.' He replied, with the faintest of smiles at the corner of his mouth. 'I thought I'd try Tom Bradbury. There's a slim chance that due to the nature of the relationship that James and Tom had in the past, James may have used it with him. Besides his guys up at Faslane use a vast amount of code and cyphers, so they have a good chance of breaking it. Otherwise I'll have to reach out to somebody I haven't spoken to in years. That's if they will even agree to speak to me.' He replied.

'Ah, I take it that relationship didn't go so well.' Devan said.

'You could say that. We had a bit of a falling out about five, six years ago and haven't really spoken since. I won't bore you with the details; to be honest I can't even remember what triggered it. Probably something really petty, that just seemed to escalate and eventually created a void so great that we couldn't find any common ground, on which to rebuild what we once had. Shame really, but even between the closest of friends, these things can happen. Hopefully Tom will be able to help and then I won't have to go down that particular path.'

'Let's hope so.' Devan replied, but she wasn't convinced. For starters she couldn't imagine that Chris would ever let something petty destroy a friendship, also the manner in which he spoke about it implied that he knew exactly what had happened and that it was far from a trivial rift. He might not have realised it but his tone portrayed a deep fracture, almost unforgivable. She got the sense that the odds would be better on Hell freezing over long before Chris made an attempt at reconciliation, let alone make a request for help.

Chris was already on the phone to Tom, before Devan had finished mulling over this latest piece of his complex puzzle, however from what she caught of the conversation between Chris and Tom; it didn't sound like they would get the result that they were looking for. Not that she could actually hear Tom's side of the call.

'… Are you absolutely sure?' She heard Chris ask, followed by a brief momentary silence where Tom was talking. Followed by yet another question from Chris. 'And you think that is the only way?' He paused again, for a slightly longer period, as Tom responded.

'Okay, thanks for trying Tom.' Chris said with a deep sigh. 'If it has to be this way, then so be it. I had hoped to avoid this. They're an absolute nightmare and the less said about the sister the better, but if there's no other option, then so be it. I'll just have to hope that dead men don't hold grudges for broken promises. Let's keep in touch and I'll let you know how it goes. Thanks again, bye Tom, bye.'

Devan's ear had pricked up at that last part of the conversation, and she suddenly began to understand at least part of what it had all been about. This wasn't about Chris at all, she realised; this was about James and his past. She had seen enough of their bond to know that either one of them would, if at all possible, keep promises made long after the demise of the other. Such was the almost unbreakable nature of the friendship between them.

She also realised just how deep Chris's void must be right about now, with James gone, a vast chasm must have been left. And she began to appreciate just how hard he must be working in order to keep a lid on his emotions and to keep everything moving, let alone come across, on the surface at least, as if it was business as usual. Even if below the surface the sea was far from calm. She hoped for his sake that this wouldn't eventually take its toll. There were after all only so many wave strikes a headland could take before it started to crumble.

'I hope you are prepared for a bumpy ride.' Chris said as he slipped his phone into his pocket.

'I take it that Tom can't help?' Devan replied, knowing fully well what the outcome had been.

'Can't or won't, I'm not a hundred per cent which. He sounded a bit cagey on the phone. It's as if he was expecting the call but not about that particular subject. There's definitely something he's not telling me but at the moment I'm not sure what it is. But yeah, the short answer is that he can't help. He doesn't remember using that code with James and his cyber gurus are all tied up with current chatter. Apparently there's been a recent spike in activity, suspect Comms from a few places of interest, which means we would be at the back of a rather long queue. And as we don't have an official sanction there is absolutely no chance of jumping a few places without questions being asked at a much more senior level than Tom is prepared to take on. And to be honest I agree with him, he'd be risking his job if the higher ups started poking around into what we are doing and which assets we have already used. Re-tasking that satellite to track the *Astronomer* was enough for a court martial, let alone the incident in Belize, best not to push our luck. We're on our own for this one. As much as the stability of Tom's position is a concern, I find the question of how we are going to decipher that code a much more disquieting one.' He said.

'I got that impression. But I think you are going to have to be a bit more forthcoming than that. Who is this person that holds the key and seems to fill you with dread every time you've not mentioned them. I got the notion they are from both yours and James' past. And that you are trying to fulfil a promise made to him.' Devan said in a much more direct way than she had on previous occasions. She was fed up with tiptoeing around subjects that seemed to be taboo. She wanted answers and she had finally come to the conclusion that she would keep forcing the issue until she got them.

'How long have you got? It's quite a long and rather complex affair.' Chris replied.

'They always are with you two. How about starting at the beginning and go from there. Firstly who is this person?' She asked.

'They, or rather she is called Chestnut Adams.' Chris replied as a vexed look of torn loyalties creased his brow.

'And exactly who is she to you and James?' Devan asked more determined than ever to get to the crux of the thing.

'For me she was once a close friend; to James, she's his ex-wife. Yeah, didn't think you were expecting that.' Chris replied, as he saw the shocked look on Devan's face.

'Well, of course I had picked up that he had once been engaged shortly before he left the forces but I never realised that they had been married.' She replied.

'That's a different person. James left the forces as a result of losing his fiancée, Lucy. But he had been married, although rather briefly years before that, to Chestnut.'

'Ah okay, that makes more sense. He hasn't had a lot of luck has he?' She replied now rather regretting pushing quite so hard for answers.

'No, I suppose not. I still don't actually know what happened to Lucy. I'd always though he would tell me when the time was right; unfortunately he never got the chance. I suppose I could try and find out from the MoD reports, but doesn't really seem like there's much point now, maybe it's better left in the past.

Chestnut and his first marriage on the other hand are a completely different kettle of fish. I know exactly what happened.

They first met whilst we were going through officer training at Sandhurst. I can't remember exactly how he said they met, was at some social event or possibly at one of the dinner parties in the mess. I didn't actually find out they had been seeing each other until much later. James had kept the whole affair rather secretive. Looking back on it, I should have realised much sooner that something was going on. I had on occasion found him smiling at small notes, which were quickly hidden away if anybody happened across him. Once I found one lying on his bedside and was intrigued enough to look but it was just a string of numbers. Numbers that meant absolutely nothing to me and actually didn't really raise any questions. Ever since I had know him, James had been dabbling in cryptography, and I'd just presumed that this was one of his works in progress.

It was purely by chance that I uncovered the relationship and put two and two together, suddenly all those cryptic messages made sense. I'd had a day's leave from the camp and had popped into Little Sandhurst to post a few letters and collect some supplies. Walking up the High Street, I'd caught a glimpse of somebody, through a pub window, that I thought was James. However by the time I looked again he had vanished. Then I heard the sound of somebody running off behind me. Turning I clearly saw him charging off down the street. All my shouts were ignored, so I waited until I got back to the base and after throwing several drinks down him I finally got him to crack and discovered that he'd been sneaking off whenever he got the chance to see Chestnut. Tickled me a bit at the time that the pub I'd spotted them in earlier that day had been called *The Bird in Hand*. Anyway the relationship really blossomed after that, as much as I'm sure that they both enjoyed the covert weekends, it may have just remained a fling had it not become public knowledge. I honestly can't remember a time when I had seen him so happy and content with life. Whenever we had the odd day to ourselves, which bearing in mind were pretty seldom, such is the life of an officer in training, you could guarantee that you'd find them arm in arm out for a stroll or giggling over some private joke.

Needless to say this didn't last forever, it had to cool off as we passed out and were relocated to our respective regiments. James' manner changed as well, he became quite moody and I occasionally caught him brooding, especially in the evenings at the officer's mess. They were still seeing each other, of course, but it was less frequent and I think it started to put a strain on the relationship. You could tell that he was torn between love of country and love of her. I don't think he ever did get to make up his own mind. Our first tour out to Afghan killed it completely and truth be told I thought that would be the end of it. He got suck into the campaign and seemed to be well over it. But I was wrong, we returned to the UK briefly before being posted out to Germany.

One evening we were guests at the embassy, to this day I don't know how he knew, we couldn't have been there for more than a few minutes before James turned to me and said, 'She's here, I can feel it.' At the time I didn't even realise who he was talking about, Chestnut didn't even cross my mind. Before I'd even had the chance to ask him what the hell he was talking about he'd disappeared into the crowd, leaving me to fend for myself and battle my way out of being dragged into conversations about politics and country relations, all of which I can tell you is like being subjected to the worst kind of torture imaginable. The fakery and smarminess, argh all that sleaze, still makes my skin crawl when I think about it. One world I don't think I would be able to survive in for too long. Anyway before I digress, I probably didn't see James for at least an hour before I spied him in a corner with his arm around a girl's shoulder whispering and joking. From the angle I couldn't actually see who the young lady was. But she'd evidently captured his attention.

I would have probably left them to it had it not been for the fact that one of the junior foreign office members had been trying to chew my ear off all night and before he made another pass I decided that I needed to look occupied so I crashed James's party.

It was only when I got closer that I realised who he was so enamoured by, and I must admit at the time the thought *here we go again* crossed my mind. Hoping that it would either be over by the morning or that the outcome would be better than last time.'

'How come she was there?' Devan asked, interrupting Chris' story.

'Oh, well it turned out that she was working as the PA to the CEO of a media company. They were currently in talks with a German news agency and had been invited by the ambassador in order to make some new connections that maybe of use during the negotiations. The deal itself would take a few months to finalise and although she was due to fly out the next day, she would return several times over the next few months.

As you can probably guess that resulted in the covert dating starting up all over again. Nevertheless, there was something different this time, or at least he was different. I think his previous attempt had left a desire that he wanted more. There was a determined look in his eye that he wasn't going to let this one slip away again.

I think, even you had known him for long enough, to get the idea that once he decided that he wanted something, he would pursue it until he got it. And on this occasion he wanted her, there was absolutely no doubt in my mind that this time he would not allow anything to get in his way. Needless to say they were married within ten weeks of reconnecting.'

'Wow, that's fast.' She remarked.

'It was, but I also think that you'll find that more common than you might think in the forces. Having said that in this case it's not like they had only just met, they were really picking up where they'd left off and at the time I really believed they had every intention of being together forever. Unfortunately for them, events outside of their control shattered that dream.' He said.

'You mentioned a sister?' Devan said now very much engaged in the story.

'Okay, hold on, I'm getting to that part. Do you want the whole story or just the highlights? So anyway as I was saying, things seemed to be going very well, even if James was away quite a lot. Chestnut appeared to settle into the role of an officer's wife rather well. She was in her element when it came to entertaining James's peers, not only was she an excellent hostess but also very proactive and hands on. She soon became involved in a number of weekend clubs on whichever base they happened to be living on at the time, including helping out with children's clubs, even though they didn't currently have any themselves. I suppose her activeness may have partly been to do with the fact that being an army wife can be quite lonely, especially when your husband is galavanting away in some far off land. Keeping busy must help to keep the thought, however small it might be, that something tragic could happen at any moment out of one's mind. In her case, I have a sense that this didn't really have much of a bearing, she was after all still working for the same media company, so she tended to be down in London most of the week. I think she just wanted to create a role for herself within the community and had found a niche that she could make her own. However, as happy as they were. It had come at a cost, which I'm sure because of how quickly events had unfolded, they were not aware of. The one thing that they hadn't really done was to involve their respective family's in any of it. In James' case that wasn't a surprise as I'm sure you have discovered by now, there was a long period when he wasn't really on speaking terms with his father. Chestnut on the other hand had been very close to her family, especially her elder sister, Carla. That is, until she met James. From what I understand the two sisters had almost been inseparable, and if they weren't together, they kept in regular contact. This had all changed as Chestnut's relationship with him had developed.

Their wedding had been a small and intimate affair, of course they had invited Chestnut's parents and her father gave her away. But for some reason and I don't know why; Carla had not been present. As far as I know she had been invited and yet she did not attend. I'm sure at the time this had been rather upsetting for Chestnut, nevertheless, she carried herself that day as if she was the happiest person in the universe.'

'That must have been a huge slap in the face. I couldn't imagine someone so close not turning up to celebrate and show support for such an important day in one's life. She must have been absolutely devastated when her sister didn't turn up.' Devan commented.

'I believe she was, and it took quite a long time to make a reconciliation. I have a suspicion that Carla felt that James had driven a wedge between them and laid the blame firmly at his feet. Something that couldn't have been further from the truth. He would never have intended to do that and certainly didn't feel that he had prevented them from seeing each other.' Chris said.

'I'm presuming as the marriage didn't last, that the reconciliation between siblings had been rather brief.' Devan commented.

'Sort of, it's actually slightly more complicated than that; I'll try to keep it as straight forward as I can.

It really comes down to the nature of what Carla was or did. I'm sure that even her sister wasn't aware of her chosen career, if one could call it that. If she was, she was a far better actress than I had thought.' Chris replied.

'Why? What was it exactly that she did?' Devan asked, her curiosity spiking once more.

'She was what one might term within those murky waters as *a fixer*.'

'You mean she was an assassin?' Devan half gasped.

'Well, yes and no. She could be contracted for a number of things, of which I suppose murder could be on the agenda. Of course, nobody realised this until much later.

James first began to suspect that something wasn't quite right with her, when she began asking some quite probing questions about the nature of what we did, although he gave her the benefit of the doubt at the time and put it down to casual curiosity. And to be honest even when they did talk about things, strictly between family, he never went into enough detail for any harm to have come of it. However, he began to notice that the questions started to become more probing over the next few years, it was subtle but definitely more precise in the nature of what he was being asked.

Then late one night, after they'd said goodnight to the last of their dinner guests, he noticed one or two things marginally out of place in his study. He didn't know if Chestnut had accidentally moved them when she'd been tidying or whether someone else had been in there. At the time he put it down to the former and left it at that. But when a similar thing happened on a further two occasions he became deeply concerned. There wasn't anything top secret in there, those never left the ops rooms, but there were documents of a confidential nature, mainly training documents. Nothing current, but still he was troubled that someone was going through his papers.' He said vividly remembering how concerned James had become over the whole affair.

'Surely it would have been very easy to work out who was behind it.' Devan said.

'It should have been but actually there had been several people that had been present at all of the parties so he had to come up with another ploy to catch the culprit. He decided to host another party with all those who could have been responsible. During which he'd setup a small camera in his study connected to his phone, activated by motion so when the perpetrator stepped foot inside he would know and be able to confront them. I don't think even he had expected it to be Carla.

Of course, she initially tried to talk her way out of it. But he was having none of it. And so when that didn't work she picked up a letter opener and flew at him.'

'Hold on just a second, you mean she tried to kill him? How can you be so blasé about that?' Devan exclaimed.

'You have to remember this all happened a long time ago. But yes, you are right, there was nothing more shocking than one's sister-in-law trying to skewer you with a letter opener. To be frank she was lucky that she was Chestnut's sister otherwise I think James would have broken her neck. Trust me, he came pretty close. And that was effectively the straw that broke the camel's back. Chestnut couldn't forgive him for throwing her sister out of the house and he couldn't believe that she hadn't known about what Carla was up to.

There were two more attempts on his life that year, which he suspected were at least arranged by Carla, if not actually carried out by her. And that was it; the marriage was over.' Chris said bluntly.

'Hence feeling that you would be breaking a promise if you make contact with her. I can see your dilemma.' Devan said realising just how hard the struggle with his emotions must be for Chris right that moment.

'Pretty much, unfortunately Tom reckons that those little romantic messages they used to send each other used that coding, so really there isn't any other alternative. If she can decode the professor's journal then we have to talk to her. Just have to hope that Carla isn't around when we do. She'd definitely try and kill me.' Chris said in such a tone that Devan couldn't actually work out if he was joking or not.

'I'm presuming you can't just call her?' Devan asked.

'No, I'm afraid this is one of those things that is going to have to be done in person. And that means that we are going to have to take a trip to the mainland.' He replied as he made up his mind as to the course he would have to take.

'Oh, I didn't realise that you wanted us both to go. Who's going to stay and look after the house not to mention check up on the professor.' Devan replied slightly taken aback that he wanted her to accompany him.

'Rachel's here.' Chris replied.

'Are you sure after everything she'll be alright on her own?' Devan asked, think that this wasn't the best timing in the world.

'I've given it a bit of thought and to be honest I think she'll surprise you, she's more resilient than you might think. They'll both be fine, the prof will be in good hands and the house isn't suddenly going to run off of its own accord. And there's no need to be apprehensive about Chestnut, she wouldn't hurt a fly. At least, I don't think she would. Might be a bit awkward at first but she's really a sweet girl. Just unfortunate that her sister is the polar opposite. You'll be fine and I'll be there. So don't fret, it'll be perfectly safe.' He replied having made up his mind.

'Do you know where she is living now?' Devan asked.

'Tom told me when I spoke to him, apparently she's living on Beaufort Street in Chelsea, think he said No. 5, Burleigh House. I'll text him later, just to make sure.' He replied.

'She must be doing well for herself if she can live around there. Chelsea's stupidly expensive.' Devan remarked.

'Well, as far as i'm aware she's still working for that media company. Oh, what was it called *Between the Lines*, I think. But not as a PA, Tom mentioned something about editing. She had been quite instrumental during that deal in Germany, and she'd pushed hard after that to take on a more central role within the company. So i'm not surprised where she's now living. Besides she always did socialise with that set.' He said.

'You'd better let the boys know we're coming up.' Devan suggested.

'That's a good point they should have met with at least one of *The Order* by the time we get there. Plus I can make sure that Ollie hasn't gone too far off script.' He joked.

'Judging on the last time those two were let off the leash, God only know's what mayhem those two may have caused by now.' Devan replied as her mind turned to the prospect of meeting James's former partner.

Chapter Six: Drop Zone

The loud rush of air gradually subsided as the tube slowed to a halt at Oxford Circus Station. Ollie and Gaz almost fell out of the carriage like two marbles bursting out from a packed tin, such was the over crowded nature of the midday service.

'Freedom at last, don't think I could have survived in there for much longer.' Ollie said regaining his balance on the platform edge.

'Yeah, was pretty tight in that one, in hindsight probably should have waited for the next one. Although I doubt it would have made any difference, this was always going to be one of the busiest places in the city.' Gaz replied.

'Where exactly are we going anyway?' Ollie asked eager to get out of the packed station.

'To find John Snow's legacy, and no before you ask I'm not talking about the ruggedly handsome fictional character.' Gaz said.

'You realise I have absolutely no idea what you are babbling about.' Ollie replied.

'You really are totally ignorant when it comes to London's history aren't you? We're going to Broadwick Street, next drop's at John Snow's water pump.' Gaz replied.

'What the hell's so important about a water pump?' Ollie asked.

'Okay, so Dr Snow traced the origins of a cholera outbreak in 1854 to contaminated water from this source, before that it was thought to be caused by poisonous air and the low moral standards of the poorer classes.' Gaz replied.

'Alright, maybe that is a pretty important discovery.' Ollie conceded.

'You think, he probably saved hundreds, if not thousands of lives and eventually changed the scientific community's understanding of Cholera outbreaks . I'd say that's pretty impressive. Now which way out of this place? What does your box of tricks say?' Gaz asked.

'Exit 8 gets us onto Argyll Street, just follow that down onto Carnaby Street.' Ollie replied as he slipped his phone back into his pocket.

'Those things make life so much easier. Crazy to remember how people used to get around this place.' Gaz said.

'Yeah, technology's great. That is until it doesn't work.' Ollie replied as they made their way, along with the droves of other people out of the humid underground network back into the daylight.

The pair weaved their way through the throng of people around Oxford Circus, down Argyll Street. Passing several Italian restaurants abuzz with tourists and city dwellers alike, enjoying the vibrant atmosphere of London's busy shopping district, before turning left and then right onto Carnaby Street and leaving Little Italy behind them.

'What's the time? I'm famished, got time to grab a quick bite, haven't we? The sight of all these eateries, and their lovingly plated dishes is making my stomach cry out for sustenance.' Ollie remarked, as they passed yet another restaurant.

'I suppose we could pop into a fast food joint, got to be one around here somewhere.' Gaz replied.

'You've got to be joking, right? With the choice of all of these amazing dining experiences, you want to go to the bargain basement of the food industry. I refuse to put that junk anywhere near my mouth. I wouldn't feed that stuff to my cat.' Ollie replied.

'Ol, you don't have a cat. And if you did, you wouldn't feed it anyway. As I recall, you once remarked that unlike a dog, a cat is a particularly tenacious, arrogant and fiercely independent creature, that is perfectly capable of looking after itself. In fact I seem to remember that you called them great manipulators of people, only giving affection because they know it's an easy way to get food, where as dogs, require attention because they lack self esteem, they need the constant reassurance of being loved otherwise they would become the manic depressives of the animal kingdom.' Gaz remarked.

'That's not the point, and I don't recall ever comparing dogs to manic depressives, that would be wrong on so many levels. What I actually said was that you can tell when a dog isn't getting enough affection because their general demeanour comes across as being very depressive. Just goes to show how easy it is to take things out of context and misconstrue what someone meant. Have you ever thought about going into politics or journalism, they're good at that kind of thing.' Ollie replied slightly put out by Gaz's recollection.

'Mate you know I'd make a lousy politician, I'd last less than a week before becoming so frustrated with the system that I'd have to resign in order that I didn't shoot somebody.

What about this place to eat?' Gaz asked changing the subject as he spotted a Hawaiian burger joint halfway down the street.

'Now that's what I'm talking about, something authentic, that doesn't taste of cardboard.' Ollie replied, his eyes bulging at the brightly coloured signage.

True to form Ollie ordered the largest burger on the menu, devouring it at such a rate that it was as if he was concerned that given half the chance it might leap off the plate and scurry back to greener pastures.

'That, was great. Filled the gap nicely.' Ollie said wiping the excess ketchup form his lips.

'That's outrageous. I'm surprised you could even taste it. Where the hell do you put it all? You're as thin as a rake and yet you eat like it was going out of fashion.' Gaz joked.

'Just got a quick metabolism.' Ollie replied half considering a dessert.

'Won't last forever, sure it will comeback and bite you on the arse and then you are gonna be fat as well as banterless.' Gaz replied.

'Well, at least I can learn from your experience of that.' Ollie retorted.

'Touché.' Gaz replied with a grin, knowing that he'd walked right into that one.

'You, done? Or do you want some help with that?' Ollie asked eyeing up the remainder of Gaz's burger.

'Hey, you've had yours. Just because I prefer to actually chew my food doesn't mean that I'm not going to eat it. You really are just a vacuous chasm aren't you?' Gaz replied waving Ollie outstretched arm away from his chips.

'Growing lad, got to keep the energy levels up. Besides, when I'm out with you, never know when we're next going to stop and eat. All go, go, go with you.' Ollie replied.

'Yeah, well we've got a fair amount of ground still to cover if we're going to contact the remainder today. Speaking of which I think it's time we made a move.' Gaz replied as he finished the last bite.

'Just as I was starting to relax. No rest for the wicked. At least it's not that far from here. Before we make a move would it not make sense to write the message we're gonna leave?' Ollie suggested, thinking that they may look a bit odd standing in the middle of a street writing a note just to leave it on the water pump.

'Not a bad shout to be fair. Now where did I put that pen?' Gaz said as he began rummaging around in his pockets. 'Ah ha, here it is, whoever said that an Englishman can never have too many pockets was clearly delusional.'

Dear Doctor,

The long winter is breaking; and with it the epidemic can once again flow freely through our streets. If left unchecked it will sweep through our world as a rampant fire, the like of which hasn't been seen for millennia. Time to dust off those deductive powers before the ferocity of the blaze becomes inescapable and once again unearth the source of the contagion for the sake of all humanity. Non est vivere sed valere vita est.

W. Farr, 4th April 1906

'There, that should do it.' Gaz said as he finished the note.

'I have absolutely no idea what any of that means but I'm sure you're going to enlighten me.' Ollie remarked as he stared at the note with a look of complete incomprehension.

'It's quite simple really, the motto at the end gives the location, the date and year refer to a date and time, in this case four days from now at six minutes past seven.'

'Ah okay, now I understand. What's the rest of it about?'

'Just a load of bullshit really, to disguise the info. But I suppose it does sort of pass on the message the he needs to get his arse in gear and get ready for some proper work. Anyway I suppose we should make a move and drop it off by the pump.' Gaz said as he got up and began to walk out.

'Dude, we need to pay.' Ollie called after him.

'Oh shit, yeah, almost forgot that bit.' Gaz replied walking back into the restaurant to pay at the counter. 'Sorry about that, my mind was preoccupied.' He said to the hostess at the counter as he dug into another of his pockets for his wallet.

'Happens to the best of us, at least I didn't have to go chasing off down the street after you.' She replied with a smile.

'Maybe I should have done that after all, not very often I'm chased down the street by a beautiful woman. Thanks again. Great food, really very good.'

'Thanks you're welcome, enjoy the rest of your day.' She replied blushing slightly at the compliment.

'Same to you.' Gaz replied as he turned to leave for the second time.

Just before reaching the end of Carnaby Street they turned left onto Broadwick Street.

'Keep your eyes peeled for this pump, not sure how easy it is going to be to find. Pretty sure it was meant to be at one end of the street somewhere.' Gaz said

'Can't be that hard, only bollard shaped thingy with a handle, surely?' Ollie replied.

'And that would be where you are wrong because it doesn't have a handle, it was taken off during the cholera outbreak. So now, this replica is left like that as a memorial to Jon Snow and his work. Look they've even got a bar named after him now.' Gaz said pointing to the public house a few meters down from where they were standing. 'Hmmm guess it must be at the far end then as it definitely wasn't at the Carnaby end and we're about halfway down now.' He added as he stepped into the middle of the road to walk round another set of pavement works. They found that the street widened at the far end, enough for a few mobile stalls to set themselves up.

'Mate, I'll take that side, you have a look round here.' Ollie suggested as they began to scan the surroundings.

'Find it?' Gaz asked as they met in the middle.

'No definitely not on that side.' Ollie said pointing back at where he'd just been.

'Fuck, I don't understand. It's definitely meant to be at one end. Must have missed it when we hit the top end. Come on, we'll have to go back.'

'Really? You seriously gonna get me to walk all the way back up there. I've just fricking come from there.' Ollie protested, he didn't really mean it but he liked to get a rise out of Gaz whenever he could.

'Mate, gotta find it. Can't just leave that note anywhere.' Gaz flatly replied not rising to Ollie baited hook.

'Fine.' Ollie despondently responded as he began to deliberately labour his way back up the road.

'Not that bad only like three, four hundred meters.' Gaz said.

'Yeah I know, I can just guarantee that you'll end up getting me to do this for the rest of the day and it'll be like midnight before I get to put my bed together.' Ollie remarked.

'Oh yeah, shit. I totally forgot that your bed's arriving this evening. It'll be fine; we'll be back ages before then.' Gaz said.

'We better be. Are you sure you got the right street, 'cause I can't see a bloody pump at this end either. You better not have taken me to like completely the wrong part of London. Which let's face it would not be the first time your crap nav has got us wandering round in circles. Do I need to bring up the Mont Blanc incident?' Ollie said having another swipe at Gaz.

'Oh come on, that was hardly my fault. How was I supposed to know that the chalet was beneath us having been wiped of the face of the mountain by an avalanche and buried under 20 meters of snow? I don't understand it, sure the website said it was on this street.' Gaz replied annoyed that Ollie might prove to be correct.

'Right, leave it to me I'm checking this. Know what your like with technology.' Ollie said as he whipped out his phone. And waited for the search to kick out some results. 'You're such a dick!' He exclaimed as he read the blurb. 'This says it's on Broad Street not effing Broadwick Street. I can't believe you've done this not only have I had to tramp all the way across London to get here. I've then had to walk up this street not once but twice, all to find out that you brought me to the wrong effing location, un-bloody believable. Such a .... grrr can't even find the word to express my displeasure of you right now.'

'That can't be right, sure I checked it twice this morning. Give me that.' Gaz said as he snatched the phone out of Ollie's hand, and scrolled down through the rest of the article.

'Umm, excuse me. Had you bothered to read the rest of this I think you will find that I was right, in the first place. They changed it's name, it used to be called Broad Street, but they changed it to Broadwick Street. So I was right. Now who's the dick.'

'Oh, shit, sorry. Maybe you're not quite such a prick after all then.'

'Err, not a dick at all. Thank you very much.' Gaz replied.

'Anyway while we are on here, where does it say the pump is located?' Ollie asked snatching his phone back before Gaz had a chance to answer him. 'Ah ha, here we are it's at the intersection between Lexington and Broadwick, near that pub. Must have walked straight past it.' Ollie triumphantly said.

'Guess we'll have to go back down. Come on.' Gaz said as he turned and sauntered off in search of the pump.

'Oh my god, not again.' Ollie muttered to himself as he followed in his friend's footsteps, closely avoiding yet another set of pavement repairs in progress.

'So, umm where the eff is it.' Ollie asked as he finally arrived at the spot where it should have been.

'Now I am confused, definitely said it was here. I just don't understand it. That site definitely said this spot at the back of the pub.'

'Right, that's it. I'm going for a pint while you find that damn thing by yourself.' Ollie replied as he marched into the boozer slamming the door behind him.

'Pint of your finest, please landlord.' He announced catching the eye of the man behind the bar.

'Sure, Pride okay' The man asked.

'That'll do nicely.' Ollie replied.

'Your mate, not havin' one?' The barman asked as he pulled the ebony handle.

'Nope, he's trying to find some stupid water pump bollardy type thing. But I think he's fucked up somewhere.' Ollie replied.

'You mean Jon Snow's water pump?' Asked the man.

'Yeah, that's the badger.' Ollie replied.

'Well, he's gonna 'ave a bit of a job with that one then.' The barman replied in a rather thick east London accent.

'Oh why's that.' Ollie asked, now genuinely interested in what the man had to say.

'Well, they only went and removed it last week 'cause of 'll the pavement improvements. He'll have to come back in 'bout eighteen months if he wants a picture of 'hat.' The landlord said.

'Ha, I'll kill him, he's only bloody had me walking up and down this street looking for the damn thing.' Ollie replied digesting the information necking half the pint.

'Been on the council website for a while now. Just a week too late I'm afraid fella.' Replied the man.

'Ah well, c'est la vie. Cheers for the beer.' Ollie replied as he drained the last of the pint.

'No worries, sorry couldn't be of more help.'

'Just one of those things. Suppose I better go and break the news to

Shackleton out there.' Ollie said with a large dose of sarcasm, as he began to leave the bar. 'Oi numb nuts, the ruddy thing's been taken away 'cause of all the pavement works. So what are we gonna do now?' He called out as Gaz retraced his steps inspecting every possible place it could be.

'Oh bugger, when are they putting it back?' Gaz asked feeling rather stupid.

'In about eighteen months time. Somehow don't think we can wait that long. So got any other bright ideas?' Ollie replied.

'I'll have to ring Chris, he only gave me the one drop point.' Gaz replied, franticly rummaging in his pocket for his phone. 'Hey Chris, it's Gaz we've hit a slight snag. Jon Snow's water pump has been removed by the council due to road works or something. So there's nowhere to leave a note. How else can we contact that member of *The Order*?' Gaz asked.

'Yeah, that is more than a slight problem. From what I know he frequents a bar near there called *Cahoots*, it's in Kingly Court built into a disused tube station. Try there, if not we'll have to get one of the others to contact him directly.' Chris replied.

'Right you are then, Ollie and I will give that a go. Hopefully we'll get lucky.' He said.

'Good thing you called, I was just about to ring you. Devan and I are actually on the way up to London, turns out the one person who might be able to decipher the code is living there. So we may well meet up with you in the next few days.' Chris said.

'Oh, okay cool. Just give us a bell when you get up here.' Gaz replied.

'Will do, good luck with finding him. How many more have you got to contact?' Chris asked keen to know how much progress they were making.

'Only done the one so far, so got a few more to go. Hopefully the rest won't be as testing as this one. Catch you later.' Gaz replied.

'Yeah, okay. See you in a day or two. Bye.' Chris said before hanging up.

'So what did he come up with.' Ollie asked as he hadn't caught any of the other side of the conversation.

'Said to try a bar near here called *Cahoots*, apparently the guy goes in there quite a bit. Oh and he's coming up with Devan in a few days; apparently they found someone in London who can help with the professor's code.' Gaz replied.

'Ah, sweet finally we get to go party. Where is this bar?' Ollie gleefully replied, totally ignoring the fact that Chris was on his way up.

'In an old tube station in Kingly Court. Wherever that is.' Gaz replied.

'Ah, I saw the entrance to that place as we came down Carnaby Street. Not that far from here.' Ollie said.

'Good lad. Knew there was a reason I put up with you. 'Bout time you made yourself useful.' Gaz replied.

'That's rich coming from the man, who's just dragged me up and down a street three times to look for something that isn't even here.' Ollie retorted.

'Fair, point. Not really my fault though. Anyway, come on, let's see if we can find this bar.' Gaz said as he began to walk back up to the top of the street that intersected with Carnaby Street.

'That's it. Told you we'd passed it earlier.' Ollie triumphantly said as he pointed to a light bluish green archway, with Kingly Court written above in gold lettering. 'At least one of us can find what they are looking for.'

'Not gonna drop it are you?' Gaz replied.

'Nope, milking this one until the cows come home.' Ollie said with a smile.

'Such a prick. One mistake and you make out like it's the worst thing that has ever happened.' Gaz replied.

'Well I'm not the one who's adamant that they are always right. So where is this *Cahoots* place anyway?' Ollie asked as they entered the small courtyard full of boutiques and small cafes.

'What does that sign say?' Gaz asked, as he began to scroll down the list of proprietors on the three levels. 'Ah, here we are, entrance is on the ground floor.'

'Well, der your not exactly gonna find a disused tube station on the second floor, are you?'

'Oh yeah, forgot Chris had mentioned it was in an old tube. Well can't see it in the main courtyard, must be off down that side alley.'

'That's it. Shame it doesn't open till four.' Ollie said as he peered through the firmly locked steel gates preventing their entry down the steep steps to the bar.

'Fuck it. Just not our day. We'll have to come back later this evening. Come on, not sitting around here till four, let's do the next one.' Gaz replied.

'How did I know that was what you were gonna suggest, said you'd end up dragging me all over the city. As long as we get back for my bed, I'm easy.' Ollie said hoping that the next one wasn't that far away.

'Yeah, fair point. We'll do this next one, then go back sort out that bed and then come back here later this evening. Sound fair?' Gaz replied.

'Works for me. So *Shackleton*, where are we off to now?' Ollie asked.

'Let me just get my list, The Tate apparently. Hmm, that's gonna be a bit challenging.' Gaz replied wondering how on earth they were going to leave something in a highly secure museum without causing a scene.

'Yeah, how the hell you gonna leave a note there, not sure they will appreciate you defacing the art. Let's face it *Banksy* you are not.' Ollie joked.

'We'll work it out later, let's just get there first. Suppose we better go grab another tube.' Gaz replied.

'Once more into the breach, does feel a little bit like being continuously shot through the barrel of a gun. Guess Oxford Circus is closest.' Ollie replied.

'Pretty much, lets just hope we get an empty one for a change.' Gaz said.

'Yeah right, doubt that's gonna happen. Got more chance of Britain leaving the EU than getting an empty tube from here.' Ollie said.

'I wouldn't joke about that if I were you, that independence lot's becoming pretty influential these days.' Gaz replied, dreading the thought of a split from their European partners.

'Oh come on, they're pissing in the wind. Anybody with half a brain can see that if we left the EU we'd be buggered. You can't just leave and not expect there to be massive consequences.' Ollie replied.

'Yeah, but some people just want to see the world burn.' Gaz said.

'Suppose, it'll never happen though. I mean lets face it. Even the Tories wouldn't really allow it, would they?' Ollie naively asked.

'Who knows, they've always had a bit of a fractured identity within the party when it comes to the EU. Only takes the sceptics to be allowed into influential positions and who know's what could come about.' Gaz replied as he made his way through the turnstile and stepped onto the escalator.

'Which stop we getting off at?' Ollie asked steering the conversation away from politics.

'St. Paul's, just a step across the river from there.' Gaz replied.

'Ah, is that the one that takes us across that wonky bridge.' Ollie asked.

'Think they've fixed it since then Ol, but yeah, we do cross the Millennium Bridge.' Gaz replied.

'Nice, always wanted to walk across that. Couldn't believe that epic fail when they first opened it. I mean really come on, thought we were meant to have like some of the best engineers in the world.' Ollie replied.

'Yeah, but let's face it everybody makes mistakes once in a while.' Gaz said.

'I suppose, maybe they're related to you?' Ollie quipped.

'I thought we were done with that.' Gaz snapped.

'Oh come on, you not gonna throw your toys out with the bath water. Just a bit of banter.' Ollie said realising he might have pushed the boat a bit too far.

'Yeah, might be wearing a little thin.' Gaz replied.

'Okay, I'll stop. But you gotta admit, it was a pretty epic fail.' Ollie replied, finally giving up on roasting Gaz over the elusive water pump. 'Ah, tube is pretty empty.' He added as the carriages swooshed into the station. 'Maybe we'll have Brexit after all.'

'Ugh, couldn't think of anything more stomach churning. Can you imagine every time you visited the continent after that. You'd be treated like some sort of social pariah, like a bad smell that refuses to go away. Regardless of which way you wanted it to go. That sort of taint is hard to scrub off.' Gaz said as he took up one of the empty seats. 'Ah finally, nice to be able to get off one's feet's for a bit. Even if it is only for a few minutes.'

'Oh yeah, four stops.' Ollie remarked as he scanned the city tube map. 'Next time, can we not just grab a black cab or something.'

'Yeah right, we'd end up spending a small fortune, by the time we'd 'ave got round everywhere that we need to go.' Gaz replied.

'True, but at least my feet wouldn't feel like the bone was beginning to blister.' Ollie stated.

'Pretty sure that can't happen.' Gaz said with a snort.

'Oh, you know what I mean. You're just being pedantic. Get it, Pedantic.' Ollie replied.

'Oh, very droll. Bet you're really pleased with that one.' Gaz said rolling his eyes.

'You know sometimes you really can be just such a buzz kill. So things haven't been going quite to plan, not the end of the world, you really do just need to lighten up, just chill. The least you can do is laugh about it otherwise this is gonna be one hell of a long day.' Ollie said.

'S'pose you are right. Ah, this is our stop.' Gaz said as the tube arrived at St. Paul's. 'Come on, time to hit the bricks again.'

It didn't take the pair long to exit the station and make their way around the impressive structure of the Cathedral, and down towards the river.

'What the hell are those meant to be?' Ollie asked as they waited for the lights to turn green at a pedestrian crossing. 'Very random take on a gate if you ask me.' He added as he just about managed to read the label for the modern sculpture, on the far side of the road.

'Yeah, they are a bit novel. But that's modern art for you.' Gaz replied as they passed through the geometric archways before walking onto the pedestrian suspension bridge that elegantly curved its way across to the Tate on the south bank.

'Did Chris's note give any indication as to where in the Tate this note needs to be left?' Ollie asked.

'Something about the turbine hall. It's right at the heart of the building.' Gaz replied.

'I know that, I have been there before. I'm not completely devoid of culture you know.' Ollie remarked.

'Could have fooled me. Had you down as more of 'a three year old could have done that' school of thought.' Gaz replied sniping at his friend.

'Never heard such utter nonsense. You know what they say *one man's rubbish, is another man's Turner Prize.* Or something along those lines.' Ollie replied.

'True, pretty sure one year it was exactly that.' Gaz replied as they entered the museum, skirting one of the many gift shops and descended the stairs into the vast open space of the turbine hall.

'Ha, they've turned this place into one gigantic playground. Check out all these swings, that's so cool. Dude, sorry I know we're here for another reason but I'm sorry I'm gonna have to be a big kid for a bit.' Ollie exclaimed with excitement, his face beaming with delight at all the chain swings one would normal expect to find in a local park or playground, not something that would typically be associated with a modern art gallery.

'No change there then. Knock yourself out, you'll fit right in with the ten years olds in the corner there.' Gaz sarcastically replied.

'Oh come on. Stop being a spoil sport. While you're here, you may as well join in, and for once in your life take the tie off.' Ollie retorted. 'I don't understand what's gotten into you lately, I can remember a time when you'd be straight on there. I don't know this serious person you seem to have become. Good to throw caution to the wind every now and again.'

'Throwing caution to the wind can get you killed, Ol.' Gaz bluntly replied.

'Ah, I see what this is all about. This is about what happened to James, isn't it? And you're trying to fill the void. Mate, what happen was terrible and rather careless on his part. But you're not him. And you certainly can't change who you are, you gotta be true to yourself. Stiff upper lip just doesn't suit you and probably trying to be something you're not is more likely to get you killed than just going with the flow.' Ollie replied.

'Ugh, maybe you're right, come on I suppose we got time for a quick spin, or swing in this case.' Gaz replied finally giving into Ollie's childish notion.

'That's the spirit. It'll be fun.' Ollie replied as he almost leapt straight through the nearest swing in his over excited state. 'Take that one, we'll see who can go the highest.' He shouted to Gaz.

They spent the next few minutes in childlike rapture as they swung higher and higher, that was until Ollie decided to attempt a mid-swing dismount, culminating in a trip, fall, role and messy heap on the ground.

Wiping the tears of laughter out of his eyes, he picked himself up and dusted himself down. 'Nobody saw that right?'

'Hmm only this half of the museum.' Gaz replied trying to hold back the laughter. 'You really can't be taken anywhere in public can you?'

'Well, you know, always here to entertain.' Ollie replied before turning and in a slightly louder voice addressed to the on lookers 'Thank you, I'm here all week.' Before bowing.

Gaz jovially put his arm high around Ollie's shoulder, 'Come on you fool.' Adding to the gathering crowd, 'Sorry, ignore him. They only let him out from the circus once a month.' Causing a light ripple of laughter from their new audience, as they pair sauntered off and the crowd's attention turned back to the genuine exhibits.

'So you come up with a plan yet as to how to leave a message in this place, it's pretty vast and so packed with people. And you can't exactly write on an exhibit.' Ollie asked

'No but I reckon I can subtly tie a tab on a piece of string to one of those chain swings. If it's low down and on a very short string I don't think anybody would notice it unless they were looking for it.' Gaz replied outlining his idea.

'Ah, nice. I like your thinking. You got any string?' Ollie asked.

'Not yet, take your shoe off.' Gaz replied.

'Huh, what. You've got to be effing joking if you think you're using my shoe lace. If you wanna do that, use yours.' Ollie indignantly protested.

'Sorry bud, don't have any.' He replied raising his trouser leg ever so slightly to reveal a pair of tan loafers.

'Oh for heaven's sake, I bet you've done this on purpose. Fine, but next time we're using yours.' Ollie begrudgingly said as he leant up against one of walls of the turbine hall, taking one of his shoes off and dragging out the lace. 'I'll remember this. You owe me big time.'

'Thanks, Sport.' Gaz replied. 'Suppose we should find somewhere to write then.' He added, looking around before walking off towards the slope at other end of the turbine hall, where a few visitors were sat just admiring their surroundings.

'Could have done that before I took my lace off.' Ollie muttered as he tried to follow Gaz in a rather awkward fashion as his left shoe, now loose from it's bindings, indiscreetly attempted to escape and slip away to freedom.

'Nah, come on *Hop Along*, keep up.' Gaz replied over his shoulder as he reached the carpeted slope, sitting down and proceeded to scribble a message down onto a small scrap of paper, as the large ball continued its pendulum like movement high above his head.

Hampered by his shoe Ollie never actually got to see what Gaz had written, by the time he arrived at the far end of the slope his partner in crime had finished jotting down another cryptic message.

'Which one of those swings do you think would be the best to attach this to? The one's in the middle are too open, but don't want it to be obscured too much by hiding it in a corner 'cause they might miss it. What do you think?' Gaz asked, tilting his head slightly to one side as he looked up at Ollie.

'How about one of those ones just next to the back of the staircase from the ground floor. Not too open and yet will be some of the first to be seen after they've descended the stairs.' Ollie suggested as he quickly scanned the room for the best option.

'Yeah that should work nicely actually, those ones are overshadowed a bit by the floor above so the tag wouldn't be noticed unless one was looking for it. Just have to wait for one of them to become available now.' Gaz remarked noticing that currently all of the swings in question were currently occupied by some of the museum's many visitors, all rapturously being transported back to a time when responsibility was just a word grown-ups used. 'Ol, take this.' Gaz said, handing him the note. 'I reckon by the time you hobble over there, one of those swings will be free. See I knew that lace would be helpful.'

'Such a prick.' Ollie replied as he snatched up the note, and made his way over to the cause of so much childish behaviour. He had to hover close to one of the swings as the joyous occupants were less than willing to give up their source of fun just yet.

Eventually a swing became available, and for someone who was hampered by a loose shoe, Ollie move with the speed and grace of a gazelle, leaping the last few feet onto the swing.

There were too many people around to tie the note straight to the chains without being noticed. He needed a distraction he thought as he looked around for something to use. And then it came to him, and he began to urge the swing into motion, building up the momentum, more and more, until it had reached the max. He released his shoe.

The crowds of visitors were caught off guard, their eyes fixated upon the unexpected result of the installation, as his shoe cartwheeled end over end through the air, before crashing onto the floor some fifteen feet away from where its unsanctioned flight had begun. Ollie quickly tied the note to the chain of the swing before everybody's eyes swung back, to point accusingly at whoever had disturbed the natural order of the museum.

'Bloody thing.' He exclaimed, neatly covering up the deliberateness of the act. 'Sorry, my lace snapped.' He added.

'Come on, Trouble. Let's go before you end up getting us kicked out.' Gaz said before turning to a slightly bemused looking curator. 'Apologies for him, he really can be an absolute handful sometimes.'

'Not to worry, no harm done. Happens more often than you might think.' The curator replied. 'Enjoy the rest of your visit.'

'Thanks, been great so far.' Gaz replied trying his best to keep a serious face, before rounding on Ollie. 'Right numb nuts, let's go before you get us barred. I know you needed to create a distraction but really of all the things you could have done, you had to go and fire your shoe halfway across the effing room. Exactly how stupid are you? ... Don't answer that.' He added as he recognised the signs of wheels beginning to turn on Ollie's face. 'Come on, let's go sort your flat pack out.'

The pair were soon back with the tunnellers whizzing their way through the labyrinth of tunnels running deep below the streets of the metropolis towards Dolphin Square. By the time they arrived at Pimlico, the skies above had darkened and great drops of rain had begun to pour down.

'Crap, I left the roof down.' Ollie said as they stepped out of the station onto the now sodden streets.

'You did what?' Gaz asked, before realising what Ollie was talking about. 'You left the roof down on the car. You absolute cretin. You better run, Chris'll kill you if that car has any damage. Think you're gonna be doing more than putting a bed up.'

'Fuck it.' Ollie exclaimed as he began to sprint off, totally forgetting the lack of a shoelace, resulting in yet another heap on the floor about halfway down the street. Abandoning both shoes he picked himself up and tore off barefoot in the direction of the car park. Gaz watched him disappear around the corner and followed at a much more leisurely pace, collecting the disowned shoes along the way. *God only knows how that boy manages to function on a daily basis.* He thought, picturing the scene when Ollie arrived at the Cobra, sort of hoping that a wave of water would burst out when Ollie opened the door. Luckily for Ollie it hadn't been raining for that long so apart from some rather wet upholstery the car was okay. If anything having sprinted through the downpour he was wetter than the seats.

Gaz arrived just as Ollie finished attaching the last of the hood.

'You look like some kind of drowned water rodent.' Gaz said as he took in the sight of Ollie's drenched and bedraggled hair.

'Sort of feel like one too.' Ollie replied, spitting the excess water from around his mouth.

'Come on then Ratty, lets get you into the dry. Must be karma coming back at you after all the chaos you caused at the museum.' Gaz replied, trying not to laugh at him in his current state.

Chapter Seven: The Storm's Rider

The bleak and desolate landscape was the closest to what hell would look like if it ever froze over. Huge storm driven waves rolling across the small bay crashed into the beach with such fury that the surf erupted into the aether with so much force that the spray bursting onto the sand was as white as the snow covered dunes scattered with barbed wire, relics of the war without end that had torn the peninsular apart all those many decades ago. Many of the surfers had come off the water by this time as the tempest had reached a level that they couldn't handle. They huddled together on the edge of the windswept shoreline, specks of sand whipped up by the swirling winds stinging their ankles like a swarm of angry bees. Only a handful of the hardiest wave riders could be seen braving the strong rips in search of the perfect wave. Even from the beach the tense anticipation could be seen building on their faces as they paddled hard to maintain their position, waiting for the next set which might bring that one perfect break. An illusive wave that just didn't seem to be forthcoming, gradually all but one of the boarders was left on the water.

'He's got to come in soon, this stuff's getting real heavy.' One of the rider's said to the remaining guys watching from the shoreline.

'Nah, man he's gnarly. I've seen him out in bigger than this. He's been hell bent on catching that wave ever since he arrived. What's it been six weeks? He won't give up, that one. It's almost like he's searching for an answer to a question, but never seems to get a reply. Either that or he wants to meet God on his own terms.' Said another.

'Well, he's come to the right place. Can't get a more gnarly place to surf, if the waves don't break him then maybe the demilitarised zone will.' The first replied.

'True that. I just don't wanna be the one that has to go out to rescue him. I'm beat, that last wave wiped me out.' The girl next to him replied.

'Trust, if it gets to that point, he won't expect you to go. Should have seen him the first week. He misjudged a break and got dragged all the way through the reef. All you could see for ages was a dark red line running just above the coral. Then he just appeared, wetsuit torn to shreds, blood streaming down his back and a massive grin on his face. He just laughed, and went back out. Not many I know that have been through the washing machine that hard and continued.' He replied as he wrapped his towel close about his shoulders trying to keep the heat in.

'Yeah, even the couple of pro's that were down that week couldn't believe it.' Another of the surfers added. 'Aw check it, that one's massive. Come on dude, paddle, paddle.'

'He's not gonna make it. Shit, check out that pop up off the board. So smooth, wish I could do that.' The first said as he watched the lone surfer, effortlessly transition into a goofy stance, before pulling a tight switch back and dropping down onto the fade of the wave.

'He's going for the green room, That's sick. Go on man, you can do it. He's gonna have to work it, she's closing fast. Go on, go on. Did he just grab the rail, that's bitchin'. He's gonna have to pump it now or he's gonna get locked in. Ouf, that's gonna hurt in the morning. Glad I haven't been wiped out like that for a long time.' Another said as they watched the wave catch the rider and roll him up in its powerful jaws just as he almost made a clean break into fresh air.

'Where is he? Can anyone see him? That rip's gonna tear him apart.' The girl said.

'He's good, over there.' One of them pointed as the solitary figure of the surfer rose up out of the shallow surf further down the beach, dragging his board behind him. A fresh tear in his wetsuit clearly visible across his left shoulder.

'So close man, looked epic. You done for the day now?' One of them shouted over the howling wind.

'Yeah, almost had it. Ah well, maybe next time.' The man replied picking up his board and joining the others. 'You boys should have stayed out for a bit longer, that last set was awesome.'

'Nah man, too heavy. We leave those for the 'crazies'.' One of the locals replied.

The man didn't reply he just laughed.

'Axe, you up for a beer?' One of the spectators asked thinking it was about time to get off the beach and find somewhere to chill.

'Yeah, Jin. That would be great. You boys joining?' He asked.

'Sorry dude, I'm gonna have to bail. Got work this evening. Rain check?'

'Ah yeah, forgot some of you have to get back to the real world. Catch you next time Jung, been a pleasure as always.'

'You too man, take it easy.' Jung replied as they made their way off

70

the beach, and across the snow covered dunes towards civilisation.

'So where do you boys fancy? Mi Sun's?' The storm rider asked as he chucked the board into the back of his battered van, and stripped off the remnants of his wetsuit.

'Sure thing, best place to crash after a session.' Jin replied. 'As long as you're buying.'

'No worries, gonna need a few after that last one, proper creased the board. Definitely going to have to look at replacing some of the quiver. Had a few bad dinks over the last few days.' Axe replied as he finished towelling himself down and pulled on a pair of well worn jeans and canvas style top with the words: *Better a bad day on the water, than a good day in the office*, printed across its back.

'Yeah, especially if you're still planning to go up to Machajin-ri. Proper bitchin' up there, and that's if they even let you onto the beach. Even the locals struggle to get on it, what with all the anti-landing fences, the military are pretty strict about that area.' Jin replied.

'Can imagine, might have to go for a cheeky night surf.' Axe replied in such a way that Jin couldn't tell if he was joking or not.

'Rather you than me, man. Not sure I'd like to play chicken with all the searchlights scanning the beachhead.' Jin said with a great deal of anxiety resonating through his reply. Although he had only known Axe for the last few weeks they had become close friends. It still hadn't crossed his mind to ask the man his real name, the surfing community was funny like that. To them it really didn't matter where you were from, what your past was or for that matter what your name was. For them a shared passion for the sea, catching the next wave and above all an unbreakable unspoken trust that you'd help each other no matter the stakes was all they needed. All that being said they had to call him something, so due to the his nature of always trying to push the boundaries, resulting in some pretty heavy wipeouts they'd started referring to him as Axe. 'You still waiting for that new sled from Busan?'

'Yeah, should be here next week. But judging on this week, might have to order another one as well. There's almost as much dink stick in this one now as there is original board.' Axe replied with a grin.

'That's what happens when you keep chasing the heavy stuff. Gotta keep pushing though, right.'

'Always, what you drinking?' Axe asked as they approached the shack like bar, just across the street from the entrance to the beach.

'Bottle of Hite would be great, thanks.'

'Hey Dong, how's it going? Can we have two bottles of Hite, please?' Axe said to one of the guys behind the bar.

'Sure thing, how was it out there? Looked like it was really pumping today.' The barman replied.

'Yeah was kicking off big time. Hasn't been that big for a few weeks. Took a real pounding on the last set. This one chickened out, something about too heavy. Whatever that is.' Axe replied.

'Ha, yeah right. What he means is that some of us actually like to stay on the wave rather than coming back looking like a half chewed bit of shark bait.' Jin defiantly replied.

'Thought I did okay today, only got the one small tear in the suit.' Axe replied grinning.

'Yeah, but your board looks like it's been through a cheese grater.' Jin replied.

The barman just laughed as he cracked open the two bottles. 'Still taking on the big stuff then. You know one day, you're gonna take on more than even you can ride.'

'We'll see. Can I order some fries as well? I'm starving after that.' Axe said feeling a pang of hunger begin to stir.

'Can you make that two.' Jin added.

'Yeah, sure thing. Two fries coming up.' Dong replied, before shouting to the kitchen out the back in his native Korean. 'What you boys got planned for the rest of the day?' He asked after placing the order.

'Ah don't worry Dong, we're gonna be here for a while yet, the evening is still young. As a friend of mine once said *if you've been up early soaring with the eagles, you may as well stay up late and hoot with the owls.* You only live once so may as well enjoy it, right?' Axe said with a broad smile.

'Very true, just don't blame me in the morning if you can't stay on the board.' Dong said, chuckling as he walked off to serve a few of the other surfers that had decided to stay for a few cold ones.

'Cheers man. Been a good day, hopefully more of the same tomorrow.' Axe replied.

'Morning should be good, meant to start to drop off towards midday, really just the tail end coming through. From what I've heard it's then gonna be quiet for a while; but I'd take that with a pinch of salt. They said that before this brewed up and look what happened, doesn't matter where you are in the world, they can never be one hundred per cent when it comes to the weather.' Jin said.

'I know exactly what you mean, have exactly the same problem back home. One forecaster has never lived it down.' Axe replied laughing. 'Ah, can't beat a good cold beer after being on the water. Even if it is about to start snowing again.' Axe added as he looked up at the sky as the first few flakes of the evening began to fall.

'Well, if the beer gets too cold, we can always move onto the Soju.' Jin suggested.

'Ha, you've got to be joking if you think you're getting me onto that stuff again. I don't think your sister will ever forgive me for the last time.' Axe replied.

'Nah, think you're pretty safe there. She just puts that scathing face on for show. I think she has a bit of a crush really.' Jin replied with a smile.

'Wouldn't even dream of going there, man. She's your sister after all.' Axe said.

'Ha, that won't stop her. Once her mind is made up nothing on this earth will sway her from attaining it.' Jin replied knowing his sister all too well.

'Sounds familiar, I knew one like that a long time ago. I'll be sure to watch my six. You having another?' Axe asked as he drained the last of the bottle.

'Yeah why not. I'll have the same again, but I'm buying.' Jin offered.

'Nah, I got this.' Axe replied.

'Don't be stupid, you got the last one. Besides I think I owe you one from last night.' Jin replied.

'Ah, dunna worry, it's only a couple of beers.' Axe said as he got up and walked to the bar. 'Two more Hite, please Dong. Can you put them on my tab, just tell him his money is no good here or something.' He added.

Dong just laughed. 'You two are crazy. Never known people to argue over who's buying the next round before.'

'Ha, just a bit of friendly banter. Oh and stick one in for yourself.' Axe replied with a friendly smile.

'Cheers man, I'm not gonna argue with you.' Dong replied still grinning. 'Oh shit, your chips, I totally forgot. I'll get them now.'

'Cheers man. To be honest I'd forgotten too. No rush, don't think we'll be going anywhere for a while.' Axe replied, picking up the fresh bottles and returning to Jin. 'Here you are man, apparently they don't accept money from people who chicken out of the last set.'

'You're such a dick.' Jin said as a friendly smile spread across his face. 'The next two are definitely on me. I'll get him to bar you if I have to.' He added laughing, just as Dong came over with two bowls of fries.

'You boys want any sauces?' He asked as he set the chips down on the table.

'Got any of that homemade sweet chilli sauce left?' Axe asked, remembering the first time he'd encountered the thick sweet sauce, that flipped in his mouth, suddenly becoming like a ball of fire rolling around his tongue. He almost had tears rolling down his cheeks the first time he'd tried it, not because he couldn't handle it, more because he hadn't been expecting such an explosion of heat. Since then he'd grown accustomed to it. 'Nothing like a good burst of heat to warm you up after being on the water.'

'Got some in the back. Fresh batch, been maturing for a while, should be just right by now. I'll pre-warn you though, it's a bit hotter than the last lot. Been experimenting with a new chilli supplier.' Dong replied.

'It'll be fine, bit of heat never hurt anybody.' Axe replied.

'Okay, but don't say I didn't warn you.' Dong said disappearing into the back of the bar to dig out the fiery bottle, returning shortly afterwards with a luminescent red bottle and a glass of milk.

'What's that for?' Axe enquired.

'You, when your mouth explodes.' Dong replied with a knowing smile.

'Oh, don't be so silly. Give me that.' Axe said grabbing the bottle and shaking a good dollop of the sticky sauce over his fries. Jin didn't say anything he just watched the spectacle unfold as Axe placed the first chip in his mouth.

'See it's fine, got some good sweetness to it.' Axe said as the sweetness tickled his tongue.

'Just wait.' Dong replied with a glint in his eye.

'Bit of heat, nothing seri…' Axe began to say, before the real heat that had been lurking in the background began to kick in, and his face began to turn a deep shade of pomegranate. 'Oh fudge, eff me. Jesus, where the hell did you get these from. Christ!' He exclaimed as the tears began to form, and he necked the glass of milk.

Dong just laughed. 'I told you.'

Axe didn't reply immediately, he needed to compose himself first. Wiping the water from his eyes he said. 'Okay, you win. Jesus that was hot.

You been raiding Kim's atomic supply or something? Christ, that is truly wicked stuff; like St. Helen's suddenly erupting. Seriously, I like hot but that's just ridiculous. You can't serve that, it'll kill half your customers.' He added in between deep breaths, in a vain attempt to reduce the temperature in his mouth.

'I think it's all right.' Jin said, finally joining the conversation after trying the sauce.

'What? You can't be serious.' Axe replied.

'Yeah, it's all right, nothing special. Have had hotter.' Jin replied taking another mouthful.

'You people are just insane.' Axe replied staring at the bottle.

'Nah, we're just hardcore. Nice to have finally found something you can't ride.' Jin replied with a smile. 'See these westerners just can't handle the heat. All talk and no action.'

'Yeah, yeah. We'll see who can't handle what, come the morning.' Axe replied with an ominous and yet friendly glint in the corner of his eye, as the heat in his mouth finally began to dissipate and the tingling across his lips returned to normality.

'Better get him another beer. He's probably gonna need it.' Jin said to Dong as he finished his chips, and began to make himself comfortable for the night of partying that would no doubt ensue.

The smell of fresh coffee wafting across the room was the first thing Axe became aware of. His head felt a bit fuzzy and there was a distinct almost vodka like hint of Soju in the back of his dry throat.

Not again, knew he'd end up getting me off the wall. He thought as he started to drag himself out of bed. Shortly followed by *what the hell did I do with my clothes?* Scanning to room to find no sign of any of his kit. *Fuck it. Please done say we did naked challenge again. Fuck.*

Before he spied the note on the pillow next to him.

Clothes are on the line, not sure why you guys decided it was a good idea to go for a night swim fully clothed but sure you will have a good explanation. Dressing gown on door.

Meena

Oh crap! That's even worse. Gonna be one of those days. Axe thought digesting the contents of the note, and the potential repercussions, as he pulled on the gown. 'Time to face the music.' He muttered to himself as he descended the stairs into the kitchen.

'*Ah, The Wanderer rises.* Heavy night huh. Hope you boys had fun. Certainly sounded like you did when you crashed in here at half three.' Meena said with a look that could have vaporised the devil.

'Yeah, sorry about that. I told him Soju was a bad idea. Evidently he didn't listen.' Axe replied rather sheepishly.

'Oh, don't go blaming him. You're perfectly capable of being responsible for yourself.' Meena replied with no sign of that look softening anytime soon.

'Fair comment, we'll try and stay dry next time.' He replied.

'Oh, don't even go there. I've spent the last half an hour sorting this floor out. Sometimes I really don't know what I'm gonna do with you two.' She retorted planting her hands firmly on her hips.

'Well, I could think of one or two things.' Axe's cheeky reply was dispatched by the frostiest look he'd ever seen. 'Okay, okay. How about we'll cook this evening to make it up to you.'

'I suppose that's a start.' Meena replied, as her scowl began to give way. She knew she couldn't stay angry with them forever. She just wanted to see Axe squirm for a bit. 'Oh, and you can clean the bathroom while I'm out this morning.' She added.

'I'll think about it.' Axe's joking reply almost brought a half smile to Meena's face but she managed to just maintain her composure.

'You better, or you will be in trouble.' She replied in an equally banterish way. 'Right, I've gotta go pick up a few groceries. I'll be back a bit later.'

'See you in a bit, think we're gonna head back to the surf once Jin's up.' He replied.

'Well that bathroom better be sparkling before you do.' She said as she walked out the door.

'Glittering, promise, scout's honour.' He called after her departing figure. Meena didn't reply, she just kept walking. She'd had her say, and she knew that she'd put her point across so there really wasn't anything else to add. She was well aware that it would undoubtably happen again. She didn't really mind, she just enjoyed making out that she did and watching him squirm.

'Jin you up?' Axe shouted up the stairs from the kitchen.

'Working on it man, what's the time?' Came the reply from upstairs.

'Time to get up, we've got some waves to catch. Oh, and a bathroom to clean apparently.' Axe called back.

'Huh, what?' Jin replied.

'Part of the reparations in the ceasefire agreement. Pretty sure it's non-negotiable.' Axe remarked.

'Oh yeah, maybe swimming was not such a good idea.' Jin replied.

'You remember that? I have no recollection after the first couple of Soju's. I told you they were a bad idea.' Axe said stretching the stiffness out of his back.

'Dude, you were the one that bought them.' Jin answered.

'Did I? Oh, shit so I did. Well, I'm still blaming you.' Axe replied laughing. 'Where do you keep the cleaning stuff?'

'Under the sink, where else would you keep them?' Jin called back.

'Sorted. Right, I'll clean, you sort the food out.' Axe suggested.

'Yeah, okay. Be down in a sec once i've found a fresh pair of boxers.' Jin replied in the middle of pulling on a cleanish pair of socks.

It was a good ten minutes before Jin made his way downstairs and began rummaging around in the cupboards to find something to eat.

'Don't seem to have a lot in the way of food, apart from a box of Oreo O's.' Jin said having discovered the cupboard was looking particularly bare.

'That'll do, at this point I could pretty much eat anything.' Axe replied from the bathroom, halfway through scrubbing the shower.

'Got no milk though.' Jin replied as he stuck his head into the fridge.

'I'll eat it dry, I really don't care. Thought you were gonna get some milk yesterday.' Axe called back.

'I was, until you dragged me off to the bar.' Jin reminded him.

'Oh, so it's my fault is it?' Axe replied.

'Yep. I'll pick some up later after surfing.' Jin mumbled through a mouthful of the dry chocolatey cereal.

'You better leave some for me, or you'll be the one cleaning the sink.' Axe called down over the noise of the shower head.

'There's at least half a boxful, well maybe just under.' Jin called back, tipping a few more into his bowl.

'Well, I've finished anyway.' Axe said as he walked down into the kitchen, putting the cleaning products away before grabbing himself a bowl and pouring what was left of the cereal into a bowl. 'Text Jung, and find out what he's up to. Pretty sure he's off Wednesdays.' He added as he dived into the mountain.

'That's a good point, where is my phone? Must have left it upstairs.' Jin said. 'Give me a sec.'

'Think I saw it on the landing, charging.' Axe replied through a mounthful of biscuity goodness.

'Oh yeah, forgot I'd put it there.' Jin replied as he headed back upstairs. 'Apparently put it on silent too. Got like six missed calls and a text from Jung.' He called down.

'What's he said?' Axe inquired.

'Surfings out, wind's swung round too much, so they've headed up the coast about 10 clicks to Sokcho beach that's good for kitesurfing in these conditions. You up for that?' Jin called back.

'Sure, if surfing's out. That sounds like a good alternative. Pretty sure my rig's in order. Haven't had it out for about two weeks. But should be fine.' Axe replied.

'Sweet let's do that. Take your van, no point both of us driving up there.' Jin suggested.

'Yeah man, plenty of room for your gear in there.' Axe said.

'Sweet, let's do this. I'll go grab my stuff from the shed.' Jin replied as he opened the door from the kitchen to the side of the house, where a narrow sandy path ran between his and the next door house down to a small garden plot at the rear. In the far corner there was a ramshackle shed Jin had thrown together using whatever he could find to keep all of his water sports gear safe and dry. He began to chuck out various bags, sails, boards etc, as he dug his way towards the kitesurfing gear that he wanted for the day's excursion.

'Jin, I'm just gonna wander down to the beach car park and pick up the van, while you sort yourself out.' Axe called out from the side door.

'No worries man, should be ready by the time you get back, see you in a bit.' Jin replied dragging out the first of the two kites that he wanted to take for the day, as Axe sauntered off to collect his van.

While he was walking down to the van he took the chance to check his messages. For what seemed like decades now, he'd been waiting to receive one in particular. Ever since arriving, all he'd been doing was killing time, polishing up on the local dialects, scouting beaches and waiting for that one message. The one that would tear him away from his new found friends and send him out into the unknown and all the dangers that would accompany it.

Nothing, still silence. Axe began to wonder if it would ever come, or whether the man that had dragged him back into this world would release him and allow him to return to the loved ones that he'd been forced to leave behind. He didn't begrudge being resurrected but it had come at a price. A high price, one which he felt may turn out to be catastrophic. His mind returned to those left behind and to how they were managing to continue with what they had all set out to do and those that had already been lost along the way. He hoped that they had found what he had left and hadn't ventured down the path he'd tried so hard not to take. A path that would lead to more death and destruction and could ultimately end in failure. All he could do for now was to have faith that they would choose wisely.

Chapter Eight: A Path of Broken Seeds

Chris caught the door just as it was about to slam shut. He and Devan had been waiting for what seemed like an age in the cold light of the evening sun just outside Burleigh House for that moment when a resident opened the door. They couldn't just ring the buzzer because Chris knew that Chestnut Adams would never allow them up once she realised who it was. With a deep breath to compose himself for what was to come he grabbed the handle as it was swinging shut behind one of the residence and stepped through.

'Let me do the talking. This can only go one of two ways. I just hope it's the easy way.' Chris said to Devan, skirting the subject of what the not so easy way would involve.

'You sure this is the only option?' Devan asked, as the allusion of dark things began to dawn on her.

'If there was another way, we wouldn't be here.' He replied icily as they climbed the winding stairs up to the second floor. 'So not looking forward to this. Some things really should stay in the past.' He said as he rapped his knuckles on the dark green door of number five. Almost hoping that Chestnut was out, delaying the inevitable for just a while longer. Alas, it was not to be, as the sound of a metal chain sliding across its runner and the click of a lock being held back seeped through the door. *Once more into the breach.* He thought as the door began to open and they were greeted by the sight of Chestnut Adams standing in the way.

'Oh, it's you. You'd best come in, no point standing around in the cold for longer than you already have been.' Chestnut's statement totally blindsided Chris. Not because she didn't say hello or refer to him by name but just by the fact that it was so nonplus, as if she had been expecting them. But surely that wasn't possible, was it?

'How did...?' Part way through asking how she'd known they were coming, Chris was cut short as Chestnut raised her hand.

'No doubt you have many questions, but they can wait. It's good to see you, Chris. I really mean that; it's been far too long. And you must be Devan, I presume. Would you like some tea? Please come into the drawing room, no point lingering in the hall.'

If Chris had been slightly caught off-guard before; he was now totally confounded, so much so that the only thing he could do was to go with the flow and see where it would lead them. He was obviously missing some vital piece of info that would explain what the hell had just happened.

'Erm yeah, sure. Tea would be, err, lovely.' He replied as she led them down the hallway into a large drawing room bathed in the golden warmth of exquisite table lamps .

'Won't be a minute, just need to boil the kettle. Make yourselves at home. Would you prefer China or Indian?' She asked as she disappeared into the kitchen.

'There's a difference?' Chris asked turning to Devan, still reeling from the surrealism of the situation he found himself in.

'Typical man, absolutely oblivious to the details. China would be lovely.' Devan replied.

'I don't like this. Something doesn't feel right.' Chris whispered to Devan, while Chestnut was out of the room.

'Oh behave, you just don't like the fact that the bull in the china shop routine has been put on hold. I'm sure there is a perfectly reasonable explanation if you allow the time to find out.' Devan whispered back.

'Well, I still don't like it.' He replied.

'Don't like what?' Chestnut asked as she reappeared carrying a tea tray.

'Oh, erm, all that fruit tea malarkey. It's not really proper tea is it?' Chris's attempt at a logical answer was met with a highly sceptical raised eyebrow from Chestnut. As if to say *Yeah right; like that's what you were really talking about.* He shifted uncomfortably in his position on the sofa. He always had a severe dislike for not being in control of a situation, especially with somebody whom he'd shared so much history with.

'Milk?' Chestnut asked as she placed a cup on its saucer.

'Just a dash for me, please.' Devan replied.

'None for me thanks, black's fine.' Chris replied, he didn't want the taste to be masked by milk, in case there was something other than just tea in the cup. Pausing momentarily before deciding to tackle the issue head on. 'Chestnut, I don't mean to be rude, so please don't take this the wrong way. But can you please explain what the hell is going on.'

'Something's never change I see, he never was one for small talk.' Chestnut said directing her reply at Devan.

'Yes, I have noticed. He doesn't like it when he's not in control. But then he is a man so I suppose one can't expect the earth.' Devan replied.

'Hmm, I'm not so sure. I think it's a Chris thing. Has he gone through his grumpy PMT stage yet?' Chestnut replied handing a cup to Devan.

'Oh, once or twice. He does get quite broody especially when things aren't going his way.' Devan replied.

'Erm, I am in the room you know.' Chris interjected.

'See what I mean. Just can't handle it. James is exactly the same; they were so similar when I first met them, almost like they'd been cloned.' Chestnut said.

'You know, come to think about it I can see similar traits. Although I think this one isn't quite as methodical, shoots from the hip and asks questions later.' Devan replied with the hint of a smile.

'True, James is generally about twenty moves ahead of everybody else. Takes after his father in that respect. Shame he couldn't be here really, although I do understand his reasons.' Chestnut said with a longing sigh.

'I know, I'm truly sorry about that. You knew that once his mind was made up he wouldn't listen to anybody. In the end I just wasn't strong enough to stop him. I just hope we can pick up where he left off.' Chris replied, 'Which brings me to why we are here.'

'I know why you are here, he told me you'd need the decoder ring for that, oh what did he call it, Fibonacci cypher?' Chestnut flatly replied.

'Fibonacci ghost cypher.' Devan corrected her, in much the same manner.

'Yes, that's the one. Never could bring myself to get rid of it. Was one of the only things, after the divorce, I had left of him.' Chris sat there in stunned silence, certain words had begun to cause chaotic explosions across his neurones, as he listened to Chestnut's replies.

'Hold on just a minute, he told you we'd need this?' He finally said.

'Well, that's what he said. He seemed pretty adamant that it was the only way for you to proceed with whatever it is you lot have managed to get muddled up in. He said you'd know when to come for it. I didn't ask too much at the time, I was just happy that he was safe.' Chestnut replied.

'Exactly when did James tell you this.' Chris asked, as he battled his way through the shockwaves resonating through his mind.

'Oh, I suppose it was about six weeks ago now.' Chestnut casually replied.

'Chestnut, I hate to tell you this but that can't have been James. He was killed six and a half weeks ago hunting down the man who shot his father.' Chris said with a great deal of concern running through his voice; concern that somehow Norwood had managed to find out about the clue and the cypher, and that they were now all in mortal peril. 'I think you are in a tremendous amount of danger.'

'Oh, you always were so overly melodramatic, besides I think I know what my ex-husband looks like even if he did appear to have been used as a punch bag by a heavyweight boxer.'

Chris's head exploded, he now had so many questions he didn't even know where to begin. Part of him was more than a little relieved that his friend was alive, whilst part of him disputed the validity of the claim, and he wondered whether she was compromised. The thought briefly crossed his mind that she might be in league with Norwood and was luring them into some sort of complexed ploy cooked up by his lordship. He couldn't comprehend why James would put them through such traumatic emotions only to let them find out from a third party that he was in fact still alive. Raising the questions of how this all came about, what happened after he'd fallen into the river and most importantly, if he had survived where the hell was he now? Surely he would have returned to Noirmont as soon as he had been able to do so?

'This must all be a bit of a shock.' Chestnut said. 'I'm sorry, but he did make it very clear at the time that I was to tell nobody until the time was right.'

'A bit, that's the understatement of the decade. You have no idea. I'll bloody kill him.' Chris blurted out.

'I think he's died enough times already, don't you? He thought you might react this way, I got the impression that if he could have found another way, he would have taken it. He left this for you. I think it will explain things.' Chestnut said handing Chris a sealed envelope. Chris didn't reply, quickly tearing the envelope and pulling out its contents, he eagerly began to read.

Dear Chris,

Took you long enough. If you are reading this then you must have found dad's coded journal and worked out that Chestnut has the key to unlocking it. It will guide you to the next part of the Codex. Trust no one, there are things at work here that in the end even I couldn't out flank. Hence why I felt I had to do this and remove myself from the board. The spectre of darkness is at its most vulnerable when it believes it has already won.

What was once whole is now shattered. The Glove has one, the other I must find and destroy. Between them they hold the legend of the Codex, without them all will remain lost.

I'm sorry but I can't tell you where I am or what I'm doing, this is the only way. Hopefully our paths will cross again, if not there is one who will show you the way. Do not look for them, when the time comes, they will find you.

And regardless of what she offers do not trust her, she will always protect me, but I don't believe her protection will extend to you, she will most likely betray you at the first opportunity.

Good luck and God speed,

James

'Is that it? He can't be serious, why does everything have to be so bloody cryptic?' Chris said feeling more than a little frustrated as he finished reading the letter for a second time, committing it to memory before taking out a lighter and setting fire to a corner of the paper, dropping it into the ashtray on the coffee table as the flames quickly flared up, engulfing it until all that remained was a mixture of blackened flakes and ash. 'For someone who went out of their way to be the complete opposite of his father, he's doing a surprisingly poor job. I guess we really are flying solo, where's this decoder ring. If it truly is the key to all this, we better get cracking.' He said.

'It's here.' Chestnut replied opening the draw in the coffee table and laying it out for all to see.

'Jesus, how long did it take him to make this?' Chris exclaimed as he starred down at the decoder ring, made up of twenty-eight independently spinning rings, each split into twenty-six sections inscribed with either letters or numbers depending on where within the wheels they fell.

'It's beautiful.' Devan said gazing down at the complexity of the discs. 'Must have taken an age to work it out.'

'James never told me how long it took to create. I just know that it takes long enough to get all the discs in the right places to end up with anything that makes sense. It just depends on how many levels down through the rings the original message has been sent. If the message is as important as he has made it out to be, it may well have been put through all of them. You said it was a ghost cypher right?'

'The clues point to that.'

'Which means that it has an added layer of security as the final layer of letters are shifted, so this could end up taking quite some time.' Chestnut said letting out another deep sigh, as she thought back to times when her heart used to skip a beat every time she discovered that James had left a coded note for her to find. Even though this one would not end up being a clue to some romantic liaison, the same feelings now rushed through her veins once more.

'We better get started then.' Chris replied.

'Would you like some more tea?' Chestnut asked.

'I think this is going to require something a bit stronger than tea.' Chris replied.

'I've got a pretty decent claret, I'm afraid spirits are rather none existent here.' Chestnut replied.

'Red sounds good to me, almost feels like being back at uni rushing to meet the assignment deadline for the next day and having to pull an all nighter.' Devan said with a laugh, pulling a transcript of the professor's coded journal out of her handbag.

'Wow, I didn't realise it was going to be so long.' Chestnut said, pouring the wine and quickly scanning the first of what appeared to be several pages of notes. 'Might be best to divide these up and each of us work on a different section, otherwise this is going to take days rather than hours.' She added, removing the staples from the spine of the notebook..

'Always were full of practical ideas. And I must say this is miles better than just being a decent claret.' Chris said taking a long draught of the deep crimson liquid and helping himself to the first couple of pages.

'Is anybody else finding that the majority of these pages is utter gibberish with the occasional proper word?' Chris asked after half an hour of trying to figure out the correct way to decode the first page.

'I haven't even found one word yet.' Devan replied dejectedly. 'Are you sure this is the right setup on the ring to use?'

'Absolutely, I have a feeling that's why there are so many pages. I think the professor has hidden the message within a text of meaningless rubbish. We will have to unravel all of it and then take out the proper words from within in the whole thing.' Chestnut sighed as she scribbled down another section of meaningless rubbish.

'In that case I think we're gonna need another bottle.' Chris said holding up the empty bottle of red.

In the end it took two more hours before they could finally sit back and read the full text.

If you are reading this then I have failed in my task of protecting the Liber Veritatis, it is now up to you. I hope that this, combined with my other notes will guide you along the way to completing what I originally set out to do.

The Codex most commonly referred to as the Liber Veritatis has appeared throughout history under a variety of different guises. During my research I have found references to what I believe to be the same collection under the following names: The Book of Sin, The Divine Test, The Torment of Man and The Fall, I'm sure there are others but these are just the ones I have come across so far. Although the details of exactly what is contained within the volumes is rather vague, the sources all seem to follow similar themes that within its pages is great knowledge and power. The ownership of which has been fought over for as long as it has existed. My work is far from complete, nevertheless I believe there is a greater purpose and meaning hidden within the Codex, which for the moment eludes me.

The Sumerians broke it when they realised that man was not ready to be confronted with whatever the true nature of the text was. So far I have been able to ascertain where five of the seven parts are or at least were, two still remain lost.

The hours of studying the one at The Mount, have revealed that there is still great danger in humanity possessing all the parts. I have therefore concluded that they must remain hidden.

There still exists the risk that those who seek them may one day possess the entire Codex, I have set out to prevent this from happening. Where I have been able to I have relocated some of the pieces to new locations.

As an absolute last resort I am prepared to destroy them, something that I am loathed to do, not just because of their great historical significance but also because I believe there will come a day when the peoples of this earth will be able to comprehend its true nature.

I lacked the resources to move the first of the five I pin pointed. For now it remains undiscovered by The Glove, so I have left it where it has lain for millennia. And to keep its resting place as secure as possible I have destroyed all bar one record of it. A record that I have in turn disguised and placed somewhere that I believe will stand the test of time.

'The seeds of the flower, will be forever protected behind high walls and great dragons, nestled amongst millions of others.'

I hope this exhibition of my dedication to protect the truth does not go unnoticed over the passage of time. And shows the metal of the man I have become.

'See, what did I tell you. Like father, like son.' Chris said as he finished reading the decoded text. 'More riddles and hidden meanings.'

'True, but I think I know what he is referring to.' Devan said as she carefully reread the final parts of the text. 'In fact combining it with the clues we already have I'm absolutely positive I know what he's talking about.'

'And are you going to enlighten us or just say that you know?' Chris blurted out, not being able to contain his frustration any longer.

'I think you need to wind you neck in and behave a bit more like a gentleman first.' Devan bluntly replied starring him straight in the eye.

'Sorry, point taken.' He sheepishly replied, he knew he wasn't behaving quite as he should. He had so much bouncing around in his head, ever since Chestnut had blindsided him at the door and combined with the rest of the evening's revelations he was struggling to think straight.

'So we know there's a China connection which is definitely backed up by the lines here referring to high walls and dragons. And then there's this recurring reference to sunflower seeds, do you remember there was a Chinese artist that did an exhibition with millions of ceramic sunflower seeds at the Tate in London?'

'I vaguely remember something about it, wasn't he arrested by the Chinese regime?' Chris remarked.

'For a time yes, but more importantly I think, is the reference here to hiding something within millions of other seeds. I think the professor has hidden the location of the next part of the codex within one of these exhibitions, the Tate only kept part of the original display, the other bits were sold off to private collectors or sent to a few other art museums. A part went to the Faurschou Foundation in Beijing. I think the Professor must have put some extra seeds into the display which contain the location.' Devan said.

'But there are like god only knows how many millions of them, how the hell would we firstly find the right ones and secondly and more importantly get access to them in the first place, museums don't tend to just let you start digging around in their installations. The security for something like that would be immense.' Chris dejectedly replied, realising that although Devan was probably correct in her assumption, the task they now faced was nigh on impossible.

'I think that's why he has used *metal* in the wrong context, it should be *mettle*. The professor would know that, this is deliberate. I think he had some made out of metal or at least contained a trace of metal so one could find them with a metal detector amongst all the rest that are just ceramic.' Devan replied.

'Great, and how exactly do you suggest we get a metal detector into a museum? And then walk out with the seeds.' Chris said without really thinking.

'I kinda figured that's your area of expertise being the highly trained military specialist.' Devan replied defiantly. 'You always say that anything is possible.'

'Under normal circumstances yes, but we are talking about China here, one of the most authoritarian, paranoid and policed states in the world. You don't just walk in there and ask for the key. I'll have to discuss this with Gaz and Ollie, they may have a suggestion, but this isn't something we can pull off over night. This is going to take a serious amount of planning not to mention a master thief.' Chris replied. 'We'd better go. This isn't something I can do from here.

Chestnut, thank you for everything and if you do happen to speak to your ex, tell him from me that he's an absolute arse.' Chris said.

'Chris, so eloquent as always. Stay in touch, I might be able to help you at some point. I have some business contacts in China that might be of use to you.' She replied in the sweetest possible way that she could bring herself to. 'Devan, lovely to meet you. Look after this one, he needs a steady hand to keep him on track.' Chris snorted at her final statement, which was immediately battered by deep scowls from both women.

'Great to meet you too. It's been a real pleasure to finally meet one of the women from James's past.' Devan replied as she and Chris began to take their leave. 'I'll do my best with this one, still needs breaking in a bit I think, but he'll get there.' She added just before Chestnut closed the door behind them, cutting off any witty rebuke Chris could come up with.

'You'd better send Gaz or Ollie a message and let them know that we are coming round.' Devan said as they wound their way back down the stairs and out onto the damp, now floodlit street.

'Yes, I suppose I should but I think we will pay them a visit tomorrow, it's late, I'm tired and I have a feeling that they will be otherwise engaged at present.' Chris replied, quickly sending a message to Gaz to say they were in London, had made good progress and would be round in the morning to discuss the next moves. 'Best thing to do now is to find a room for the night.' He added as he spied an available black cab making its way towards them. He flagged it down and told the driver to take them to the nearest hotel. All he needed at that moment was sleep to help mull over everything he'd been bombarded with over the past few hours. Hoping that a new day would bring fresh insights.

Chapter Nine: The Woman

The apartment at Dolphin Square now resembled a child's playroom with giant pieces of Meccano scattered across the room. This was Ollie and Gaz's second attempt at putting the flat pack bed together.

'Dude, I don't think that bolt goes there.' Gaz said to Ollie watching him trying to force a bolt into part of the metal frame.

'It will go.' Ollie replied through gritted teeth as he put all his might behind it.

'Well, it might go, but according to the instruction it's meant to go over there.'

'You don't need to follow the instructions, what do they know?' Ollie replied.

'Well, generally how this all fits together. Oh, just give it here. We can't spend all night on this.' Gaz said as he pushed Ollie out of the way and relocated the bolt in the correct position. 'See, the bed actually folds down now. Right where's the other one?' He said as he scanned the floor for the next component.

'Fine, you sort it, I'm clearly just in the way.' Ollie grumpily replied, he hated it when Gaz proved him to be in the wrong.

'Wouldn't be the first time.' Gaz snapped back, after spending the last half an hour battling with Ollie regarding how to build a bed, he'd finally lost his rag. 'Look it's almost done, just go make some coffee, we've still got a long night ahead.

'Fine, can't believe I've been demoted to kitchen bitch.' Ollie replied stomping off to find the coffee.

'Finally, I can make some progress on this thing.' Gaz muttered under his breath and well out of Ollie's earshot.

A light knock at the door, prevented Gaz from putting the final piece in place and he darted into the kitchen.

'Ol, we've got company. Are we expecting Chris yet?' Gaz called out.

'No, he hasn't messaged to say he's on his way.' Ollie replied.

'Okay, then you stay here. I'll get the door, and be ready for anything.' Gaz said concerned that they might be about to receive an uninvited guest. As he heard another light rap on the door.

'Won't be a minute.' Gaz called out, as he left Ollie scrabbling around in the kitchen for anything that could be used as a weapon if this turned out to be an unfriendly, and crossed through the lounge to get the door. Pausing for the briefest of moments readying himself for whatever might be about to come through he opened the door to be met by the sight of a woman, in a red skirt, crisp white blouse and black jacket, who in his opinion must have been in her late fifties. He was so taken aback by the sight of the woman, as she was not like anything he had been expecting, that for a brief moment he lost the use of his tongue.

'Aren't you going to invite me in.' She said bluntly. 'After all, it was you who extended this invitation. Was it not?'

'Err, err, yes. Erm who are you exactly?' He half blurted out as his brain attempted to re-engage.

'Well, honestly, I could tell from your craft that you were a little green around the edges, but I hadn't imagined that you would be quite so dull.' She replied in the same icy tone in which she had begun.

Finally cottoning on to what she was implying Gaz opened the door as wide as it would go and she breezed passed him as if this was just a casual visit.

'And you can put that down, before you hurt yourself.' She calmly said catching sight of Ollie, who was standing in the middle of the lounge brandishing a rolling pin in his right hand. The only potentially lethal thing he had managed to find before Gaz had opened the door.

'Oh, um, yeah. Sorry. Can't be too careful these days. Can one?' He replied.

'I suppose that's one way to put it.' She replied shutting him down in much the same manner as she had shown to Gaz. 'Honestly, I would have thought that my nephew would have trained you better.' She remarked.

'Nephew?' Gaz asked in an exceedingly puzzled voice.

'Well, I'm assuming Christopher sent you.' She nonchalantly replied as if it was the most obvious thing in the world.

'Oh right, yes. Don't think I've ever heard him being called that before.' Ollie said

'Strange, I thought it was common practice to call someone by their name.' The woman bluntly replied.

'I just meant...' Ollie began to respond but she cut him off.

'Yes, yes, I know. But I hardly think this is the time to split hairs.' She said waving her hand around in such a well practiced autocratic manner, that both young men were rather at a loss as to what had just hit them. 'Is that coffee I can smell?' She asked.

'Er, yeah. I was just boiling some.' Ollie replied, finally remembering his manners, ' Would you like one?' He asked.

'Has nobody ever taught you that you don't boil coffee? But yes a coffee would be just the ticket.' She replied making herself at home in an armchair in the lounge. 'Don't just stand there like a wet lettuce.' She said turning her attention back to Gaz, 'Come sit, we have a lot to cover and one is not accustomed to talking up to people.'

Still trying to process exactly what had just happened, and not really noticing that he resembled a shell-shocked lost bunny in the middle of no man's land. Gaz slowly sat down on the sofa opposite the lady. He found her sharp icy demeanour more than a little intimidating and he was sure that even now as they sat there he was being eyed up, weighed and measure like a butcher's joint.

'Sorry where I my manners, I'm Gaz and that's Ollie and you are Mrs...?' Gaz finally said as the fog began to clear.

'I know who you are and it's Ms Sharpe, there is no mister.' She flatly replied.

'I must apologise for the state in here, we weren't expecting to have company.' Gaz said slightly embarrassed by the room's chaotic state.

'I'm not surprised, judging by your antics today. Your craft is unpolished, at best and quite frankly sloppy. A twelve year old could have caused less fuss than you two have managed to kick up today. Luckily apart from myself there wasn't anybody around of any significance to have noticed. You are fortunate that it was myself you contacted first and not one of the others. They would have been far less understanding. They are not ones to be coaxed out without reason and when they are, they expect it to be done in a manner in which they can slink back into the shadows free from consequence. If not they would make damn sure that no trace remains. I hope I'm making myself clear.' Ms Sharpe said.

'I get the picture.' Gaz replied. 'Speaking of which we still have two on the list to contact. And we've hit a snag with one as the drop point is no longer viable. We have a backup plan of sorts but maybe you have a better idea of what our next steps should be.'

'Yes, I've noticed that your information is rather outdated. We haven't used that particular drop point in months. Who else is on the list?' She enquired.

'Oh let me just find Chris's note.' Gaz replied as he thrust his hand deep into his trouser pocket and pulled out a now rather crumpled scrap of paper. 'That's all Chris gave us. So far, apart from yourself we've only managed to leave a message for the third one. The remaining two we were planning on targeting tomorrow.' He said as he handed it over to her.

She scanned the list, raising an eyebrow as she read the third name on the list. 'I wish I had seen this earlier. I would have advised against contacting that specific person, ah well, too late now. We will have to deal with those consequences when they arise. As for the others, it is no longer necessary to pull both out of their current situations. The task that lies ahead of us requires a very specific skill set. Only one of the remaining names has those attributes. The others should and will be left well alone for now. It is vital that they remain where they are for as long as possible.

We must act fast, before events completely overtake us, the specialist we need must be contacted as soon as possible. I will accompany you, he will not appreciate being dragged into the centre of the fray. And if it is done in the wrong way you two won't be around long enough to realise how displeased he was. Whilst you two have been prancing around, wheels have been set in motion that you could not even begin to comprehend.' She said as Ollie came through with a tray of coffee mugs. 'Thank you.' She added taking one. 'I have it on good authority that Lord Norwood is in the process of relocating the books and the map to a more secure premises. As I'm sure you are aware, they need to be retrieved.'

'Of course, but that isn't part of what Chris, sorry Christopher, tasked us with. We have just been asked to make contact with other members of the order. And then await further instructions from him.' Gaz replied.

'Yes, well, I'm giving you further instructions. He was unaware of the full picture, time to adapt or die gentlemen. The pace is picking up and none of us can just tread water anymore. We have to move and move fast if we have any chance of stopping what has now been set in motion. If you aren't up to the challenge, you better step off now, because from here on out the waters are going to get very rough indeed.' She warned.

'Where's a boat when you need one.' The look that Ollie received from Ms Sharpe as he tried to lighten the mood was so piercing he felt like he'd just been skewered like a spring lamb and tossed into a furnace.

'This is not a laughing matter, young man.' She snapped cutting him in two with her hawkish glare.

'Sorry, I didn't mean to cause offence.' He said sheepishly.

'You didn't, just think next time before you open you mouth. We've got enough clowns meddling in this city already, we don't need another. Come on, get whatever you need to keep warm, we've got a long night ahead of us.' She finished, picking up her clutch and rising from the sofa.

'We're going now?' Ollie asked, surprised that she wanted to leave quite so soon after arriving.

'Of course, the man in question doesn't stay in one place for longer than absolutely necessary.' She replied as she waited for the pair to grab their coats. And they left the apartment. Hailing a black cab on the street, Ms Sharpe instructed the driver to drop them at the corner of Upper St. John's and Beak Street.

The twenty odd minute drive, was one of the most uncomfortable Ollie and Gaz had ever had, they felt like two schoolboys being chaperoned around under the beady eye of a Dickensian governess. And they were glad when the cabbie pulled up at their destination and they escaped the cold dark silence of the hackney carriage.

'Right, Gentlemen. Time to go to work. Down that passage and take a right down the steps inside. Order yourselves a drink and enjoy the music. I'll be in shortly. Remember you're just there for a casual evening, so try not to stick out like a sunflower in a bed full of pansies.' She said waving her hand in the general direction of a passageway on the far side of the street.

'Okay, whatever you say.' Gaz said as he and Ollie left her and wandered over to the entrance.

'I know where we are, this is Kingly Court.' Ollie said noticing the lettering above the alleyway. 'She's brought us back to where we'd planned to go to anyway.'

'Looks like you are gonna get to party after all then.' Gaz replied. 'Come on, may as well just go with the flow and enjoy it.' He added as the pair began to relax for the first time that evening and descended down the old tube steps into the world of the roaring '40s.

The underground bar full of memorabilia and trinkets from the era of Django Reinhardt created a warm and welcoming nostalgic atmosphere that immediately whisked them back to the surreptitious and frivolous jocularities of Soho's nocturnal past. Even the band in the corner with their lively mix of Gypsy Flamenco and Swing seemed perfectly at home nestled amongst travelling cases, vintage milk bottles and hip flasks brimming with black market liquor.

'Hi man.' Ollie said to the tall man behind the bar. 'Great place you've got here. Love it, got a great vibe.'

'Thanks, we like to think so. You gents after some drinks?' The man behind the bar enquired.

'Yeah, what would you recommend?' Ollie asked.

'You on the ales tonight or do you fancy treating yourselves to one of our illicit cocktails?' The barman asked.

'Now there's a question. What are your thoughts, Gaz?' Ollie asked turning to his companion.

'Hmmm I think in this place in would be rude not to have a cocktail or two. Can I have a look at the menu?' Gaz enquired.

'Certainly, here you are, Sir. Our classics are currently half price for happy hour. Just give me a shout when you're ready to order.' The barman said as he left them flicking through the stylish green leather bound menu, whilst he served another customer.

'What do you reckon, Ol?' Gaz asked as they flicked through the comprehensively enticing list of intoxicating elixirs and heavenly tonics.

'Struggling to decide, I'm torn between The Count's Mistress and The Hatter's Tea Party, you?' Ollie replied with a wide eyed look of wonder and amazement similar to that of a child that had just walked into Hamleys for the very first time.

'Oh, I know what I'm having. Gotta be a Smoked Old Fashioned in a place like this. Bourbon and Swing just go so well together.' Gaz replied as his hand began to tap the bar top to the beat of the music.

'True, I just don't fancy such a slow drink, besides with so much choice why would you just go with something so mundane? Right, I've decided I'm going for the Hatter's.' Ollie said finally making up his mind.

'You know that's meant for two?' Gaz remarked.

'Yeah, all the more for me, haha.' Ollie jovially replied.

'Well, you're carrying yourself home. I'm not going to be responsible for you this time. Took me ages to get the smell out of my suit last time you went on a bender.' Gaz said.

'Whatever dad, she told us to enjoy ourselves so that's exactly what I'm going to do.' Ollie retorted, grabbing the barman's attention. 'Hey man, think we are good to go. Could we have one Smoked Old Fashioned for *Mr no Thrills* here, and a Hatter's Tea Party for myself, please.'

'Sure, the Old Fashioned will be a few minutes, if that's okay. Takes a bit of stirring that one.'

'No hurry, can't rush perfection.' Gaz replied with a smile.

'Ha, try telling the rest of my customers that, especially when it's ten deep at the bar. Absolute nightmare of a drink to make when it's rammed. Lucky it hasn't picked up yet, but it will do later.' Said the man as he picked up a shaker and shovelled some ice into the bottom.

'I can imagine, and I'll bear that in mind. Have a feeling we'll be here for the long haul this evening.' Gaz replied as he watched the bar tender expertly pour vodka, elderflower liqueur, lychee liquor, pineapple, apple and lime juice into a shaker before slamming on the top and vigorously shaking the mixture, before draining the concoction into a teapot with dry ice crystals.

'One Hatter's Tea Party.' He said as he handed over the steaming pot, accompanied by a cup and saucer.

'Ha ha, that's awesome. I'll take that over a Smoked Old Fash'd any day of the week.' Ollie squealed with childlike excitement as he eyed up the smoky indulgence.

'Would you prefer the Old Fashioned to be smoked with cedar, maple or cherry and applewood?' The mixologist enquired as he began to gather the ingredients together.

'Wow, that's a fair selection.'

'Would have been bigger, we we're going to try sapient pearwood. The problem was that it kept running away.' The barman joked.

'Ha, yeah don't think Twoflower would've been too impressed either if you started burning 'The Luggage'.' Gaz replied picking up on the iconic magical reference to one of Pratchett's Discworld creations. 'Hmmm, I think I'll try the cherry and applewood.' Gaz replied.

'Can I suggest, that you go with the Bulleit Bourbon, we'd normally use this one.' He said holding up a bottle of Woodford Reserve. 'But personally I think the Bulleit works better with that particular smoked wood.'

'Sounds good to me, you're the expert after all. I'll go with what you suggest.' Gaz replied as he intently watched the man skilfully add the bitters to the sugar, flick some ice high into the air, catching it in the heavy rocks glass, with a great deal of flare before adding the bourbon and then the long stir. The man finished it by smoking the drink with shavings of the fragrant wood over the rocks glass and a flash of orange peel.

'Here you are, Sir. One Smoked Old Fashioned. Would you like to pay now or would you prefer a tab?' The barman asked as he handed over the wispy infusion.

'Fantastic, love the way you guys come up with these. I think we'll start a tab if that's okay?' Gaz replied, taking his first sip of the smooth smokiness. 'Must admit I was beginning to wonder where she had got to.' He said to Ollie as Ms Sharpe entered the bar. Not that she even acknowledge them, she made a beeline for a space at the other end of the bar, ordered a classic French Martini and took a table in the far corner of the room opposite where the band were positioned.

'Guess we'll just have to wait and see what happens. Can't see anybody that looks remotely interested in any of us yet. Maybe they haven't arrived yet.' Gaz said as he lent back into the high back of the stool and let the music wash over him.

'If they're as good as she makes them out to be, maybe they are already here and are just biding their time.' Ollie suggested. 'Or maybe she's just testing us before taking us somewhere else, she's a bit of a dragon that one.'

'Yeah I know what you mean, no wonder there's no mister.' Gaz replied, thinking back to their initial encounter with Ms Sharpe. 'She is a pretty intimidating person for one of relatively short stature. I thought she was going to bite your head off earlier.' He added.

'Ha, I thought she was going to do far worse than that. Could eat children without blinking that one.' Ollie replied just as the band's first set came to an end and their lively playing was replaced with a generic playlist from behind the bar.

'Hey man, can I get four espressos, thanks.' The lead guitarist said to the barman as he approached the bar.

'Sure thing, Juan. Sounding good tonight.'

'Ah thanks, dude. It's okay isn't it. Could do with a bit more of a vibe in here, but hopefully it will pick up. First set's always a difficult one to judge, don't wanna play all the up beat stuff straight away, you know what I mean.' The guitarist replied.

'Yeah, gotta keep some in the tank for later.' Replied the barman.

'For sure, always want to end on a high, you know.' Juan said.

'Anything else I can get for you?' Asked the man behind the bar.

'A hareem full of semi naked women... ha ha I'm only joking. My girlfriend would kill me.' Juan replied as he was joined by the rest of the band.

'Is she joining you tonight?'

'I think so, I'm not a hundred percent sure, she's having a girls' night, and you know what they are like. They could end up anywhere. I remember I once got a call to say that they'd got a bit carried away and were spending the rest of the weekend in Paris, so we'll see what happens.' Juan said.

'Paris, that's nuts.'

'Yeah they can get pretty wild. But I got my own back. Although she wasn't so impressed when I told her I was in Istanbul. Ha ha.' Juan replied laughing.

'Nice, bet there were fireworks when you got back.' The barman replied with a smile.

'She calmed down once I'd explained about the hair, check it.' He said as he lifted his dark blue fedora to reveal the signs of new growth on his balding head.

'Ah nice man, I remember you saying you were thinking of getting it done. How long does it take to fill in?' The man asked.

'About eight months, then I'll have go back for the rest of the procedure. Takes a long time though, this took like seven hours having follicles taken out from my face and neck and then re-planted, definitely now know what it's like to be a pin cushion. But yeah it's great, soon I'll have enough to flick it around again.'

'How come you had it done in Turkey?' He asked.

'Best place for it, everybody gets it done over there.' Juan replied.

'Nice, you boys want anything else?' The barman asked.

'Nah, coffee's good for now. We'll be back on in a bit.' Juan replied as he finished the last of his espresso.

Ollie and Gaz couldn't help but overhear the band's hyper conversations about past gigs and what they had planned for the rest of the weekend.

'Hey guys, enjoying your night?' The boisterous guitarist asked sauntering up to Gaz and Ollie.

'Good thanks, loving the music.' Ollie replied.

'Thanks, man. Always nice to know it's appreciated. You guys just visiting? Don't think I've seen you in here before.' Juan said in his usual friendly manner.

'Yeah, just in town for a few days on business and thought we'd pop in. Where you guys from?' Gaz asked.

'Spain originally, but been living here for just over six years now. Got a great music scene in London.' Juan commented.

'Yeah the big smoke has got a pretty colourful nightlife. You guys just do bars or do you do other stuff as well?' Ollie asked.

'Oh we do all sorts, bars, clubs, weddings, private parties and so on. Pretty full on most of the time. You should checkout our website, you never know you might have a gig one day that requires our skills.' Juan replied handing Ollie his card.

'Thanks man, I'll check it out for sure.' Ollie replied taking the card and dropping it into his pocket.

'Right these guys are waiting for me to go play but maybe we can finish this conversation after the next set.' Juan said as he nodded in the general direction of the rest of the band that had moved back to the stage.

'Yeah, that would be great. Thanks.' Ollie said as Juan moved back to the stage.

'No worries, hope you enjoy the next set. Second set's always a bit livelier.' Juan replied before heading back to join his fellow musicians.

'Seems like a pretty cool guy.' Ollie said as the band started up again.

'Yeah bit eccentric, but guess that's par for the course in the music scene.' Gaz replied. 'Let's have a look at that card.'

'Hold on, I put it in here somewhere.' Ollie said as he rummaged around in his pocket pulling out his wallet, phone and eventually finding the card. 'Sweet picture.' He added looking at the cover photo of the band all dressed up in tails and top hats. Before flicking it over to read the band's blurb on the back. To his surprise there was a hand written note on the back.

Blend in more. Get drunk. We'll talk after the next set. J

'Dude, I think he's the contact.' Ollie said handing the card to Gaz.

'Crazy, talk about subtlety. Would never have guessed it would be him. See what she meant now about these guys being smooth operators.' Gaz replied. 'Just don't get too drunk, regardless of what that note says, need to have all your faculties to hand when the time comes.' He added, licking his finger and smudging the handwritten note.

'I'll try, got a taste for it now, but I'll do my best.' Ollie replied as he necked the last of his cocktail. 'What?' He asked catching sight of Gaz's sceptical look. 'Can't change the routine too much or it will look suspicious.'

'Such a liability.' Gaz muttered deciding that he was going to have to be the sensible one, after all he had a slow drink so could take his time, and he'd just have to put up with whatever state Ollie ended up in.

'She hasn't even batted an eyelid.' Ollie said glancing over in Ms Sharpe's direction. The lady hadn't changed her demeanour one iota, she just sat there in the corner as if nothing had happened.

'I'm sure she will find an equally creative way of entering the conversation when the time comes.' Gaz replied far more concerned with the fact that Ollie had now moved onto Mojitos. He was definitely on a mission to get absolutely plastered, there would be no stopping him now regardless of what the stakes were.

Ollie was certainly well on his way by the time the band's second set drew to a close. So much so in fact that Gaz had to order him a pint of water, just to get him to slow his roll.

'Come on you fool, you gotta sober up, you're in no state for this now.' Gaz said in a stern voice as he tried to get Ollie to concentrate. 'Get this down you.' He added passing him the glass.

'I'm fine.' Ollie slurred as he tipped the pint up getting more on his face than he did in his mouth.

'You boys okay?' Juan asked as he approached them.

'Yeah, this one's just had a bit more than he can handle, got a bit over excited I think.' Gaz replied.

'That might actually help things a bit. Sorry I couldn't be more open earlier I needed to be sure that you hadn't be tailed on you're way here. Can't be too careful, things have been manic ever since that thing with James. We've had to be far more vigilant.' Juan said, all the while appearing to be giving Ollie some assistance in his drunken state. 'Come on fella, get a bit more of this down you.' He added helping Ollie to drink some more water.

'Is your friend all right? Can I help at all?' The now familiar cutting voice of Ms Sharpe asked, having finally left her position at the table and wondered over to the group.

'I think he's okay, just had one too many. Juan Montego Lopes, at your service madam.' The flamenco player said.

'Pleasure to meet you, Juan. Great sound, I have an event coming up that your finger tips would be well suited to I think. It's at a small intimate venue called *The Vault*, do you know it?' Ms Sharpe asked.

'Yeah, I think its name has come up before. I understand it can be a hard place to crack.' He replied.

'It sure can. But I'm sure that a man of your calibre will have no problems.' She replied.

'Sounds great, what dates are you looking at?' He asked pulling out his phone to check his calendar.

'Oh well, would the day after tomorrow work for you? I realise it's quite short notice, unfortunately we had to bring the date forward due to conflicting interests.' She remarked.

'Would be tight, doesn't leave a lot of time to prepare. But I'm sure we can work something out. Here's my card, if you add us on facebook and message me the details I'll have a look and see what I can shuffle around and get back to you.' Juan replied, passing her one of his cards.

'Wonderful, I'll have my secretary send you over the relevant information in the morning.' She replied. 'Lovely to meet you, and I hope these two don't become too much of a handful. Gents enjoy the rest of your evening and we'll meet up soon I'm sure.' And with that she left.

'Now that's all sorted, you boys may as well enjoy the rest of your night. If he ends up being a real handful I can probably give you guys a lift after we've finished our final set.' Juan said as he watched the departing figure of Ms Sharpe.

'Cheers man, hope the rest of your set goes okay.' Gaz replied realising that the whole thing had been arranged with such speed and ease that it really didn't matter if Ollie was hammered or not, although he wasn't looking forward to the task of getting a very inebriated Ollie back to the apartment.

He was part way through ordering another pint of water and a drink for himself when he was alerted to the fact that he had received a text. It was a very brief message from Chris to say that he and Devan were in London and that they needed to see them and would be paying them a visit in the morning.

'Right Ol, you're gonna have to neck that. We gotta go, Chris is coming round in the morning.'

'W-what, but i'm just getting started.'

'Trust me you're done, that's enough for one night. You're still gonna be a mess in the morning; god he's gonna kill me.' Gaz replied as he removed the random unclaimed shot, in front of Ollie, out of temptations way.

Necking his drink, and settling their tab, he dragged Ollie up from his seat. 'Right, let's go find a cab, shouldn't be too difficult around here.' He added as he left the club, with Ollie in tow stumbling up most of the stairs on the way out.

Chapter Ten: A Parting of Ways

The early morning sunlight streaming through the curtains stung Ollie's eyes as he tried to cling onto sleep, his head was banging as if all the drummers in the world had suddenly been crammed inside. He had a very hazy recollection of the night before and absolutely no idea at all how they had got back to the flat. Eventually the burning desire to relieve himself became so great that he had no choice but to drag himself up out of bed, tripping over his shoes that he'd unceremoniously kicked off before crashing into his bed the previous night. He lay splayed out on the floor for a few seconds starring at the ceiling, pondering when was the last time he had ever been so drunk. Today was going to be a long day he thought, before remembering that he still needed to take a leak.

'What's all the banging and crashing about?' Gaz shouted from the adjacent bedroom as he was rudely awakened by Ollie slamming into the floor.

'Standard recriminations the morning after the night before.' Ollie replied, gradually becoming aware that his body was catching up with him as aches and pains began to spring up. 'Definitely going to be paying for that one today.' Ollie added.

'Well, I have no sympathy for you. You were properly going for it last night. Haven't seen you that drunk in a long time.' Gaz replied remembering the difficulty he'd had bungling Ollie into a cab the night before.

'Yeah, probably wasn't one of my finer moments. I'm starving and feeling as rough as sandpaper, what we got to eat? Not that I really want to eat, but better have something to kickstart the recovery.' Ollie remarked.

'Bacon sarnies is about the best we can do at the mo, that's one thing we didn't get round to yesterday.' Gaz replied. 'Want a coffee?'

'Oh hell no, my stomach can't handle coffee just yet, tea's fine.' Ollie replied, as the mere thought of coffee on an empty stomach had caused his gut to clench uncomfortably.

'You do the drinks and I'll sort breakfast.' Gaz replied grinning at Ollie's sickly state. 'Oh, you are a one aren't you, what will we do with you?'

'No idea, as long as I never see another cocktail again I'll be fine.'

Ollie replied.

'Yeah right, like that will ever happen.' Gaz replied as the mouthwatering smell of sizzling bacon gradually filled the room.

'Ah, that smell's making me feel better already.' Ollie said as he finished making his tea. 'You having tea or coffee?'

'Coffee, can't beat a cup of the black stuff in the morning.' Gaz replied as he began to plate up the bacon on some thick crusty bread. 'You want some ketchup on this?'

'We got any brown? Nothing better than HP with bacon.'

'Have a look in that cupboard over there, think I saw a bottle lurking on one of the shelves.' Gaz replied shaking a good dollop of ketchup out onto his breakfast.

'Ah sweet.' Ollie triumphantly replied, locating the bottle hiding at the back of a shelf behind the mustard pots.

'You got enough sauce there?' Gaz asked as he watched Ollie continue to pour the thick tangy sauce over the rashers until he could barely make out that there was any bacon on the bread.

'Gotta do it right, nothing worse than not having enough sauce.' Ollie mumbled through a mouthful of bacon just as a knock at the door caused him to almost choke and he had to swallow hard to force the ball of food down.

'Bet that'll be Chris and Devan.' Gaz remarked as he strode off to greet whoever was at the door.

'Hi guys. Good to see you.' Gaz said as he opened the door. 'Fancy a coffee?' He asked as the pair entered the apartment.

'That would be great thanks. Where's *Trouble*?' Chris asked.

'Just finishing his hangover cure.' Gaz replied.

'Oh, please tell me he didn't go too far off script and make a fool of himself.' Chris said with visions of Ollie's inebriated state.

'Nah, he played his part to a tee. Maybe a little bit too enthusiastically, hence feeling a wincy bit delicate this morning but all in a good cause. How did your fact finding go?' Gaz asked.

'On the whole pretty good, although it has left us with some decisions to make as to how we proceed. Looks like we may have to split the team up for a bit. We'll explain in due course.' Chris replied as they wandered through the lounge and into the kitchen area. 'You all right Ol, you look a like shit. Heavy night?'

'Urgh, don't go there. Did I overhear you'd like a coffee?' Ollie asked quickly changing the subject.

'Yeah, please mate. Just a dash of milk, no sugar.' Chris replied.

'Same for me, with one sugar, please.' Devan added.

'Think I can just about manage that. So what's new?' Ollie replied grabbing two extra mugs from a cupboard.

'Well, as I was just saying to Gaz, we've had a pretty productive trip up. However, due to the information we've managed to get from the Prof's code, we may have to go our separate ways for a period. It appears that the next part of the Codex or at least the coordinates of where it is are in China.' Chris said.

'China, Jesus, that's a bit of a trek. The Prof really does enjoy treasure hunting on a large scale. I'm presuming that you and Devan are planning on going?' Gaz remarked.

'More than likely, but because of how the Prof has concealed the information we are going to have to enlist the help of a thief in order to retrieve the info.' Chris replied.

'Ah we just made contact with one of them. But that's going to cause a problem. Your Aunt requires his services. And on that note, thanks for the heads up.' Ollie said. 'Bit of battle axe that one.'

'Oh yeah, sorry. She can be a bit blunt.' Chris smiled as he replied, thinking that she must have been a bit of a shock to the system for the pair's laid back approach.

'A bit, that's the understatement of the century.' Ollie replied.

'Oh, she's not that bad. But we're digressing, why does she need a thief?' Chris asked, caught off guard at the mention of a thief.

'Because she has been reliably informed that Norwood is relocating the parts of the Codex he already has to a vault somewhere in the city. So to retrieve them we are going to have to crack it.' Gaz replied.

'Ah, that's inconvenient, but not unexpected. I had a feeling he would do something like that after your exploits at Glympton. Do you know where she is now? I had hoped to catch her here.' Chris remarked.

'She's gone to find out where the books are being taken to. She mentioned that a source had contacted her to say that Norwood had dispatched Chamberlain with them, and that he was arriving in London today to deposit them. So I can only assume that she is planning on following him. I can't tell you much more, because she hasn't disclosed any more than that. Another one that keeps cards close to her chest.' Ollie replied.

'Hmmm, old habits, I'm afraid. I had hoped she would be a little more open, but I do understand the motivations. She's been in deep for a long time and she won't take any risks which might jeopardise that.' Chris replied.

'Yeah, she made sure we got that message. So we have rather left her to it. So whereabouts in China is this thingy that you got to half inch?' Ollie asked.

'At the Faurschou Foundation, an art museum in the Dashanzi Art District, northeast of central Beijing.' Chris said.

'Ha yeah, funny. Seriously where is it?' Gaz replied.

'He is being serious.' Devan interjected, before Chris had a chance to snap back.

'So hold on, let me just get this straight, you want us to go into one of the most highly policed states on the planet and steal something in one of the tightest controlled areas of said state and just walk away.' Gaz said.

'Pretty much.' Chris replied with a slight smile.

'Well, I'm sold.' Ollie said.

'Why am I not surprised. Well, I suppose if he wants to do it, I can't really refuse, can I? After all someone's got to be there to save his arse when he drops the ball.' Gaz added.

'That's great boys, I appreciate the enthusiasm, but I think you are forgetting that someone's got to stay and help Aunt Tabitha.' Chris replied.

'Ah Tabitha, so that's her first name. We had begun to wonder if she actually had one.' Ollie smirked. 'So I guess we have to stay here then?' He added slightly deflated after the notion of being let off the leash in a foreign land.

'For now at least, yes. I think if you continue with whatever she has planned for retrieving what you can from wherever it is that Chamberlain ends up stashing the Codex parts and the Map, whilst Devan and I travel to Beijing and get the lay of the land. This isn't going to be something that we can do in a few days, it's going to require meticulous planning to pull off a job of that magnitude. You'll have to join us later. Just look at it this way at least you'll get a warm up here before the main event.' Chris said.

'I guess so. That's if we survive *The Tabby Cat*.' Ollie's laugh vanished as abruptly as it had begun as he was hit but the full force of Chris's glare.

'Such a good thing she's not here to witness that. You'd be all kinds of dead by now, had she been.' Chris said swigging the last of his coffee. 'Right well, that's about the gist of everything to date. We are going to have to bid you adieu, got a lot of travel to sort out. Oh and you won't forget to tell my aunt to drop me a line, will you?' He added.

'Yeah, we'll tell her. Still using the same protocol at the moment?' Gaz asked.

'For now, yes. We're not due to switch for another few days. See you boys and try not to have too much fun without us.' Chris said as he stood to leave.

'Take care guys.' Devan added as she joined Chris at the door.

'You didn't mention James, to them.' Devan said in a questioning tone as they descended in the lift.

'The timing isn't right. I need them one hundred percent focused at the moment, not wondering about where he might be, if indeed he is still alive.' Chris replied.

'But that note.' Devan interjected.

'That note, just tells us he didn't die in the river. We've no way of knowing what's happened since.' Chris replied coldly.

'I suppose that's true.' Devan replied not forcing the issue, realising that Chris was also trying to keep his focus on the job at hand . 'So what's next?' She asked as they stepped out of Hood House.

'Good question, a good travel agent seems to be the order of the day. And I think I know just the one.' He replied with another one of those teasing looks as they wandering away from Dolphin Square leaving Ollie and Gaz to wait for the return of Ms Sharpe.

Chapter Eleven: A Red Sky in The North

Lord Norwood rubbed his bloodshot strained eyes as he tried to focus on the document he was scrolling through on his desktop. Since Chamberlain had left for London with the two parts of the *Liber Veritatis*, Lord Norwood had turned his sights on locating the next piece of the ancient codex. All he had to go on was a tenuous link to the Prince of Gui, the *Black Dragon Seal Scroll*. A scroll that he had not been able to possess because Professor Middleton had beaten him to it and hidden the document. As a result he had been forced to get hold of as many books and other sources as possible regarding the lesser imperial figure, even trawling the internet for any snippets of information about the last few years of the obscure Prince's life. So far all he had managed to learn was that Zhu Youlang, the Prince of Gui had been the seventh son of Zhu Changying and had ascended to the throne as the fourth Southern Ming emperor in November 1646 during a period when the Ming, as a ruling dynasty, were in their twilight. Their influence was being sapped and under constant attack from the Manchu, by the time the Prince of Gui had converted to Christianity he had been forced to flee to the South Western region of the empire, eventually being caught in Burma by the turncoat General Wu Sangui in 1662, who promptly executed the sole remaining claimant of the Ming dynasty, personally strangling him so slowly that the last of the Ming reportedly begged him to be quicker so that he didn't have to look upon the traitor's face for a second longer. In a final act of humiliation the Prince of Gui's body was torn into five pieces, his head was hung on display in the capital, whilst the remaining parts were dispatched to the furthest reaches of the empire. Acting as a constant reminder that the Manchu and Qing Dynasty were now holding the reins of power.

The questions that persisted were how any of this could be relevant to the location of the next undiscovered piece and would he ever find it? Nevertheless his overwhelming zealous desire to wield the whole codex drove him to keep searching.

The sun was gradually creeping up, casting far-reaching shadows with the long blades of grass in front of Glympton by the time Lord Norwood found the reference he had spent days searching for, a small note in the *Junjichu lufu zouzhe* recording where in the empire the rent body parts of the Prince of Gui had been dragged off to. In the North East, Liaoning, to the South East, Fujian, to the South, Guangxi and to the North West, Xinjiang.

Out of the four provinces Liaoning was the most intriguing, it was the heartland of the Manchu, surely out of all the Chinese provinces they controlled it would be the least likely to foster rebellion. It was not until he read further down that Norwood realised, that this was not the final resting place for the severed quarter, from Liaoning it was taken to Pyongyang and mounted on display amongst the Goguryeo Tombs Complex, in present day North Korea. The Joseon Dynasty, that had ruled all of Korea centuries before the North-South divide, had been tributaries to the Ming Dynasty and had initially supported them when the Manchu had begun their invasion until the Manchu had utterly destroyed the Ming and brought Joseon to heel. It was evident that the Manchu wanted to send a clear warning to their Korean subordinates that any kind of insurrection would be swiftly dealt with in the most severe way imaginable. According to the text a number of the Prince of Gui's possessions had accompanied the body part, including an ornately inscribed medallion which was later rumoured to be the key to unlocking the source of all the Ming's power.

Lord Norwood rubbed his hands together with glee as he read the final part of the source. He could sense that he was now closer than he had ever been to finding the third part of the *Liber Veritatis*. Although he realised that it would take all his guile and a great deal of luck to gain entry into a country that for centuries had pursued isolationist policies, limiting contact with foreign countries long before the rise of the tyrannical Kims.

It was at this moment that Miss Carla Adams effortlessly glided into his study.

'Have you had any luck, my dear?' She asked in a voice that could have melted the thickest of ice.

'I believe I have found it or at least something that will lead us to it. But it won't be easy to obtain, out of all the places that it could be, the key to finding the next piece is in North Korea. And I'm sure you are well aware that they are not exactly the most welcoming of nations. I think I will contact Conrad, he's had dealings with them in the past.' Norwood replied.

'Yes, I seem to remember the last time I met Mr Du Bois he mentioned he had just brokered some sort of oil deal between the North

Koreans and Russia. And I'm almost certain he has contacts at the North Korean Embassy, if one can call it that. It's not much more than a town house well outside the centre of London. Where's your address book? I'll phone him and see if he is available to start making the arrangements.' Carla asked, keen to get the ball rolling. She had been starting to get itchy feet as she had been at the manor for such a long time just waiting for her next assignment. She very much hoped that his Lordship would send her out to do what she did best.

'There's a Filofax over on the window sill.' He replied pointing to the huge sash windows. 'I think it would be best to try his office number, I'm sure he won't be at home at this time of day.' Norwood added glancing at his watch to see that it was already half past ten in the morning and suddenly realising that he had been wading through various texts for a good twenty odd hours. 'Is that really the time? I think some coffee might be in order to restore my spirits.' He said, giving a rope dangling down from the ceiling just behind his desk a sharp tug. A soft ding-a-ling of a bell could be heard echoing far away in another part of the great house. To be answered by the appearance of Mr Jacobs a few minutes later.

'You rang, My Lord.' Mr Jacobs said as he entered the warm study.

'Ah, yes Jacobs, would you be so kind as to fetch some coffee. I'm in need of blowing the cobwebs away.' Lord Norwood said.

'Very good, My Lord. Would you prefer hot milk or cream, this morning?' His valet attentively asked.

'Oh, hot milk will be perfectly adequate this morning. Thank you Jacobs, you really are very good to me.' He added, realising that his valet had been exceedingly proactive of late and hadn't really received the praise that he was due.

'Thank you, My Lord.' Mr Jacobs replied, rather surprised by the unexpected gratitude that he had just received. In fact he couldn't ever remember a previous occasion when his Lordship had shown even the slightest sliver of appreciation for the duties that he carried out; something very momentous indeed must have just occurred to put his Lordship in such high spirits Mr Jacobs thought as he strode down the stone passageway to the kitchen in the East wing of the manor.

Carla flicked through the alphabetised contacts until she found Conrad's details and picking up the receiver she dialled the number, waiting as the phone began to ring until Conrad's distinctive voice answered.

'Hi Conrad, it's Carla. I trust you are well?' She asked.

'Very well indeed, my dear and much the better for hearing your voice. I hope all is well and that things are progressing as planned.' He replied.

'Oh, you're such a charmer. Yes, in general things are good at this end, however we have come to a slight impasse that we were hoping you might be able to help with. His lordship has discovered that the key to locating the next part of the book is buried somewhere near the capital of North Korea, and as you have avenues of contiguity into there, we were hoping that you would be able to organise safe passage into the country to retrieve it.'

There was a brief pause before Conrad answered. As if he were weighing up the risks versus rewards of utilising a network he had taken a considerable and painstaking amount of time and effort to bend to his will. 'I believe it would be possible. Yes, I have a man in their embassy that I think should be able to make the arrangements, tell his lordship that I will undertake the necessary ground work. I'm presuming that you will be traveling privately? How many permits will be required?' He asked as he began to make some notes on a pad.

'I should think four including one for yourself should be sufficient and yes we will take the jet. I don't think there are that many public flights into the country, and besides you know how his lordship feels about public transport.'

'Ha, yes. Very true. Just remind his lordship that they will want something in return, nothing comes for free with that lot.' Conrad replied.

'Thanks, Conrad. I'm sure he will find something of sufficient value to trade in return. Speak to you again soon. All my best to the family.' She replied before hanging up.

'Does he think he can do it?' Lord Norwood asked.

'Yes, he will make all the arrangements. I've asked him for four permits, one for each of us and as Chamberlain is otherwise engaged I presumed you would like Mr Leach to accompany you.'

'Well, I suppose an extra pair of hands can't hurt, although I must admit he is beginning to wear out his usefulness. I suppose I can always leave him with the Koreans; although even they might see that as more of an insult than a gift.' Norwood replied with a wry smile.

'Speaking of which Conrad did mention that you should be prepared to give the North Koreans something in return. I got the impression that they can be very difficult to deal with.' Carla replied.

'Hmmm, yes. He has a point. I'll have to think carefully about that one. We have a few trinkets left in the hangar that might be of use to them, failing that I have been keeping something tucked away for just such an occasion.' He said mysteriously. 'But don't worry about that for now, I'll re-assess the situation nearer the time, they certainly wouldn't have been my first choice for such a gift; but needs must when the devil drives.' His brow creased for the briefest of heart beats, as if even he was perplexed by whether it was sound logic to travel down that particular road

'Would you like me to begin preparations for the trip?' Carla asked, deliberately avoiding the question of exactly what it was that he had been saving for just such an occasion. She knew that had he wanted her to know he would have told her, so there was no point even asking. Whatever it was, if he didn't want her to know, it might well be something that even she would think twice about before giving away. Certainly his last troubled fleeting glance out of the window gave her the impression that it was something that he might actually fear.

'Yes, you better go and make sure the jet's ready for a long trip. Oh and get the captain to file a flight plan, best not make North Korea the destination. Tell her to make it somewhere close and then we'll have to make mid flight adjustments due to mechanical issues or something similar, sure you'll be able to work it out between yourselves.' He said before adding; 'Oh, and make sure the plane is fully equipped with expedition gear, North Korea may not be our final destination. If we do find this medallion, I'm not going to waste any time. Captain Flack must not be allowed to get his hands on another piece before me, if he's found the scroll the professor hid, the next part may well already be within his grasp. Which reminds me I must call Chamberlain and make sure he has the up to date code to access the vault.'

Carla left Lord Norwood in the process of contacting Chamberlain and set out for the private airfield just outside Oxford where the Gulfstream G550 jet was currently being stored for the winter. She knew she would have a lot to do over the coming days to ensure that they were ready to go as soon as the permits were granted. At least she finally had some action to look forward to she thought as she drove out of the gates at Glympton.

Chapter Twelve: The Vault

The huge figure of Chamberlain, carrying a package wrapped up in brown paper and string, arriving outside the Safe Deposit building had not proved hard to track. Ms Sharpe had been trailing him from Paddington Station across the tube network and the streets of London ever since she had received information from her contact within Glympton Park that he had been dispatched by Lord Norwood with both pieces of the *Liber Veritatis*. Ducking into a shop doorway, she watched him enter the building. The Depository was one of the oldest established in the area, and although she was sure that their security systems would be state of the art, the building itself was beginning to show its age. A weakness, perhaps one that could be exploited, she thought. However, getting into the building wasn't the only problem, once inside they would have to get into the vault without detection and most importantly get out without anybody being any the wiser, something that many had tried over the years, generally without much success. At this stage the crucial step was to get a good look at the vault.

It was a good fifteen minutes or so before the lumbering hulk of Chamberlain re-emerged from the building, leaving without the package that he had been carrying. Deciding that there was no longer any need to continue to track his movements, Ms Sharpe switched her attention to the building and made the swift decision to gain entry and if possible get a peak at the vault itself. All of which would be of vital importance for what would have to follow.

She spent the next few hours flitting in and out of a number of high end jewellery stores until she had acquired a few items that would pass scrutiny. She'd heard that sometimes the deposit companies would check what was going into their boxes just in case someone was trying to pull a fast one to access the vaults.

Chamberlain was long gone by the time she returned to the Safe Deposit company, putting on the air of somebody going through a great deal of stress and worry she entered the building.

'Good afternoon, Madame.' Said the burly security guard just inside the doorway. 'Do you have an appointment?'

'I'm afraid I don't, everything has happened so quickly that I rather panicked, jumped in the car and rushed down here as soon as I could.' She replied. 'I'm sorry, I must apologise, I'm all of a flutter. Somebody broke into my next door neighbour's, you see, and well it rather put the wind up, I have been keeping some rather expensive jewellery given to me by my late husband. I wouldn't be able to forgive myself if the same thing happened to me. So I jumped in the car and came straight up. I didn't even stop to think about making an appointment, and of course now I have all of these things with me. Would it be at all possible to speak to a manager.'

'I quite understand.' The guard replied, totally taken in by her distressed look. 'Can I take your name and I'll see if the duty manager is available.' He added.

'Oh, you are kind. Honestly, I've been in such a tizzy since it happened. It's Mrs. Trickle.' She replied, using an alias that she had used many times in the past and one that she knew would pass all the relevant background and security checks.

'Please, take a seat Madame. While I see what I can arrange for you.' He said, as he began to radio through to the management and explain the situation.

She had not been sitting in the reception area for more than a few minutes when a lady in her early forties came to greet her.

'Mrs Trickle, good afternoon. I'm Sarah Connors, the Deposit Manager. I understand you are looking to rent a box from us. And may I add that I'm very sorry to hear of the events leading to you seeking us out, it must have been very frightening and upsetting for you.' Sarah said.

'Thank you dear, yes it was rather shocking. I haven't slept a wink since.' She replied.

'Would you like to follow me and we'll see what we can find that best fits your requirements. Can I get you a drink, tea or coffee perhaps?' She asked as she ushered the lady she believed to be Mrs Trickle into her office.

'Oh you are kind, a cup of tea would be very nice dear, thank you.' Ms Sharpe replied as she took a seat in the deposit manager's office.

'Do you take milk and sugar?' Sarah asked as she poured some hot water from the electric urn in the corner of her office.

'Just a spot of milk, thank you.'

'So I understand that you have some jewellery that you would like to deposit.' Sarah said as she fished out the spent tea bag with a spoon and slung it into a waste bin.

'Yes, they're probably not particularly valuable compared to some of the items that you no doubt come across, but they do have an enormous amount of sentimental value to me as they were given to me by my late husband.' She explained.

'I quite understand. Would I be able to take a look?' Ms Connors asked.

'Certainly, I've got them in my bag somewhere. Let me just find them.' Ms Sharpe replied as she opened her handbag and began pulling out the leather jewellery cases laying them on the desk in front of Ms Connors.

'Oh, those pearls are lovely.' Sarah remarked as she looked through the boxes. 'We have a few different sizes of box, but I would say that you would only require our smallest, which is two hundred pounds a year and will insure the contents for up to ten thousand, so I would have thought we may have to up the insurance a bit for these. Shall we say thirty-five thousand? Which would be an additional sixty pounds a year. '

'That sounds fine dear. A small price to pay for peace of mind.' Ms Sharpe replied.

'There's just a few formalities and paperwork to go through and then we can go down and sort out the box. If I can just have a look at some identification, and ask you to fill out this form for our records that would be great.' Ms Connors said.

'Would a driving license be sufficient? I'm afraid I didn't bring my passport with me.'

'That would be absolutely fine.' Sarah replied as she handed Mrs Trickle the form.

'Could I borrow a pen?' Ms Sharpe inquired as she passed her driving license over to be scanned.

'Certainly, have this one.' Sarah replied, passing her a Biro from her desk.

'Thank you, dear.' Ms Sharpe replied as she began to fill out the form whilst Ms Connors scanned the ID. 'Right I think that's all done.' She said as she finished dating her signature.

'Prefect, that all looks in order. If you would like to follow me, I'll take you down to our deposit area.' Sarah said as she took a card out of her office draw, unaware that Ms Sharpe had slipped the Biro, she had handed her earlier, into her bag as they left the office. Ms Sharpe followed Sarah across the foyer to a lift on the far side that would transport them deep into the belly of the building.

Ms Sharpe began to take careful notes of her surroundings, where the fire exits were, the fact that the lift required the swipe card to descend down to the deposit area and that entry into the room itself was unlocked by a finger print scanner.

'As you can see all our security systems are pretty high tech, we have constant CCTV here that works on heat and motion, the walls of the vault itself are made from reinforced concrete and the vault mechanism was designed by Withy Grove Stores in the 1880s and installed not long after that. Unlike some modern vaults these older models utilise much thicker steel in the door construction and as such are much harder to break into, so you can rest assured that your belongings will be perfectly safe. If you do need to access anything out of our normal hours, there is a number you can call to arrange for a special collection. Let me just fetch you a box.' Sarah said as she walked around the counter to fetch an empty box. 'Here we are, and this is your key set to the box.' She said handing her a set of two keys and a card with a chip similar to that used in bank cards. 'If you would like anybody to be a key holder we can have others cut for you. The company itself does not keep masters or a spare, so if you ever lose yours or we end up repossessing your box due to failure to settle your accounts then the locks will have to be drilled out by a locksmith. But I'm sure that won't be the case.'

'I should hope not.' Ms Sharpe replied. 'Would it be okay for me to take a photo of my things in the box for my records?'

'Certainly, that's absolutely fine.' Sarah replied as she began to open the vault for the box to go into.

Ms Sharpe carefully laid all of her jewellery boxes into the metal case and took several photos ensuring that she had the vault itself in the background. From what she could see the walls of the main vault were approximately 15 inches thick. Finally she closed the lid of the box and locked it before handing it back to Ms Connors.

'If you would like to accompany me into the vault we just need to setup the final parts of the security. We use a triple key system on the outer door of our deposit boxes, firstly one of the two keys on your set, then there is the lock that requires the card from your set and finally there is an alphanumerical code lock. So if you would like to type in a code that you can remember. It's amazing how many customers put one in and forget it and we end up having to get a locksmith to drill the locks out.'

Sarah said.

Ms Sharpe choose a code that incorporated the date of the Battle of Trafalgar and the initials of her top five favourite authors.

'I think that will suffice, this certainly seems to be a very comprehensive system.' She said as she finished typing in the code and waited for Sarah to store it in the lock's memory. 'I'm assuming if you have a power cut there is a back up for these electric locks?'

'Oh yes, we have two emergency generators that are designed to cut in on such an occasion. There we are, all done.' Sarah said as she locked the outer box door. 'Here's your key and card for the deposit unit. And as I say don't hesitate to call if you need to access your valuables or if you require to make another deposit. I should just add that due too the Easter bank holiday this weekend we will be closed from noon on Friday until noon on Tuesday, so if you need anything out for the weekend you might want to keep that for now.'

'Thank you dear, but I shan't require any of these this weekend, I'm not as much of the socialite that I once was in my younger days.' Ms Sharpe replied.

'In that case if you'd just like to reopen the box to ensure that everything is set up correctly, we'll pop these safely inside.' Sarah said as she handed the keys back to Miss Trickle.'

'Thank you so much dear. I feel I can now put my mind at ease. I must say you have been so very helpful and accommodating.' Ms Sharpe replied after she carefully placed the box with her belongings safely inside.

'Don't mention it. It's our pleasure to be able to provide you with peace of mind.' Sarah replied as they entered the lift to return to the surface.

Ms Sharpe thanked Ms Connors and the guard on the door once again as she left the building. Now in possession of all the information she needed to pass onto Juan in order to make a plan of attack she wandered back to the nearest tube station and worked her way back to Dolphin Square where Ollie and Gaz were waiting for her to return.

Chapter Thirteen: The Isle of a Single Stone

The stiffening wind sweeping across the ancient causeway reinforced Glen's determination to finish the crusade he had embarked upon regardless of how insurmountable the blocks placed in front of him might seem. Just like the previous day, he was sure that progress was going to be slow; the Atlantic seemed to be just as unwavering in its resolve to throw everything it had towards the small rocky isle, inevitably delaying the marine investigators' work on the salvaged fishing boat made fast in the marina, as he was on getting to the truth. The one and only positive which sprung to mind, as he watched awestruck by another boat breaker erupting over the outer stonework, was that at least the vessel was well inside the protection of both the inner and outer harbour walls.

After his storm tossed passage to Saint Michael's he had come to the conclusion that although he had the stomach for it, he lacked the skill to be anything more than a fair weather sailor and was best advised to keep his feet firmly on solid shores during a heavy blow.

Pulling up in the marina car park, he braced himself for whatever Orcus might unleash upon him, and made a dash for the marina office.

'Morning.' He said, greeting the receptionist on the marina desk, as he finished wiping the dampness from his face.

'Back again? Would've thought you lot had enough punishment yesterday.' She said.

'You'd think so, wouldn't you?' He replied with a warm smile. 'Anybody down there yet?'

'Yeah, Jamie's been down there since dawn, mentioned something about strengthening the lines. Can't say I blame her, it's forecast to get a lot worse over the course of the next few hours.'

'So I understand, at least there's only below deck left to process, thank god. Right, I suppose I better go and brave the maelstrom. Catch you later.' He replied as he finished signing in before stepping out of the office's shelter to commence battle with the elements once more.

He was glad he'd taken Jamie's advice and borrowed a set of offshores from the marina the previous day. By the time he reached the pontoon, had he worn his customary Harris tweed he'd have most certainly resembled some scraggy breed of wet dog.

'Hey Jamie, you ready for round two?' Glen shouted above the clamouring roar of the wind to the lady he could just make out through the partially steamed windows of the wheelhouse as he clambered aboard.

'More or less, what you turn the heating off for? It was so nice until you turned up.' She jokingly replied.

'I know, crazy right. But I guess this is pretty typical for the season. What's the order for the day?' He asked.

'Tea with one, would be lovely.' She replied.

'Ha, yeah. Can't argue with that, as good a place to start as any on a day like this.' He replied entering the wheelhouse and sliding the door to. Shaking off the rain from his oilies as he hung them up just inside the door to drip dry.

'Hey, gloves first mister.' She reminded him as he was about to disappear down the cabin steps to the small galley. 'Got enough to do in here without you getting your wet paw prints all over the place.'

'Fair point.' He replied half kicking himself for the rookie mistake. 'Brain obviously not functioning in these conditions.' He laughed.

'I know, I almost did the same thing yesterday. Been a while since I've had to process one of these on the water. They're normally well inside a shed or a dry dock by this point, unfortunately just no way of operating a hoist safely in this howling gale.' She replied.

'Ah well, I'm sure we'll manage. The more we can get now, the more info I can pass onto Carline. I'm sure we'll get her into the dry at a later date for a final once over. But you know as well as I do that sometimes speed is the key.' He said as he waited for the kettle to boil.

'True, hopefully there'll be a bit more in here than there was outside, all that spray and rain pretty much destroyed any decent prints on the decks. Got a few very iffy partials but I'm not gonna hold my breath. I was thinking, if we process the wheelhouse first then we can go below and work our way aft from stem to stern, if that makes sense.' She said.

'Yeah, I got no problem with that. I'll just follow your lead. After all I'm not the expert, especially when it comes to boats.' He replied warmly.'

'Just remind me to dip the holding tanks, when we get to them, I didn't take a water sample when we were on deck yesterday, so I must get one today.'

'Sure thing, where exactly are they on this tub? Just so I know when to remind you.' Glen inquired, as he actually had no idea about the internal layout of the small fishing vessel.

'Should be somewhere just aft of amidships, can't miss them really, they take up quite a lot of space.' She replied.

'I guess, easy for someone that knows what they are looking for. But from my perspective it's like a rab…'

'For god's sake don't finish that word!' She exclaimed.

'What rabbit?' He asked without thinking.

'Ugh, you have no idea what you've just done.' She replied.

'I don't understand, what's so bad about rabbits?' He innocently asked.

'Oh for the love of God. He said it again, I can't believe he said it again.' Jamie fretted talking to the air and shaking her head in her hands.

'What's so bad about ra…' Jamie punched him hard in the arm before he could get it out for the third time.

'I'll explain; just promise me you're not going to say it a third time, Lord only knows what would happen.' She said.

'O-kay, although I have absolutely no idea what the hell you are on about, you do realise you sound like a crazy bunny lady right now?' He replied.

'To you maybe, but I assure you it will make sense. Okay so you know that Portland's famous for its stone, it's been quarried here for centuries, and as does happen from time to time those working in the quarries were tragically killed due to landslide, on a number of such occasions our furry foe were often seen surfacing just before the rockfall. So the local superstition is that bad things happen when they are referred to by name. They are generally only referred to as, *underground mutton, long-eared furry things,* or *bunnies.* Even fishermen have been known to refuse to go out if they hear that word. And you've just said it not once but twice.' She said.

'You're joking right, you can't seriously believe in that sort of thing, can you?' He replied.

'Does this face look like I'm joking.' She replied raising an eyebrow as if to say: *Don't even, fucking go there!*

'Okay, ok, I get it. So any counter for it like with that silly one about the play that must not be named?' Glen asked trying to keep a serious face.

'Not that I know of, we'll just have to hope they weren't listening too hard.' She replied.

'You guys should really put up a sign or something about this, you know just to warn unsuspecting tourists.' He remarked.

'Yeah, because that would be a great idea, wouldn't it? You can almost picture the scene can't you, hundreds of tourist flocking to this isle just to see all the locals' reactions when they casually drop it into conversation.' She said

'Haha, I see your point. Maybe that's not quite such a good plan. You gotta admit though its pretty strange, but then again what's that saying, there's nowt so queer as folk.' Glen replied.

'No more so than that of Jack the Giant killer and the giant's stone heart at St Michael's Mount.' She replied so sharply as if to say, *we're not the only one's with local folklore and that the subject was now; taboo.*

'All right, I promise I won't say it again, but you gotta admit that going down the bunny hole doesn't have quite the same ring to it.' He said.

'Ha, no but I think *The Hef* might have missed a good one liner there.' Jamie mused, blushing slightly as she quickly busied herself by unpacking one of her SOCO cases. 'Can you set these up over there?' She asked pointing to the chart table and handing Glen a variety of powder kits they would use throughout the day.

'Exactly how much dusting are you planning on doing, not gonna be able to see for dust if you get through all of this.' He remarked.

'You'd think wouldn't you, but there's a huge area to cover here. Plus all these different surface materials mean we've got to be really careful about selecting the right powder or we won't get a good lift. Don't worry, I'll make sure you've got the right one. Just stick to the usual target areas: door handles, hand rails, taps, etc. I know it's a boat and potentially you could find them anywhere that someone has put a hand out to brace themselves, but let me deal with those. I've got a special tool to find those.' She said.

'Hey no worries, don't need to tell me twice. I'm just the help.' Glen replied beginning to wonder why on earth he had allowed Carline to talk him into this, when he could be enjoying a pleasant weekend in Penzance with his wife and son. He'd only been away for a few days, yet those final harsh words from his wife were still ringing in his ears. He regretted leaving so abruptly without appeasing the situation. But it was just one of those times when he was torn, ultimately he knew he would have to make a heartfelt reconciliation, but for now he just had to go with what his head was telling him, that it would all work itself out in the end. She'd known what she was signing up for when she said yes.

Chapter Fourteen: The Art of Conspiracy

It was late in the afternoon, for those lucky enough to be in the right part of the city to see the sun's rays brilliantly split by the prism like shape of The Shard as it dropped in low behind the new icon of inequality, when Ms Sharpe finally returned to Dolphin Square. Chris and Devan had long since departed and were well on their way to meet up with Louis who had returned to the city not long after James's demise to research the orb like object they had received from the mysterious clergyman of St Pauls, who had seemingly disappeared since his meeting with Michael.

'Right, gentlemen. We have a lot of work to do before Friday so you better be ready to put in some long hours between now and then.' She stated in the brisk manner that Gaz and Ollie had become accustomed to over the past few days.

'I take it you managed to find Chamberlain and the stolen pieces?' Gaz asked.

'Oh that was child's play. He isn't the most inconspicuous of figures, even in the crowds he sticks out like a Texan cowboy in a Tuscan village. I watched him go into a safety deposit building with a package and depart without it. So I would say it's safe to assume that's where he left them.' She replied.

'Oh great, so we're expected to just go in and ask for them.' Ollie said with slightly more sarcasm than even he had intended to use.

'Less of that, thank you very much. Certainly it is by no means the best outcome we could have wished for, nevertheless, neither is it impossible. It's just going to require some careful planning and a high degree of professionalism that I hope you are both capable of drawing upon. And before you ask the answer is, no. You're not going to get to play with your toys. Chris has kept me well informed about your antics and special skills, but we need to be able to leave quietly and therefore a big bang is just not what the doctor ordered, I'm afraid.' She replied.

'Damn, just when I was beginning to enjoy this trip. Oh, well Ol, we'll just have to hope that Chris lets us play with some in China.' Gaz remarked.

'If we make it that far.' Ollie muttered under his breath, he was far less confident that this was going to end well.

'I think we best make a start, I'm sure Juan will be here shortly.' Ms Sharpe began, pulling out a pad of paper and setting it on the dining room table. 'This is the layout of the ground floor.' She said as she began to sketch out what she had observed. 'The entrance usually has a guard on it and there are several dotted around the foyer come meeting area; on the far right hand side from the entrance are some public toilets. And to the left of reception is the duty manager's office. I didn't go onto the floors above but from reading the signs I gather there are just offices and a staff area up there.' She said as she began to outline the layout of the building.

'I take it the vault is underground?' Gaz asked.

'Yes, it's reached via a single lift, which requires the duty manager's swipe card to operate it. Although there maybe other members of staff who also have access cards.' She replied.

'Well, a card is easy enough to get hold of or at least copy.' Ollie mused.

'I agree, it's the finger print scanner to access the deposit room itself once you exit the lift which will be harder to fool. But don't worry about that, I've already got that covered.' She replied.

'What do you mean, by got it covered?' Gaz asked. 'I don't want to sound agnostic but as this isn't going to be a walk in the park I'd like a little more detail than: I've got it covered.' He added, finally coming off the fence.

'Point taken, I kept the pen the duty manager handed to me to fill out the forms. So it should have enough of her prints on it to make up some latex copies.' She replied.

'Forms?' Ollie asked raising an eyebrow.

'Oh, did I not mention, I had to have some sort of a reason to be in the building so I bought a few trinkets and rented a box. You didn't just expect me to ask the duty manager for a tour did you?'

'Er, er, no. I suppose not.' Ollie replied, now feeling rather stupid for raising the question.

'Which of course also gave me access to the vault area and I managed to take a few photos of the vault door and the concrete it's set into. By the looks of it, the door itself is pretty bomb proof.' She said, feeling that she had to further clarify her statement by the expression on both their faces. 'Don't miss understand me, I'm sure you gentlemen would be able to blow it apart with ease, but not without either damaging everything else in the process or as would be more than likely alerting ever police officer in a two block radius, which would rather defeat the object. It's an old Victorian construction and so is a far sturdier design than some of the modern safe doors.'

'That doesn't sound like the sort of safe one is easily going to break into without a bit of a bang.' Gaz remarked.

'Generally I would agree, but there is a weakness; the walls. They are by no means as thick as the steel door. I'd estimate them around about fifteen inches.'

'That's still pretty thick.' Gaz replied. 'But as you say, that's not impossible to do something with, we can get specialist drilling equipment that could handle a wall of that thickness, without much trouble. I'm assuming there are some kind of sensors in there that will have to be circumvented.'

'There are, however the duty manager never had to do anything after she had used the finger print scanner, I expect that is connected to the alarm system and disables all the sensors when an authorised print is detected. And just to bear in mind, she mentioned that the concrete walls are reinforced.'

'Ah that's no problem, we'll factor in some cutting equipment to deal with the rebars. What about the boxes themselves?' Ollie asked. 'Do they require two keys to open them?'

'I wish they were as easy as that. No, they use a triple lock system, a physical key, a card and an alphanumeric code. I don't think we are going to have the luxury of opening these conventionally. Interestingly, she mentioned that if one of the keys is ever lost, they would have to get a locksmith in, to physically break into the box and replace it. So it would seem that the boxes themselves, although very secure, aren't connected to any alarm circuitry.'

'Well, if Juan is as good as you say he is. Then that should be a piece of cake for him.' Ollie said, just as there was a knock at the door. 'Ah, speaking of the devil, I bet that's him now.' He added.

'Hey kids, how's tricks?' Juan warmly said as he entered the flat. 'The tube was a nightmare, rush hour madness as usual. Hope I haven't missed much.'

'Not at all. I was just giving these two an overview of the situation. I'll catch you up while these two have a look at the footage I recorded.' Ms Sharpe said.

'Footage?' Ollie asked incredulously raising an eyebrow.

'Oh yes, this brooch has a small camera concealed in it, should have some footage while I was walking around, will give you a better idea of the field of play.' She said.

'Nice, very Roman Nagel of you.' Gaz nonchalantly remarked.

'Who? Sounds like some sort of exotic body piercing.' Ollie said.

'Ha, no. He's the tech guru from that Ocean's series.'

'Oh yeah, that guy, now I know who you mean. Right, so speaking of tech how do we get this thing to work on the TV?' Ollie asked.

'Just plug this Bluetooth dongle into the USB port and it should auto play.' Ms Sharpe said, tossing him a device not much bigger than a thumbnail.

'Cool. Lights, camera, action, as they'd say in Hollywood.' Ollie joked as he leapt across the sofa, locating the USB port and sat back to watch the slightly shaky film.

'I see what you mean about the security being quite comprehensively spread about the atrium. They've definitely done their research into the most effective placement, got almost everywhere covered with intersecting arcs of sight. Ex-military I'd hazard a guess by their general manner and appearance. Yeah these guys definitely know their stuff, although I'd say not ex-specials.'

'Oh, why do you say that?' Ms Sharpe asked.

'Well, for one, if they had that sort of background they wouldn't be working for a deposit company, when there are far more lucrative contracts available for people of that calibre and secondly they wouldn't have left a blind spot on people going in and out of the toilets.' Ollie replied. 'That maybe our in, depending on whether they do a check before shutting up for the night.' He added, as the film continued.

'Hmm my initial thoughts are to use Oxy-Acete...' Juan was saying to Ms Sharpe just as he was cut off mid-sentence.

'Um, we may have a problem here.' Gaz called out grabbing Ms Sharpe's attention away from Juan. 'Your brooch just stopped recording as you entered the lift.'

'That's strange, it didn't get knocked. Does the picture come back at any point?'

'Oh yeah.' Gaz said as he forwarded the film on. 'Just as you're putting the jewellery into a metal box.' He added.

'Hmmm maybe one of the wires is loose, I'll have to get it looked at.' Ms Sharpe stated, as Juan interjected.

'They've probably got some sort of EMI device installed to prevent electronics from being used in the room.' Juan suggested. 'They're not that common outside of the military, but I have heard of a few cases where they are being used. The manager probably has a remote on her person or a switch somewhere in that room to disable it, which she triggered just before you started taking photos so you wouldn't have noticed it. Not a complete game changer but I'll have to do a bit of research, if we can't disable that there is no way we're getting into those boxes.' He added. 'I'll make a few calls and see what I can find out. Maybe we'll get lucky.'

'Yeah, we had something like that out in Afghan, but the ones we used would totally destroy electronic devices. I did hear they were working on one that would just temporarily disable electronics within a certain radius but I didn't think they had perfected it.' Ollie said, carefully disclosing just enough about the tech without revealing everything about its uses or exactly how far its development had got. There were certain things that he still believed should remain outside of the public domain, especially as he was well aware of how many lives had been saved and were still being protected by advances in military tech.

'Well, I've got a list of pretty much everything that we would need to get through that wall.' Gaz said, after a long period of concentrated silence. 'If Ollie and I go on a shopping spree and Juan goes to find out whatever he can about that EMI stuff. Do you think you can get us the blueprints of the building from public records?' He asked turning to Ms Sharpe.

'I don't think that should be a problem. Just of that particular building?' She asked.

'Hmmm, maybe the one next to it as well. Getting in is the easy bit. It's getting out that I think may prove to be more of a sticking point, but until we see the lay of the land it's difficult to say for sure.' He replied.

'Don't forget it's Easter Bank Holiday, so there won't be anybody there from Friday afternoon until late Tuesday morning. Ms Connors, the duty manager said they were not open again until midday Tuesday, so I suspect the staff will be back in by ten-ish. So you've got quite a bit of time in there to play with.' Ms Sharpe replied.

'Better window than I'd been thinking of, and less need to worry about the noise that drill's going to make as it cuts through all that concrete.' Ollie said.

'Oh and gentlemen, don't forget you are going to need a van.

Whatever you do, don't hire it. Try and find a trader that'll take cash, no questions asked. The less traceable the better.' She suggested.

'I thought we're just after the books?' Ollie said.

'We are, but we're going to have to take more than that otherwise Norwood will realise that it was us that took them rather than just thinking that it was a bad choice to pick that particular vault. Remember normally a job like this would take months of planning and recon not just a few days, but unfortunately we don't have that cushion, but it's still got to look like a full heist not just a specific target.' She replied with almost the hint of a twinkle in her eye as if she was beginning to drop her abrasive demeanour and enjoy the moment. 'Well, what are you waiting for. Off you go.' She added quickly snapping back into character.

It seemed like they had been waiting an age for Louis to arrive when in fact they themselves had only been there for no more than ten minutes, however the biting chill of the easterly wind currently cutting through the city streets gave a false impression of the passage of time. His familiar swagger walking up the street was enough to warm them momentarily against the backdrop of a house connected to so many painful memories.

'Hi guys good to see you.' He said as he warmly embraced both of them. 'Hope you haven't been waiting long.'

'Long enough.' Chris replied. 'This wind is just bitter. Shall we go in, before we all catch our death?'

'Yeah, I've got the keys here somewhere.' Louis replied. 'Took me a while to find where the hell I'd put the spare set. I'd almost forgotten that James had given them to me, don't think I've ever had to use them before. I bet it's going to be like the Baltic in there. That fire won't have been lit in months. I hope he left some wood or coal before he decided to depart. If not there's gonna be a few less dining chairs before we leave, not like he's going to need them.'

'It does have central heating, you know.' Chris remarked as Louis opened the door of James's old house, judging that it wasn't quite the right moment to reveal that James may still be alive.

'Oh, well in that case I won't. Do you know where to turn it on?' Louis asked.

'No, but I'm sure it can't be that hard to find, even for you.' Chris said.

As luck would have it, they discovered that James had left the house with a full supply of logs for the fire, and it wasn't long before they were all sat in the smoking room around a roaring fire reminiscing about old times.

'Seems weird to be here without him, somehow it doesn't feel right.' Louis said after a while.

'I know what you mean, but I think he will approve.' Chris replied.

'You say that like he is still here.' Louis remarked.

'Well, yeah about that.' Chris began and continued to fill Louis in on everything that had transpired at Chestnut's flat. 'So you see, there is a good chance that he's around; at the moment I haven't quite managed to put all the pieces together, although I do have a working theory. I'm just not quite ready to pull that particular thread and see where it leads. As much as I would like to be able to go galavanting off in the hopes of finding a trace of a ghost, we have our own endeavours to pursue. One which I think you will agree may well be just as perilous as hunting for the resurrected.

'Yeah, about that. Just exactly how do you propose to break into a museum in Beijing, steal part of an almost priceless piece of art and not end up being detained indefinitely without trial?' Louis asked.

'Well, to put it simply, I don't. We're going to be invited.' Chris replied.

'Huh, what? How does that work?' Louis asked in bemusement.

It took several hours but eventually Chris and Devan finished explaining their plan to Louis and although his head was still reeling with the amount of detail and information that he had just been battered by, Louis finally managed to drift off into the world of dreams, only to be tormented by images of that orb and the sound of hammering metal on rock echoing though his mind as he floated through an orchard of tress, that he was still no closer to understanding.

Several times in the night Louis woke in a cold sweat from the vivid imagery, he finally gave up on a peaceful night's rest and got up around five. There was just something about those scenes, he was sure his subconscious was trying to tell him something. Something in his research that he had overlooked. Pulling on a dressing gown he went back down stairs and began rifling back though his notes.

By the time Chris and Devan rose Louis had long gone. He'd left the keys and a note on the kitchen table.

Sorry I didn't wake you, but I promised James I'd find out about the orb and I think I've finally worked out its origin. Good luck in China, I'll be in touch.

Louis

'Fucking knew he'd do this.' Chris said as he read the note. 'Guess we'll just have to manage with a man down.'

'He can't have got far maybe you can get him back.' Devan replied.

'No time for that now, we've got a plane to catch.' He said looking at his watch. 'We'll just have to make do. I suppose I shouldn't really be that surprised he always would do whatever James asked him to do. Come on grab your passport, let's go.' He sighed swiping up the keys from the table.

Chapter Fifteen: Clipped Wings

'Are you absolutely sure this is the only way?' Carla asked the captain as they poured over the flight plan.

'It's the only way it will look convincing, any other way and I suspect there will be more questions raised than simply mechanical failure.' She replied. 'I'm still not a hundred percent convinced myself but I can't see a better option at the moment.'

'What happens if we stopped here first?' Carla asked pointing at the map. 'Citing a suspected issue, and then continue on, where we then encounter further difficulties and are forced to make an emergency landing?'

'Actually, yes that may well work, depending on exactly where our destination is. I'll have to work out a point in the flight where it is the only resort left without ditching in the sea, it could be conceivable that something could be overlooked, especially if it is inconclusive as to the initial cause of the fault. An electrical fault is probably a good one to go with, some of these modern lithium-ion batteries are notoriously unpredictable and can suffer from thermal runaway. In fact I'm pretty sure I have one that we had to change out due to suspected degradation.'

'Get it done, I want to be off the tarmac in the next twelve hours.' Carla tersely replied as she left the pilot scratching her head as to exactly how she was going to pull it off, and went to check on Leach's progress, who was busy loading the hold with all the gear they would require for their expedition.

'Hey, careful with that one! Damage that, and it won't just be the remainder of your fingers you'll lose.' She snapped as Leach and another man almost dropped an oversized crate they were struggling to get onto the loading ramp.

'Well, a little bit of help wouldn't go amiss.' He replied with a grimace, trying to hold back the anguish of the memory when Chamberlain hacked off his finger.

'Oh man up, and get on with it.' She bluntly replied to the wiry man. 'His lordship will be here within the next few hours and everything better be ready by the time he arrives.'

'Fucking bitch.' Leach muttered under his breath.

'What was that?' She barked, just about catching the later part of his comment.

'Oh nothing, just telling him to get on the winch.' Leach replied.

'For your sake, you better hope that was it.' Carla forcefully replied, intimating she knew full well what he'd said, but in her eyes he was such a pathetic little runt of a man that he wasn't worth her time of day. She had far more pressing things to finalise than kicking the shit out of such an insignificant creature, which although pleasurable would only result in further delays. There was still the plane to fuel, not to mention chasing Conrad for all the documents and codes that by now he should have confirmed with his contact.

Conrad hated leaving things to the last minute, to him it felt sloppy, however on this occasion there was nothing he could do to speed up the process. It was out of his hands, something he had come to expect from the North Koreans. He was sure they were just flexing their muscles to demonstrate that they were the ones calling the shots. He would just have to hold his nerve for a little bit longer, if he pushed too hard they'd no doubt over react and pull the rug out. Even so they were cutting it very fine indeed. He'd already been waiting for over an hour at the embassy and he was getting to the point when he would have to push back.

Enough was enough he decided and was in the process of standing up from where he sat to find someone to get the ball moving again when a young girl approached him.

'Sorry for the delay, Mr Du Bois the ambassador had some urgent business to attend to. He can see you now. If you would please follow me.' She gestured towards a door at the end of the corridor.

'About bloody time.' Conrad muttered under his breath, careful not to be over heard, these were delicate negotiations and he couldn't afford to blow them when he was so close to achieving his goal.

The room he entered was small in comparison to some of the national outposts he had frequented, not that he was that surprised, they weren't exactly flavour of the month with the West.

'My apologies, Conrad. Your request has raised a few eyebrows and well to be honest the debate has been raging back and forth for the last few days. Naturally my countrymen are cautious when it comes to requests of this nature and as I'm sure you are aware goodwill only gets you so far. As much as we would love to aid you in your archaeological exploits, we feel that there is little for us to gain from such a partnership. We have our own experienced archaeologists who have already done and are continuing to work at the site in question and we don't feel that outsiders can offer anything that we can't already do ourselves.' The ambassador said flatly. 'I'm sorry if this isn't what you had hope for but at present there is just not enough in it for us. I hope you understand.'

Conrad took a moment before replying, he had to be careful how he approached this subject matter and he also didn't want to come across as overly anxious.

'We understand your position, before you make a final decision can I suggest you take a look at this. I think a man with your previous work experience will appreciate it. I am right in thinking you still consult for SMG; remind me that's The Special Missions Group isn't it? I forget, you people have so many acronyms and bureaus within the MSS that I must confess I do sometimes get them mixed up.' He said casually taking a folded piece of paper out of his jacket. He was taking a huge risk not only in mentioning the Ministry of State Security but also revealing that he knew about the man's broader role. But a risk that he felt would get the man off the fence. 'This was a recent discovery, an artefact that we feel would greatly impact on your country's cultural and historical understanding. We believe this would be a fair trade for whatever we uncover.' He added continuing in the casual manner he had adopted.

Conrad's statement was met with a deafening silence, the ambassador initially said nothing. The reference to the MSS had rather caught him off guard. It was not very often that people even within the intelligence community would be quite so blatant with that sort of information, besides they'd carried out their checks on Conrad prior to his arrival and there was absolutely no indication that he was tied to an agency, so the next question was where the hell had he got this data from?

Conrad could tell when the man's eyebrow twitched for the briefest of moments that he'd got him on the hook.

'Interesting, you seem awfully well informed for a business man.' He finally replied.

'Well, I find it pays to know who one is dealing with, sometimes it helps to create a door in space that isn't always there.' Conrad replied.

'True, but I would tread carefully. Wisdom may open many things but just because there is a way in, doesn't necessarily mean there's going to be a safe exit, gravity can be funny like that sometimes.'

'Believe me, unlike some politicians I know; I never do business without having a comprehensive strategy.'

'That's reassuring to know. So this is a recent find you say. Can I ask whereabouts this was discovered, just so that I can verify it.' He probed.

'Of course, it was located deep in the Hatteras Plain.' Conrad replied. 'I'm sure your colleagues in the 121 Bureau won't find it to hard dig up the relevant material.'

'Oh, I don't think I need disturb them, it's not really their field of expertise, but then I think you already know that. I believe an artefact from this period would be significant. It's a shame it's not from the western province nevertheless I feel sure that a broken arrow from that particular era would certainly be something that we would like to have for further study. Shame it's not complete. If you can wait while, I will see if this will have an impact on your travel status. I think we maybe able to come to some sort of an arrangement that satisfies both parties.' The ambassador said as he rose from behind his desk.

'Of course, I should add that this is a limited one time offer. We have other parties that are also interested, so we will need to know by the end of the day.' Conrad lied, he knew full well that his lordship had not approached any other parties that might have been interested in such an item. He just hoped his gambit would kick the Koreans into gear.

'I'll make sure they understand the position.' The man quickly replied as he opened the door and hurried out. Conrad smiled as the Korean left, he knew this wouldn't take long. There was no way that they would be able to resist a carrot that large.

The ambassador reappeared within minutes carrying a plastic wallet full of papers. 'They find your trade acceptable, here's everything you will need to benefit from our hospitality. I hope you have a safe trip.'

'Thank you, hopefully this will be the start of a long and mutually prosperous relationship.' Conrad replied as he shook the ambassador's hand before departing.

Carla smiled as she read the brief text she had just received from Conrad to assure her that everything was now in order and that he was on his way to the hanger. Everything was falling into place, his lordship was surely on his way by now and as soon as Conrad joined them they would be winging their way to their destination.

'Leach, have you finished loading the plane?' She called out from the fuel dump.

'Yes, we've just finished. Everything listed has been loaded.' The man thinly replied.

'Is it secure, we can't afford for anything to be damaged in transit.' She replied.

'It is, I secured it myself. Do you need any help fuelling the plane?' He asked, the one thing he wanted to avoid was being seen to be more of a waste of space than he believed he was already perceived to be. Ever since his attempts to capture Middleton and the girl had failed he had felt there was a cloud hanging over his head, one that he was battling to prevent from engulfing him and smothering the glimmer of his life. He felt that if the cards would just land right for him once, then he would be back in the game.

'No, I think between myself and the ground crew we've got it under control. But you can go and see if the captain needs some help getting those batteries onto the plane.' She replied, giving him a sliver of hope. She knew he was just trying to be helpful, however it didn't change her opinion that he was as toxic as single use plastic and the quicker he was phased out the better for the long term health of the organisation.

Leach took the half dead olive branch, he knew it was about all he could expect from her. He had never witnessed what she was capable of first hand but the stories he had heard did nothing to fill him with a sense that things were going to improve anytime soon. At least Norwood had personally chosen him above Chamberlain for this particular mission so there was still the smallest glimmer that he was still seen as being useful, the only question was, useful for what? He decided not to dwell on it, as in his current frame of mind that could be twisted into something just as malignant as it might be magnificent.

'Captain, I understand these need to be stowed on board.' Leach said to the woman still pouring over the flight plan laid out in the office.

'They do, but actually in the passenger section, not in the hold. They'll be absolutely no use to us if they're in the hold. Just give me a minute and I'll give you a hand. No way you'll manage them by yourself.' She said as he scribbled the finishing touches to her flight plan onto the form. 'Right that should just about cover it, I hope.' She remarked in a less than confident tone.

'Jesus, I didn't think they'd be weigh that much.' Leach stated as he picked up one side of the first of two batteries they had to get onto the jet.

'Yeah, you won't be needing to go to the gym after these two. I just hope it works otherwise nobody will be going to a gym ever again.' The darkness of the tone surrounding the captain's statement was so deep that Leach decided he didn't even want to know what she was talking about. Sometimes it was far better not to know what the potential outcomes might be. 'Come on man, put your back into it.' The captain added as Leach wrestled with gravity attempting to maintain his balance as he clawed his way up the stairs onto the plane, just managing not to loose his footing before he reached the doorway. 'Good lad, just one more to go. Think we'll get the other one on board before we get them into place.'

'G-give me one sec, just to catch my breath.' Leach panted. 'Fuck me that was heavy.'

'Come on, only one more to go. The sooner we get it done, the sooner we can get this bird up.' The captain replied.

'I suppose. Okay, I'm good.' He said.

The second was surprisingly easier, possibly because he now knew what to expect, or more likely because the captain had realised that it would be better for Leach to be at the top, enabling the pilot to be able to put all of her weight behind it to force the pack up the stairs.

'Nice one, can you find the service hatch for the electronics compartment and open it up, should be down there, just a bit further. Yep that's the one.' The captain said directing Leach to the hatch in question.

'Um, there's already batteries in here.' Leach remarked, slightly surprised as he opened the hatch.

'I know, we're taking *backups*. Should just slot in nicely.' She replied.

If Mr Leach had been less that happy about what they were about to embark upon then this a latest revelation was more than a little unsettling to say the least. Not that he knew anything about aircraft design or flight preparation, but he was pretty sure that they didn't normally install backup batteries just before they were about to take off. But if the captain was doing it then there must be a logical explanation for it. She was the expert after all.

'Don't worry about the wiring. We'll do that later, can't do it while she's fuelling unless you want a big orange ball.' The captain remarked as they dropped the last one into place. 'Tend to find fuel and sparks don't interact very well with each other.' She joked.

If Leach had begun to have thoughts about jumping ship before takeoff, then he was out of time. Lord Norwood's Jeep could be seen just clearing the gates into the private airfield and he would be there in a matter of minutes.

The tall muscular man, stepped out into the crisp evening air, with a sense of eager anticipation as he surveyed the scene of last minute preparations going on inside the hanger. For him this was another step closer to another glorious triumph.

'I see you've got everything in hand.' He said as he warmly embraced Carla in his arms. 'Is Conrad here yet?'

'Not yet, I expect him any minute, so long as he hasn't encountered any delays. We're almost ready to go, we just need the landing details that our friends have provided and then we can file the flight plan.' She replied.

'Excellent, I'll just get these guys to load the stuff from the car and hopefully Conrad will have arrived by then. I assume you had no problem getting the special cargo onboard?' Norwood replied as he gave instructions to the men that had accompanied him to chuck the last of their gear onto the jet.

'Well, it was a bit of a tight squeeze getting it into the hold but it did just go. Would you like to check the flight plan we have come up with?' She asked.

'No, I'm sure whatever you have come up with will tick all the requirements.' He replied. Unlike some under him, he had the utmost faith in Carla's abilities. 'Ah prefect timing.' He noted as he spied a car's headlights pulling up beside the corrugated metal hanger.

Conrad pulled his jacket close around him as he stepped out of the car into the cool evening air. The temperature had dropped significantly since he had left the leafless London suburbs. Grabbing his travel case and the Korean file off the back seat he strode into the unit.

'Let me get that for you, Sir.' One of the men standing by Lord Norwood said as he approached the group.

'Thanks.' Conrad replied handing him the case before he warmly shook Norwood's hand and passed him the file. 'I think you will find everything is now in order. They were a little bit cagier than I had anticipated. So we may have to watch our backs.' He remarked.

'I expected as much, but they will be in for a surprise if they try and fuck me on this one.' Norwood replied with a knowing grin. 'Right, anyway lets get this show in the air. We can go through all of this on board.' Norwood added eager to leave England far behind.

It wasn't long before the plane was up to cruising altitude and as far as the tower was concerned was now safely on it's way to Osaka International. Most of the passengers settled in to the plush interior of the private jet and were soon soundly asleep as Norwood, Conrad and Carla went over in detail the documents that the ambassador had provided them with.

'So where exactly is this place that they want us to land?' Norwood asked.

'Looking at these coordinates it's Orang Airbase, out on the North East coast, and about a seven and a half hour drive to the complex of The Koguryo Tombs.' Carla replied. 'Interesting though. These don't take us to the official airbase but rather to what as far as I can tell is a runway that ploughs straight into a mountain.'

'Oh don't let that fool you, they have quite a few of those. They use the mountains for cover, keeps the American's prying eyes at bay. There are a number of those Underground Facilities, UGFs as they call them, used for storing and servicing aircraft and as I understand it some are suspected to house mobile ICBM launchers as well.

Given the nature of what we're transporting it makes sense they'd want to get it under cover away from those prying eyes as soon as they can.' Norwood replied. 'But we'll have to stray along way off course to make for that field, what's your thinking?'

'Oh, we've got that well in hand. There never was going to be any chance of landing directly in North Korea without raising an alarm so Laura and I put a flight plan in place to cover that.' Carla replied. 'We may as well get some rest it's going to be a long time before anything needs to be done.' And without elaborating further Carla left the two men to continue their other plans for the trip and ventured to one of the two custom sleeping compartments towards the rear of the plane.

'Likes to keep you guessing, doesn't she.' Conrad remarked once Carla was out of earshot.

'It's just her way. She's always had a very dominant personality, I'll let her have her moment. She has a point anyway, this is going to be a long flight and we are going to be fully occupied once we near their airspace. Have they provided any travel details for after our business has concluded?' He asked, changing the subject.

'Not really, but then we don't really know where we are going until you've retrieved whatever this artefact is. We must be careful though, you know as well as I do it's one thing to get into this country, it's quite another to get out.'

'Don't worry about that. I have the necessary leverage in place if they decide they want to try and change the rules. Just enough to ensure that they keep to their side of the bargain.' Norwood replied almost as cryptically as Carla had been with her arrangements for how they would get into the red state. 'Right what's the time? Hmmm, just about time for a night cap I think before I too retire. Quick Scotch?' Norwood offered.

'Ah, that'll be prefect. Need one after dealing with those sneaky little blighters.' Conrad replied. 'I swear they'd try and take the shirt off your back if one wasn't on one's toes.' He joked.

'I know they're all the same.' Norwood replied handing him a large crystal tumbler. 'To the victor, the spoils.' He added raising his own glass and taking a good swig of the fiery spirit.

They must have had a few more than they were intending as they drifted off into a deep slumber. The next thing that either of them were aware of was the emergence alarms blaring throughout the entire fuselage of the plane.

'What the hell is going on?' Norwood bellowed as he awoke.

'Nothing to worry about, dear. Just had to make this bit convincing for the flight recorders.' Carla replied as she casually sat down beside him.

'Now I know why you didn't tell me what was going to happen, you always did enjoy giving me a rude awakening. Where exactly are we?'

'Just coming into Chinggis Khaan International Airport, with a suspected electrical problem. It was the only logical place to land with a suspected fault, gives us the necessary background story for having to make an emergency landing in Orang later. I don't expect us to be here for too long, hopefully just long enough to have some engineers check over the diagnostics, find nothing wrong and get us back in the air again. Couple of hours at the very most.' She replied.

'Well, at least there's enough time to get something to eat I suppose.' He replied realising that he was feeling a little peckish. 'Good thing we're in Mongolia I could probably eat a camel, they have some great little steamed dumplings I seem to remember. Buuz I think they call them.' He said recalling one of the dishes he'd tried the last time he'd had occasion to visit the rugged open country.

'Sounds delightful, not sure I've ever had camel before.' Carla replied.

'Not that bad, once you get over the hump.' He jokingly replied as the plane juddered to a halt on the runway.

They were met by a number of emergency crew, who quickly directed the plane to an area away from the main terminal in order for ground crew to run a full diagnostic on the plane in an attempt to find whatever the fault was that had caused the aircraft to make the unscheduled stop.

'Any body round here speak English?' Laura could be heard asking as she attempted to explain what they had been experiencing. Eventually an interpreter turned up and it was not long before the engineers were busy plugging devices into the plane's diagnostic system to ascertain what the problem was, while the passengers were ushered to a small room used for private arrivals to wait until the fault was rectified and they were allowed to continue on their way.

Laura who had stayed with the service crew, joined them about half an hour later to announce that the crew had found that one of the battery banks wasn't maintaining its voltage and that it was this fluctuation that had triggered the alarms.

'So the ruse, worked. Excellent, how long before they clear us to fly?' Lord Norwood enquired.

'At least another two hours, my Lord. They are insisting that they carry out the full diagnostic. I have tried to reason with them but to no avail. It's not very often they get the chance to tinker with this type of jet and I think they're going to make the most of it.' Laura replied.

'Two hours, you've got to be joking! Where's that swine of an interpreter? Stay here, I'll sort this out. There's no way I'm sitting around here all day, whilst they have a jolly with my plane.' He said as he strode out onto the tarmac to find the woman.

Carla watched from the window. Even though she couldn't actually see it, she could tell that a wave of red mist had engulfing both the translator and the head of the service crew. She couldn't help but laugh at the expressions on their faces as Norwood laid into them. Whatever he had said obviously had the desired effect as the crews were now running around like an army of ants on a mission. He'd clearly put the fear of the reincarnation of the Airport's namesake into them, as they didn't appear to stop after that.

'That's more like it.' Norwood said as he came back in. 'We'll be leaving in twenty, so you best grab anything else you want and get yourselves back up on that plane.' He added.

'What exactly did you say to them?' Carla innocently asked.

'I merely intimated that if they didn't pull their fingers out and get my bird back together and ready for takeoff in the next hour, then they and their families would all be disappeared to a Siberian Gulag for an indeterminate period of time. Knew my Russian would come in handy at some point.'

Carla just laughed. She could well imagine the thoughts which would have run through their heads at the insinuation. She'd heard whispers that the Mongolian government had on occasion used its close relationship with Russia in order to remove political undesirables to the Siberian Tundra; never to be seen again.

In the end it had taken just shy of three hours before the plane began to briskly taxi back out onto the runway and depart the airport, continuing on its supposed route to Osaka.

'Better get those faulty batteries set up now that we are back on track, won't be long before we will need to put the rest of this ruse into practice. I just hope that it doesn't backfire and become uncontrollable. This isn't tried and tested, there is a real danger that this might actually down the plane.' Laura said to Carla. 'If I was you I'd connect one in now and leave the other until the very last minute, that way I'll have at least half a chance of regaining control if the batteries catch fire.'

'I thought this would just simulate a battery problem.' Carla said, now actually slightly apprehensive about what they were about to do.

'Oh no, there isn't a way of 'simulating' a battery fire, we are actually going to have to do it. I thought you understood that, hence why I only suggested it as a last resort.

'Ah well, it's too late to come up with another alternative now. I just hope to God this'll work otherwise we're all going to be swimming. Does it matter which one I plug in first?'

'Nope they're both fucked so it's not going to make a jot of difference. Whichever one you prefer.'

'Okay, I'll give you a count down as I connect them so you know when it's linked, just in case you have to do some of that crazy pilot shit.' Carla said as she left the cockpit and headed to the rear of the plane where the battery compartment was located.

'Ready.' She called out after opening the compartment.

'Ready.' Came the pilot's reply from the nose of the plane.

'Three, two, one, Now!' Carla shouted out as she connected the final wire to the battery's terminal.

The plane gave a momentary lurch as the wing flaps twitched from a drop in power due to the compromised battery being integrated into the circuitry, before the voltage in the circuits stabilised and the plane resumed normal cruising.

'Looks good, so far.' Laura called out. 'Temperature is fluctuating a little bit, but then that was to be expected. Leave it like that for now. Connect the second one in about thirty minutes, by then we'll be about ten minutes out from where I'll need to put in that emergency call. I expect when you connect the second it will be enough to ignite the batteries within a matter of minutes. Their temp will sky rocket with two fucked cells wired into each other. I'm gonna start the climb, we're gonna need every bit of altitude this puppy can give us to make that strip when that thing goes bang.' She added throttling up and pulling back on the stick, and the plane responded by dropping into a steady climb graciously rising from their current cruising height of thirty-two thousand feet towards its ceiling of fifty-one.

Chapter Sixteen: The Winds of Change

'That's the last of it.' Jin said as he threw the final kiteboard into the back of the van. 'We best get going or we're gonna miss the best of the conditions.' He added as he hopped into the passenger seat next to Axe.

'It's gonna be epic. Just seen an instagram post by Jung and it looks like it's properly going off up there. Can't wait to get back out on the water.' Axe replied as he drove out of the small town.

The coastal journey was pleasant enough, and apart from the odd stretch of rusty barbed wire you'd hardly realise that this had once been a land ravaged by one of the bloodiest conflicts to have ever been waged.

'Turn right up here. It'll take you down to the car park just above the beach.' Jin said as he directed Axe for the last few hundred meters of rough track.

'Those breaks are looking sick from here, arrived just about the right time by the looks of things. Shame we can't park right on the beach.' Axe said as he pulled up. 'Right let's get this gear and go find the others.' He added, jumping out of the battered van and grabbing as much gear as he could physically carry before making his way down the sandy path to the beach.

It didn't take him long to spot Jung and the other kiters thirty or so meters further up the beach. Dumping his kit down with the rest of the thrill seekers' mound of gear, he and Jin wasted no time in setting up their kites, lines and boards.

Axe wandered down to the water's edge and waded in until the water was just below his knees, there was something about the feel of the sea swirling around his legs that gave him a small buzz of anticipation, while he surveyed the building swell before him, searching for the perfect line to take when he was ready to leave the beach and blast off across the small bay. Taking a few deep breaths of that crisp salty air, he picked his line before making his way back to his gear. Stripping everything off he pulled on his pot marked wetsuit, and without wasting any more time strode back out to do battle with the elements.

By the time Jin joined him out on the water, Axe was already quite a way out into the bay and for a time they just raced each other back and forth, throwing in the odd jump before Axe decided to go in search of the bigger waves further up the shoreline. Now that he'd got his eye back in he was eager to push himself to the limits, not only because he had a desire to see just how big he could go but he also knew the time was fast approaching when that would be the only way. A time when he would have to dig deep and jump higher and further than he'd ever been; it really would be a case of go big or go home. The only thing was; going home wasn't an option and he knew it.

After a couple of hours of pretty mixed results and a few major wipeouts on the landings Axe came back to the beach.

'Looking good man, considering we haven't been out with these rigs for a while.' Jin said as Axe set his kite down.

'Was all right, need to work on my landings a bit. Think I must be edging very slightly, I'm sliding out on the landing every now and again. If it wasn't so choppy I'd probably get away with it, but the waters around here are pretty unforgiving, especially on a day like today. Might have to go back to the smaller stuff for a bit just to iron out the kinks.' Axe replied with a sigh, moderately irritated with himself that he wasn't where he thought he should be by now, he knew the call could come anytime now and he needed to be ready. In this game you didn't get second chances.

'Well, far better than anything I could pull off at the moment, seem to end up paddling every time.' Jin replied.

'You just need to stop weighting your trail leg so much as you drop back down. That's what's causing your wipeouts. The tail of the board's just digging in, kills your speed and you end up stalling.' Axe said with a few hand gestures to highlight what he meant. 'Just keep practicing man, it'll come. Tides' going to turn quite soon, should flatten off a bit, then you'll have near prefect conditions to practice that landing. Fancy a brew while we wait? Swear I packed that Kelly kettle in here somewhere.' He said as he began routing around in one of his kit bags.

'Hell yeah. You sort the brews and I'll pop the shelter up. Bit exposed here; get too cold and we'll never get back out this arvo.' Jin replied, already starting to feel the cold now that he'd come off the water.

'Thought you'd have toughened up a bit after all this winter surfing you've been doing.' Axe retorted.

'Yeah right, you know as well as I do that in the water is okay, but out of it, with this windchill it's enough to even give a Yeti a nipple erection.' Axe almost chocked with laughter at Jin's bluntness.

'That's certainly one way to put it.' He replied as he wiped a bit of water from the corner of his eye. 'Here, you want sugar?' He asked, passing Jin a steaming mug of black tea.

'If you've got some, may as well keep the energy levels up. Besides your tea generally taste like I've sucked on half a dozen dandelion stems.' Jin joked.

'Ha, fine. Make it yourself in future.' Axe sarcastically replied as he nestled himself into the doorway of the shelter, and watched the ever rolling waves crash across the sand. The bleak and desolateness didn't help his mood much, he knew that he would soon have to leave his new friends behind and venture into a world that he had tried so hard to free himself from, a world that seemed determined one way or another to suck him back in.

A sharp dig in his ribs from Jin; broke his train of thought.

'Hey you okay, you looked at bit lost for a second there.' Jin asked. 'Thought you'd be well up for today, it's been all you've talked about for at least a week.'

'Ah sorry, I was just trying to work out how to smooth out the edges. Sometimes when things aren't quite where I'd like them to be I can look a bit melancholy. Especially if I'm trying to think it through.' Axe replied, not wanting to go anywhere near what was actually driving the maelstrom in his mind.

'You guys coming back out?' Jung asked as he ran up from the waterline. 'You're missing out on the best of it, that messy chop from this morning's flattened right off. As perfect as you are gonna get now.' He added.

'Right come on.' Axe said snapping back onto his feet. 'Let's have another crack at it. He's right, we can't sit here any longer. Time to get back on it. May as well leave the shelter up, might come in handy later.' He added stripping off his fleece and wandering back over to his rig.

The sun was beginning to drop onto the horizon by the time Axe, Jin and the other kiters finally came off the water and began to pack up.

'Not a bad day in the end. Shame we couldn't stay out for a bit longer, but I don't think I'm up to speed to go kiting in the dark just yet.' Jin said as he rolled up his kite and stuffed it into its case.

'I don't know, don't think you're that far away from having a night sesh. Maybe later on in the week we could have a short one.' Axe replied.

'Argh, wish I could but I'm gonna have to actually go and do some work at some point this week. Not sure I can stay longer than tomorrow. And besides isn't Meena expecting us back for dinner this evening?' Jin reluctantly reminded Axe.

'Oh, I'm sure she will understand that we've got to make the most of the conditions while they last.' Axe replied.

'You do remember who you are talking about right? The one who will literally crush your manhood in a vice if you leave the seat up.' Jin joked.

'Hmmm, fair point. Shotgun, you tell her we won't be back for dinner.' Axe said.

'Argh you swine, why would you do that? We maybe related, but that doesn't mean she'll go any easier on me. I bet this is how you've survived for so long, by putting other people directly into the firing line.' Jin protested.

'Yeah, but you love me really. And trust, I've fought my fair share over the years when required.' Axe replied with a grin as he hoisted up his gear.

Jin was right though, the afternoon had been great. In fact it had been so good that he'd completely forgotten about the things that had been plaguing his mood earlier. That was until his phone started vibrating in his pocket, opening it to find a new message. The message, the one he'd been waiting so long for; but hoped might never come. He had to think fast and send Jin home.

'But you might be right. Tell you what, how about I set up camp here and you take the van back and appease your sister. You can pop back later in the week when you get a free day.' Axe suggested

'You sure that's okay man, not going to be lonely all up here by yourself?' Jin asked.

'Nah man, pretty sure the others are popping back up here over the next few days, and besides I've got all these waves to play with. I'll be fine, plus I might be able to get in a cheeky night sesh before you get back up. I've got your number so can always ring for a lift if I decide to cut it short.' Axe replied as a large grin spread across his face.

'Well, if you're sure. Would be the better option for me. What gear do you need out of the van?' Jin asked.

'Just the tent. Oh and there's a black dry bag I need to dig out from under one of the bench seats. That should be enough.' Axe replied as he began tossing gear left, right, and centre out of the van to get to the locker which contained the bag that he could never be without.

Chapter Seventeen: The Great North Run

Axe huddled just below the dunes in the growing darkness and waited for the moon to reappear from behind the clouds before he put out to sea for what could be his final venture. Jin had long since said his goodbyes and made his way back home, and although he didn't realise, it would be the last time he would see Axe. He would return to the beach a few days later to find a deserted tent and this note:

Gone walkabout, catch you on the flip side. Take it easy man and keep the van. Axe.

The breeze was stiffening and by the time the moon had reappeared it was gusting twenty-five to thirty knots. At least it was going to be a steady reach all the way up the coast before the serious work would begin. Making a final check of all his gear, Axe tightened the rucksack like straps of his dry bag and blasted off out from the beach. Spray flying up all around him through the gloominess as he battled with the kite for the first fifteen minutes of the gusty conditions making his way round the headland before bearing away on to an almost perfect reach up the coast.

Axe could see the high wire fences and watchtowers looming up in the darkness as he approached the beaches of the North. The relative safety of the tree-line was a good fifty metres beyond the beach's defences, all he needed now was a mega gust and the perfect wave to pitch him up and over the high wires. He bore away hard, picking up speed, timing it just as the watchtower's searchlights began a fresh sweep of the bay he hit his line and caught a wave perfectly, propelling himself skyward.

Come on, come on. He thought as the kite took him ever higher. *Just a little bit more. Shit, shit, shit not gonna make it.* As the fence line appeared to be more than a bit too close for comfort. Leaving it to the last possible moment before crashing straight into the fence he quickly jerked on his control lines looping the kite, and eking out that last little bit of extra air. The bottom of the board literally scrapped the metalwork as he crossed over the razor wire before he and his kit crashed through the bushes on the far side, disappearing into the thick undergrowth before the scanning searchlights had caught up with him.

The lights may not have caught him, but the dogs had definitely picked up on his presence, as he heard low growling and barking from one of the towers, raising the alarm that all was not well. Wasting no time at all Axe quickly slipped on a pair of running shoes and without even bothering to attempt to hide the kite and the board, he bolted off in the direction of his final rendezvous, weaving his way in between the boulders, tearing through bushes and trees, putting as much distance between himself and the gnashing teeth that would surely by now be hot on his heels. He just hoped to god that whoever he was due to meet would already be waiting for him. Otherwise the game would well and truly go up several levels of difficulty.

The terrain somewhat reminded him of his training days in Snowdonia as he scampered and scrambled up and over the rough rocky landscape of the North Korean peninsular. Occasionally he thought he could hear the dogs and men growing ever closer, but then the noises would die off again. He maintained the relentless pace and by the time he reached the crest of the ridge he was blowing hard, a quick glance back in the direction he had come confirmed that the patrols had indeed picked up his tracks but their bouncing lights were labouring up the steepest part of the hillside a good click adrift of his current position. Down below in front of him he could just pick out the faint trace of the train tracks and the drab silhouette of the station buildings, but no car or vehicle of any kind. *Was he early? No, if anything he was running a few minutes behind.*

With no time to second guess where his contact was he set out again down the bank, with as much speed as he dared without risking a cheese roll like tumble, that would be the last thing he needed at this point. Reaching the last hundred or so metres of the slope he spotted a pair of dim lights, growing in intensity as they wove their way towards him along the road running parallel to the railway tracks. This must be his contact and if it wasn't, he'd already decided he'd be commandeering the vehicle, there was no way he was going to be a guest of the PDRK forces, not now that the hardest part was out of the way.

Crouching behind a clump of thorny bushes at the side of the rugged track he waited until the vehicle was almost on top of his position before emerging so suddenly that the driver had no option but to slam on the breaks and come to a screeching stop less than a yard in front of him. The bright beams almost blinded him making it impossible to see anything other than the outline of the occupant, nevertheless Axe was sure they were not Korean. Shielding his eyes as best he could his squinted stare remained transfixed on the driver.

'Oi Ghost Rider, you only live twice. So unless you intend on making this a cameo. Get a wriggle on!' The voice that called out through the darkness was somehow familiar and yet he couldn't quite place it. 'No time for brinkmanship, Middleton. We need to go, like now!'

There was a split second in which he inwardly smiled at the sound of his own name, a name that he hadn't heard for a good few months. Nonetheless James didn't need to be told twice. And as he jumped in through the passenger door, the car roared back into life almost spinning on the spot and his heart leapt at the sight of a familiar face, the face of Josh Palmer.

'I see you're getting all the holiday destinations. Great to see you, Josh.' James said beaming, glad that the powers that be had sent someone whom he already knew. It would make things a lot easier in the coming days.

'You too man, I heard about what happened on your return, nasty business that. How's your father doing?' Josh enquired.

'To be honest I really don't know. I've been totally off the grid. As I'm sure you have too. So I know about as much as you do I reckon. Nevertheless, if there is one person who just through sheer stubbornness will not leave this world quietly and without a fight, it's my father. Even if it was just to be a pain in my arse for a little bit longer, he'll get some sort of kick out of it.' James laughed. 'Right, what's the plan? I guessing you've been here for a while and should have a much better feel for the lay of the land than I do.' He added.

'Been in country for about a six weeks, under the guise of a UNESCO representative, gave my *Guide of the People* the slip but if I'm not back at my meeting point by 1000hrs then we may have a problem. Although to be honest that's not what I'm worried about. The distance isn't the problem, it's the route. The quickest and pretty much only way takes us past some of the most militarised areas in the whole country. I would have said we had the element of surprise on our side but judging by those lights just coming up over the brow of the hill behind us I'm not sure that is the case anymore.' Josh replied.

'Oh don't worry about them, they'll be so scared of what might happen to them if they notify a superior that someone may have sneaked into the country the night before *The Day of The Sun* celebrations are due to start that they won't even dare mention it. Which should give us a clear run all the way through, there will be so much last minute rushing around to make sure tomorrow is just the way *Rocket Man* expects that they won't be looking out for one insignificant vehicle. Besides I'm assuming this has got a smuggler's hole build into it somewhere.' James confidently replied, or at least giving his best impression of not having a care in the world. He was after all far more experienced at this kind of work and knew full well that this was a big step up for Josh from the sun bleached beaches of Belize. He had to front up and give off an air of total control otherwise he could see his younger companion's head exploding.

'Yeah there is one set into the floor in the back, which actually you better jump into; we're coming up to where the road forks, might be a checkpoint off to the Kosong Naval base.' Josh replied.

'Keep driving.' James stated as he started to clamber between the front seats and into the back of the car. 'Whatever you do don't stop.' James said as he lifted the floor and ducked down into the belly of the vehicle.

'Trust me, I've got no intention of stopping.' Josh replied as he began to accelerate around the bend, putting on as much speed as he dared before the straight where the road split. He could see a small checkpoint had indeed been set up, but luckily it was a couple of hundred metres down the road they would not take, not that he had any intention of slowing. To slow now might actually work against them. He made sure the checkpoint was a distant spot on the rear horizon before he gave a tap on the floor to signal that all was safe for James to reemerge from his hiding place.

'Jesus it's cramped in there, wouldn't want to stay down there for too long. ' James exclaimed as he wriggled his way out of the floor.

'Sorry didn't have a great deal of materials to work with fitting that. Not something that is easy to come by over here and funnily enough rather difficult to make when you feel like you have someone attached at the hip watching and questioning almost everything you do. I'm surprised they didn't demand that we should be bed buddies.' Josh replied.

'Not knocking it man, you've done a great job for someone that's been properly dropped into the thick of it. Not many as green as you have been given this type of assignment, I'd take that as a very good sign if I were you. Well either that or you've properly pissed someone off.' James joked trying to keep the journey as light as possible, he was very well aware of what lay ahead, Wonsan. 'Only small observation the next time you make one of these, don't leave spikes sticking out. Generally live cargo doesn't appreciate feeling like a pin cushion.'

'Spikes? Oh, I forgot about them. They're not spikes, but now that you've found them we better pull over and sort them out.' Josh replied, coming to a stop on the verge. Getting out he opened the back and dug around in the modified floor until he found what he was looking for. Pulling out two short poles with North Korean flags on them.

'Good thinking, with most of the windows blacked out, nobody's going to dare stop a car with those on tonight.' James said as he helped Josh to attach them to either side of the bonnet. 'Right, we best get moving. I'll jump back under the floor when we're about half an hour out from Wonsan. Guaranteed there will be lots of activity around there tonight, they'll be gearing up to move some of their toys up for the parades tomorrow, if they haven't already started.' James added, as they set off again.

'Did Tom, tell you exactly where this suspected arms deal was being done?' Josh asked.

'Something about some ancient tomb complex just outside the capital.' James replied.

'About as much as he told me, had a quick recce of it a week ago, it's certainly a tomb complex how old it is, is questionable. One of the things the Kim's have not been so transparent about. Parts of it could be very old indeed, but they have done so much cosmetic work to it to show off the greatness of the country, you know the usual propaganda stunts, that it's now rather difficult to tell what it would have originally looked like.'

'That doesn't surprise me in the least, did he mention to you what the nature of the weapons were?' James asked.

'No, I don't think anybody managed to work out exactly what it was that was being supplied. They just got the impression from the chatter that it was something the Koreans were very excited about. Which generally means it's nothing good. The odd thing was that it came across as if the Koreans also had something of significant value and yet there was something very ambiguous about the reference, there was no real clear indication as to what it was, only that it was something very old and very important.'

'But important to whom and why? Those are the questions that have been bugging me.' James replied half lost in deep contemplation.

'Hmmm, all very curious. Keep driving, I'll jump into the back from here.' He added as they drew nearer to their next big obstacle.

Josh kept a steady speed as he drove into the outer suburbs of Wonsan. Noting the vast amount of heavy vehicles in and around the area, all accompanied by more troops than he would ever entertain coming into contact with solo. Luckily so far the flags were doing their job and keeping any of the more quizzical amongst the soldiers at bay. 'Jesus, that's a bloody ICBM transporter, and another one.' Josh exclaimed, not being able to contain his surprise.

'Yep, was expecting as much. This is one of those bases, you just concentrate on the driving.' James said in as low a voice as possible.

'There's two coming up that look like they're gonna turn off onto the highway we want to get onto, what shall I do?' Josh asked as it dawned on him just how serious their situation was.

'Keep you're nerve, just fall in behind them, and overtake when the opportunity presents itself. Let the flags do the rest. You'll probably find the outriders will wave you on passed.' James replied from underneath the floor.

'Okay, I hope this works. Otherwise we're buggered.' Josh replied trying to stay as calm as possible. It wasn't exactly everyday that he followed convoys of trucks transporting nukes down the road.

This was one of those times when James really didn't like being where he was, he had very little control over how this played out, all he could do was trust that Josh wouldn't do something stupid and that nobody paid too close attention to the car. Darkness was their ally, a passing glance in the moonlight wouldn't warrant a second, had they been trying this in daylight he doubted very much that the car would stand up to scrutiny.

'They're waving us on.' Josh's relieved voice called out.

'Perfect, just take it easy. Don't ram your foot down and we'll be fine. Easy does it.' James replied, crossing his fingers as he began calculating the size of the convoy by the changes in traffic nosies as Josh warily made his way up the side of the monsters.

'That's the last of them.' Josh called out. 'Better stay down there, just in case we come across anymore up ahead.'

'Great, I always wanted to know what it was like to be a pilchard.' James replied from the confines of the hole in the floor. 'You got any dry clothes? This wetsuit's starting to chafe.'

'Yeah, but you're going to have to wait, not like we can stop now. Unless you want those nukes to catch up with us. Will sort you out when I drop you off.'

'How long we got to go?' James asked.

'About an hour, maybe a bit longer depending on what else we come up against. Will try and get you as close as I can to the site.' Josh replied.

'In that case, I'm gonna get a bit of shut eye, never know when the next time will be to get any sleep.' James said, trying to find as comfortable a position as possible, closing his eyes and allowing the constant vibrations of the car to ease him off.

The next thing James was aware of was the engine noise dropping out and a ratter tap tap, on the lid of his coffin like box.

'We're here, time to get moving.' Josh said as James started to drag himself out from the tin can. 'The main complex is about half a click up that ridge. This is as close as I can get you without driving up to the main gates and introducing you to the security staff. Take this.' Josh added tossing James a black rucksack.

'Cheers man, hopefully catch you later.' James replied.

'Hopefully, I did request access to the site today. Right, I better get a move on to make it back to my digs in time for morning role call otherwise I'll be going somewhere that even god doesn't visit.' Josh replied jumping back in the car and disappearing back down the dusty track towards the main highway.

James surveyed the hillside in the growing light of the new dawn, shaking the last of the tiredness off, he darted off in the direction of what appeared to be a small copse of trees to the west of the main site where he hoped he might be able to find a bit of cover and hideout until the site opened up for the day's tours, when he might just be able to blend in with the crowds.

Chapter Eighteen: The Tango's Tarnished

Gaz and Ollie weaved their way down the twisty narrow back streets of East London until they found the one they were looking for. The dilapidated terraces didn't fill them with confidence as they finally arrived at the small industrial estate where the garage they had found on the net had a van for sale, described as a tidy runner.

'Mate I don't want to stay here for any longer than absolutely necessary so don't try being clever with the price. As long as it's in the right ball park just give them what they want.' Ollie said to Gaz as they pulled up in one of the roughest areas they had seen since they had arrived in the sprawling metropolis.

'We'll see, this car's not going to help much on that one me thinks, kinda screams money.' Gaz said.

'Yeah, in hindsight probably should have taken the tube.' Ollie replied. 'Right, now where is this garage.' He added as he began to scan the buildings on either side of the road, paying close attention to the assortment of signs on the units as they cruised round the estate.

'Ah, that's the one. Halfway Autos.' Gaz said pointing to a unit fifty yards further up the lane on the right. 'Not exactly a name that shouts quality is it?'

'As long as it runs I suppose it doesn't matter too much, not exactly like we're gonna trek across Europe in it.' Ollie said as Gaz parked the car and they wandered over to the dingy looking building with just over a dozen vehicles out on the forecourt.

'Hiya man, Dave about?' Gaz asked a rough shaved burly looking man, in the process of washing one of the cars on the forecourt.

'In the office, mate.' The man replied pointing to a door on the left of the unit.

'Cheers fella.' Gaz replied before heading off towards the office door.

The first thing that struck them as they entered the office was the grimy orange carpet, straight out of the seventies and judging from its general condition hadn't been cleaned since.

'Ugh, here we go.' Ollie muttered under his breath, just as a tree trunk of a man emerged from a room at the very rear of the office.

'Yes, gents. What can I do for you?' He asked.

'Alright bud, looking for Dave.' Gaz said.

'That's me. What you want?' Dave replied.

'Perfect, we rang earlier about the long wheel based Transit.' Gaz said.

'Ah yeah I remember, unfortunately I've literally just had a fella pop in and buy it for cash.'

'What about the one on the forecourt?' Ollie asked, having clocked it just before they entered the office.

'Yeah, sorry. That's the one. He's picking it up next week.' Dave replied. 'Got a real tidy VW transporter, little bit more pricy but in a much better condition.'

Ollie didn't say anything out loud but just gave Gaz the subtlest of looks just to say *I told you something like this was going to happen.*

'Oh that's a shame, really needed a Transit. Bit of a wasted trip then, was gonna pay cash too. Ah well, guess we'll have to go elsewhere.' Gaz said, not rising to the bait.

'Hold on, don't be too hasty.' Dave said as Gaz was about to turn and walk out. 'I've got another Transit round the back, she's not a great looker, got a few bumps and scrapes, but the engine's sound enough. I wouldn't normally let it go in that condition but if you are really after a Tranny, I could let her go for say two.'

'Two hundred, sounds okay.' Ollie said before wishing he hadn't opened his mouth.

'Nah, two grand mate. You havin' a bath? Not gonna get anything around here for a few squid.' Dave bluntly replied.

Gaz stopped Ollie from replying with a sarky comment. 'Let's have a look at her first and then we'll talk money.'

'Sure. But I gotta make something on her.' Dave replied ushering them round to the back of the unit.

Gaz and Ollie spent a good amount of time looking over the van. Dave wasn't lying it certainly had been bumped around a bit, nevertheless the engine seemed to be smooth enough for the age.

'Take eleven fifty for cash?' Gaz finally offered as he closed the hood.

'Nineteen hundred.' Dave replied.

'Fourteen.' Gaz shot back. 'After all she does need a bit of body work doing.'

'Can't really go lower than eighteen, to be honest geez.'

'Tell you what I'll meet you half way, sixteen.' Gaz said.

'Seventeen fifty cash.' Dave replied putting his hand out.

'Seventeen.' Gaz said shaking Dave's hand before the guy had a chance to retract it.

'Oh go on then. Fair play, drive a hard bargain you do.' Dave said, slightly annoyed with himself at the rookie mistake of allowing Gaz the opportunity to knock a bit more out.

'Tidy. Let's get the paperwork done then.' Gaz replied. 'Ol, get on the blower and sort the insurance out. You know the one to use don't you?' Gaz half asked not really expecting a reply as he walked back into the office with Dave.

It didn't take them long to finalise all the relevant documents. The only thing left was for Gaz to pull out a wedge of cash in an envelope, remove a couple of hundred to keep back and handed the rest over.

'Cheers bud, pleasure doing business with you.' He said to Dave as he left the back of the office, chucking the keys at Ollie. 'You can drive.'

'How did I know you were going to do that.' Ollie half protested at being kicked out of the comfort of the Cobra. Gaz didn't reply he just kept walking back towards the sportster. Briefly waiting for Ollie to drive round to the front.

'You best follow me mate, we've gotta go pick up the rest of the gear. Just have to hope Juan's sorted all that EMI stuff and had a look at the building plans by the time we get back.' Gaz said as Ollie briefly pulled up next to the Cobra.

'No worries, lead on MacDuff. Sure the Spaniard will be in his element by now.' Ollie replied.

Juan was indeed on the verge of making a breakthrough regarding the EMI that would disrupt the vault's security systems, having almost exhausted his list of tech savvy associates. As a last resort he had pitched a hypothetically scenario onto a dark web message board he occasionally used to contact a hacker collective known as *Omnes*, and was now waiting to see if he would get a nibble. He just hoped that unlike his previous encounters with the group, their enthusiasm for setting, what they saw as entertainment, wouldn't turn out to be quite as humiliating as the last couple of challenges they had demanded he complete as payment for their assistance. The repercussions of the last such challenge were still a bit raw.

He was in the process of working out how they were all going to get back out of the deposit building when the now familiar springing boing-boing sound emanating from his tablet alerted him that *Omnes* had sent a response, as an animation of Zebedee complete with bristling moustache clutching an envelope bounced and cartwheeled across the screen. 'Some like it hot, haha.'

Purely from the hackers' choice of animation Juan knew that they were definitely in a particularly mischievous mood; not delaying the inevitable he tracked the cursor onto the envelope and clicked. *Omnes* were on form today, out of the envelope popped Dylan, another character from *The Magic Roundabout*.

'Hey man, We got the gear you need. But first you must take a trip. Your mission should you choose to accept it, is so close and yet so far out. This one is gonna be one hell of a wild ride, so strap yourself in and remember to hold on tight. This train is about to leave the station. Oh and Dude, whatever you do, don't walk on the grass.' Dylan said before jumping back into the envelope. Only to be replaced by Zeebad.

'Right you spineless slime-spreader, listen up and listen good. I'm free at last, you must raise my Standard on the palace of this land. It's time for the big chill, haha.' And with that Zeebad exploded in a puff of blue smoke. Juan couldn't help but laugh at the cheeky concept of the challenge and yet quite how he was going to achieve it stumped him for a few moments. Then an amused smile began to spread across his face as the flicker of an idea began to emerge. In fact he realised that it might even hold the key or at least part of it for making a swift and inconspicuous getaway from the heist.

By the time Ollie and Gaz returned to the flat having picked up all of the equipment they had identified for the operation Juan was just putting the finishing touches to what would in his mind might well be the prank of the century.

'Hey guys, how was it? All set for tomorrow?' He asked with a massive smug grin.

'Yeah bro, what are you so pleased with?' Ollie asked.

'Ah it's a surprise, my dear. No spoilers, that's not my style.' Juan replied in an equally mischievous tone. 'Do you love me babs? I feel you have a burning desire for me.'

'Only on Wednesdays.' Ollie replied. 'Have you sorted the electro magnetic stuff?'

'Of course, honey. Never in any doubt. All that's left to do is to go over how we are going to dance our way out of the building and skip arm in arm down the street.' Juan replied with a wry smile.

'Er okay, whatever floats your boat.' Gaz replied slightly bemused by Juan's random choice of phrase.

'Come on, I'll fill you in. I'm so excited I just wanna get naked, you know what I mean, babs.'

'Crazy fool, let's leave the nakedness till after shall we?' Ollie said trying not to laugh at Juan's overly buoyant mood. 'Then you and Gaz can get up to whatever shenanigans take your fancy.'

'Hey speak for yourself, no way I'm being left with this overly sexed maniac.' Gaz responded. 'Can we keep on script for the time being?'

'Oh you two are so uptight, got to loosen up a bit boys. A heist like this is a very sensual thing. You gotta be gentle at the start, don't rush things, gotta get those juices flowing. Wham, bam and Thank you mam, gets you stuck in all manner of shit. No, gotta take the time and treat her right.' Juan replied as he began to pull out the blueprints laying them out on the kitchen table for the boys to see the full layout. Before he proceeded to thrash out the main points for getting in and out of the depository and where they should aim to leave the van etc.

By the time Juan had finished going over every aspect of the deed, dancing his way across the detail as if he was performing a passionate tango, Ollie and Gaz were in mesmerised awe of the sublime subtleties, colourful flourishes and deft little touches Juan was painting.

'Right boys, I don't know about you, but I could do with getting some kip.' Ollie said rubbing his eyes. 'I can tell it's gonna be the start of a long few days and I for one need to recharge the batteries before this epic begins.'

'Yeah, I'm with you on that one bro.' Juan replied. 'So which one of you am I bunking up with?' He jokingly asked.

'Yeah, right.' Gaz replied. 'That ain't happening. You can have the sofa.'

'No worries, I've got an errand to run first anyway. I know when I'm not loved.' Juan replied as he gathered up his things. 'I won't be back till late. So don't wait up, babs.' He said.

' Better take a key in that case.' Ollie said tossing him the set before he left.

'Cheers man, I knew you loved me really. I'll try not to be too noisy when I get back, not sure what time it will be, I may well be some time. Sweet dreams.' Juan said as he left to embark on the undertaking set by the hackers. The results of which wouldn't become apparent until Monday morning and all being well would unfurl just as they crossed the finish line.

Ollie and Gaz never even heard Juan return several hours later. He slipped into the flat so quietly that not even a mouse would have noticed him tiptoeing across the room and curled up on the sofa full of contentment and soon fell asleep with a beaming Cheshire Cat like grin on his face as he began to dream about the ripples that would surely fan out across the country come Monday morning.

For once they slept in late, their antics would not commence until early afternoon so there was no need to rise as early as they had been over the last few days, in fact it was almost twelve by the time the mixologists even contemplated rolling out of the comfort of their respective sleeping arrangements.

'Brew's up.' Ollie called out, just as Gaz wandered out of the bedroom.

'Nice, that's exactly what the doctor ordered.' Gaz replied taking a steaming mug from Ollie. 'You ready for this?'

'Born ready mate, you know me just living the dream. This is gonna be awesome.' Ollie replied, having seen Juan's plan, he was now far more confident that they would come out the other end unscathed.

A light rap on the door caught their attention. It was Ms Sharpe carrying a parcel address to Juan.

'Someone left this outside for you.' She said as she entered.

'Sweet, perfect timing, I had wondered when they were going to drop it off.' Juan said. 'It's the EMI device.' He added spotting Ollie's quizzical expression. 'Not going to get very far without it. Just hope it actually works, wouldn't be the first time one of their creations hasn't quite performed as advertised.'

'I thought these guys were experts.' Ollie said, as his confidence in the plan momentarily waned.

'Well it's not an exact science, and to be fair they've never produced something that fails. Just sometimes have unintended consequences, occasionally gone further than the required remit. You know like instead of blowing the doors off, it might blow up the van kinda thing. But I'm sure you guys know all about that.' Juan replied with a grin.

'Oh yeah, Gaz knows all about that.' Ollie replied with a laugh.

'Ha speak for yourself. As I recall it wasn't me that overcooked the charges on that bridge and took out an entire dam.' Gaz gibed.

'Oh come on, that was a joint effort. Had you told me you'd added Semtex to the mix I might have used a kilo or so less.' Ollie fired back. 'Mr Perfect, my arse. More like Mr Messy.'

'That's rich, coming from the one that mislabelled the containers. Was a cool wave though.' Gaz replied.

'Haha, true that.' Ollie smirked. 'But yeah, we get the idea, might not just knock out the depository. Ah well good thing it's a bank holiday, not like anybody's gonna notice. I suppose we best get a move on otherwise they'll have locked up and gone home before one of us is inside.' He added.

Juan and Ollie left first taking the tube, follow shortly after by Gaz and Ms Sharpe. Having already been into the depository, Ms Sharpe could not go back in whilst it was still staffed as she risked being recognised by the staff. So she and Gaz drove across the city in the battered tranny van. The traffic at that time of day on Good Friday was as congested as it could possibly be making it a bit of a nightmare trip especially having to avoid colliding with the aggressive city dwellers who would barge into any available gap in the traffic or in some cases forcing the issue to create a gap that wasn't there. They weren't in any particular hurry to arrive so in a way it suited them as they really didn't want to be hanging around outside for too long whilst they waited for the building to be locked up. Nevertheless Gaz was rather irate and blue in the face having vented his frustration at what he referred to as *the effing cretins* that he had to deal with on the roads.

Juan and Ollie in comparison had a very smooth if slightly crowded trip across on the tube arriving twenty minutes before the safety deposit was due to close. Making their way up the steps and entering the building Juan headed straight for the toilets whilst Ollie distracted the nearest guard by asking if he could speak to the manager as Juan slipped unnoticed into the gents, quickly locating an air vent above one of the cubicles and hauling himself up into the conditioning unit's tight pipework until the building had emptied and been locked down.

'Good afternoon, Sir. How can I be of assistance?' Sarah Connors said as she meet Ollie in the foyer.

'Good afternoon, are you the manager?' Ollie asked.

'Yes, I'm the duty manager today. Are you looking to use our facilities?' Sarah asked.

'Well potentially yes, I represent someone who has some very rare items that has empowered me to find a suitably reputable establishment to store said items. So I'm really just sounding out the various options in the area.' He replied.

'Well we are in the process of closing for the bank holiday but I'm sure I have got a bit of time just to run you through our facilities and maybe book you in for a more detailed consultation when we reopen next week. What sort of value are we talking about?' Sarah inquired.

'Oh I'd say on today's market value somewhere between twenty and thirty million pounds, sterling. Depends a bit on which collectors are bidding.' Ollie replied, making sure that he put enough bait on the hook to spark her interest.

'Well in that case, I'm sure I can spare a few minutes. Would you like to follow me and we can go over a few details in my office.' Sarah replied, totally sucked in by the figures Ollie had mentioned. She would be in line for a hefty bonus if she managed to attract a long term client of that calibre.

'Perfect, I've seen a few today and I must admit I haven't been overly impressed with all of them.' He replied, stoking the flames a bit more.

'Well I can assure you, we take the utmost precautions for all of our clients and their valuables.' Sarah confidently said as she ushered him into her office.

Ollie was careful not to over cook the goose so to speak as he continued with his ruse, after all he had an entirely different motive for talking to her. Whilst she was jabbering on about the security and other benefits of the company he was using an RFID reader to scan and copy her access card which he and the others would require later to get into both the lift and vault area. A light vibration in his pocket indicated that the scan had been successful.

'Well it all sounds very comprehensive.' He finally said as he began to wind up the conversation. 'Let me see, ah yes, I've got a free gap on Thursday next week.' He continued as he pretended to flick through his phone's calendar. 'Shall we say one thirty Thursday afternoon to have a full tour. Might even bring my employer along, availability dependant of course.' He added.

'Of course, we would be more than happy to arrange that. Very nice to meet you.' Sarah replied as she jotted down his bogus details in her appointments book.

'I shall look forward to continuing our conversation then and hopefully working with you into the future.' She said with a very warm and friendly smile, shaking Ollie's hand before he left the building.

Ollie caught sight of the battered van parked on a side street a few hundred meters further down the road. He took his time to walk down to meet Gaz and Ms Sharpe.

'All good so far, he's in. They really were incredibly sloppy, take the utmost precautions, my arse. I wouldn't trust them with my hair trimmings. Anyway, the hard part's almost done. Better find somewhere to stash this van for a bit. Not exactly the most conspicuous of things is it. Especially around this area, Maseratis are the norm here.'

'I had noticed. There's a multi storey just across the way, better drop it there and grab a coffee and a feed. Can't do much more until dark.' Gaz replied as Ollie jumped in and they moved off.

By the time the next phase of the scheme was due to start, Juan had a serious case of pins and needles in his legs, having had to cram himself up into a pipe not much wider than he was. He'd been laying there in almost total darkness since the security guards had been round turned all of the lights off and locked up for the evening. The only light he had was the faint greenish yellow glow from the dial of his watch and due to the restrictiveness of the tube he could only just cock his head very slightly to one side and peer down at it's face every now and again. This by itself wasn't particularly out of the ordinary considering the nature of his profession, but the one thing that he had overlooked was that it was part of the heating system, and still being the tail end of winter, the warm air circulating through to regulate the temperature in the building was slowly cooking his goose. *At least it'll be easy to wriggle out.* He thought as the sweat ran down his face.

In fact it wasn't and it took him a good few minutes to manoeuvre himself out of his hiding place dropping down just as cramp began to rip through his right thigh, immediately sending him into one of those bizarre hop, hobble, stretch, hop stretch, hobble, stretch awkward dances everybody goes through when the nightmare bites. Once the burning clench had subsided he climbed back up onto the toilet bowl and retrieved the rucksack he'd stashed. Fumbling around inside it he located a small head torch and the box of tricks he would require to bypass the alarm system.

He knew he had thirty seconds to get across the foyer to the control panel and deactivate the system before the silent alarm was triggered alerting both the police and the private security firm that the building had been breached. Taking a few calming breaths, he opened the door and sprinted across the room to where the panel was near the main door. His adrenaline was pumping as he quickly connected the box to the panel and watched the sequencer reel through a string of combinations. His heart was beating hard as the seconds ticked off. *Come on, come on.* He prayed as the device began to narrow down the possibilities. *Eureka, thank you.* He thought as it finally cracked the code with the smallest of margins to spare before all would have been lost.

Following the blueprint in his head Juan went to the side of the building and picked the lock on the emergency fire exit. Cautiously poking his head out, the coast was clear. The side street was almost completely deserted apart from the battered looking van, that the others had brought round from the car park a few minutes before. He didn't;'t even need to wave to them, they had seen him open the door and had already begun to grab the gear they would need for the vault. Gaz and Ollie raced across from the van with the tanks of Oxyacetylene, drill and cutting tools they had picked up the day before. Ms Sharpe slammed the sliding door of the van shut and without even hanging around to wish them luck disappeared with the van, not planning on returning until the arranged time on the Monday. They had discussed leaving the van in the alley over the weekend but in the end they had all agree that would be asking for trouble. It was so battered and scruffy that it would undoubtably attract unwanted attention.

'Did you miss me, babs?' Juan asked as he shut and relocated the door.

'Yeah man, take it everything was okay here?' Gaz replied.

'Bit sticky, but yeah everything seems to be in order so far. You got her card?' Juan asked.

'Copied it, just need to pop a blank into the scanner and copy it and we are good to go.' Ollie replied as he took out a blank card and inserted it into the device he'd used earlier to clone Sarah Connors' security pass. 'One sec.' He added as the machine began to transfer the data onto the card. 'Done.' He said taking the card out and handing it to Juan.

They dragged all the gear across the polished marble to the lift, and Juan deftly swiped the card. The lift doors smoothly swung back accompanied by a soft ping. They piled in, selected the basement level and watched the doors close. Nothing happened.

'Shit! They must lockdown the lift mechanism. We're stuck on this floor. Can you bypass it?' Gaz asked Juan, as the panicked thoughts began to roll through his head.

'Possibly, gonna take some time. Depends if it's an electrical or physical lock. Just bear with me.' Juan replied as he began to take apart the lifts control panel to access the wiring.

'This isn't good.' He said scratching his head after fiddling with the wiring loom. It's not electrical, or at least not done here. I can't bypass this.'

'Well that's tarnished your tango, what the fuck are we gonna do now? We've only got this one window. Shit.'

'Don't panic, man. Chill, there is another way. Just not gonna be quite so easy. Hope you boys can climb. Juan said looking up at the lifts emergency panel in the ceiling. Gonna have to go up to go down.'

'But we haven't got any ropes. This gas tank's not exactly light you know.' Ollie replied.

'I got that covered.' Juan replied as he took out a knife and began to cannibalise his rucksack to create a makeshift back harness for the tank. 'This will have to do. Just hope it holds.' He said as he finished attaching the webbing around the tank.

'Right up you go.' Gaz said to Ollie as he set himself into a position to give Ollie a leg up.

Ollie scrambled up through the opening, leaning back through to haul up all of their gear before helping the other two up onto the top of the lift.

'At least the framework in this shaft looks pretty solid.' Gaz said surveying their next obstacle. 'Shouldn't be too bad. Just that one bit half way down that is a bit of a step.' He said. 'Ol, I'll take that. Just shadow me in case I go.' He added picking up the gas tank and slinging it up onto his back.

'I'll do my best but if you go I don't think I'm gonna be able to hold both you and that tank.' Ollie replied with a noticeable degree of trepidation in his voice. As he climbed down along side Gaz. Just as he reached the halfway point Gaz's foot slipped, Ollie missed his arm, but just managed to catch hold of the back of his collar.

'That was a close one, try not to kill both of us.' He said as Gaz steadied himself before continuing their descent down into the darkness of the shaft.

'That's me.' Gaz called out as he reached the floor of the shaft just before Ollie dropped down next to him.

'Nice, a few more trips and we're done. Definitely earning our Scooby snacks today.' Ollie replied as he began to make his way back up, nimbly swinging between the metalwork to where they had left Juan with the rest of the kit. The whole exercise took forty minutes in the end to ferry all their stuff down into the depths of the building. Catching their breath for a few moments they examined the basement exit doors just above. Now that they didn't have the assistance of the lift they were faced with having to prize them open with a crowbar and a lot of brute force. In the end it took both of them, with Juan wriggling through the gap to get into their end goal, the vault room.

'Finally, well that was a lot harder than it needed to be. Don't know about you boys but I think a quick bite to eat and then kip for a few hours before we start on this concrete.' Gaz said as he arched his back stretching out his muscles after carrying the heavy tank.

'Sounds like a plan, can't rest for too long. Have a feeling this wall is going to be a pain in the arse as well.' Juan said having started to inspected the smooth solid grey mass that stood between them and the inside of the vault.

It was about five in the morning by the time Juan awoke and roused the other two from their slumber.

'Right babs, time to dance, you got that one ten transformer?' He asked as Ollie wiped the sleep from the corner of his eyes.

'Er, yeah over in that corner.' Ollie replied as he began to wake up. ' I'm shattered remind me never to go rough sleeping, feels like I only just went to bed.'

'Ah, I think we've slept on worse.' Gaz said as he began to set up the drill. 'Let's just hope that this baby is up to the job.' He added as he connected it up to the transformer and set the head of the drill up against the concrete. 'Okay, ready when you are.'

The sound of the drill roaring into life was deafening and it reverberated around the walls of the enclosed room.

'Good thing we're well underground, this isn't exactly quiet.' Gaz shouted out above the noise and plume of dust spraying out of the wall as the drill bit into the tough stone and ever so gradually made it's way through.

There was a loud crack. Gaz had to stop and wait for the dust to settle. 'Got another head? This ones had it.' He said when he finally saw what had happened, pulling out what remained of the drill bit, which had decided that it didn't fancy continuing the battle of attrition against the reinforced concrete and had sheered off.

'Yeah, got several. Had a feeling one wouldn't cut it. How far we got?' Ollie replied.

'About two inches, this stuffs brutal man. Think they must have used granite in the mix. Gonna be most of the day before we get through I reckon. Take over for a bit, my knuckles are starting to go white.' Gaz replied flexing his hands trying to stimulate the blood flow back into his extremities, after all the vibration from the drill.

'Oh go on then, never send a boy to do a man's job.' Ollie chuntered picking up the drill, for his stint. They rotated the work between the three of them and little by little the distance between them and their prize began to reduce, until great chunks around the rebar began to flake off. Still it took them the best part of four hours to get half way through.

'Gonna have to cut these out, all this rebar's just in the wrong places to go any deeper.' Juan said as he pulled out the drill.

'Yeah no worries, I'll get the torch here setup, not gonna take the Oxy long to dispatch them, will; be like a hot knife through butter.' Gaz replied as he brought the gas tank across, attaching the blow torch to it. He was right, unlike the stubborn concrete the rebar capitulated within moments of being set upon by the plasma like intensity of the flame.

'If only there was one of these for the rest of it, we'd have been through hours ago.' Ollie said and he swept out the hole. 'Should be wide enough, well for me and you at least.' He said to Juan. 'Not sure about *Roly-poly* over here.'

'Ha, talk about calling the kettle black. *Roly-poly* indeed, dick.' Gaz replied wiping as much of the whitish grey cement dust from his face as he possibly could. 'Looks like you've already eaten all the pies in the bloody bakery and started munching on raw flour.' He laughed. It was true they all did just look like they had been caught in a large explosion of flour such was the nature of drilling such a concentrated amount of stone for what had started to seem like an eternity.

'Come on boys, let's have a break, bite to eat.' Juan said before the two-way banter got too heated. He knew it was a hard slog, and they were just blowing off steam in their own way, but not knowing their banterish nature that well he could be excused for worrying if it would erupt into something more serious.

Ten hours it took in the end to break through into the vault, and then they still had to activate the EMI device, and for Juan to work his magic breaking into every single box individually until they found the one containing the two parts of the *Liber Veritatis*. His fingers were needless to say well and truly worn out by the time he opened the one they sought.

'Gotcha!' Juan exclaimed as he cracked the triple locking mechanism, of by that point the umpteenth box, he'd lost count after the first hour's worth.

'Bastard, fucker's kept the map. Ah well, that'll just have to wait for another time.' Gaz said as he retrieved the objects. Right better just chuck all these onto the floor, empty a few and go, fuck me it's almost that time.' He added as he glanced at his watch.

So intent had they been on their mission that they hadn't even bothered to keep track of the time and had worked, bar a few breaks almost solidly for the entire weekend.

'What is the time.' Ollie asked.

'Ten in the evening, Sunday. By the time we've staged this lot, and had a snuggle it'll be time to get the eff outta here.' Juan replied.

'Need to make sure we time it for about nine, my surprise should be well and truly working it's magic by that point.' He added beaming with a cheeky grin.

'Oh yeah, you still haven't told us what that is.' Ollie replied, eager to know exactly what it was that had kept Juan out for so late on Thursday night.

'Sorry babs, not spoiling it. You're just going to have to wait until the morning.' Juan replied still grinning.

The heavens had opened up a good half an hour before the intrepid thieves made their way out of the depository, just enough time for Juan's surprise to unfurl and cause bemused chaos and in certain circles a degree of indignation as they stepped out into the alleyway where Ms Sharpe was already waiting for them.

Sirens could be heard wailing far off in the distance. As Juan closed the door behind them.

'Dude is this you?' Ollie asked catching the familiar noise of police sirens.

'More than likely. Juan said tossing him his cell phone open on the BBC's news app. 'Sure it will be on there by now.' He added.

'Haha that's genius.' Ollie said as he looked at the main headline, that read: *Royally Fooled on 1st April,* accompanied by what should have been the Royal Standard flying above Buckingham Palace, it looked similar but there were noticeable differences, instead of the quartered red, blue and yellow, it was red and black and where the Scottish Lion and Irish Harp normally sat, there was in their place the familiar taunting smile of Guy Fawkes's mask grinning out across The Mall.

'How the hell did you put that up there without being seen?' Ollie asked in awe.

'Oh I didn't, they hoisted it themselves. I just intercepted the flag that was being set down from the producer for Easter and replaced it with one that changed when it got wet.' Juan nonchalantly replied.

'Brilliant. That's gonna be viral forever.' Ollie replied still laughing at the shear audacity of it.'And the irony that it happens to be April Fool's as well, is just perfect.'

'Haha you should see the tabloids headlines.' Gaz laughed as he read out one in particular. *'Bucking Hell! It's a Royal April Fool's.* Genius, good thing we're going out to China. They won't leave any stone unturned trying to find you.' He added as they jumped into the van and disappeared whilst the world was preoccupied by anonymity.

Chapter Nineteen: States of Sleep

Rachel sat in the high backed chair, as she had done everyday since Professor Middleton had been admitted in to the ICU at Jersey General Hospital. There had been very little change in his condition since he'd slipped into a coma. The doctors still seemed hopeful that he would come out of it, although from what she gathered they were a little baffled as to why he had not already come round. They said that his brain activity was not what they would expect from somebody in a coma, but that there seemed to be something they could not pinpoint which seemed to be preventing him from waking. It was almost as if he was stuck somewhere between REM and NREM sleep floating in an inexplicable kind of paralysed sleep. All they could do was to wait and see if his brain activity stabilised enough for them to try injecting him with a prototype stimulant which, fingers crossed might help to break the cycle. They were hesitant to try it whilst his cortex activity was so erratic especially when the drug's effectiveness in this type of case was not fully known.

All Rachel could do was pray that he would pull through, she looked as if she hadn't slept in days, big dark slightly puffy rings were clearly visible around her eyes and her joints were sore from the stiffness of not having had a decent nights sleep.

'Oh honey, are you still here?' A nurse called Noura, whom Rachel had come to know quite well asked, as she came into the room to check on the machines hooked up to the professor. 'Come on, time you went home for some proper rest. You keep this up and I'll be looking after you too if you're not careful. Come on, Let's get you a cuppa tea in the nurses' room and then young lady you need to go get some rest. Nothing's going to change by tomorrow and if it does we will ring you straight away, I promise.'

'Argh, maybe you are right. I just feel like I should be here you know. I just feel so; argh, I can't even think of the word for it.' Rachel replied with the emotional tired expression that Noura had seen all too often.

'Come on; tea, taxi and bed. Sister's orders.' Noura replied taking charge of the situation.

The hot cup of tea did indeed begin to restore Rachel's spirits and she almost thought about staying but she knew from previous experience that the concept wouldn't wash with Noura, once the nurse had decided to evict her she wouldn't change her mind. In her heart Rachel knew it was the right call to make, she was desperately tired and realistically it was very unlikely that the Professor would suddenly wake up. And even if he did, it would still be sometime before he was able to stay awake for more than a few minutes. The recovery process from what she had read could take several days before a patient was up for more than a few hours at a time.

By the time the taxi dropped her off at Noirmont the only thing Rachel wanted to do was to collapse on to her bed. But bed would have to wait. She was almost at the top of the stairs when Chris rang to check on how she was doing.

'Hi Rach, just thought I'd call to make sure you are okay. How's things? Any change?' Chris asked.

'I'm okay, bit tired but ok. He's the same as he has been. The doctors seem positive but I get the impression that they are a little bit stumped; I don't think they are too concerned but his current state is something that they don't usually see so they are, hmmm how do I put it? Winging it and hoping that it will resolve itself in time. I just feel a bit helpless really as there's nothing I can do. I talk to him a bit and read bits to him but I've got no idea whether it's getting through or not. It's just such a demoralising situation, I'm just so tired and a bit dejected if I'm honest.' Rachel despondently replied.

'Hey chin up, he's a fighter. He'll pull through one way or another, of that I have no doubt. I know it's a bit erratic but to have any brainwave activity has got to be a positive thing. So, I'm pretty optimistic. He'll be up and around in no time, you'll see.' Chris replied trying to keep her as positive as possible.

'Thanks Chris, you always were good at knowing what to say.' She replied feeling slightly better for being able to talk to a friendly voice. 'How's everything going with you all? Gaz and Ollie still causing chaos?'

'Oh you know those two, chaos and carnage go hand in hand with them, but joking aside they're actually being surprisingly well behaved. We left them yesterday working on getting in to some safety deposit where Norwood's secured the codex pieces, so by now I expect there may well be more chaos and carnage. Not like I can keep them on the leash all the time. The rest of us are flying out to Beijing, the Prof certainly knows how to set a big Easter Egg Hunt, that's for sure.' Chris laughingly replied.

'Ha yeah, for someone in a coma he certainly knows how to keep you lot occupied, doesn't he.' Rachel said smiling. 'How long are you going to be away for? Would be nice to get some company around here at some point. Definitely the hardest part, being stuck in this massive house all alone on the island.' She replied.

'Ah, I can't really say to be honest, I just don't know how far this thread is going to lead us. But if you want some company, let me have a word with Aunt Tabitha, once she's finished helping Ollie and Gaz, she may well be able to come over. Besides it would be useful for someone to keep plugging away at the Prof's notes. There must be more clues as to where the remaining parts are hidden or where he thinks they might be.' Chris replied.

'Oh, that would be so nice. I haven't seen Great Aunt Tabitha in ages. I always enjoy chatting to her. Promise me you will be careful out in China, won't you?' Rachel said.

'Well I'm not planning on starting World War Three. Nevertheless there is a certain degree of risk, we'll be as mindful as we can be given the circumstances. Anyway, look I best get off, we've got a long day of flights tomorrow and you sound like you could do with some sleep too.' Chris replied.

'Yeah, my bed is definitely calling. Good to talk to you and stay safe.' Rachel said hanging up the phone and without even bothering to disrobe she lay back on her bed, closed her eyes and slept like she had never slept before.

Chapter Twenty: The Faurschou Conundrum

Devan stood sipping a cup of the finest Da Hong Pao tea, as she had done every morning since they had arrived in Beijing. Looking out from the private rooftop terrace of the Four Seasons' Imperial Suite she admired the sublime vision of one of the oldest cities in the world, where ancient and modern met, blending perfectly to create a rich tapestry displaying the evolution and achievements of the people's great nation state of China. Beijing certainly did have a deep rich vein of tradition and pioneering development and yet it also represented some of the darkest, most brutal sides of human nature. Devan mused for a time over the sights changed or unseen, not because they were obscured but because they no longer existed as they once did, like the Yuanmingyuan, more commonly known as The Old Summer Palace, looted and burnt to the ground by the British in 1860. Retribution for the torture and murder of two British envoys, a *Times* journalist and their escorts. An event which certainly by today's standards would be seen as neither proportionate nor chivalrous in its response and was still a poignant sticking point of immense pain and anguish for the Chinese government, not only because of the heritage that had been looted and still remained to be retuned but also the hypocritical attitude of old imperial western powers that constantly preached about letting bygones be bygones, and looking towards forging stronger trading relationships in the future, and yet cried out themselves with incredulity at the barbaric actions of groups such as the Taliban whenever they destroyed another site of cultural and historical importance and yet continued their failure to see the similarities with their own past behaviour. As a historian she could see both sides of the argument, although she did wish that sometimes her fellow countrymen would just for once show a bit more humility and at the very least make a symbolic gesture if not a full apology for their forebears actions. Of course the irony of what Chris and the Order were about to pull off in the city was not lost on her either. Draining the last of her tea, she wandered back into the sumptuous interior of the deluxe suite.

Chris had cunningly contacted the Australian billionaire, Jack Whiting, whose drug cartel problems they had been instrumental in dealing with. Chris and James had always thought when they had agreed to help out Mr Whiting that it wouldn't be a bad thing to have a pocket billionaire up their sleeves. Chris had given Jack the inside track to invest in the mega media deal that was about to take place and in return Jack had gone all out setting them up to give the impression they were ultra high net worth individuals looking to invest in the joint venture between Chestnut's media firm and a Chinese competitor. As soon as Mr Whiting's name was mentioned the staff at the hotel had immediately blocked out the suite indefinitely. He was one of their *super clients*, only ever staying at The Four Seasons when on business in the capital. When he clicked his fingers, they jumped; ensuring that the colossal suite which actually occupied the entire twenty-seventh floor atop the hotel was available until his business was concluded. It really was the epitome of extravagance, from the library stacked full of first editions, the grand piano nestled overlooking the vibrant cityscape, to the plunge pool and fire pit on the private veranda no expense had been spared. Jack himself would join them later; on the morning before the launch party of the new venture. The party would play host not only to all the VIPs, investors, media types and other guest of the two great media outlets but also unknowingly the daring heist that Chris had to pull off in order to be one step closer to the next piece of the codex.

It had taken Chestnut and her Chinese counterpart several days of negotiation with the Faurschou Foundation to be allowed to host the gala at the museum, where the heist would take place, including a sizeable donation towards securing the foundation's future. Everything was almost in place, all they needed now was a master thief, a thief that had only just finished rocking the status quo back in England.

At that very moment whilst Devan made the most of everything the lavish suite had to offer Chris was eagerly awaiting the arrival of his specialists at Beijing International Airport and then the rollercoaster would really start to shift into another gear.

Chris couldn't fail to miss Ollie and Gaz as they walked out of the terminal, accompanied by a deeply tanned man of shorter stature, he assumed was Juan, wearing a multi striped shirt, well worn red cords and a hat that he mistakenly thought was a fedora. It was in fact a cross between a pork-pie and a fedora specially made for the Spaniard, who referred to it as *The Mendoza.*

Juan Montego Lopes to give him his full name had been born in Poland four years before the fall of the Berlin Wall. Both his parents were missionaries and had travelled extensively around the world doing good works with their ten children in tow. By the time Juan was twelve he had already been to more countries than most would visit in a life time, and in some places experienced first hand the squalor and depravity that most people only read about in books. Being home schooled was not the easiest but it did allow him to embrace his passion, music. He had a natural gift, especially for flamenco; and spent much of his younger days practicing the guitar wherever and whenever he could, but he was also exceptionally ambitious albeit in a rather unconventional way. He had a keen eye for detail and turning his hand to anything that he could make money from. It had not taken him long to realise that the dexterity acquired from playing the guitar, had resulted in great feel and touch, he'd picked his first lock by the age of five and by the time he was eighteen he was breaking safes that were said to be uncrackable. His flair for making a statement had inevitably attracted the attention of Interpol, who had added him to their *Most Wanted List* under the pseudonym *The Spaniard* due to the little sheets of flamenco music he would leave behind for them to find. In fact the heist he had just pulled off in London was the first occasion on which he hadn't left his trademark calling card behind at the scene for them to find. Ms Sharpe had been unequivocally crystal clear that he was not to leave any such signature behind. The last thing any of them wanted was to attract the unrelenting dogged microscopic gaze of Interpol and their global network of investigators. He had reluctantly agreed not to leave one in the vault, nevertheless that hadn't stopped him from having one sewn into the hem of the flag raised above Buckingham Palace. That was as far as he was prepared to compromise, at least he would still know who had pulled it all off even if nobody else ever managed to join the dots together.

'Alright boys, how was your trip?' Chris asked as he greeted them.

'Long and cramped, why they insist on treating you like cattle in a milking parlour, I will never understand.' Ollie replied. 'Didn't help this one doesn't understand the concept of personal space.' He added with an accusing glance at Gaz.

'As I explained before, not my fault your shoulder was perfect for a pillow, although you might want to bulk out a bit so it's less boney next time.' Gaz replied.

'Somethings, never change.' Chris muttered. ' And you must be Juan, nice to meet you at last. I've heard a lot about your talents.'

'Likewise, I'll try to live up to expectations. Although it has been a while since I've done a job in China, so we'll have to see if I'm still quick enough with the Mahjong tiles to rob a Kong like I used to.'

'I don't think you'll have any trouble with this particular Gordian knot, everybody will be so distracted by the party's attractions that they won't even notice what's happening. You'll have a good thirty-minute window without any guests in the museum to find the professor's hidden treasure. By the time people realise the hand's been played it will be far too late for them to do anything about it. Oh this is us.' Chris said as he approached a sleek black stretched limo complete with driver.

'Sounds good, man. Not like we are having to break into another vault. But can we go over the particulars later? I'm not gonna lie am a bit shattered, travelling always makes me sleepy.' Juan replied with a half yawn. Not even batting an eyelid at the manner in which they were about to travel.

Ollie on the other hand had questions. 'Who the hell did you have to con to get this? Explains why we had to fly economy, talk about double standards.' He indignantly exclaimed whilst attempting to pick his jaw up off the floor.

'I didn't, it was complimentary.' Chris grinned. 'And don't worry boys, I got you covered. Twenty-five minutes and you'll be in the best beds money can buy.'

'You better not be joking, I've had my fair share of crap sleeping arrangement over the last few days to last me a lifetime.' Ollie said as they pulled off back towards the business district.

'Nah man, you're in for a treat. Whiting has proper sorted us out.' Chris replied with a knowing grin.

'Ah well, if you'd said that in the first place, I wouldn't have worried. Next time, lead with that.' Ollie retorted as he stretched out as much as he could in the plush comfort of the limo and was almost asleep by the time they pulled up in front of the hotel.

It was late in the afternoon by the time the journeymen had recharged their batteries enough to continue going over the plan of attack. Although it had taken Chris a few minutes to convince Ollie that he wasn't dreaming and that the plunge pool would still be there after they'd got the business side of things ironed out.

'I know all the guests will be outside but what about the museum security? I'm presuming they won't all go outside with the guests.' Juan was saying as he surveyed the floor plan of the Faurschou complex.

'Most will go out because of who some of the guests are, but you're right there will be a wandering patrol that will remain inside with the exhibits, and of course the CCTV operator. A minor drunken distraction outside one of the rear fire exits should suffice, I think. You're quite well practiced at playing the drunken fool aren't you, Ol.'

'Oh now hang on just a minute. There's no tom-foolery involved I take pride in my cameo rolls.'

'That's the spirit, as for the CCTV, you've brought that EMP box of tricks with you I presume?' Chris asked turning his attention back to Juan.

'Course babs, I wasn't going to leave my new favourite toy behind.'

'Then that should just about do us. I've managed to get Whiting a personal tour of the exhibits earlier in the afternoon, so you boys can get a first hand look at the layout under the guise of his close protection team.'

'Great, nice not to go in completely blind for a change.' Gaz remarked.

'Yeah well, I thought you would appreciate that.' Chris replied.

'What about actually finding the pieces, amongst all those other sunflower seeds? I'm presuming you're not actually expecting us to sift through all of those... what millions of seeds, to find the ones we need. That would take like forever.' Ollie said.

'Nope, from the prof's clues we're almost certain that the replicas that he had made have a very small piece of metal in them whereas the actual art work is made entirely from ceramics. Should just require scanning the whole area with a metal detector and then filtering a small amount to find the exact ones.' Chris confidently replied.

'And exactly how do you expect us to get one of them into the building?' Ollie enquired with a degree of scepticism in his voice.

Gaz turned to Ollie, giving him a look at is to say: *did you really just come out with that* before turning on his compatriot. 'Do you ever engage your brain before you speak? Just think about it for a second... acting as close protection. Do you really need me to join the dots. Come on, security wands. Pretty standard when you think about it.'

'Oh yeah, good point. Haha, nice touch, I like it.' Ollie replied as he finally began to complete the jigsaw and realised just how simple the whole thing appeared to be. 'Just what have you got planned to act as a distraction to get all of the guest outside whilst we are busy with the art?'

He added, after a moments thought.

'Ah, that's a surprise you will have to wait and see. Which reminds me, Devan and I have got to go and finalise those arrangements. So make the most of your evening. Whiting is due to arrive in the morning and I want to make sure everything is in place by the time he gets here.' Chris replied as he gathered up the blueprints, packing them away in a safe place before he and Devan left to fit the last cog into the intricate plan.

'So where are you taking me?' Devan asked stepping into the black limo, ready and waiting for them outside.

'It's a surprise, no fun in giving away all of my secrets.' Chris replied as the limo pulled off and they were soon cruising down one of Beijing's many busy highways. It didn't take them long to reach their destination, as the car pulled up outside a large rectangular stone building with huge posters hanging down between square columns.

'Ooh, are we going to see the acrobats?' Devan exclaimed in excitement as she read the Chinese signage on the front of the theatre. 'I've always wanted to see them live. They're meant to be amazing.'

'I thought you might like it.' Chris replied with a beaming smile. 'Although we're not just here for pleasure. My show stopper for the party is doing some work here at the moment.'

'Are you planning on asking some of the acrobats to perform?' She asked. 'That really would be an amazing distraction to keep the guests occupied.'

'In an sense yes, but not in quite the way you would expect. All will be revealed in due course.' Chris replied, knowing full well that his aloof response would have once again piqued her curiosity, as they entered the foyer before winding their way up the ornate staircase to their box.

The awestruck oohs and ahhs from the audience as acrobats performed daring feats defying gravity, nimbly throwing delicate female performers balancing rice bowls on an outstretched foot above their heads between strong male bases really set the atmosphere for the show. By the time motorbike riders appeared on stage and entered a cage of death the audience were hooked. Circling the metal globe in ever quicker and tighter loops, adding in more and more bikers until eight riders were almost circling wheel to wheel, before they began an intricate weaving pattern of criss-crossing lines, if their timing was out by even a millisecond they would almost certainly collide, in almost total darkness they raced, faster and faster. Only the flashing red and blue lights on the bikes were visible, so enthralled were the audience that by the time the bikers departed they did not know what to expect next, as two Chinese dragons danced in, closely followed by three human lions balancing on huge decorative balls that rolled onto the stage and began swirling around each other.

The audience was buzzing by the time the interval arrived and the crowd gradually filtered out from their seats to enjoy the refreshments and vibrant bars on the mezzanine floor. Chris and Devan left their box joining the flow of people to the VIP lounge. He took two glasses of champagne from the hostess as they entered, passing one to Devan and began to scan the room for the individual he had arranged to meet. It did not take him long to spot the man standing at one end of the bar, chatting to a couple of the theatre's directors. He just managed to catch the man's attention with a quick wave as they snaked their way through the busy throng of people.

'Hi Rups, good to see you again. May I present Professor Devan Valentine.' Chris said as he introduced his companion to his old friend and the rest of the group.

'Devan, lovely to meet you. Hope you are both enjoying the show.' Rupert replied as he warmly greeted her with a friendly kiss on the cheek.

'Oh yes, it's fantastic. Very impressive, especially those girls at the beginning. How they managed to keep balancing those bowls on the souls of their feet whilst being thrown into the air was just amazing.' Devan enthusiastically replied.

'I know right, you'd almost think they had magic glue or something. I can tell you hours and hours of practice goes into that particular routine. They really are something else. But the best is yet to come.' Rupert replied with a beaming smile.

'You're more than welcome to join us for the second half if you like.' Chris offered.

'I would love to, but I'll have to sneak in about halfway through, after my bit.' Rups replied.

'Oh, I hadn't realised you were doing part of the show, I'd just thought you were mapping bits and pieces.'

'Originally yes, but then a few days ago during a rehearsal break I'd been playing around with the kit, and one of the directors had caught part of it and really liked it so they asked if I would be able to incorporate some of it into tonight's show.'

'Nice man. Looks like you might be getting a preview of what's going to happen tomorrow evening after all.' Chris said to Devan. Who was now more intrigued than ever about what he had planned for the showstopper.

'Can't wait, you know he's been so elusive about the whole thing for ages. Dropped loads of teasing hints but never actually given the game away.' Devan said.

'Ha, that sounds about right. Well you'll only get a brief taste of it tonight. Tomorrow night is going to be on another level compared to this evening.' Rupert replied with an equally evasive smile.

'Oh you two are as bad as each other with all this theatrical mystery. All I can say is, it's going to have to be something really spectacular now that you've hyped it up so much.' Devan replied.

'I'll let you be the judge of that. Right, I best go and make sure everything is good to go, I'll catch you both in a bit. Devan really a pleasure to meet you. Enjoy the second half.' Rups said, before making his way out towards the theatre's technical box.

'I suppose we should also be making our way back to our seats.' Chris commented, noticing that most of the guests had already begun to filter back and settle in for the continuation.

Whether it was the champagne or the intoxicating experience itself Devan couldn't stop chatting about the second half of the circus as they made their way back to the hotel, so mesmerised had she been by Rups's addition to the show that she'd missed some of the other acts front of stage.

'I can see what you guys were talking about now. That was just so captivating, I can see why you wanted to book him for tomorrow. The intricacy and detail, let alone all the choreography was just stunning, so clever. It'll be perfect.' She exclaimed beaming at Chris. 'Thank you for such a wonderful evening.' She added letting her emotions from the evening take hold, and catching Chris off guard, firmly planting a passionate kiss on his lips.

A small voice in Chris's head was pleading with him not to get carried away in the moment, that he should keep his focus on point, but his heart had already overruled. They'd been stuck in this game of playful flirtations for weeks now, he could hold back his desire no longer and gave into his primal masculine instincts. Fate gave them a final nudge as they found the suite empty, and their fiery passions continued into the master bedroom until the small hours of the morning.

A light rap on the door roused Chris at about half eight, not that he'd been asleep. After a night like that; sleep was the last thing on his mind as he gently ran his fingers through Devan's hair, admiring the contours of her face her as she peacefully slept.

'Be right with you, give me a sec.' He called out trying to be quiet enough so as not to disturb her, softly slipping from the bed he left the room.

'Not a word.' He said before Ollie even had a chance to open his mouth.

'Yes, boss. Er, just wondering what time we're going to steal the museum's cherry so to speak?' Ollie asked with an air of mischievous innocence. Knowing full well he'd hit his mark just right as he received a sailing too close to the wind glaring look from Chris. 'Whiting's due in about eleven, so aim for that. I'd get as much rest as you can before then. It's gonna be a long night.'

'Looks like some of us already have had a long night.' Ollie winked, scuttling off before Chris managed to fire something back at him. Chris just sighed. *Can't really be too pissed off with him, shouldn't have expected anything less. Fucking rookie move.* The last thought aimed at himself for letting his heart rule his head. He knew he'd broken the golden rule; don't mess with the streak. So far everything had gone according to plan, the first parts of the codex were safely back in their possession and it would not be long before the next part was within reach, he just had to hope that one night of passion wouldn't turn the fates against them.

'Morning beautiful, how are you feeling?' Chris asked as he returned to Devan, who was just waking.

'All the better now that you've brought you're sexy ass back.' She replied holding out an outstretched arm invitingly.

'As tempting as the offer is, and trust me it is very. We're going to have to put round two on hold for a bit.' He replied, knowing that he may as well have just stepped on a bouncing Betty, as the look he received from Devan cut him straight in half. 'I know, but lets just slow things down for a bit, at least until after the media launch.' He knew it was the worst possible thing he could have said as the words left his lips but he couldn't think of a better option, he'd just have to get a very large shovel and fill the hole back in later.

'Well just don't expect all of this to come running whenever it suits you. I can tell you now, that isn't going to happen.' She replied with a steeliness that he didn't want to encounter again in a hurry. 'And if that's off the table, you may as well make yourself useful and make me breakfast.' She added in a lighter voice.

'Now that I can do. Tea?'

'Please.' She replied admiring his rippling topless body as it disappeared out of the room. *And I thought it was women that were meant to run hot and cold. Typical, why do I always end up with the business before pleasure type? At least the sex is good.* Devan thought to herself, reflecting on the passionate night they had just spent together, as she finally got up, walking into the marble bathroom to wash away any last hope there was of morning sex.

They spent the rest of the morning going over the last few details of how the day would play out; by the time Whiting arrived Chris could tell that Ollie and Gaz were itching to get on with it.

'Looking sharp boys.' Jack said as he walked into the Imperial Suite, to find them all suited and booted ready for their new roles as his close protection team.

'Good to see you again, Sir.' Ollie said warmly shaking Jack's hand. 'Hopefully will be a bit smother than the last time we met.'

'Wasn't that bad, was it? Nothing like a bit of chop.' Jack replied smiling as he referred to the tempestuous voyage in which his super yacht had been tossed around like a rag doll by the ferocious winds and waves of the Atlantic's winter wrath.

'If that was just a bit of chop I'd hate to know what you'd class as the perfect storm.' Ollie jokingly replied.

'You should meet my ex-wife, then you'll know.' Jack laughed before clapping his hands together. 'Right, I guess we best get cracking and kick this game into action. The driver's waiting downstairs.' He added, being as eager as everybody else to discover where the cards would land.

The Faurschou museum was abuzz with visitors taking in the new installations of a fresh exhibition; *The Book of Kings* by *Shirin Neshat*, inspired by the mass protests of the Arab Spring and the demonstrations by the Iranian Green Movement against the totalitarian regime, perfectly complemented the themes addressed by the permanent collections, including the pièce de résistance, part of Ai Weiwei's *Sunflower Seeds*. Originally commissioned as one hundred tonnes of porcelain sunflower seeds for the Tate Modern in London, the work had been carved up and sold off, of which the Faurschou had acquired one hundredth of the work. Although not anything like the scale of the original the symbolism and relationship between the individual and the masses still resonated.

'Good afternoon and welcome to The Faurschou Museum. My name is Lena, I will be your guide. Our Director, Kristian sends his apologies but he will not be able to join you, he has some last minute bits and pieces for this evening's gala to finalise. May I just say what an absolute pleasure it is for us to have you here, Mr Whiting. And thank you so much for your generous contribution to ensure the gallery's future.'

'My pleasure, I've always believed it's one's cultural duty to help preserve and promote art and artist alike, especially if one has the means to do so. I must say it's quite bold of you to have run with this theme of *Exiled Voices* considering your country's record on such matters.'

'I suppose to some it may be seen in that light; but this is modern China, Mr Whiting, and this is part of a vision for the future. We feel that if the foundations for a dialogue are set in place then as long as it is done respectfully, hopefully over time we can achieve some degree of change. In these particular cases it is all about context, perception and interpretation. Take this piece for example.' Lena said turning and pointing to a black and white photographic portrait of a man inscribed with handwritten Farsi poetry. 'This is part of Shirin's *Book of Kings*, can you see his face has no expression, he gazes at us and we at him, there's a sense of expectant waiting. The covering text, which fades out towards the bottom, projects this idea that something has happened, that this man is part of a rich tapestry of actions. And yet the question lingers how is he destined to be judged? Be he Martyr, Villain or Patriot? His actions like so many others pictured in the series have already been written and yet their story in culture is far from over. It's interesting how the artist has chosen to confront the complex questions and relationships between history, politics and philosophy. And the fact that she offers no answers; leaving it open for future generations, emphasises that point perfectly, culture is always changing and evolving so one generation's freedom fighter could very well be the next's terrorist.'

'Yes, interesting. I see what you mean. And from that stand point as long as the museum remains neutral this work does not openly criticise any current regime.' Jack remarked.

'Exactly, we are blurring the boundaries, asking the difficult questions that should be asked and at the same time challenging the individual to form their own interpretation.' She replied.

'Very good. I like it and your knowledge of the work is very impressive. I can see we will have a very stimulating and pleasurable working relationship between our cultures.' Jack replied as he continued to admire the installations.

Ollie and Gaz exchanged a glance as if you say: *did he just flirt with the Manager?* They both just smiled.

'So tell me Lena, I see most of the installations are not behind glass, how do you ensure that the works are not damaged or stolen by wandering fingers? I wouldn't want to be in the business of having to repair or replace these on a regular basis.' Jack casually asked as they continued the tour through to the permanent collections.

'Rest assured, although we chose not to put these behind glass as we felt it detracts somewhat from people's overall interaction and experience of the pieces, the security of the works was forefront in our mind when the interior of the gallery was designed. We utilise state of the art heat, motion and laser beam technology to ensure that nobody gets too close. Also as you can see there is a curator in every room backed up by CCTV. The museum's automatic shutters will completely seal the building if somebody tries to remove something from it's place.'

'Sounds very comprehensive, nice to know it's a secure investment. Now where are these sunflower seeds I've heard so much about?' Jack asked.

'Right this way, we were very fortunate to have been able to acquire a piece that has such artistic and cultural significance. As you can imagine it is a highly sought after creation, especially within China.'

'Yes, I came quite close to winning a bid for a part of it myself last year, unfortunately another private collector was prepared to go just a bit further. Although now that I see this piece in the flesh, I think it would have been lost in my collection. Far better for it to be on display for everyone to enjoy. Do you always keep it in the same configuration?' Jack asked looking at the rectangular shape that the sunflowers had been arranged in.

'Oh no, we change the shape every now and again. Just like the way that the individual can effect change on the masses, the relationship is in a constant flux of evolving so it doesn't make sense for it to be permanently in one state. In fact that reminds me, I must talk to the curators about closing off this area for a bit, as we are planning on changing it's shape for the gala this evening.' Lena replied. 'I will leave you gentlemen to enjoy the rest of the exhibits.' She added as she bid them farewell.

'What do you think boys?' Jack asked when she was out of ear shot. 'Think you can pull it off?'

'It will be a challenge for sure, but I can see a few areas that they haven't got covered.' Juan replied. 'Timing is going to be key, we won't have a big window especially when the power goes out. Keeping security busy for as long as possible is the main thing. At least it's in a separate area, if it had been open plan all the way through we'd have a real problem.'

'What about getting out afterwards? The fire escape won't be an option because Ollie will be out there, presumably under a heap of guards by that point. Can't really walk straight out into that.' Gaz said.

'Keep it simple. You don't need to over think that, these things are so small, not like your trying to walk out with the Venus de Milo.' Juan replied.

'And bear in mind that this place will be almost empty, everybody will be outside by that point.' Chris added. 'You done taking photos?' He asked Ollie.

'Almost, just need to go and wander round the back and get a few of the back of the building and then I'll be good to go.' Ollie replied.

'You and Juan do that and we'll meet you out the front.' Chris replied, looking at his watch to see the time was ticking down and they needed to make a move in order to get ready for the night's festivities.

The outside of the gallery look like it was hosting a film première by the time they returned later that evening. Orange glowing lanterns had been hung along the museum frontage, and small floating vessels with candles in the pools framed the red carpet stretching out from the entrance. All manner of high end chauffeured cars dropping off the respective guests were lined up along the street each waiting for their moment in the spot light. In the centre of the paved courtyard facing the entrance a tower of scaffolding had been erected for Rupert's evening display. Chris could just make him out, setting up his equipment atop the tower as he, Devan and the others exited the limo and made their way down the scarlet fabric to join the party.

It was the first time since London that he had seen Chestnut, she had been so busy with actually finalising the deal and overseeing the majority of the evening's events that they had only spoken over the phone a couple of times, mainly to confirm where Rupert would set himself up and the timings of when that part of the show would begin.

'Looking the picture of elegance as always.' He said as he greeted her just inside the entrance.

'Thanks, not sure how I managed to find the time in between all of this. Just something I threw together rather last minute.' She replied. 'Devan lovely to see you again. I hope he hasn't been too much hard work. I'm sure by now you've realised what he gets like when he's in mission impossible mode.'

'Tell me about it. And I thought he was bad enough before, but now he's running the show he's twice as bad.' Devan replied giving Chris a slight squeeze around the waist just to say: *I'm only teasing.*

'Oh, let me introduce you to Mrs Keller, she our Chairwoman.' Chestnut added as a tall woman in her early fifties entered.

'Mrs Keller, this is Chris Flack and his partner Devan. Chris is the one who got Mr Whiting to come on board.'

'Very nice to meet you both, I hope you enjoy our little gathering.' Mrs Keller warmly said.

'Charmed, nice to finally meet the one that keeps this one on her toes.' Chris replied as he greeted the media magnate.

'Oh she doesn't need my help, she has been absolutely fantastic, she's a real asset and done wonders for us. I don't think this merger would have been pulled together had it not been for all of Chestnut's hard work. She really has been tremendous.' Mrs Keller said beaming at the woman that she had come to see as her protégé.

'Oh you give me too much. I just got all the players together, it was you that really sealed the negotiations.' Chestnut sweetly replied.

'It was a team effort, but I think you underestimate your part. Now did I just spot, Jack? I must catch him before the Premier arrives, if I don't catch him now he'll be tied up in trade deals for the rest of the evening, knowing him. Lovely to meet you both and please enjoy yourselves.' She said before leaving them to catch up with Jack Whiting, who had already settled into a deep conversation with a Chinese tech developer.

'The Premier is coming here?' Chris asked after Mrs Keller had left, with a degree of anxiousness in his voice.

'It must have been a last minute thing, even I didn't know until now.' Chestnut replied. 'Is that going to be a problem?'

'A problem. Losing one's invitation would have been a problem. This is FUBAR on a whole 'nother level. Have you any idea the amount of security that's about to descend on this place.' He stated, frantically trying to redesign the plan on the fly. 'Where did Ollie and Juan go? I need to find them ASAP.'

'I think they went to check out the Weiwei piece, as Lena said they were going to change its configuration.' Devan replied.

'Fuck sake, why is it always the best laid plans that go out the window. You and Gaz stay close to Whiting, got to at least keep up some of the pretence of close protection.' Chris said storming off through the mêlée to find his co-conspirators.

Chris eventually located the pair in deep discussion in front of the sunflower seeds.

'Jesus, I knew they intended on re-shaping it but that's just something else.' He exclaimed as he saw what the next glitch in the plan would surely be. What had been a very simple rectangle had been meticulously moulded into two hands reaching for each other in a very similar way to Michelangelo's fresco on the ceiling of the Sistine chapel.

'Yeah, not exactly going to be the easiest to put back together once we're finished digging around in it for the one's the professor hid.' Ollie said stroking his chin with his hand as he tried to work out the best way to do it.

'Well that's the least of our worries, it appears that the Premier has decided to make a last minute appearance to this little soirée. So you acting as decoy definitely goes out the window unless you fancy spending the next decade or so in a detention centre, if they don't just decide to execute you on the spot.' Chris said hastily. 'So you boys got any fresh ideas? Otherwise we may as well sack it off right now.'

Juan stood there in deep thought for a few moments before he said anything. 'We might be able to use this to our advantage, his arrival could be the distraction, or at least the bits leading up to his arrival because they are sure to turn up with all sorts of pre-arrival security that will draw a great deal of attention, will take them a while to get round the whole building. Otherwise I suppose I could always try reconfiguring the EMP and cross wire it with one of the security wands to create an electro magnet that might be strong enough to pull the metal seeds out from the rest.' Juan suggested.

'Will it work?' Chris asked, hoping that the odds wouldn't be too long.

'I'd be somewhere in the region of fifty fifty. The circuitry is there but it's not tried and tested. Not really what either of them were originally designed for, there's a lot of power in this box, will just have to hope that the wand's wiring will cope with the load.'

'I'll take those odds at the moment. Do it and we'll try and stall the Premier's entrance.' Chris replied. 'Ol, you come with me, I think it's time to move Rupert's schedule up a bit.'

Just before Chris left, Ollie noticed that he whispered something in Juan's ear. But he didn't think much of it apart from maybe Chris giving him a bit of personal encouragement.

'I think I can see where you are going with this.' Ollie replied as he and Chris hurriedly made their way out towards the courtyard leaving Juan to work his electrical magic. Catching Chestnut on the way Chris quickly explained part of the situation. 'No time to fully explain, but I'm reworking your party schedule. Get the guests out into the courtyard.'

'How did I know you were going to say something like that. I'll do the best I can; I better still have a job at the end of it otherwise you and me are going to have a big falling out.'

'If it works out I think you're more likely to get a promotion.' He replied as he continued to rush past her out of the doors. Sprinting the last few meters he clambered up the scaffolding to where Rupert was stationed.

'Sorry to do this man, but slight sequence change. You ready to go?'

'I can be. Why the sudden change?' Rups asked before he really had a chance to properly formulate a response.

'The Premier has decide to make an impromptu appearance, and I need you to give him a big welcome. Can't go into all the reasons why. The less you know the better to be perfectly honest.' Chris said.

'Say no more, it's done.' Rupert replied, realising whatever the reason, it was probably better not to ask at that very moment. He was sure he would find out in due course. Chris had never asked him to do something without a very good reason and if he said that it was best that he didn't know everything that was good enough for him. He quickly flicked a switch before typing in a few commands on his tablet, and not before time as Chris saw the first of the Chinese Premier's cavalcade coming round the bend of a street a few blocks away from the museum. No sooner had Rupert began to type, a projector splashed an array of dramatic colours and dancing figures across the front of the museum all choreographed to electro-swing, as the first of the guest began to make their way out of the gallery and by the time the Premier's train had begun to enter the courtyard, the place was packed with so many people both from the party and passers by who had stopped to watch the display.

All Chris could do now was hope that this would give Juan enough time to do whatever it was he had in mind to drag the individual seeds from the masses. From his view point high up in the scaffold tower he could see the irritated expressions on some of the Premier's guards as they had to wave and shout at the onlookers to get out of their way as the procession slowly made it's way across the last few hundred meters through the crowds. Rupert was also quickly tailoring the display on the fly so just as the Premier's car arrived and the doors opened, a patriotic flourish of flags and ancient Chinese warriors and Emperors flashed up onto the building. The armed guard, were taken aback slightly, they hesitated not sure whether they should proceed and secure the building or to secure an area in the square. As Chris had hopped, they waited to take their lead from their supreme leader, and were soon quickly darting around his car to form a protective barrier from which he, his wife and their guests could watch without risk.

Suddenly everything went out. Darkness engulfed the whole area, a gasp went up from the crowd, not sure if this was part of the show or a power outage.

'Please tell me this is you.' Chris exclaimed to his companion on the tower.

'Nope, I've lost all power.'

'Shit, Juan's fucked it.' Chris replied, just as the display flicked on again as quickly as it had vanished. And as luck would have it a spotlight span into the direction of the Premier and his entourage to excited applause from the crowd.

'Thank fuck for that. I just hope whatever he did worked.' Chris said breathing a huge sigh of relief. 'Far too close for comfort.'

'I've no idea what you guys have just done but let's not do it again. Not sure I'd enjoy a permanent residency here.' Rups replied. 'I thought for sure had those lights been out any longer we'd have seen what Tiananmen Square was really like.'

'Yeah agreed. Good job man, and the timing on that spot was just perfect.'

'Ha, more luck than judgement on that one.' His friend replied with a relieved smile. And they both leaned over the railings and watched as the beam of light continued to trace a path for the Chinese Premier as he made his way up to the red carpet, to be greeted with more resounding applause and warm handshakes from all the directors from both media companies and the Museum. A stream of military police continued passed the group and entered the building to ensure it was secure.

'Well that was a bit too close for me. I'm gonna leave you to it man. Hope the rest of show goes okay and catch you again sometime, hopefully with a little less theatrics. Take care.' Chris said to Rups giving him a warm embrace before he descended the tower to join the rest of the guests who were by now beginning to make their way back inside.

Ollie was the first to speak to Chris. 'Juan's gone, I can't find him anywhere. I think he's done a runner with the seeds. I knew that little fucker would pull a fast one.' He said trying to hold back his anger.

'Little bastard, when I get hold of him. I'll break all his fingers, then we'll see how good his flamenco is.' Chris replied loudly enough that the people around him could hear.

'What's happened?' Chestnut asked, having caught the last few words.

'The Spaniard's double crossed us. And done a runner.' Chris replied.

'Do you think he's going for the codex by himself?' She asked.

'Not sure, he could be working for a third party.' Chris replied careful not to mention Norwood by name around her, there was still something about the last few lines of James' note that were bugging him. 'Get the boys, we're leaving, no point staying here. Where's Devan?'

'Still with Jack. I get her.' Ollie said.

'Don't bother, I need to say goodbye to Jack anyway.' Chris replied as he spotted the two talking to a couple of business types. He strode over to them putting his arm around Devan as if everything was going to plan. 'Jack it's been a real pleasure, but I'm afraid we are going to have to make a move. Thank you for all your help and I'm sure we will see each other again at some point.'

'Leaving so soon, I thought you would have stayed till the end. I hope everything is okay and you managed to find what you came for.' Jack replied slightly disappointed at the news that they were leaving. 'I had hope to discuss a few things with you.'

'Unfortunately, other business requires our attention. I'll be in touch. I hope all goes well with the merger.' Chris replied.

Devan was also rather taken by surprise by Chris's announcement, but she knew better than to question him in public. If he said they were going it probably meant something hadn't gone quite as expected.

'Well you'll be missed, boys. I take it you won't be at the hotel when I get back later?' Jack asked.

'It's unlikely.' Chris replied. 'Thanks again and I promise we'll stay in touch.' He added as the five of them left Jack and Chestnut to enjoy the rest of the gala.

'What's happened?' Devan enquired once they were out of earshot of everybody.

'Not now.' Chris snapped, immediately regretting the harsh tone.

Devan half felt like giving him an earful, but decided it wasn't the time or the place. Something had clearly got under his skin and he needed sometime to cool off before she approached the subject again. She wondered if it would be the same if James was still here. Chris had definitely changed since the loss of his closest friend, he'd become more closed off and pensive as if he was gradually giving way under the weight that had suddenly been shackled to his back. She wished she could find a way to help him with the burden, but it was always going to be difficult if he refused to let her in. The turmoil in his mind was clear for all to see and yet he flatly refused to share the load, it was as if he was punishing himself for something that wasn't his fault. Time would tell if it would make or break him, she just hoped it would be the former.

Oh, James what the hell have you left us with. I hope you are happy with yourself. She thought as they left the turbulent city far behind.

Chapter Twenty-One: The King's Tomb

The pouring rain flecked James's face and mouth with mud, bouncing up from the puddles pooling around him, he felt like he was back in the wilds of Wales patiently biding his time until it was just right to rise up out of the long wet undergrowth and ambush unsuspecting new recruits. Tucked in as tightly as he could against the boulders and rocks to the East of the main monuments dotted through the ancient burial complex he watched and waited for the first of the tourists to arrive, this was the less glamorous side of covert work, staying concealed in one place for days and just taking a pounding from whatever the elements threw at him. At least on this occasion he only had a few hours to safely navigate unlike the week he'd spent out in Afghan baking under the unrelenting rays of the arid sun for that one moment when his scope filled with *Charlie*, allowing him that one soft squeeze on the trigger, and blood to explode across his vision from the distance. However, this time was purely reconnaissance, and as far as he knew he wouldn't be called upon to hit anything. That was unless he was in imminent danger and there was a genuine risk to his life, his orders were crystal clear; gather what intel he could and slink back across the border. Better odds of getting out alive than one man verses an entire country gradually hunting him down.

As soon as Josh had dropped him, he'd wasted no time finding a gap in the fence surrounding the heritage site and scouting out the best possible positions from which to covertly watch the goings on at the complex. It hadn't proved hard to find the area he now lay in. The large boulders rising up from the ground, gave him good cover to his rear, and the scattering of trees to the North further up the slope obscured him from all but the most eagle eyed of patrols, not that there were many. By his count the entire site had two pairs of roving patrols, three guards on the entrance and another handful, placed as far as he could work out in the most pointless positions, with poor visibility and obstructions in virtually every direction from where they were stationed invariably delaying a quick response to any incident, set his mind at ease. *Just a walk in the park*, he thought as he tracked the movements of the closest patrol.

Away to his South he could see the road winding away into the valley from the main gates, far in the distance just above the horizon a cloud of dust was clearly visible, the first of the day's many visitors he mused, and with them the first opportunity perhaps to be able to stretch his aching legs that had begun to stiffen having been in an almost perpetual state of dampness ever since setting out from the Southern side of the DMZ over nine hours ago. The rain was one thing but these first few days of a particularly cold April, really didn't help matters. The combination of wet and cold was gradually nibbling away at his energy levels, little by little he could feel the tiredness kicking in. Rummaging around in one of the side pockets of the rucksack he eased out an energy gel sachet; what he really wanted was to brew up something hot, that not being an option without the risk of revealing his presence, the sweet gooey substance would have to do for now. Tearing off the top of the wrapper, he sucked it down; *ugh peaches, I fucking hate peaches* he thought as the sickly sweet taste lingered in his mouth, *ah well could be worse, at least there aren't any biscuit browns this time.*

His attention was drawn back to some frantic activity on the main gate. The guards were scrambling around as quickly as they were able to get the gates open, something had clearly spurred them into action; that cloud of dust was much closer now. Close enough to start to make out a vehicle convoy, but it didn't even remotely resemble a coach load of tourists; these were military.

Let the games begin, James said to himself as he set about mentally preparing himself for whatever was about to unfold. Pulling his body even tighter into the boulders he observed four jeeps and two open trucks, one full of soldiers and the other transporting two large wooden crates, roll in through the gates and precede on up to a flat gravel area just below the stone steps flowing up to the main tomb. The soldiers quickly jumped out, forming two lines either side of the steps, before the occupants of the jeeps had disembarked.

James was a little surprised to see a couple of Generals exiting the second jeep but that was nothing compared to the sight of Lord Norwood and others that he could only assume had travelled with his nemesis exiting the rest. He saw a woman with a cap pulled low accompanying Norwood, she seemed vaguely familiar but he couldn't make out her features clearly enough over that distance to make a positive identification. Four soldiers detached themselves from their positions as one of the officers in charge launched into barking a string of orders, they proceeded to unload one of the crates from the rear of the truck. Cracking the lid they began to pull out an assortment of digging equipment, and embarked upon lugging it all up the steps and into the tomb.

The sight of Norwood had caught James off guard, he had been told there was a deal of some sort due to take place but Tom had failed to tell him that Norwood was involved, more than likely he had deliberately held that snippet of information back fearing that if James knew in advance that the man responsible for so much pain would be there James would not even take a moments hesitation before embarking on reaping carnage regardless of the consequences. As it was, James just about managed to stem the rage rising up inside him. He continued to watch until the majority of the group had vanished inside the tomb, this was his moment to act. Taking out his Sat-phone from the other side pocket he sent a very quick communiqué to say that contact had been established, and a brief outline of the situation.

It did not take long to get a response to his message. A response that he had expected but nevertheless vexed him greatly.

'Hold station, photograph everything you can, and under no circumstances are you to engage.'

That didn't deter him from opening the main compartment of his rucksack to pull out an SRS - A2 Covert sniper rifle, now that he knew Norwood was here his mind was already made up that if the chance presented itself come hell or high water he was determined to put that man down. He was just tightening the suppressor onto the end of the muzzle when he received another message.

'What part of do not engage did you not understand?'

Fucking satellite surveillance. He thought, turning skyward and defiantly giving whoever it was at the other end of the eye in the sky the middle finger. Before clarifying his position by replying:

'Understand perfectly, just a precaution. Now piss off and let me do my job.'

He didn't know if it had the desired effect that he hoped it would, but whoever was at the other end decided it was best not to respond. Laying the rifle down where it was in easy reach for when he would require it, he began taking as many photos as he could of the vehicles and troops, until the Generals and Norwood's team reappeared from the tomb, he notice that one of the Generals was carrying something, he slid the scope off the rifle so he could get a clearer view of it. A small medallion with a random cracked pattern. Then it clicked, this must be a way to locate that part of the codex his father had intimated was lost somewhere in China. This wasn't so much an arms deal as a swap. The medallion for whatever was in that other crate.

He watched Norwood triumphantly marching down the steps, waving two of his companions to offload the second crate. James almost let out a gasp as he saw what was inside. He'd seen enough diagrams to know exactly what it was, a gyroscope from an ICBM. *Norwood you complete lunatic, you can't be seriously entertaining the idea of giving that to them. Nothing on earth can be worth giving them that capability.* He thought as he attempted to run scenarios, what was the best course of action? Would this be reason enough to engage? If so, how would he get away unscathed? He didn't get a chance to make the decision as his Sat-phone vibrated.

'If you have clear shot, green light to use tracker round, and tag crate. Use of lethal force not authorised. Repeat, non lethal force only. Tag and get out. Use secondary evac point.'

James desperately wanted to put that man in the ground more than ever, but even he had to concede that he didn't have the ammo or the position to get into a firefight with so many combatants by himself. He reluctantly changed the clip in the rifle, taking his time to wait until all the exchanges had been made and the truck with the gyro was on its way out before he fired a single round with the isotopic tracking round into the side of the wooden crate. The noise of the heavy Diesel engine obscured the light thud as the shot hit the mark embedding itself deep into the pine. As far as James was concerned that was mission done. From now on he had his own assignment; her majesty's service would just have to wait.

Norwood's jeep hadn't cleared the gates yet. There was still time to take the opportunity to tag them too. James quickly reloaded and fired another tracker into the back door of the jeep. It wasn't a perfect plan, he had no idea how long they would be travelling or in what direction but it was the best chance he had. He watched them go, and then set about getting himself out of the complex as quickly as he could, that secondary evac point was a good hump over five clicks away. *Josh, you better be on time.*

He thought as he cleared the boundary fence and ran off through the undergrowth as fast as the terrain would allow.

He was blowing hard by the time he reached the rendezvous site, and sweat was streaming off his brow. But Josh was nowhere to be seen; he was about to start cursing as he cast his gaze around to see if he could make out any sign of an approaching vehicle, but there was none. Then his eyes hit upon a pile of branches that just didn't quite seem to look right. *You little beauty*, he though as he ripped them apart to find a dirt bike concealed underneath. James leapt on, glanced at the screen of his phone to get the tracking data up and without any hesitation raced off in hot pursuit of his new target.

Chapter Twenty-Two: Connecting The Double Helix

It seemed like months had passed since Jamie and Glen had processed the *Morning Star*, when in fact it had only been just over a week. All the prints, hairs and fibres they'd pulled were now undergoing a full workup by the forensic gurus, so far most had turned out to belong to the captain of the vessel, however there were several that did not match the DNA or finger prints of the body in the morgue. These had been passed onto both DCI Carline and Glen's own unit in Penzance, and Glen was now eagerly awaiting a reply from either, as to whether or not any of these matched the evidence collected at the two other crime scenes. It was an agonising wait not just because Glen's hopes of finally being able to put the case to bed had been reinvigorated, but also every minute he had to wait was another one away from his wife and child. Even thought he had eventually managed to smooth over the way he had left in pursuit of what his beloved now referred to as his obsession, he knew that there would still be repercussions when he did finally return home, and the longer it became, the worse it would inevitably be.

At least the storms battering the south Dorset coast had abated for the time being as Glen pieced together the most realistic scenario of what had happened to the boat captain. Jamie had been proven to be correct in her assumption that the man had not accidentally fallen overboard, the tests carried out on the water found in his lungs had been a match to the chemical concentration in the holding tanks, and as such it was now a full blown murder investigation. The question that remained was whether it was linked in any way to Noirmont or was it something else, only time would tell. His current theory was that somebody for whatever reason had forced a large amount of alcohol down the captain's throat, and then held his head in the holding tank's deck hatchway until the last breath of the man gave out, tied the man to a mooring line and thrown him overboard to give the impression that he had accidentally been caught in the warp and fallen overboard to be dragged by the boat; before setting the auto pilot on a converging course with the path of the storm in the hope that it would take the boat down and with it all evidence of the incident. It was only by sheer chance that the storm had veered off its original track skirting the forsaken vessel by a few nautical miles.

Rubbing his temples in an attempt to maintain his concentration as he worked his way through the most recent additions from forensics, Glen wondered if he would ever fully complete the jigsaw. Even if a link was found between all of the crime scenes from a forensic standpoint there was still a huge hole as to what was the motivation behind them all. Could it really be as simple as an organised crew targeting high value collections of antiques with the killings and injuries just collateral for being in the wrong place at the wrong time or was there something more intricate and sinister afoot? Ever since the demise of his original prime suspect and the new developments his mind had been circling the issue without really being able to light upon a coherent explanation. The more he thought about it the less the pieces as a whole made sense. Dropping the file down on his desk in frustration he was about to go in search of the coffee pot, when the phone began to ring.

'DI Harris, speaking.' He said answering in a tone that reflected his current mood.

'Glen, it's Carline. We've had a break through, well two in fact. Firstly, we've had a match between some DNA found at Noirmont and what you pulled from the *Morning Star.*'

'Ah that's great news, at least we now know we're on the right track. I'm hoping the second is you've found a match to somebody in the data base?' Glen replied, his spirits rising considerably from where he had been.

'Unfortunately not, well that's to say we haven't found a match to a person. It's a bit of an odd one to be fair and I'm still trying to get my head round it a bit. They've been flagged by The Yard. I'm sure you heard about the heist at that safety deposit place in London a couple of days ago?'

'Of course, it was all over the news. How could one forget it especially with all that hoo-ha at Buckingham Palace around the same time. You're not going to tell me it was linked to the Palace?'

'No, but Scotland Yard have flagged the DNA because it matches some found in the vault of the depository.'

'That's crazy. Man, this thing just gets stranger by the minute.'

'Sure does, anyway they've requested that you send them everything you have.'

'Ah come on, they can't take this off me now.' Glen exclaimed. 'I've worked to hard to loose control of this now.'

'Hold on let me finish, and they've asked that you go up to the city, as you are the one that's worked it from the beginning. They think your insight into how it all fits together will be invaluable. That's if you feel you are up for a bit more travelling.'

'Up for it. Wild horses wouldn't be able to keep me away.' Glen replied.

'I told them as much. How soon do you think you will be able to get up there?' Carline asked.

'I'm halfway out the door as soon as this phone goes down.' Glen replied.

'Good man, well I best let you get going. I'll give you a call when you're settled up there. Good Luck.' Carline said before he hung up.

Glen's head was sent back into a fresh tailspin as the new revelations began to sink in and mix with the jumble that was already pushing his synapses close to a critical overload. This last addition bugged him, it seemed to be an anomaly, an outlier that didn't fit the trend. Many things about it seemed to be out of character if these were heists being carried out by a slick well organised crew. For starters that depository was a highly secure company rather than a relatively unsecured private house and secondly the timing seemed off. There had been months in between St. Michael's and Noirmont, whereas if he was correct in the conclusion that the men had used the fishing boat to get back to the mainland, this new heist was only a week after they had returned. Granted it was still meticulously well planned to be able to get in and out of the building before anybody had realised what had happened but for some reason it just didn't seem quiet like their signature. Nevertheless, DNA was a pretty conclusive link. He supposed that it could be argued that the crew would have had a bigger time gap had it not been for things going horribly wrong from their perspective at Noirmont. But still it was a big step up and change in M.O. from robbing country houses to raiding safety depositories. *Just have to follow the evidence and see where it leads,* he thought as he quickly scribbled a note for Jamie about the new direction things had begun to take, and that he would call her on his way up. The last thing he did in the rustic coastal station was to email all the related case files across to the Yard and without any further delay he stuffed all his belongings into a hold-all and dumped it onto the backseat of his car and left the tiny isle of stone and its inbred bunnies sinking onto the horizon.

Chapter Twenty-Three: Legacy of an Emperor

Lord Norwood was surrounded by a triumphant glow as he turned the curved medallion over in his hands. The cracks and markings in the ancient turtle shell and mother of pearl meant nothing to him, but he still knew that it would bring him one step closer to his goal. Whilst the jeep bumped and rocked during their journey into the capital he took several photos of the artefact and sent them to a number of dubious contacts who specialised in fencing ancient Chinese antiques. He was sure that they would be wired into the right networks and find somebody who might be able to decipher the meaning hidden within.

They were heading for the capital in order to catch a train that would transport them across the boarder into China. He had thrown in the remnants of his private jet as compensation for the use of the train, not that it was in any state to be flown. The fire they had set in order to disguise their true reason for landing in North Korea had severely crippled its electronics, nevertheless it still had value to the Koreans as far as re-engineering technology that they wouldn't normally be able to get their hands on. A small price in his view for continuing his obsessive search for the *Liber Veritatis*, and finally achieving his other objective of ascending the top of the brotherhood. He was well aware that the current Grand Master of *The Glove* would struggle to maintain his position once Norwood had all of the pieces, in fact he had been gradually whittling away at the Grand Master's power base from the shadows for quite sometime without the man realising that he no longer held the reigns of power.

China was the logical step having read about the Prince of Gui's connection to the medallion, there was no doubt in his mind that somewhere in that vast country would be the location of the next piece, lying undisturbed for centuries. He inwardly smiled as they pulled into the station.

James dumped his scrambler at the corner of the street opposite Pyongyang train station, watching the jeeps pull in and begin to unload outside the main entrance. He waited until Norwood and his companions had boarded a train bound for the city of Sinŭiju on the Sino-Korean boarder. Taking a mental note of their carriage he booked himself a ticket that would take him across the boarder into Dandong. There was no way in his mind they would be staying in North Korea, the vague recollection of his father mentioning something about a Chinese scroll popped in to his head. He wished he could get a closer look at whatever was on that medallion, if he could only get near enough to photograph it he could at least then see what was on it, if not send it to somebody who might be able to fill in the blanks. For now he would just have to shadow them and wait for an opportunity to present itself. He just hoped that he would be able to do it without being recognised, even with the thick beard he was currently sporting he felt sure that if Norwood saw him the game would be up. Stepping onto the train three carriages down from Norwood's he settled himself in for the long haul and waited for the train to depart on its long winding track northwards.

Taking the opportunity, before he planned his next move, he sent a quick communiqué to Tom to keep him abreast of the situation. He felt sure he would not get a very pleasant response as he was now going way off script but to hell with the service for the time being. As far as he was concerned he had carried out his part of the deal in so much as his resurrection was concerned, from now on he would be his own man. Besides he could always argue that he was operating within the interest of national security by tracking a person not only of interest but one that had just handed over a piece of technology that would vastly speed up North Korea's efforts to create a fully functional ICBM with a much more accurate targeting system than anything they currently possessed. If Norwood was prepared to go to those extremes then it was conceivable that he may also have other deals lined up with China. Considering the man was connected to parts of the MoD, what he was now carrying out could certainly be construed as conspiring with the enemy if not full blown treason. Either way James didn't think that Tom would completely pull the plug, more likely he would begrudgingly concede and tell him to continue with the utmost caution but that if anything went awry, normal protocol would kick in and the service would disavow him and deny any knowledge of any such operation.

'I take it you weren't planning on saying goodbye.' Josh's voice wafted over from the seat behind the one he occupied.

'How the... actually don't answer that. So I've got a babysitter now, have I? Nice to know that my judgment isn't in question.' James replied as Josh got up and sat down across the table from him.

'Not so much, as soon as Tom realised Norwood was involved he thought you might need a wingman. Don't take it personally, you know how he gets when the curve balls start flying. Surprised you didn't find that tracker on the bike though, must be slipping.' Josh mused.

'Oh I see, you think the student is ready to step up and become the master. Well I can tell you right now this old dog hasn't run out of tricks just yet. But as you're here I don't suppose you've brought a fresh bag with you?' James asked with an amused smile, knowing that Josh had for once managed to get the better of him. There was no denying that he had a soft spot for Josh, maybe it was because he could see something of himself in the young agent, or that he saw that with the right mentor Josh would soon become a force to be reckoned with. His surveillance skills had definitely come on leaps and bounds since their first meeting in Belize. Granted James had been running around with blinkers on in his pursuit of Norwood, nevertheless he'd always been mindful of his surroundings so to have missed Josh highlighted to him just how much Josh had grown.

'I've got one or two things, but that really depends on what the plan is. You do have a plan, don't you?' Josh asked with a degree of scepticism in his voice.

'Yep, it's called wingin' it. Until I can get a closer look at the artefact Norwood has dug up and work out what his endgame is, shadow games is the best option.' James replied. 'I think we'll have to just wait and see where they go once we cross the border, there's too many of them in that carriage to be able to do anything whilst we're still on this train.' James paused as a thought crossed his mind. 'Or at least I can't, but you. Hmm, he doesn't know you. That's something. He's never crossed your path, maybe we can gain some wisdom after all.' There was a small glint of a plan forming in James's eye as he lent back and began to mentally run a scenario that would help them get wise, without their quarry realising.

Norwood was so engrossed in the group messages that were flying back in response to his request for specialists in Ancient Chinese artefacts that he did not pay a moments notice to Josh as he wandered through the carriage past the table where Carla, Conrad and himself sat discussing which of the recommendations they had received warranted further investigation.

'Look this one here is based in Dandong. Seems to know what she's talking about, we've got to get off there anyway so why not take advantage of the proximity and arrange a meeting.' Carla suggested as she looked through the list of potentials.

'I agree, there's no point going further in land to say Beijing only to then discover that we've got to retrace our steps back up. Dandong is well placed to shoot off in any direction once we have a better idea where to go.' Conrad added.

'But will the outer regions really have the sort of person we require?' Norwood asked not wholly convinced by the concept.

'I would think so, especially for Sino-Korean artefacts, because of its location. In fact due to the artefact's links to both countries they may well be more informed than someone based further inside the interior.' Carla replied.

'Good point, make the arrangements.' Norwood said to Carla. 'I suppose worse case scenario is we'll just have to venture elsewhere if she turns out to be of no use. Oh and you better organise some transport as well, whatever the outcome we are going to need some wheels at some point. Actually no, let's hold off on the transport for now. Not exactly like getting around our tiny island, sod's law the final stop will be half way across the bastard. In which case wings rather than wheels might be more appropriate.' Norwood stated, the visualisation of holding the next piece in his hands was becoming clearer with every minute.

'Oh bloody hell. Mind where you are going.' One of the men from the table behind Norwood blurted out as Josh accidentally on purpose tripped over his outstretched foot whilst carrying a couple of cups of tea from the buffet car back to his seat, landing right next door to Norwood's table, spilling the contents from the cups all down the occupant's shoes.

'Of all the incompetence.' Lord Norwood blasted at Josh as the young man began to pick himself up. Before apologising profusely for his clumsy wrong footedness.

'I'm terribly sorry, I must have just lost my footing.' Josh replied as he weathered the burning glare of disdain and disapproval from all of the table. 'Here let me just clear that up.' He added, bending down to pick up the empty vessels and attempting to wipe the worst off Norwood's shoes with a paper napkin.'

'Oh get off, none of that faffing.' Norwood irritably snapped.

'Sorry, can I buy you a drink or something.' Josh said trying to prolong his presence at the table for as long as possible.

'No, just... just go would you.' Came the response from the man.

'Apologies again. I am really sorry.' Josh replied turning on his heels and returning to the buffet car to reorder his drinks.

Norwood could be heard continuing to make disparaging comments to his companions about the young man's incompetence as Josh walked back through the carriage with a fresh set of drinks, although he did hold himself back from having a final little dig at Josh as he passed their table. Of course the joke was on him as the incident had concealed Josh's real motive.

'Did you manage to get it?' James asked as Josh returned. Hoping that the ruse had proved to be fruitful and they would effectively now be level pegging with his nemesis.

'Yeah, worked a treat. They never even noticed me taking a few photos of whatever that medallion thing is while they were fusing about the hot tea I spilt.' Josh replied.

'Good, I hope it burnt the fucker.' James replied with a rueful smile.

'Ah sorry, I only managed to get his shoes.' Josh said. 'I didn't want to make too much of an impression.'

'More's the pity, ah well there will be ample opportunity later to leave a proper mark on that man. Let's have a look at this object then.' James said before Josh passed his phone over with the few photos he'd managed to sneak during his little charade.

'Interesting looks like it's made out of some sort of shell. These marking are a bit random, mainly cracks, but those scrapings around the edge are curious. If they ever had been Chinese characters they haven't aged well. Looks like it will prove difficult to translate. Hmmm, I bet he must be having the same problem. We may as well keep tracking him for now. Let him do all the hard work and then we'll reap the rewards.' James said as he continued to study the photos.

'Sounds good to me, shame I couldn't get the other side as well. I did manage to overhear they are planning a meeting in Dandong. Presumably they must have located someone who can unlock its meaning.' Josh replied hoping that the symbols, if one could call them that, were only on the one side.

'Then we will know soon enough. Don't know about you but I'm gonna get some shut eye before we get to Dandong. Roughing it in a cold and wet glorified graveyard doesn't exactly make for the best of sleeping arrangements.' James said as he screwed up his jacket into a ball and stuffed it between his shoulder, head and the carriage widow as a make shift pillow.

'Not a bad idea, never quite know these days when the next bit of sleep is an option.' Josh replied.

'Welcome to the club, not so gung-ho now are we.' James smiled as he nestled his head into a more comfortable position, and gradually nodded off to the rhythmical clickety-clack of wheels running on steel.

They must have slept for a good few hours as the next thing James was aware of was the voice of the conductor announcing over a crackling PA that the train would shortly be departing Sinŭiju, the last stop before crossing the border into Dandong and that passengers should make sure that they have their respective travel documents ready.

'Hurrrgh, fuck me I needed that.' James yawned as he rubbed the remaining crumbs of sleep from the corners of his eyes.

'Yeah not bad considering this train's about as old as *The Stones*. Right time to see how well Barkley's passports stand up to scrutiny. His work's normally pretty good. Although, admittedly he didn't have a current photo of you with growth, nevertheless I think it'll just about pass muster.' Josh said as he passed James his new identification.

'Alexander Whittering, where the hell does he come up with these names, sounds like something out of Jane Austen.' James scoffed as he flicked through the fresh pages of the passport. 'Fair play, at least he remembered to put a North Korean stamp in. I've had that before, picked up docs in country and the guy who'd made it hadn't put one in; raised an eyebrow or two when leaving. Luckily I managed to explain I'd lost my original on holiday and had only just picked the new one up that very morning from the British Embassy hence not having a visa stamped inside. Thankfully as I was departing they didn't make too much of a fuss over it.' James said reminiscing about a prior op, choosing not to mention that particular mission ended up being one of those that the survivors would rather forget had ever happened. 'Think we'll wait until they have disembarked before we get off, I'd rather not risk being stuck directly behind or in front of them in the customs queue.' He added as he began to gather his belongings ready for their arrival into Dandong Station.

The train slowly trundled over the iron bridge connecting the two countries separated by the brown murky depths of the Yalu River and gradually came to a screeching halt in the raw concrete station as the dusk began to creep across the bland, almost featureless city port sprawling its way like a cancer inland from the polluted water's edge. A statue of the great leader Mao towered over the square in front of the station, hailing a warm red welcome to all the leg weary travellers arriving in the city.

James and Josh ended up with about a dozen or so passengers between themselves and Norwood's group and they casually joined the line moving towards the customs officers. Norwood could be seen talking to one of the officers as his group arrived at the desk, he had obviously made an impression as the man quickly picked up a phone and within a few minutes a couple of electric baggage cars pulled up, collecting them along with all of their belongings and whisked them off in the direction of the exit. James just hoped that they would not fall too far behind by the time he and Josh managed to clear customs. It was one of those agonising passages of time as they slowly made their way to the desk knowing that with ever second their quarry was getting farther and farther away. When it did finally become their turn, the officer took an overly long look at James's ID, glancing at his face and back at the passport's photo a couple of times before he was satisfied that it was a good enough likeness and allowed him through to where Josh was already waiting on the other side of the barriers.

'For a second there I thought he was going to be awkward.' James said as they quickly hurried off in the direction the porters had departed. 'Let's just hope they are still looking for transport.' James said as the two of them exited the station and scanned the outside area for any sign of Norwood.

'There they are.' Josh gestured with a nod in the direction of their targets, who were indeed in the process of leaving in a few taxis. James quickly hailed the next in line.

'Gēnzhe nàxiē chūzū chē.' James said pointing, as Josh just managed to slam the door shut before the taxi sharply pulled out in pursuit. Evidently his Cantonese was just about good enough for the driver to get the gist to follow those in front. They weaved in and out of the congested evening traffic staying as close to the convoy as possible, although James did tell the driver at one point not to get too close, to which he received a very quizzical look from the man. Nevertheless he did as he was instructed.

Eventually they turned onto a narrow poorly lit backstreet, just in time to see those in front pull up about a hundred yards further up the street. James immediately signalled to their driver to continue past and turn off onto a smaller adjacent alley. Giving the man half the fare, he told the man to keep the meter running and wait for their return. They stepped out quickly crossing back onto the other street. The taxis they had been following were now deserted, apart from the drivers and now parked up at the far end of the street. The only clue as to where Norwood had disappeared into was the orange glow around a doorframe set into what appeared to be a warehouse in a rather dilapidated state of repair half covered by bamboo scaffolding, midway along the far side of the street.

'Up you go.' James said to Josh, as he quickly assessed the sturdiness of the wooden framework.

'I had a feeling you were going to say that.' Josh replied dubiously, less than impressed at the idea of climbing up something that in his mind at least, looked very rickety indeed.

'You'll be fine, they were using these long before metal poles even existed.' James replied.

'Easy for you to say, some of us only live once.' Josh retorted.

James half laughed, grabbing hold of the closest upright pole, swinging his legs up he hooked his feet onto the walkway just above head hight before turning to catch hold of Josh's outstretched arm and hauled him up. The bamboo creaked as they continued their ascent until they reached the top and rolled out onto a shallow sloping roof with a number of skylights set into the tin. They crawled on their bellies across the cool metalwork until they found a roof light with a good view of the scene unfolding inside the building. From what they could see the warehouse was bursting with antiques and other objects of intrigue. James managed to lift the steel frame around the glass just enough to be able to make out the conversation taking place almost directly below them.

Norwood was talking to a woman in her late fifties dressed in fine Chinese silk robes, James watched him pass the artefact to her. Her eyes lit up as if mesmerised by the object and she took in a deep breath becoming very animated with excitement as she instantly realised what it was. She handed it back to the lord, and gestured for him to wait, before scurrying off into a back room only to return several moments later with a large, old and very worn book, which she quickly opened and began flicking through its pages until she reached a section full of brightly decorated pictures and characters. From his position high up on the roof James could not read the characters only the decorative scenes of a man wandering through a range of mountains, what he assumed to be some sort of temple or shrine and a golden dragon in the top righthand corner of one of the pages.

'May I enquire where you came across this?' She asked.

'It was recently discovered at an excavation of a tomb in North Korea.' Norwood replied, refraining from telling her exactly which tomb.

'Of course, of course. That makes perfect sense. You do realise its significance and who it belonged to?'

'Well, from my understanding it is a medallion originating sometime during the Ming Dynasty or at least has attributions to the period.' He replied. 'More than that I cannot tell you.' Norwood replied, deliberately omitting the significant parts of the object's earlier history, he wanted to test her knowledge and by holding some information back he sought to gauge whether she was being open and forthcoming with what she knew.

'That is partly correct, it is mentioned during that period as belonging to the Ming Emperors, in fact the Prince of Gui was the last known emperor to hold it. But it is far older and more significant than that. In Chinese legend it was passed down not just from emperor to emperor but dynasty to dynasty, something that only happened to a handful of the rarest and most significant relics, it is rumoured to be the key to a great source of power. If the story is to be believed; it is written:

When that which was lost, is found,
From the mountain Huanglong, the Great Dragon will reawaken,
Be the Dragon Bearer of good heart then Huanglong will usher in a new period
of peace and prosperity,
If not; great sorrow and suffering will be wrought upon the world by whomever
unleashes the beast once more.'

According to the text here the medallion was a gift from the immortals bestowed to the Yellow Emperor when he first ventured to Mount Hua in search of guidance from the gods. It is made from mother of pearl laid on turtle shell and the cracks on the surface are a result of it having been burnt on searing hot coals.' She said taking the medallion once again and with a her long boney fingers traced out those areas on its surface, before continuing her tale. 'The ancients used this technique to divine wisdom from interpreting the patterns and shapes created across the shell's surface. Unfortunately the art of reading these has all but vanished, nevertheless there is evidence that many of the emperors he was succeeded by made pilgrimages to a temple built on the Southern most peak of the mountain in search of the divine mystery. It is said that whoever possess the medallion will be afforded the same gift of foresight.'

'If that's the case, I guess they forgot to get infinity WiFi.' Norwood sarcastically replied, shaking the medallion next to his ear.

'No you miss understand, the medallion itself is not the source, rather it is the key to unlocking it. In order to attain the gift you must travel to the temple on the mountain, there you must complete the ritual under the guidance of the Celestial Mistress. If you are deemed worthy by the immortals then you will receive their divine wisdom, if you are not you will be destroyed by the guardians.'

'The guardians? Who are they?' Norwood asked enthralled by these new additions to the legend surrounding what was his unwavering belief to be the next piece of the codex.

'The gift itself, according to the mythology is guarded by a legendary band of warrior monks known as The Huanglong Sisterhood, although they are sometimes referred to as The Circle of The Yellow Dragon. But until now as the medallion had never been found it has always been though to a be fairy tale told as a bedtime story to entertain and frighten young children.' She replied.

'Ha, women in long dresses and sticks. What can they do?' Norwood scoffed.

'Do not underestimate the power of the guardians, they are not something to be mocked. Nobody can fully comprehend the extent of their potency as they have only operated from the shadows, nevertheless if the legend is to be believed, they have protected the gift and humanity for millennia. They will not hesitate to destroy all who are deemed unworthy. Awaken the Dragon at your peril.' She replied as she handed the medallion back to Lord Norwood.

'We'll take our chances. Fortune favours the brave as they say. Thank you for your help. Doubtless our paths will not cross again.' Norwood replied as he handed her a large envelope which James assumed was payment for her information, and the man and his companions began to leave the warehouse.

'So, now what do we do?' Josh asked, turning to James in the hope he'd formulated a plan in order to seize the medallion from the clutches of Norwood.

'The only thing we can do, follow them to the mountain and hope that an opportunity will present itself during whatever this ceremony is. We can't take them on here, there's too many of them, we wouldn't even get through the door before they would be upon us. No, we'll just have to carefully weave a web and spring the trap when they are at their ease.' James replied rising from the prostrate position he'd been lying in.

'They're starting to leave, we best start to make a move down to earth otherwise we'll loose them.' Josh said beginning to move back towards the scaffolding they had scaled earlier. He was about to start his descent back down the structure when James grabbed hold of his shoulder.

'Wait, look, over there.' James said in a hushed voice, pointing to the corner of a building on the far side of the road. In the shadows the warm orange glow of a lit cigarette inside a jet black car was just visible. James couldn't tell for sure but he thought there were two people inside the vehicle. They hadn't noticed James or Josh high up on the roof but as soon as Norwood and his followers began to depart in their taxis the black car stealthily pulled out and began to tail them.

'Seems we are not the only ones that have taken an interest in that medallion.' James said.

'I guess that changes things. Any idea who they might be?' Josh replied.

'Only one way to find out.' He replied grabbing hold of the bars and nimbly swing his way down to the ground in the well practiced manner of a circus acrobat, closely followed by his fellow companion.

They reached the ground just as the black car disappear around the corner at the end of the street. Josh had almost reached the middle of the road, when James stopped in his tracks, as if he'd just been struck by a thunderbolt and called him back.

'Josh, let them go, we know where they are going. I've had an idea. I think that dealer knows far more than she was letting on. That car didn't happen to be here by accident.'

'What do you mean?' Josh asked.

'I think she tipped them off. She did spend an awfully long time in that backroom, enough time for a phone call I suspect. And there was something in the tone of her warning; as if she was holding something back. I think Norwood's arrogant and disparaging remark about The Yellow Dragon gave her cause to not be quite as forthcoming as she had initially intended.' James said turning on his heels and striding back to the warehouse. The warm glow surrounding the door frame flooded out onto the dark murky street for a brief moment and then it was gone again as the door firmly slammed shut behind them.

Chapter Twenty-Four: The Southern Mountain

The misty cloud inversion swirled around the small wooden cabin constructed in a traditional Chinese style, half hidden, nestled between the tall firs and fresh cypress trees of the ancient forest at the head of the overgrown valley. Every now and again part of the nimbus would break just enough to catch a glimpse of the ageing watchtower of the Sky Stair on the wildest section of the Great Wall to the south of the sprawling suburbs of the capital. Devan was struggling to answer the question as to why Chris had suddenly decided to up sticks, leaving the city in such haste, even if Juan had double-crossed them, as far as she could see they didn't have the slightest inclination of where to begin in order to track him down. What's more, at the heart of her troubled mind was why out of everywhere Chris could have chosen to take them, did he bring them to this most remote, rugged and weather torn location. Wild was an understatement for such a place, plagued by bandits and gangs, a place where the rule of law was a naivety long since returned to dust like the decaying foundations of the defensive outpost straining to maintain its gravity defying position on the steepest mountainside along the Great Wall's snakelike passage. In her mind this was the last place they should have retreated to, surely rather than seeking out isolation it would have been wiser to have remained in the city. At least they would have been able to contact Rachel and find out whether she had uncovered any new information hidden amongst Professor Middleton's journals that may yet bring forth new light into what seemed to be an ever growing tunnel of darkness. For now all she could do was keep the faith and hope that he knew what he was doing. That this was all part of some grand plan; a plan which he would in due course reveal.

The dead vegetation squelched under foot as they approached the cabin in the growing darkness. It looked deserted, the light breeze rippling through the branches created the unnerving sense that the forest was aware its peaceful tranquility was being disturbed by these strange newcomers. Devan shuddered, moving closer to Chris as they were now within a few feet of the shack's door. Even he looked tense, which was slightly out of character, it was if he wasn't sure what he was about to find. She could see by the deep expression across his face that his senses were working in overdrive as if he was trying to detect something or perhaps someone. He paused momentarily before clasping the handle of the door with such a grip that his knuckles turned white. Opening the latch he deftly swung the door open as wide as it would go.

'Took you long enough, babs. I've been waiting here for hours.' A voice from inside the gloom announced, as they heard the scrape of a match and in the dim flicker Juan's beaming face emerged.

'I know, sorry man. Took far longer than I expected to get out of the city the right way.' Chris replied as he embraced Juan in a huge bear like hug, before anybody else had a chance to ask what the hell was happening.

'Umm, do you guys care to explain yourselves?' Ollie asked. 'I thought he'd done a bunk.'

'Oh yeah, sorry for keeping everyone in the dark. It was a spur of the moment thing. After the warning in James's note I felt it best that Chestnut should be under the assumption that Juan had pulled a double-cross.' Chris explained.

'Err now I'm really lost, did you just say James and a note. Have you some how managed to find a way to communicate through the veil.' Ollie shot back, now completely confused about what the hell Chris was talking about.

'Not quite, when Devan and I first went to Chestnut in London, she was already expecting us. James had seemingly visited her after his brush with a watery demise and had entrusted her with a note for me. Apart from filling in some gaps he insinuated we should be mindful of her. So I decided that it would be best to put some distance between us and her as soon as Chestnut's usefulness had lapsed so I told our friend here to make it look like he had run off once he had recovered the pieces, and we felt it was prudent to keep you all in the dark so that your reactions at the party were as natural as possible. Sorry, it seemed logical at the time.' Chris replied.

'Umm, hold on a minute you said after his brush with a watery grave, are you telling us that James is alive? And that you knew but didn't tell us?' The indignation in Gaz's tone ricocheted around the small cabin, like a stray bullet.

'Kind of, sorry. I felt it was best to keep you guys focused on the job at hand. And to be honest I can't say for sure that he is still alive. He was certainly alive when he delivered the note, but I got the sense that wherever he was going and whatever he was about to do would be fraught with danger. He didn't give much away, I put out a few feelers but to no avail. It's like he never existed. So he's either gone darker than he has ever been before or well you don't need me to…' Chris never got the chance to finish his sentence as Gaz's fist met the side of his face, overcome with anger at having been kept out of the loop. Chris took it and just shrugged it off. 'I guess I deserved that.' He replied as he rubbed the side of his jaw.

'So not cool, man.' Ollie said. 'I thought we were a team and didn't keep secrets from each other.'

'Apologies, and I can't promise that it won't happen again, it is the nature of the life we lead. Besides you guys know full well that had you been told at the time, you would have insisted on rushing off in some vain and foolhardy attempt to find him, searching high and low for any sign of him, chasing your tails until you were all blue in the face; all the while handing precious time to Norwood and his quest for the codex. Deep down you know that is not what James would want. It was a judgment call, maybe I should have told you. Either way, I can't turn back the clock. We are where we are, and as you are all well aware we have our own hurdles still to face. So can we put James aside for the moment and crack on with whatever the professor's puzzle is.' Chris replied still rubbing the side of his chin.

'We may have a slight problem on that subject, babs.' Juan said, as he finished lighting a set of candles to shed some light onto the matter at hand. 'The good news is having had a chance to study those metal sunflower seeds; I've worked out what I think they are or at least what they contain. Basically they're RFID chips, which would be great. The bad news is had we not used an electro-magnet to retrieve them we might have been able to read the data stored on them, but as we did, they are more than likely, to use a lay man's terms, fucked. Of course I won't know for sure until I've scanned them. I presume you brought all my gear that I left at the hotel with you?'

'Nah, Ollie and I flogged the lot, babs. We didn't think you'd be needing it anymore.' Gaz replied.

'You did what? Have you any idea how important that…' Juan began to indignantly reply, before catching the faintest smirk on Ollie's face, and realising that Gaz was just messing with him.

'Don't worry it's all here, how else did you think we would have started to track you down had you actually stepped out on us.' Gaz said, patting a rucksack down at his feet.

'Phew had me going there for a bit. Well we better see if there is anything retrievable left.' Juan said.

'Right, while you lot crack on with that, I'm going to pick a bone with someone and hopefully get some answers to a few questions that have been bugging me. Oh Juan, did you find any food in this place? I'm famished.' Chris added.

'Yeah man, kitchen's fully stocked. Just need to turn on the gas canisters outside.' Juan replied.

'All over that like a rash.' Ollie said disappearing outside no sooner than he had uttered the words, he too was feeling more than a little peckish, apart from a few nibbles he'd managed to sneak he hadn't had anything substantial since before the gala had commenced.

'While you are out there you better crank up that generator as well.' Juan suggested.

Chris left the others working on the seeds and stepped out into the forest, he'd been mulling over James's note and the conversation he'd had with Tom Bradbury before they'd visited Chestnut's London apartment for sometime. Gradually he'd come to the conclusion that the reason Tom had been so coy with him, was because he had known more than he was letting on about what had become of James after that fateful night. The more he had thought about it, the more the pieces seemed to fit. It explained why Tom seemed to have been expecting his call and at the same time was surprised about the topic. Yes, it all made sense now, he'd been expecting Chris to have questions about James and not about how to decode the cypher. Dialling Tom's direct line he waited for the familiar voice to answer.

'Commander Bradbury speaking.'

'Tom, just the man I wanted to speak to. I think you know why I'm calling, you've been holding out on me haven't you? Where is he?' Chris asked cutting through any opportunity for Tom to side track the conversation by getting straight to the crux of his issue.

'Hi Chris, I'd been wondering when you'd work it out and ask. Unfortunately, I can't tell you what I don't know.' Tom said.

'Come on cut the crap, you did pull him out of that river, didn't you?' Chris bluntly replied.

'We did have an arrangement along those lines, although we didn't really plan on it going quite the way it did. The river was a complication and yet at the same time presented a marvellous opportunity.' Tom replied.

'You mean you had a ghost to play with. So can I presume, as part of that deal, he's now doing a job for you? And therefore you know where he is.' Chris said.

'Well, yes and no. He was deployed into the field on a small operation on our behalf which I'm not at liberty to go into, so you are right in so far as we knew where he was. But James being James, things took a turn in a direction that we hadn't expected and currently I can honestly say that we haven't the foggiest what he's doing or where the fuck he's gone. Had it been anyone else I would have listed them as AWOL, however I've given him a long leash in the hope that he's following up on what he discovered and I'm holding out in hope that he will be back in contact when he deems it safe to re-establish comms. I'm sorry I can't divulge any more about an on going operation.' Tom replied knowing that his explanation would be far from satisfactory.

'So it isn't that small then, otherwise you wouldn't be quite so sheepish about it. Basically what you are saying is that you put him somewhere exceptionally hostile without backup, something didn't go to plan and now you've lost him.'

'Err, well kind of. There was a contact out there for him.' Tom protested.

'Who?' Chris butted in before Tom could continue.

'J-osh Palmer, you know the one you met when you were out in Belize.' Tom replied nervously.

'Oh, come on that's as good as having no backup, he's as green as a blade of grass. Please tell me you're taking the piss.' Chris bellowed at him so loudly that Tom was grateful there were a good few thousand miles between them.

'I can't, but he's come on leaps and bounds since you last crossed paths.'

'How long since their last contact?' Chris snapped.

'About twelve hours, since Josh's last transmission.'

'And what's you secondary, I presume you have got an emergency protocol in the event that things slide sideways in a direction you hadn't expected?' Chris asked now rather concerned that Tom had lost control of whatever his op had been.

'Err, in this particular case, that was never an option. They both knew that. And besides as you are well aware once we are in the dark we can't put anything into place because we don't know either where to start or for that matter whether they would be in a position to enact them. Until communication returns there really isn't a lot we can do. I'm hoping they're attempting to cross into err friendlier territory.' Came the vague response.

'You're a swine, you've dropped them into North Korea haven't you? Of all the half-arsed, ill-conceived brain haemorrhages, you lot have had in the past; this one takes the fucking biscuit.' Chris shouted back under no illusion of those implications.

'I-I... as I'm sure you are aware the service can neither confirm nor deny or give any comment for that matter about an on-going operation.' Tom said trying to wriggle his way out of the hole.

'So, that's a yes then. You utter nimrod. Well, I'm holding you personally responsible if James or actually for that matter Josh are sent back in body bags. At least with James I know what he's like when the bit's between his teeth. You give him a challenge like that and he will be relentless in his pursuit. He won't shy away until the job's done, but Josh; you had absolutely no business sending a novice like that into that particular nest of vipers. And you know it. That's why you're scrabbling to try and justify the utter car crash you now find yourself with.' Chris replied.

'Chris, I'm sorry we didn't have another option.' Tom replied, his voice beginning to tremble with anxiety and concern not just for the safety of his operatives but also because of the pressure he now felt having to rationalise his decisions.

'Well, if they do get out. I hope they give you a damn good kicking the next time they see you. You can be damn sure I will.' Chris shouted down the phone, with such force that the trees closest to him almost shook with his rage. Hanging up before Tom had a chance to respond to his outburst. His hands were visibly shaking with so much raw emotion as he put his phone back in his pocket that he had to walk around and compose himself before he returned to the others in the cabin.

'It's as I suspected, partial data loss.' Juan was saying as Chris walked back into the cabin.

'Is it bad, is there enough to make an educated guess or are we fighting a loosing battle against the current?' Chris asked in a tone that suggested his damp mood had just been flooded with yet more cold water.

'There's two more seeds to scan, I've got partial numerical chains from the first three. I'd hazard a guess that they will make up lat' and longitudes, hopefully there might just be enough digits to narrow the location down to a few possibilities once we factor in the other clues the professor left behind. What do you think Devan?'

'I think it is possible, I mean that ancient verse must have some other clues hidden within, I'm working on a theory that it's definitely inside China. Let's see what partial coordinates we get and as you say put the two together and see if they point to a logical position.' Devan replied trying to put a positive spin on the situation. 'Let's just hope that Norwood hasn't managed to identify the location already.' She added.

'Got it!' Juan exclaimed in jubilation as the algorithm he'd been running pulled the last piece of salvageable data from the collection of seeds. 'Haven't lost half as much as I'd feared. I think this lot will do very nicely. Only lost the last few digits from the lats and longs. We've got thirty four point, blank, seven, blank, blank, one from the first set and one, one, blank, point, zero, blank, blank, zero, blank for the other. Assuming it is a Chinese location the thirty four must refer to the 34th parallel north and on that basis the other must be between one hundred and ten to one hundred and nineteen east. Ol there's a ruck of maps in the corner over there for hikers, dig them out and see what would get close to that.' Juan said as the exhilaration of almost having the location at his finger tips gripped him.

Ollie started rummaging through the assortment of maps, chucking ones that he deemed of no use over his shoulder, until he'd narrowed it down to a handful that might cover the area. Unfolding the largest one he traced the 34th parallel with his finger until he came into the area bisected by the hundred and tenth to hundred and twentieth meridians.

'Looks like the Qinling Mountains are pretty much spot on for that, but it is a huge stretch. Any ideas on how to narrow it down? We can't go traipsing backwards and forth across that lot in the hope that we stumble across the right place, that could take months.' Ollie replied.

'Ol, don't worry. I think we can be a bit more astute than that.' Chris said.

'You can take that as a given, if I have anything to do with it.' Devan said. 'Literally just with a quick tinternet search I can narrow it down to a possible three which are culturally notable peaks along the range but only one of them falls into that particular zone, Mount Hua. Not to mention there are countless references to its links to the immortals of Chinese legend. Oh, this ones really interesting; about one of these immortal encounters on Mount Hua in Cao Pi's Zhe yangliu xing.'

'Why's that so relevant?' Ollie asked.

'Because Zhe yangliu xing translates as snapping a willow branch and if you recall the professor's bit of verse referred to weeping willows. There's also many references to the cypress trees planted by many of the Han Emperors stretching from the Palace of Assembled Spirits erected by Emperor Wu to the north of the mountain as far as the northern slopes.'

'Anything else, which might narrow the location a bit more?'

'Well, the mountain is made up of three distinct peaks, East, West and South, James' father referred to the southern peak and according to these tourist maps there's a temple complex on the southern peak, just above Heaven's Gate and the sunshine welcoming cave, which again tie in well with the professor's cryptic message.'

'Well that's me sold.' Chris said. 'How far is it from here?'

'Let me see.' Devan replied, using Beijing as a starting point. 'Says it's about eleven hours by road, or we can jump on a high speed train from Beijing and do it in about five.'

'As much as I like the sound of the faster option I have a feeling road is gonna have to be our choice. There's things we're going to have to take with us that I'm pretty sure would look a bit out of place, not to mention draw the wrong kind of attention on the platform let alone on the train itself, if you get my drift.' Chris replied with the hint of a smile. 'Which reminds me, Juan did you manage to reach out to any of those guys while you were making your way over here?'

'Yeah, I spoke to a few. Just waiting to hear back, there was at least one item that was felt to be rather rare and might prove to be a bridge too far, but otherwise they were confident they'd get the rest together.'

'Well I suggest you guys all get a good feed and as much rest as possible because I can guarantee once that gear arrives we won't get much sleep for a good few days.' Chris stated as he turned his mind back to the journey that lay before them and the prospect of what awaited them at Mount Hua.

Chapter Twenty-Five: Enter the Dragon

The interior of the warehouse James and Josh found themselves in was far larger than they had appreciated from their rooftop vantage point earlier that evening. A dimly lit Aladdin's cave bursting at the seams with treasures, everything from the finest silk carpets, jade statues and ivory carvings to terracotta warriors. The latter, presumably knock-offs to fool the untrained tourist's eye; this was China after all. They took their time just wandering in amongst the maze of passageways that had sprung up like topsy as ever more wondrous things had been added to entice collectors and tourist alike to depart with hard earned readies.

James was about to inspect a bizarre piece of taxidermy in the form of squirrel ripping open its chest to reveal a superman costume underneath as Josh picked up an extremely delicate and intricately painted porcelain vase, which he almost dropped; startled by a woman's voice calling out from somewhere behind him.

'Careful with that one, it's from the early Qing period. Very rare. Is there anything in particular you are looking for? We have some exquisite porcelain from the Song Dynasty if you are looking for something really special.' The woman whom they had observed meeting with Norwood earlier said as she appeared from behind another precariously stacked row of shelving.

'That's a bit too late, I'm interested in the Xi period.' Josh replied, carefully replacing the object undamaged.

'Oh, I believe you mean the Xia.'

'Yes, thank you. I do struggle with my pronunciation sometimes.' Josh replied, acting as if it was just a slip of the tongue.

'We don't have much from that period, mainly bronzes. No porcelain I'm afraid, as I'm sure you are aware, that did not develop until much later.'

'Of course, as I recall, the Eastern Han were the first to really perfect what we would now consider as porcelain.'

'Yes, I see you know your history.' She said smiling.

'Well I try. But porcelain isn't what we are looking for. What my colleague and I are really interested in are ritualistic objects, totems, charms, and turtle shells. That sort of thing.' He replied casually slipping a reference to the artefact into the conversation, catching her eyebrow twitch ever so slightly at the mention of the shell.

'I'm afraid, we don't have anything like that in stock. They are, as I'm sure you are familiar, almost impossible to acquire. I've only seen one in the last twenty years, this very evening coincidentally, but the owner assured me that it was not for sale.' She replied.

'How very serendipitous, amazing how sometimes the fates align. I don't suppose he left any details, did he?' Josh asked, immediately realising he'd made a slip; the woman had never mentioned the gender of the owner. Luckily for him she hadn't noticed.

'He might have left some with my assistant. Let me just go and check.' She lied sweetly, taking the opportunity no doubt to make another call from the backroom.

'Well played, just don't over do it.' James said to Josh while the woman was away looking for the so called details they both knew did not exist. 'Here she comes.' He added as he spied the woman returning through a beaded curtain draped across a doorway at the backend of the display room.

'Unfortunately it appears he did not. Maybe you can leave yours in case he has a change of heart.' She slyly proposed.

'Well we're really only passing through Dandong. A few days here and then onto Beijing, but if he does come back in the next day or two you can tell him we're staying at the Sunny Resort Hotel on Xianqian Street.' James replied, intervening before Josh gave out more than he should.

'And who should I say to ask for, Mr...?

'Whittering, Alexander Whittering.' James rolled the cover name off his tongue as smoothly as if he was accustomed to using it everyday. 'Now if you will excuse us we have a taxi waiting, so we really must be off. Thank you so much for your assistance, you have a wonderful selection here and we may very well be back to pick up a few trinkets before we continue our adventures.' He said.

'A pleasure to meet you both. I hope you find what you are looking for. Come back and see us anytime.' She replied, watching them like a hawk as they made their way back out onto the street.

'We haven't booked into any hotel.' Josh said as they stepped out in to the cooling night air.

'We have now. I took the liberty of making the arrangements while you two were discussing pottery. Notice anything of interest in there?'

'Not really, there were some nice pieces once you worked out which ones were fake. Oh actually, there was one thing; no alarm sensors. Curious, no? You'd have thought with all those antiques genuine or otherwise that the building would be secure.' Josh said.

'Well I would fill you in but as you're about to find out anyway. There doesn't seem much point. Just don't do anything stupid.' James coolly replied. As Josh suddenly noticed several men in black suits approaching them.

'Mr Whittering, you and your companion will come with us, please.' The largest of the square shouldered men said, now standing no more than two feet from James.

'I don't suppose we can respectfully decline your kind invitation.' James calmly replied.

'This isn't a request.' The man bluntly replied.

'Very well then gentlemen, we accept. We don't want any trouble.' James replied.

'No trouble. We just want to have a conversation.' The man said, letting out a high pitched whistle accompanied by a flicked wave of his right hand. Two black saloons shot up and came to a halt just beside them.

'Please, after you.' The man said gesturing for them to get into the back of the lead car. James didn't say anything he just gave a slight nod and got in. Josh was about to follow, then hesitated. James tried to grab his sleeve and drag him into the vehicle but he was too late, as Josh dodged his outstretched arm.

'Hey, what about our taxi and bags?' Josh hastily asked.

'Don't worry they will be taken care of.' The man replied, turning to one of his compatriots and saying something so quickly in Chinese that Josh didn't even have a chance to work out what he had said.

'Just get in the damn car.' James said. 'I told you not to do anything stupid. These aren't the kind of people you dick around with.'

'I just wanted to make sure we didn't lose our gear.' Josh replied as he sat down next to James.

'I'd be more concerned about losing other stuff than our gear at this point, if I was you. You don't make Triad ask twice.' The mere mention of the Triad sent a brief almost imperceptible shiver down Josh's spine. Indeed he'd sat through many a briefing on what signs to look out for, their organisational structure, and tentacle like growth across various parts of the world not to mention their sometimes brutal operational methods. But not once had he ever come face to face with one until now. As soon as the man that had accosted them, who Josh assumed was in charge, got into the front passenger seat the car pulled off and they were soon meandering their way through the unfamiliar suburbs of Dandong.

Something continued to nag at Josh as the car continued to roll on through the narrow back streets right out through the dwindling outskirts of the city and into open countryside, this was mainland China. Supposedly the Triad had failed to establish themselves in the interior because of the no tolerance stance taken by the one party state, yes, there were pockets of disorderly criminal activity but syndicates of organised crime were almost unheard of, even corrupt officials were soon weeded out. James did have more overall and China-specific field experience but surely he'd sat through many of the same briefings albeit half a decade ago, so why was he so convinced these were Triad? The question continued to bounce around his thoughts as the car continued on, but he daren't ask out loud as he was certain the men in the front would be listening in. Instead he glanced at James in such a way to get his attention and then began to tap his middle finger on the space between them on the back seat.

It had been a long time since James had seen anybody use tap code, he beamed inside at just how much Josh was developing as he began to decipher the first in a series of questions. A half grin spread across his face before he answered the first in the same manner in which it was asked.

'Security systems not needed, if paying for protection.' He quickly tapped back before waiting for a response.

'Why Triad?' Came the next short question.

'One with Black dragon tattoo on neck and three dots around eye.' He fired back.

'Which Triad?'

'Not sure, 14K possibly.' James answered along with a slight shrug indicating he couldn't say for sure.

'Why interest in the shell?'

'Leverage or profit. Let it play out.' James laid his hand on top of Josh's indicating that he didn't have anymore to add, before the young man could start another line of questioning. Josh reluctantly nodded that he understood. He had heaps of other questions he wanted to ask but he realised that what he really wanted was longer more detailed answers which weren't really suited to tap code and the longer they carried on the greater the risk became that their chaperones in the front might notice and work out what was going on. After all tap code wasn't just confined to use by covert ops but was also in frequent use by gangs and prisoners.

The car eventually rolled in through an impressive set of gates and proceeded up a long winding lane towards a vast estate house overlooking open countryside stretching out as far as they eye could see in all directions. James and Josh were ushered into the hallway and told to wait.

'They're quite well mannered considering they've probably disposed of a good few bodies in their time.' Josh said softly as they waited.

'I'd say that's a good sign. More of a chance there might be a deal to be done.' James suggested as the men returned accompanied by another. Just from the way the latter carried himself they could tell that he was far more than just a street thug.

'Mr Whittering, Mr Parker. Good afternoon. My name is Mr Li. It's a pleasure to welcome you to my humble home. Can I offer you some tea?' The man of short stature warmly offered.

'That would be very welcome and thank you for inviting us to your beautiful home. It's a pleasure to make your acquaintance Mr Li.' James replied.

'Please follow me.' Mr Li said as he made an open hand gesture towards a large sitting room with those stunning vistas below the house, where a tray of piping hot tea was already waiting for them.

'It really is idyllic here. Have you lived here long?' James asked, as he continued to weigh the man up.

'Oh well, me personally, I suppose a decade or so. It was my father's before that and his father's before him. So I suppose you could say we're part of the furniture, as you Brits put it.' He replied with a warm beaming smile. 'And yes, it is rather pleasant. There's just something relaxing and rejuvenating about country life, wouldn't you agree.' Mr Li added.

'Yes, I suppose there is. Of course we don't currently suffer from the same levels of smog and pollution in the cities as you do. But I'm sure if we are not careful we may go back to the murkiness of our industrial past.' James replied. 'I hope you don't mind if I cut to the chase and ask exactly why you have extended this kind invitation? We seldom receive requests from businessmen such as yourself.' James added, carefully choosing his words not to mention the Triad, as he suspected that would have the potential to cause deep offence. Something that they could ill afford.

'Certainly, it is nothing to worry about. It just came to our attention that we have interests that may intersect. As such I thought it would be beneficial for all of us to clear a safe passage of travel so to speak in order to avoid any unforeseen hazards. I do hope you don't feel that I have overstepped the mark, as that was not my intention at all.' Mr Li said.

James deliberately choreographed taking a casual sip of tea before he responded. 'I appreciate your candour. We are of course talking about the Huanglong Medallion, as I believe it is known. An artefact of that nature will always attract interest from a wide variety of parties. I'm sure you are already aware that we are not the only ones who seek it and that it is currently in the possession of another. However, I can assure you that even though it does have a bearing on an area we are interested in we have no desire to possess it in the long term. I hope I am also not over-stepping in my assumption that this is what you are concerned about?'

'No on the contrary, I think we understand each other very well, Mr Whittering. Let us just say that our main concern is to ensure China doesn't lose another piece of its heritage, and chiefly for us this has the potential to open a lot doors so to speak.' Mr Li replied.

'I know exactly what you mean. If I can speak plainly, we too have a tricky door within China which requires unlocking, and the Medallion is the key. Nevertheless once opened, we will have no further need for it and could be handed over to remain as a cultural icon. I trust that will be satisfactory.'

'I think we can agree to those terms. I think China and its people, I'm sure will be more than grateful and will be more than happy to assist you along your way.' Mr Li replied as another beaming smile spread across his face.

'So it's settled then. I hope that we can build upon this new foundation of friendship moving forward.' James said rising, giving a friendly and sincere bow to his counterpart.

'Mr Whittering, I look forward to our future blossoming.' Mr Li replied warmly reciprocating and shaking James's hand. 'And on that note is there anything that we can do or provide you with, since I'm sure we have already caused you some delay in your quest.' Mr Li added.

'Well as I'm sure you are well aware the vastness of your country does make travel tricky and we do have a considerable amount of ground to cover. Apart from that, a few tools to ensure we can maintain our safety I hope would not be too difficult for a man such as yourself to supply.' James replied.

'How far do you need to go?' Mr Li asked.

'As far as the dragon's lair.' James replied.

'Yes, I know the legend. I think that can be arranged. It is getting late so please stay the night and we will have everything ready for you come morning. I will have the house keeper come and show you to your rooms. Now if you will excuse me I must get the ball rolling.' Mr Li said before leaving them at their ease.

Lord Norwood's high spirits had been short lived once they'd left the warehouse with the information he desired. He had hope to secure an evening flight out of Dandong to any of the airports near to Mount Hua, but as it turned out the earliest available flight was the following afternoon. And then of course there was the issue that they would then need to find armaments on the black market at the other end, there was no way he intended to turn up without weapons in case a bit of gentle leverage was required. In the end he took the decision that it would be better to secure everything he required whilst still in Dandong, hire a few jeeps and drive. It was almost a twenty hour drive but there were easily enough people to rotate the driving, and still all be fresh at the other end for what would ensue. He had just finished reaching out to his contacts to secure the necessary equipment when he received a call from Chamberlain.

'My Lord, I've been trying to contact you for hours. There has been a development that you should be aware of, and I'm afraid to say it is not good news or at least it may not be.' Chamberlain said.

'Just spit it out man, I'm not a mind reader.' Norwood replied half distracted by the journey that lay ahead.

'There has been a break-in at the safety depository.' Chamberlain said.

'What, when did this happen?' Norwood asked, dreading what this might mean.

'Two days ago.' Chamberlain replied.

'And you are only telling me about this now!' Norwood bellowed down the phone.

'I'm sorry my Lord, the story only broke this morning.' His man replied.

'Well, the codex is it safe?' Norwood asked hoping for a positive answer.

'I cannot say my Lord, the place is swarming with police. They won't let anybody in and at present they will not confirm which boxes were broken into and which ones were left untouched.' Chamberlain explained.

'Well you better find out, and fast.' Norwood coldly replied.

'What if they have been taken?' Chamberlain asked half expecting what was to come.

'I'm surprised you even need to ask. Let me be crystal clear on this, if you dare to cross my path without them I will wipe you from the face of this earth.' Norwood shouted, before completely loosing control of his temper throwing his mobile so forcefully against the window of the taxi that both shattered. Carla thought about attempting to calm him down but realised that she was best to keep tight lipped, Chamberlain was thousands of miles away whereas she was in reach and there was no way she wanted to risk becoming a punch bag for him to vent on. She had witnessed first hand what he was capable of when he lost control. She also knew he had nineteen odd hours to calm down before they reached their final destination, Mount Hua.

Chapter Twenty-Six: Mind the Gaps

The cosy docile mood of the coffeeshop was shattered by Chamberlain's clenched fist smashing down upon the tabletop as his call with Lord Norwood abruptly ended. A few of the other customers glanced over in his direction with disapproving looks at the cause of the disruption but upon meeting the colossal size of the disturbance they hastily turned back to whatever they had been doing, before the focus of its rage swivelled towards them. Not that Chamberlain had even noticed the extra attention, he was far too consumed by his dented ego. This was the closest he had come to failing his lordship, he knew that there was no way he could have predicted that someone would break into Norwood's depository, nevertheless he certainly saw that he could have taken extra measures to keep an eye on the place while his lordship was otherwise engaged. The problem that now lay ahead of him was how to find out whether or not that particular box had been broken into, and if it had; was this the work of Flack and his meddling cohorts or had the depository been targeted by a professional crew and Norwood's box just collateral damage? After all, as far as he was aware, apart from Lord Norwood, Carla and himself nobody else had known about the vault. As his mind began to de-mist he decided the most logical thing to do was to probe the police; sooner or later the police were bound to start asking the registered clients of the safety deposit to come and check whether or not anything from their respective boxes had been taken. Norwood actually had several in the vault but there was no way Chamberlain was going to check the others, the things contained in them would get him and his lordship into a serious amount of hot water. No, his best bet was to just ask to check the one containing the codex and if confronted about the others, he'd tell the police that the main signatory was away on business and had left strict instructions that under no circumstances were those boxes to be opened without them being present.

Having made his mind up on the best course of action to take, he stood up leaving a tip beside the empty coffee cup on the table and walked out onto the busy Covent street. He headed straight for the nearest mobile shop and purchased the cheapest throw away with some credit.

Before calling the police he rang the safety depository direct just in case they'd be willing to provide information on whether or not the box in question had been hit.

'Good morning, Miss Connors speaking.' Said the voice in a tone that belied her façade; it was far from a good morning. She had lost count of the number of calls she had already taken that morning regarding the break-in and presumably this was to be yet another irate customer about to vent their ire down the line.

'Good morning. I'm ringing regarding a box I rented a few days prior to the break-in at your establishment under the name of Chamberlain. It was number 2458, if I recall correctly. I was hoping you would be able to tell me whether or not its contents are still secure?' Chamberlain calmly asked. As much as he would've liked to have scooped out her eyes with a searing hot spoon, he knew that the best way to get the information he required was to be as affable as possible. No doubt the woman at the other end would have had a torrid morning with other clients so a change of tack should probably be a welcome break.

'Oh Mr Chamberlain, firstly can I offer our most sincerest of apologies for what I'm sure must be a devastating set of circumstances. You placed your trust in us and I'm afraid we have come up way short of the bar expected by our clients.'

'Don't worry about it, there's always someone clever in the room that can get the better of us from time to time. It's all insured at the end of the day, if the worst has happened.' He replied.

'Oh that's so understanding of you and far more gracious than half the people I have spoken with this morning. You really wouldn't believe some of the things I have been called since I came in to help man the phones. In regards to your box, the police did asked that we refer all our clients to them, but I don't see the harm in checking the list for you. Let me see 2458.' She said as she ran her finger down the list of boxes in front of her. 'Ah, yes. Here it is. So I'm afraid to say it does appear that yours was broken into, although there is an extra note here to say that there were two rare volumes and a piece of parchment still in it when it was discovered amongst the mess.'

Chamberlain's heart leapt with relief at this news, if they were still there then he hadn't failed his master as he had feared.

'Miss Connors, I think your luck must be changing. Those were the only items in that particular box, so you can cross us off the list. Will I still need to go via the police to arrange to pick the items up, as I'm sure you will understand my employer has insisted that they are moved as soon as possible to a more secure location.' He said.

'Yes, I'm afraid you will have to go through them. It is still an active crime scene, and they will not allow anything to leave the premises until they have finished processing the building. But I'm sure they won't keep you any longer than necessary. I'm sorry we will be losing your custom, but I quite understand given the circumstances. I'm glad that it has at least had a positive ending for you; let's just hope a few more of our clients have your good fortune.' Sarah replied.

'Is there a direct number I can call or do I just ring the local nick?' Chamberlain asked.

'Oh, this isn't being overseen locally, Scotland Yard were brought in as soon as the news broke. I did have a card here somewhere but right this second I can't seem to find where I put it. When I do manage to find it I'll text it to you. I presume the number you are on is the best one to contact you on?'

'It is, but don't fret if you can't find it. I'm sure if I ring the Yard's switchboard they'll redirect me through to the appropriate channels. Thank you so much for your help and I do hope your day gets better.' Chamberlain said before hanging up.

His spirits fully restored now that he knew the pieces of the codex were safe, he casually took his time before calling the switchboard at Scotland Yard making an appointment to see one of the junior detectives involved with the case later that afternoon. He didn't mention that he already knew that the contents of his box were intact as he didn't want to drop Miss Connors into hot water for breaching protocol. Not that it mattered in any case, from here on out he was certain it would be a formality to arrange collection once the bobbies cross referenced the number with their evidence list. As soon as he'd made the arrangements he sauntered off towards Covent Garden tube station to make his way up to Westminster, where he intended to grab a bite before his allotted time with the junior detective.

Having dined well, Chamberlain had just a short five minute stroll up to New Scotland Yard. Striding confidently into reception he approached the sergeant on the desk whom in his opinion was a little on the short side for a member of the flying squad.

'Good afternoon, my name is Chamberlain. I have an appointment with one of your DIs. Oh, now what was their name? Steb... Stebbings, yes that's was the one, DI Stebbings.'

'Certainly sir, I'll just let her know you have arrived.' Replied the sergeant. 'If you'd like to take a seat, I'm sure she will be right down.' He added as he dialled her extension.

'Thanks.' Chamberlain smiled as he took a seat in the foyer musing as he did so at the revelation that it had been a female detective he had spoken to earlier, demonstrating just how cheap that burner actually was. He would have never have guessed from the sound quality that he'd been conversing with a woman. While he was still musing the desk sergeant leant over to say that she was just wrapping up a meeting and didn't expect to be any longer than five or so minutes.

'That's great, thanks.' Chamberlain replied, picking up a magazine entitled *The Force: Investigating Future Roles in the Digital Age*. He couldn't help but chuckle at the concept; it seemed they were already stretched enough as it was and that was just with the ordinary criminal so how they hoped to cope with those hidden amongst the binary world amused him greatly.

He was halfway down the first article identifying some of the new threats facing the force when DI Stebbings approached him.

'Mr. Chamberlain, so sorry to have kept you waiting. Our briefing overran slightly.' She said as she greeted him.

'It's fine, I haven't long arrived.' He replied. 'Besides I'd far rather you were all hot on the trail of the perpetrators, leaving no stone unturned than dealing with the likes of me.' He added with a smile.

'Well it's still early on in our investigation but we are making good inroads. If you'd like to follow me through to my office upstairs, there's just a few formalities I need to go over with you regarding your box.' She said as she turned swiping her access pass across the sensor on the door frame into the main building, he followed her up two flights of stairs, turning left and then down a long straight corridor to her office at the far end.

'Please make yourself comfortable, can I get you a tea or coffee?' She asked as they entered.

'Coffee, black, one sugar. Thanks.' He replied. Watching her as she made him a cup, trying to gauge what sort of person she was. He always felt you could learn a lot about a person by the way they carried themselves, how they dressed, the manner in which they interacted with other people. So far she struck him as confident, bright and there was a glimmer of something else that just at that moment he couldn't quite put his finger on. 'Thanks.' He said as she handed him the hot blackness.

'So as I understood from our conversation earlier you had a box, number 2458 at the depository.'

'Yes, that's the one. It didn't have a great many things in it of any particular monetary value. More sentimental if that makes sense. Just a couple of old part manuscripts by an ancestor of mine and a wooden carving. I'm hoping that it might have been tossed aside as I really can't see it being worth fencing or passing onto a third party.'

'Well, I have had a quick flick through the items we recovered and it does seem that in your particular case although the box was ripped open, nothing was taken, as you say it clearly didn't have the monetary value that they were looking for.'

'That's fantastic news. I realise you may have to do some forensic magic but I would be grateful if I can reclaim the items at your earliest convenience.' He gently suggested not wanting to approach the subject in too direct a manner.

'Apart from the box itself which was broken open, the actual items don't seem to have been interfered with like some of the others. So I'm fairly confident they can be processed relatively quickly, obviously we do need to dust for prints, swab for DNA etc, nevertheless I'd be hopeful we can have them safely returned to you within the next couple of days if that is okay with you.'

'That sounds perfectly reasonable to me, I certainly wouldn't want to deprive you of any potential evidence that might lead to apprehending the little shits. Excuse my French.' He replied.

'Great, I've got your number, so if I can just jot down the rest of your details for my notebook, I'll be in touch as soon as your items are ready to be released. Just remember to bring some form of identification with you when you come to collect them.' She said.

'I think I can do that. Here's my card, should have everything you need. And feel free to contact me if there are any other questions you might think of at a later date. ' He replied, passing her a business card he'd fished out of his wallet.

'Perfect, I think that's us done. I hope you enjoy the rest of your day and I'm glad you've had a luckier resolution than some. Are you okay to find your own way out?'

'Oh yes, I don't think that will be a problem. Thank you very much detective, and I look forward to hearing from you shortly.' He said rising to shake her hand and make his leave.

'Oh, there was one thing I wanted to ask before you leave. There were a number of other boxes that have someone with your name down as a secondary signatory alongside a Lord Norwood. They wouldn't have anything to do with you would they? None of them were touched, so they aren't part of our official investigation. More just my professional curiosity.' She asked, before he'd managed to make it out of her office.

He turned slowly back to face her before he gave his reply.

'Technically yes, I am the secondary signatory. I spoke to Lord Norwood earlier, as he is currently abroad on business and the primary signatory. He left instructions that if they had been broken into he would deal with it personally on his return. If they had not, which in this case appears to be so, then they would be moved on his return. As they can only be opened and relocated when both signatories are present I rather didn't see the point of enquiring about them, partly because he would have been the one dealing with any fallout and also because I actually don't know what they contain so I wouldn't have been much help in that respect had anything been taken. When his lordship first took me on as his head of security I had advised him to add a secondary signature as an extra measure of protection, but I was never privy to what he was storing at the vault. I hope that answers your question, detective.' Chamberlain replied.

'Thanks, that makes a lot of sense. Do you know when he is likely to be back?' She probed.

'I believe he is aiming to be back within the next seven days, depending of course on whether his business has reached a satisfactory conclusion by then. If not, he may be delayed by a day or two, but he assured me no longer than that. If he doesn't get exactly what he wants, he's not afraid to pull the plug and walk away.' Chamberlain replied.

'Sounds like quite a formidable person your boss.'

'You have no idea. And on that note, if you have nothing else detective, I have one or two appointments still to keep on his behalf, so I really must be making tracks.' Chamberlain stated, trying to extricate himself before he said something he might later regret.

'No that's great, I've got your number if I do think of anything else. I hope you manage to conclude your day satisfactorily. And I'll be in touch within the next few days about your items, if not before.' She replied.

'Thanks again detective, and I'll look forward to hearing from you.' He said smiling as he left her office.

The door was just closing behind Chamberlain as he left when he glimpsed a familiar face walking towards him. *That detective, the one from the TV. The one who'd been in charge of that murder case at Saint Michael's Mount. What the fuck is he doing here? Surely he couldn't be involved with this one could he? No, there can't be any connection between that case and this, could there? How could there be, they'd been careful and that storm must have destroyed any tangible evidence.* Chamberlain quickly darted into the gents just before Glen reached him. Locking himself into a cubicle he waited for what seemed like an age, all the while unanswered questions and paranoid thoughts began tearing through his mind. *Had they left any prints there? Oh shit, what about Jersey? That had been a bit of a train wreck. Was there something there to link the two? The boat, please tell me they didn't find that fucking boat. But that would be ruled a suicide or accidental death, wouldn't it?* A rap on the cubicle door dragged him back from the chaos of jumbled thoughts.

'Hey mate, you gonna be much longer. Not gonna lie, last night's curry ain't sitting too well.'

'Oh yeah, sorry. One sec.' He hastily replied, quickly flushing and vacating the cubicle.

'Thanks man, not sure how much longer I could've held on.' Said the man darting past him into the now vacant box.

Stepping back out onto the corridor he could see that detective talking to DI Stebbings through the glass. He could think of nothing else as he left New Scotland Yard. *What the hell to do now? Can't risk going back to Stebbings once the items are ready for collection, bumping into that man could be a disaster. What if they discover something in the mean time and make a connection that links to the other cases. But not to return to collect the items? Wouldn't that also look a bit dodgy, and pique their curiosity. The lock's been primed, can't afford a misfire now. Fuck, fuck, fuck. Come on you bastard think, for god's sake; think! There must be a way to retrieve those items without running into that detective or getting ensnared. But how?*

Chapter Twenty-Seven: Reawakening from a Dream

Rachel felt like no time at all had passed since her head hit the pillow when she was ripped back from the land of dreams by her phone's startling eagerness to inform her she had a call. At first she put out a blind sleep driven hand and fumbled around hitting the decline button, but all that happened was that the blasted thing started up again moments later. This time she made half an effort, raising her head just enough to read the caller ID, immediately bolting straight upright and snatching the handset off the bedside table as she realised the call was from the ICU at Jersey General.

'Hi Rach, here. I'm up. I'm up. S'happened?' She blurted out so quickly that to anybody else it would have made no sense whatsoever.

'Hi Rachel, it's Noura. Sorry, to wake you. No need to fret, nothing sinister. I'd promised that if there were any developments I would call, so I thought you ought to know that Professor Middleton has begun to regain what we would class as a degree of consciousness, and is displaying some localised responses to touch. He hasn't opened his eyes yet, but this is certainly an encouraging sign that he is beginning to recover from his ordeal.'

'Oh Noura, that's wonderful. I'll be in as soon as I can.' Rachel replied feeling a great weight lifting from her shoulders at the news.

'It's a good sign but don't get too excited. Just bear in mind that it's very early days, and may still be some time yet before we see any higher levels of response. So don't expect too much when you come in.' The nurse replied.

'I understand, and thank you so much. You've been so supportive through all of this. I really can't thank you enough. Will you be around later?'

'Yes, I should be. Just gone onto days.' Noura replied.

'Great, I'll see you later. And we can have a proper catch-up. Right, I best sort myself out. See you in a bit, bye.'

'See you later and take your time, no need to rush. He's not going anyway. Speak shortly, bye.' The nurse replied before hanging up.

Rachel breathed an overdue sigh of relief as she laid her phone back down on the nightstand. Her long-standing hopes that James's father would recover were on the way to being realised, yet she knew not to let herself get too carried away, as Noura had said, this was still the first in a long line of steps and stages along the way to a full recovery, if that was even still a possibility. After all, while he was still in the coma there was no way of knowing exactly how much of the brain had been damaged by the stroke, only time would tell. *At least the spark of hope's now growing a little brighter.* She thought as she stepped into the shower.

The morning had almost departed by the time Rachel arrived at the hospital having decided to have breakfast at Noirmont and compose herself ready for whatever was awaiting her at the Intensive Care Unit. The lift up from The Parade entrance to the second floor seemed to take far longer than she remembered, such was the way of things when one desperately wanted to be somewhere, stepping out she was about to turn and make her now familiar route across to ICU when she was spotted by Noura from her vantage point at the nurses' station and called her over.

'Rach, you won't find him there anymore. I forgot to mention earlier, now that he's showing signs of recovery, we've moved him from ICU to the HDU on the Plemont ward, just across the way. Close enough to ICU should he take a turn for the worse but also allows us to have an extra bed in the ICU should we need it for someone else.'

'Good thing you caught me otherwise I'd have been panicking when I didn't find him.' Rachel replied with a smile. 'Has the consultant finished his rounds yet?'

'You literally just missed him. He wouldn't have told you much more than I already have. He seemed happy enough with how things stand but if you would like to speak to him. When you come in tomorrow aim to get here for around half ten, I'll ask him if he can give you a bit more detail on what to expect over the coming days etc.'

'Oh would you? That would be very kind. Just to understand a bit more about these stages would just help to give me a bit more peace of mind if that makes sense.' Rachel replied.

'Of course no trouble at all. It's not just about patient welfare, your's is just as important.' The nurse replied with a reassuring smile. 'Come on, lets go and see how he's doing.' She added stepping out from behind the desk to accompany Rachel to the ward the professor had been moved to.

The professor's room on the ward was just like any other, devoid of decoration and character, clinically clean and functional. There was barely a sound in the sterile environment apart from the rhythmical bleeps emanating out of the machines keeping him stable. His bed was centred off one wall surrounded by all manner of gadgets hooked up to his frail body, monitoring his brain activity and life signs, an IV drip and most importantly a respirator helping him to breath. Rachel just managed to hold back a tear at the sight of the withered looking man, a mere distorted reflection of the charming and cheery gent she had first met those many months ago.

'For some reason I'd expected he'd been taken off the respirator when you rang this morning.' She commented.

'It was considered, in the end I think the consultant wanted to keep him on for a day or two longer just to make sure.' Noura replied, glancing at the watch pinned to the front of her uniform. 'Right, I'll leave you two, I've got to go off on my rounds. But I won't be far away if you need anything.' She added. Leaving Rachel to settle into the chair next to the professor's bed.

'Oh Peter, I wish I knew what was gong on inside that head of yours. Or that you could give me some sort of clue, just an indication; anything to point me in the right direction.' Rachel sighed as she took the professor's hand in hers with a tender caress. She'd half expected for Peter to reciprocate after all that Noura had told her, but she didn't perceive any discernible notion of cognisance. 'Maybe it's me, my words are just not familiar enough are they. I wonder if a stronger, more emotive bond will stay your mind and bring you back to us.' She mused, taking out a collection of envelopes she'd found lovingly tucked inside a few of his journals. Before she had even opened them Rachel had realised that they must have been written by someone very dear to the professor indeed to have been so carefully persevered with all the hallmarks of being well read amongst his most prized possessions. It had only been on opening them that Rachel had realised they were from James's mother. Which shouldn't have been a surprise. After all, it was only natural for lovers to keep and cherish the tokens that they sent to each other. Gently removing the first from its envelope she hoped that the contents would reignite a flame inside the professor's mind.

My Darling,

I trust that this finds you well and that your spirits have much improved since your last letter. I was very disheartened to hear that your dig has been beset by delays. I know how much your work means to you, and how beautiful the light inside your soul sparkles every time you recant the stories of your adventures to your son upon your return. Everyday my heart aches a little more for your safe homecoming. And I pray every evening that you successfully find what you are searching for quickly in order to hasten our reunion, not just for my sake but also for your darling son's, seldom seeing one's father is not a good thing for a young boy.

Oh you should see him now, James has grown so much since you departed and he is turning into quite the little explorer, just like his father in that respect. Only just the other day, when we'd been in the kitchen making cupcakes, and I turned my back for a matter of a few seconds to fetch some flour from the pantry only to return and discover that he'd pulled another of his disappearing acts. I searched the house high and low but he was nowhere to be found. I was almost at my wits end when I spied, the little terror, through the window on the landing, half way across the hundred acre field with the dogs. The 'troublesome trio' as I have come to call them, they always seem to be off on some sort of adventure and generally up to all sorts of mischief. But I never worry about him when he is with them, Raffie and Meg seem to have taken a shine to him and I am always reassured that he'll be safe when they accompany him. Raffles in particular seems to have a very strong bond with him. They never go anywhere without each other, so I suppose I should have guessed where he had gone when I didn't find Raffles. Needless to say he has now been firmly informed that he should always tell someone before he goes running off. But knowing who he takes after I doubt that will last for long.

We both miss you terribly and I do wish you would come home soon, there is a sense of emptiness here without you. But I'm not suggesting that you cut your trip short, I realise that your work is important and I wish you every success and hope that those Greek gods you are so fond of, bestow good fortune upon you and your endeavours.

My heart as ever is yours,

Catherine.

A smile welled up inside Rachel as she read the letter, her heart warmed by the glimpse into James' childhood, a part that he'd never spoken about. She could picture the whole scene in her mind's eye, and was not surprised at all that he was just as much of a handful as a small boy as he was in adulthood. The next letter she picked out was of much the same vein as the first although there had clearly been developments at the dig site and the professor's luck had appeared to have changed.

Rachel's eyelids slowly began to drop as she moved onto the third letter, being woken early by Noura's call was catching up with her, she shook her head in an effort to focus but lulled by the sweet dulcet tone of the third letter she eventually lost the battle and as she nodded off in the chair next to the professor's bed. The letter slipped from her hand and softly floated down onto the cold sterile floor. Her mind wandered as she slept and she was soon transported off to the household of James' childhood, picturing him and his two canine companions darting about the house re-enacting a somewhat embellished version of his father's latest exploits, all be it with a few more dragons and monsters and a little less cataloguing and paperwork. In her dreams James was always wearing a silver crown encrusted with diamonds, which Rachel's subconscious had conjured from a section of the third letter in which Catherine had thanked Peter for his extraordinarily generous gift of a diamond tiara that she referred to as *Ariadne's Corona* unearthed by her husband on his latest dig site in Crete. The intricate detailing of a Greek mythological scene around the lower banding was just coming into focus when Rachel was dragged back into the real world. She had slept through the professor's hand gently squeezing hers but the sound of his raspy voice calling out his love's name was like a starting pistol going off inside Rachel's head, and she bolted upright from where she had been dozing just as Peter called out for his beloved Catherine once more.

'I'm here Peter, its okay you're safe.' Rachel replied. To which Peter just replied.

'C- Catherine, my love. I-is that yo-uu?' Rachel hesitated for a moment before she replied, she was about to say no and tell him it wasn't Catherine, but then she changed her mind and decided to go with it.

'Yes my love, it's me Catherine. I'm here by your side, you're safe now.' Rachel replied feeling a little disingenuous for the deception.

'C-Catherine. James, the key. He must find the key. Must find it, Catherine.' The man withered as he feebly tried to move his arms.

'What do you mean, Peter? What key?' Rachel asked, half wondering whether the professor was just babbling on in a kind of confused delirium as he began to come out of the coma.

'Cath-erine, you must tell him Catherine. He will know where to find it. Yes, he will know.' The professor continued completely oblivious to the question of what the key actually was.

'I will tell him, my love. But you need to tell me what the key is? What does it look like? Focus Peter, think, what does it look like?' Rachel pleaded with him to remember what it was.

'James, find James. He knows where. The gift, Diony… He knows where. Dionysus's… yes he knows where…' The professor sank back into his pillow, passing out through exhaustion before he ever completed his ramblings. Leaving Rachel in a state of stunned bewilderment.

'Is everything okay? Rachel, you look like you've just seen a ghost. Are you okay?' Noura asked as she bustled her way into the room.

'Hm what?' Rachel began to reply before shaking herself to catch up with herself. 'Noura, the professor, he spoke. He actually spoke. Just for a few moments and nothing that coherent but he did, he spoke.' Rachel exclaimed still reeling slightly from the surreal experience.

'That's wonderful and a really good sign.' The nurse replied beaming at her, and giving her a much needed and reassuring hug. 'I told you there would be some light at the end of the tunnel.'

'True, I mean it was only for a few moments and then he passed out again, but he was definitely there. You could feel a change in the room as another presence became… well present I guess. It was really quite strange. And then he departed again almost as swiftly as he arrived.' Rachel recounted, gradually starting to turn her attention to the details concealed within the professor's wording.

'That's quite usual, I wouldn't worry about that too much. Patients don't tend to stay awake for very long in the days after coming out of that kind of state. It takes a lot of effort, but bit by bit you'll notice the amount of time he is up for increases and he should become much more coherent, of course this will depend on how much damage the stroke caused and I'm afraid only time will tell on that one. Did anything he said make sense? They often don't.' Noura replied.

'Not really a bit of a mishmash really, he thought he was talking to his wife Catherine and something about his son.' Rachel sighed. 'I don't know maybe it makes sense but I'm not sure I'm the one who can work it out.'

'He may have just been dreaming, or coming out of one. They often do at this early stage of recovery. Anyway chin up it's certainly a very good start. Come on let's go grab a cuppa tea, he's going to be asleep for quite a while now. And you need a change of scenery.' Noura suggested seeing the all to familiar look on Rachel's face of so many raw emotions bombarding her on all sides that she was being overwhelmed, even if she didn't realise it herself. 'Oh and don't forget that letter.' Noura added as she scooped up the loving note that had slipped from Rachel's grip while she slept and handed it back to her.

The night was fast approaching by the time Rachel found herself fumbling for the key to open up Noirmont, she felt dazed to the point of numbness, as if she been trapped in a perpetual spin cycle until the mechanism finally gave out. She could have quite easily dropped down into the nearest sofa and fallen asleep, had it not been for the professor's words still bouncing around just enough to keep her going. Whether it was a gut feeling or some other higher power guiding her, she did not know why she discovered herself standing in front of that particular section of a bookcase in the professor's study. Or for that matter out of all the books in that section, she seemed drawn to a small cluster part way along the central but one shelf. She pulled them off the shelf and unceremoniously swept some of the clutter straight off the desk and onto the floor to make room.

The first few were of very little help or significance. Rachel had already made the connection that the mumblings about Dionysus, must have been a reference to the Ancient Greek god, and although the volumes did indeed contain much about the ancient civilisation. They really only dealt with their political and social structures and nothing centred around the Olympians, their origins and myths, let alone Dionysus himself.

Having flicked through the last pages of the second she sighed in frustration and was in the process of picking up the third when a handful of loose pages slipped from the book onto the floor. Scooping them up she glanced at them to find a page number to return them to their rightful place in the book only to discover that they weren't part of the book at all, instead they were another hand written letter by the professor. And she was immediately sucked in by the story contained within:

Dear Jamie,

By the time you read this you will be old enough to understand its significance. I can only hope that it is not too late in the day and that there is still time to do what must be done. You were so small when I made my greatest discovery and so for your own protection it was decided not to tell you about it until the time was right. There are many myths surrounding the Liber Veritatis, and I have myself been taken down many a wrong path. This will not lead you directly to the Codex itself, but it will point you in the direction of that which holds the key.

Long before the destruction of Troy, and the songs of the glories of heroes now made legend; the Codex was broken. The labours of Gods and Men, I sing, across land and sea they bore the burden of knowledge so great that the natural balance between the heavens and the earth would break. From lands deserted they did depart, with good intent the brave of heart sought to remove the seeds of envy. Yet for all their efforts they could not escape a cursed hand and twist of fate. I know not all that passed. Yet that which I do, I now impart. A tale of woe and great sadness, of ill-fated travellers and vengeful gods, of scheming kings and shattered dreams.

In fairest Athens this doth begin. For a challenge by Zeus, Athena did win and claim their favour above another. With dented pride and battered ego, Poseidon's everlasting hate did rile deep inside. And so it was that this course was set, long before our brave souls were met:

Poseidon watched as the Sumerians boarded a small fleet of Athenian ships at Tyre, plotting his revenge while they sailed across the Levantine Sea, as they reached the Strait of Kasos, Poseidon rose from the deep pools of his great watery halls and brandishing his trident aloft, called out to Aeolus, Keeper of the Winds sitting in his high citadel to unleash the great winds upon the ships carrying the Sumerians and their treasure in order to drive them onto the rocks.

Aeolus replied: 'But why, O great King, what have this race of men done to cause such great offence?'

To this Poseidon responded: 'They have chosen to cross me by aligning, and lavishing great gifts of wisdom upon those who spurned and cast me aside by favouring the Goddess Athena as their patron. If it is wisdom that they desire then let her bestow it upon them. Overwhelm and chase their ships in all directions. Strike them onto wretched shores and scatter their bodies across the seas. Do me this service and I shall grant you free passage to come and go across my oceans as you please. To whip up the waters or to becalm them at your leisure.'

'That would be a great honour indeed, but why O mighty King, who has the power of all the oceans at his command, does thou ask this of me?' Aeolus enquired, perplexed as to why the all powerful father of the seas did not just summon Scylla and Charybdis to tear the tiny fleet of ships apart and damn their souls to an eternity in Tartarus.

'The dispute for Athens was settled by a challenge from Zeus. As such my hand

cannot be seen in this. To go against my brother would be to tear Olympus in two. But you have no such restriction.'

'As you command. Your right, my King, is to convey your wishes. Mine is to honour and obediently enact your orders.' And with these words Aeolus struck his mighty sceptre against the craggy mountainside, from deep within the vast caverns the winds seemed to swirl and writhe into a column and pour out from the open gates to blow a hurricane over the entire Earth.

In whichever direction the terrified sailors turned; death starred back. In desperation the Athenian crew called out pleading for their patron to deliver them from utter ruin.

Athena, meanwhile, observed the tumultuous upheaval of the oceans by these airs so foul. And yet she knew that it was not within her jurisdiction to quell the vicious uproar as she could not wield the trident that knows no pity. Nevertheless emboldened by a burning desire to protect the innocent and uphold justice she snatched up her shield, spurring on her horses she drove her chariot headlong into the maelstrom.

Restraining the most powerful waves as she skimmed the crests with her chariot wheels and deflecting the surging winds with her golden shield, the noble goddess sheltered the storm tossed ships to the nearest landfall, the safe harbour of Heraklion on the isle of Crete.

Having been outflanked by Athena, Poseidon enraged that the Sumerians had survived Aeolus's onslaught, commanded Morpheus to weave bad omens of death and destruction into the dreams of the Cretan king. That night while Minos slept soundly, the God of Dreams stole into his bedchamber, casting a nightmare in which strangers from the east beset by a storm, landed at his fair city of Heraklion. They came with sweet honeyed words of peace and friendship, but in fact had been on their way to deliver on object of great knowledge and power to Athens, an object that the Athenians would use to wage war on Crete and tear down his great Palaces.

Minos awoke as the sun broke revealing the devastation from the storm. At first he thought nothing of the dreams that had so tormented his sleep, until a messenger arrived from the port to announce that five Athenian ships from Tyre carrying men from the east had been forced to seek shelter in the harbour. Their ships badly damaged required repair and that the Sumerians offered great riches and the hand of friendship if Minos would set their ships to right and enable them to continue on their way.

Wary of the warning contained within the dream Minos responded to the messenger: 'Go with all haste to these weary travellers, extend to them every courtesy and aid that they require. And tell them that they are invited to the palace this very night as my guests.'

'As you command, my King.' Replied the messenger, departing as fast as his

legs would carry him down to quayside. Meanwhile, Minos plotted and schemed. For the Cretan king had no intention of allowing these men to ever leave his shores alive. Once he had secured this great treasure for himself, he would dispatch these treacherous Sumerians to the Underworld.

That evening, Minos threw a sumptuous party in honour of the men from the east and their new found friendship, ensuring that their wine goblets were never empty. Full of wine and barely able to stand, the travellers accepted Minos's offer to sleep in the palace, and return to their ships the following day. Unbeknown to his guests, Minos had instructed his palace guard to put them all to the sword while they slept. Dispatching his finest assassins down to the ships to ensure that none of the Athenian crew that had stayed onboard to keep watch survived. By the time the cock began to crow the palace's great hall was as crimson as the sky above and the Sumerians' treasure was his.

Intoxicated by this new found power Minos boasted that even the gods would now have to answer whatever prayer he offered them. Dedicating the first altar to Poseidon, whose waves had delivered this great prize to him, he prayed that a great bull might emerge from the sea. Poseidon smiled, not only had his plan to destroy the Sumerians been for filled but Minos recognised the god's part in his new found power. At once, a dazzling white bull, sent by the father of the oceans, swam onto the shore. However, Minos was so taken by the beauty of the beast that instead of sacrificing it upon the altar, he sent the great bull to become part of his own herd and slaughtered another in its place. Poseidon was once again enraged that a mere mortal insolently presumed that the extent of their power was now so great that they no longer needed to honour and pay homage to the Gods. In order to punish such foolish vanity, Poseidon summoned Aphrodite.

'O great Goddess, wilt thou help to avenge the dishonour shown to me by this conceited king. If it is beauty that he covets more than any other, then wouldst thou cast thy spell upon his fair queen? So that she spurns the sanctity of their wedded bed in favour of the beast he dared to keep. Instead of a handsome masculine heir, may his firstborn be a monster; half man, half beast. To act as a cruel reminder that no mere mortal will ever rule above our golden thrones.

'If this be your wish O great king, then so be it.' Aphrodite replied. So it came to pass that the goddess of love weaved her spell and Minos's wife fell deeply in love with the magnificent bull that the Cretan king had sought to keep. But she was by no means the only goddess at work, for Athena too had kept a close watch on both Poseidon and Minos. The wisest of all the Olympians, seeing what Poseidon had set in motion sent Daedalus the great architect whom she herself had taught, to the queen. Daedalus constructed a great wooden bull in order that the queen would be safe from

Minos's wrath and carry out her lurid affair in secret. But this was not Athena's final plan, for she saw that in the birth of such a thing some good could come. She realised that Minos wracked by shame would attempt to hide his wife's offspring from the world.

And so it was that when the queen gave birth and Minos beheld the monster that had been created he instructed Daedalus to construct a great labyrinth underneath his palace in which the beast might live out its days. Dutifully the master craftsman diligently toiled to construct the complicated maze in which the beast could be housed without fear of it escaping into the kingdom. Exactly the way that Athena had foreseen. Using this to her advantage she visited Daedalus telling him of the great treasure of knowledge that Minos had stolen from the murdered Sumerians, warning him that whilst it remained in Minos's possession all of Athens was in grave danger. She persuaded him that in order to ensure peace, the Codex must be removed from the hands of men. Daedalus agreed and while he had free range inside the palace he snuck into the great treasury, stealing the Codex to hide it in the heart of the labyrinth, inaccessible to all men whilst the Minotaur still lived.

Upon discovering the Codex was missing Minos flew into an almighty rage, believing that somehow the Athenians must have discovered what he had done and contrived a way to retrieve it. At once he gathered his fleet and launched them against Athens.

The war dragged on for many years, and the Athenians were on the verge of being wiped out as Zeus sent a plague and famine to ravage the city in answer to Minos's prayers, but they overcame this be sacrificing four daughters of Hyakinthos at the tomb of the Cyclops Geraistos. The famine and plague were vanquished but the war continued to drag on. The Athenians learned from an oracle that the war would continue and eventually result in their destruction unless they paid whatever tribute Minos demanded.

Minos insisted that they return that which they had stolen from him, but they could not return what they did not have. So he issued them an ultimatum that until they returned what he believed they had stolen, seven young men and seven young maidens must be sent to Crete every year to be eaten by the Minotaur. Heeding the warning of the oracle with heavy hearts the Athenians agreed. And so it came to pass that every year seven young men and maidens were sent to Crete to meet their fate in the maze of the Labyrinth. That was until Theseus reunited with his father took it upon himself to become one of the sacrifices in order to slay the Minotaur.

So vainglorious was Minos that the king of Athens had resorted to sacrificing his own flesh and blood, he arrogantly proclaimed that should Theseus navigate his way out of the Labyrinth then Athens would not longer have to pay tribute. So blinded was Minos by his own arrogance that he was unaware that his daughter Ariadne was deeply enchanted by the heroism of Theseus, so much so that she felt that she must do all within her power to aid the young prince. She sought out Daedalus and together they conspired, not only to help Theseus by weaving a ball of golden thread but also to retrieve the Codex. That night Ariadne slipped silently into the cells, passing the golden thread to Theseus and telling him about the Codex hidden in the centre of the maze that had been the cause of all their woes.

The next day Theseus entered the Labyrinth, and as he turned a corner came face to face with the Minotaur, he battled with the monster for several hours and eventually slaughtered the beast severing its head from its body. In his triumphant haste to be reunited with his love he forgot to retrieve the Codex. Needless to say so great was the victorious confusion as Theseus reappeared from the maze that he and Ariadne managed to flee from the city and set sail for Athens.

But they were never destined to be together; tired and hungry they made land fall on the Isle of Naxos and as they slept, Theseus was visited by Athena who told him that the Island belonged to Dionysus and that he must return to Athens leaving Ariadne behind for the god. It was during her despair at the betrayal by Theseus that the god, Dionysus took Ariadne to be his bride gifting her a dazzling Argyroupolean silver crown engraved with the legend of the Codex and set with gems fallen from the heavens themselves. Upon her death many years later Ariadne's crown was returned from whence it came.

Jamie, I am sure you will know where to find it, my greatest discovery lying with my greatest treasure. I can only hope that she and the fates are smiling favourably upon you.

Your loving Father.

'I'm sure he does. But that doesn't help the rest of us.' Rachel muttered. 'And who's this she? The cat's mother?' A spark of realisation surged through Rachel mind as the words left her lips. It was James's mother, as she recalled the letter she had read in the hospital. It was so obvious now and yet it had been so unclear hours ago. The thought hadn't even crossed Rachel's mind at the time that she might be involved. James had rarely spoken of his father and it had been very evident whenever he did that they were not on the best of terms, nevertheless he had featured. Whereas there had never been a mention of his mother, which in itself was strange. Normally the two people that one is raised by and who share the deepest of bonds are mentioned at some point or another and yet his mother was distinctly absent. Rachel wondered what could have happened to cause James to have carefully enamelled her out of his story.

Any hint of Rachel's exhaustion had been swept away with the sudden stream of adrenaline now coursing through her veins. Yanking every one of the drawers out of the professor's mahogany desk down onto the study floor she began rifling through all that which was contained within, searching in vain for anything that might shine a light through the shadows, but nothing; just boxes of spare keys, the odd battery, a battered corkscrew, old chequebook stubs and countless felt tip pens long since dried up from years of disuse. The only thing that stood out wasn't in the drawers but on the desk itself; a small bronze statue of a British soldier, steadfastly readying his bayoneted rifle to defend his charge, come what may, upon which hanging from the bayonet was a small key on pewter fob with ESLM 77 stamped into the soft metal. Rachel found herself being drawn towards the key, what was it about this particular key that set it apart from being treated like all the others? She scoured the house, trying every lock that she could find but to no avail. Eventually she gave up, returning to the study she reunited the key with its custodian and set about tackling the diaries on the shelves, flicking through them and tossing them aside when they revealed nothing. Suddenly she stopped, as soon as she saw the words on the page, Rachel understood.

James must have been about seven, when his mother had passed. Retracing the diaries that she had been so quick to discard Rachel learnt of Catherine's short but agonising battle with cancer, everyday had been a living hell and then one day as quickly as it had arrived, in the snap of one's fingers it had departed taking Catherine with it. Rachel forced down a lump in her throat. So caught up in the hunt, that she had forgotten the human cost. *How much time had the professor lost searching for a mythical book that decades later he was still no closer to finding; time that he could have spent by her side. And now James, how many more would there be?* Rachel wondered. None of them were superheroes, just your average Joe on the street caught up in something that she still didn't fully comprehend.

Rachel cried herself to sleep that night.

Chapter Twenty-Eight: Ariadne's Corona

The sound of the door knocker dragged Rachel back from her tormented sleep. Rubbing her tear stained tired eyes she composed herself to greet whoever it might be that had roused her from the dreams that had been so vivid and relentless in harrowing her through the night. Still dressed in her night clothes she crossed the hallway and opened the door.

Although Rachel hadn't seen her cousin since she was a small girl, Rachel instantly recognised Ms Sharpe from Chris's description and having been trying to cope for so long on her own Rachel could hold back her raw emotions no longer, breaking down into a flood of tears; more out of joy that there was now somebody to shoulder the burden she had found herself with than from despair. Instinctively Ms Shape dropped her travelling case she was holding and swept Rachel up in a loving embrace.

'Oh Cousin, come here. Looks like I've arrived just in time. Had Christopher told me more about the situation I would have been here weeks ago. I shall be having words with him. Absolutely criminal to leave you here all by yourself. Right come on, I know exactly what you need.' Ms Sharpe said, as she retrieved her case from the step and in a motherly fashion set about putting Rachel's world to rights.

By the time Rachel joined Ms Sharpe in the kitchen after taking a long hot bath at her cousin's insistence she was beginning to feel like herself again. A feeling she now realised had been missing for weeks.

'I can see that's done you a world of good. Now how about a nice cup of tea and you can tell me all about what's been going on.' Ms Sharpe said.

'Thanks, I do feel like the weight's beginning to lift. I don't think I appreciated how much of a toll the last few months had taken until I saw you on the door step. I must have just tried to put everything surrounding James to the back of my mind rather than dealing with it and it's just been festering there every since.' Rachel replied with a deep sigh as she mentioned James by name. 'I miss him terribly, there seems to be a massive void where he had been and I think what hurts the most is that I never got to tell him how I really felt and of course now I never will.' She added holding back the tears as the memories of the man she had begun to fall for resurfaced.

'Of course, I feel for you. But in a way at least you hadn't been more involved and to be honest I'm not sure it would have been a great idea. His lifestyle and the risks surrounding it would have always been ever present and I think if your relationship had developed it would have always had the potential to end in tears. But I wouldn't have wished for this outcome. How's his father?' A scowl briefly rippled across Rachel's brow at the insinuation that somehow she was better off, but she didn't have the energy to muster a rebuke and moved onto the subject of the professor's health.

'He's beginning to show signs of recovery, which is remarkable. But it's early days so we'll have to see just how far that goes. And then at some point bridge the subject of James. Couldn't really tell him while he was still in a coma, and something I'm not really looking forward to, whenever the right time comes, if there ever is such a thing.'

'Yes, I think it might be best to leave that for Christopher when he resurfaces. Better coming from him I think. After all he was James's closest friend and knows the professor very well. Speaking of Peter, how are you getting along with his journals? I remember being shown some of them and thinking that if they were ever needed, he better still be around to decipher them otherwise Hell may as well open the gates.' Ms Sharpe remarked.

'Oh they're a nightmare, every individual page takes so long and even when you do finally get somewhere with them, they're so cryptic. I have just found something but I'm not sure I can get any further with it, I was hoping Chris might know something.' Rachel replied.

'He might but I expect it's a long shot. What is it?' Asked Ms Sharpe.

'Oh, a letter about a piece of jewellery the professor gave to his late wife.' Rachel said.

'That wouldn't be Ariadne's Corona he gave to Catherine by any chance?' Mr Sharpe enquired.

'Yes, how do you know about that? Until I'd come across the letter, I'd never even considered that she would be a part of this twisted web.' Replied Rachel.

'Well you must remember I've known them a lot longer than you and it did come up in conversation but I must admit he failed to mention it's significance. I'm now presuming that it does hold some.' Ms Sharpe mused.

'Very much so, from what I understand it may reveal the location to a part of the codex. I don't suppose he told you what happened to it? All the letter says is that James would know where to find it.' Rachel said.

'Well, actually I do as I was here when Catherine's wishes were carried out.' Ms Sharpe replied, as she vividly recalled the day in her mind's eye.

'Well that explains what he meant by his greatest discovery now lying with his greatest treasure. But please don't tell me we've got to dig up his wife.' Rachel exclaimed at the thought of having to dig up yet another body.

'Oh no it's nothing as sinister as that. Luckily she wasn't buried, as it was her wish to be cremated, I was here when she was set in her final resting place with the corona. It is on the property, but it's still not going to be easy to retrieve. Had I known how important it was I would have counselled against it. But I'm sure he had his reasons.' Ms Sharpe said.

'So where is it?' Asked Rachel.

'It will be easier to show you than to describe it.' Ms Sharpe replied, rising from her seat. 'I hope you're in the mood for a few more cryptic puzzles.' She added as Rachel followed her out of the kitchen and into the study.

'If I'm not ready by now then I doubt I ever will be.' Rachel replied as she watched Ms Sharpe remove some books from a corner of the bookcase before retrieving the key from the battle hardened soldier.

'So that's what it's for. You can't begin to imagine how long I spent the other day searching for the lock to fit that key. I knew it was important.' Rachel said.

Ms Sharpe didn't reply directly to Rachel's statement just sighed, closing her eyes as she muttered the words *Ego sum lux mundi* under her breath, then scribbled a line onto a scrap of paper which she stuffed into her pocket before turning the key to unlock what Rachel had always assumed was part of the bookcase. Only that is wasn't a bookcase at all but a door that swung back to reveal a flight of stone steps descending deep down below the house.

'From here on out the only key is knowledge.' Said Ms Sharpe as she descended a little way into the darkness to flick a light switch. A wavy line of bulbs warmly illuminated a long passageway stretching far off into the distance, disappearing into the darkness round a bend in the tight tunnel. Rachel strained her eyes trying to gauge the length of the passage, but to no avail, for all she knew it could go on forever.

'How far is it?' She asked curious as to how much time they might have to spend down there.

'Oh god knows, I think one part goes as far as the point, the island's resistance were in the process of tunnelling up to the bunker built by the Nazi's occupying forces, but I'm not sure if they completed it before the armistice was signed, not that we are going as far as that nevertheless it's probably a good kilometre or so if one takes into account all of the twists and turns. The distance isn't the problem, it's all the traps and puzzles along the way that make this a rather perilous journey.' Ms Sharpe replied emphasising the danger posed by various boobytraps that lay inside the tunnel. 'So make sure you have your wits about you, they won't give you a second chance.'

'Why were they created? If they were going to use it to attack the battery, would it not have been safer without the traps?' Asked Rachel.

'Oh I wish these had been put in by the locals, alas no, James and his father installed most of these, there might be the odd remnant from the occupation but the vast majority are much more potent than what they could manufacture in the 40s.'

'Great, just what I need, a love that can reach out and kill me from beyond the grave.' Rachel muttered as she descended the dull stone steps in pursuit of her companion.

They encountered a series of locked doors along the rocky passageway, each with its own Machiavellian puzzle to solve in order to disarm and unlock the next section. They had just safely bypassed the sixth device placing thirty pieces of silver onto a set of scales to balance out the statuette of the *Judas Tree* on the other side, as Rachel began to wonder how many more of these traps there would be before they reached their goal, and what would happen if they got one wrong.

The passageway that had been running level for quite sometime suddenly dived deeper into the earth, gradually widening out into a small antechamber, dimly lit with Gothic lights hanging from the walls. Between them and the door on the far side lay a chess set on a small circular table accompanied by a chess clock, and a single walnut chair sat empty in waiting on a steel pressure plate.

'This is it, this is the last one before you get to where Catherine lies.' Ms Sharpe said noting that the chess clock unusually only had one dial with four seconds remaining on its face, just enough time if one was already on one's feet to reach the door. Rachel was about to sit down and play out the game when Ms Sharpe grabbed her back.

'Wait, stop.' She said noticing the brass plaque fixed to the table in front of the board engraved with a curious poem.

> *A broken crown for the battle ground,*
> *American Beauty checked her mate,*
> *And with one step; sealed her fate.*

Ms Sharpe picked up the black queen moving it from c3 to g3 and pressed the clock's button, as the circuit's connection was made the magnetic lock on the door buzzed open; but as soon as she removed her finger the lock re-engaged as the hand of the clock halted with just three seconds remaining.

'So be it, Peter.' She sighed in a low whisper, as the significance of Frank Marshall's famous game finally dawned on her, before turning to Rachel. There was a glint of sadness in her smile as she took Rachel by the hand. 'I'm afraid this is where we must part, cousin. I can go no further, that is not my destiny. Promise me you will see this through. And whatever you do, don't look back. Now run!' Ms Sharpe commanded pushing the note and the key from the study firmly into Rachel's hand.

'But I don't understand.' Rachel replied in bewilderment as Ms Sharpe sat down at the table.

'You don't need to understand. Now run, child. For god sake run!' She shouted as she held down the clock's button unlocking the door, and the timer resumed its count down. Rachel didn't wait to be told a third time, as soon as the lock was released she ran and burst through the door, reaching it just as the ceiling of the antechamber exploded. The lights in the tunnel flickered and went out. Everywhere around her shook; rock, stone and earth tumbled down sealing the room behind her. Once again she was alone in the darkness.

Rachel had no notion of how long she sat huddled tightly wrapped up with her arms around her knees; the rough stone wall digging awkwardly into her back, but she didn't care. She no longer cared about that or anything else. Her fragile world had just imploded.

The rubble now filling the antechamber behind her shifted slightly breaking the deafening silence, and as the spasmodic flickering of the lights returned she remembered the note and key still clenched tightly in her fist.

Ego sum lux mundi. I am the light of the world. Translating the Latin phrase in her head. Somehow, whether it was the phrase itself or the return of actual light in the tunnel, she caught hold of the glimmer of hope. She couldn't stay here and she couldn't go back, the only way was forwards. Now that most of the dust had settled she could make out a great stone archway carved right at the very end of the passageway. *That must be it,* she thought as she wiped her tear stained muddy face, putting the key on its fob into her pocket, and easing herself up from where she sat.

The chamber she found herself in was not what she had expected as she walked under the arch. There was no great pomp or ceremony or flashiness of any kind, just a simple stone alter block still in its roughly hewn form in the centre of the room, Ariadne's corona in all its splendour delicately resting on the stone top with the urn containing Catherine's ashes set inside the silver crown. Apart from a small alter upon which stood a globe of ceramic and metal bands, at its heart a pure white candle with red numerals, at the far side of the room. There was nothing else, not even a door. *Not even a door,* she thought. *Am I the beneficiary of some cruel joke. To lose so much and yet find what I seek only to be trapped within the earth somewhere between the heavens and hell. No, there must be a way. Professor, you must have known that there would come a time when this would be needed. But that tunnel was always going to be destroyed, so you must have another way. Think, nothing has face value with you. There is always something hidden.*

Rachel walked all the way round the stone block in the centre inspecting every little defect, and found nothing, so she turned her attention to the small alter and the globe. But again there didn't seem to be any significance, certainly no mechanism that would open a secret door. *What about the walls, maybe there's some stone I need to press like at Yaxhá.* She was about halfway round feeling every stone as she went when she suddenly stopped. *Two sevens,* thinking about the red numerals on the candle. *Two sevens, where else have I seen two sevens? Not on the note nor the key. But wait the fob. The Fob!* The thought exploding in her head as she quickly scrabbled around in her pocket for the key. Turning the fob over in her hand, there they were the two sevens at the end of the engraving. She hurried back to the alter. There must be something she'd missed. *But what? What's the relevance? What does a candle, a globe and two sevens have in common? No there's got to be something else. What about the letters? There weren't just numbers on that flat piece of metal.*

The instant her eyes lit upon them she knew. E.S.L.M weren't a person's initials as she had first thought. They were an acronym of the Latin phrase Ego Sum Lux Mundi, and that key and fob, weren't just a key and fob, they were also a flint and striker. Which meant that ceramic on the globe wasn't there for decoration. Striking the key against the fob, as the sparks flew out, the candle burst into flame and Rachel pivoted, running in the opposite direction and snatching up the corona as she leapt over the granite block to the safety on the other side, landing just as the ceramic charge of the explosive detonated shattering a section of the rock wall behind the alter.

Daylight; she'd never been so happy to see daylight. The only question now was with all that underground tunnelling *Where the fuck was she? She couldn't still be under the house.* As she neared the boundary between fresh and stale air, the sound of crashing water could be heard below and she knew that she must be right on the coast. In fact she wasn't just on the coast, the section she'd blown out was part of the cliff face. *Bastards!* She thought as she slung her arm through the crown, pushing it as far up as possible and began to climb.

Chapter Twenty-Nine: The Treasures in Tea

Chris was just finishing his breakfast when he heard the familiar sound of wheels pulling up on the rough ground outside the cabin.

'Juan, they're here. The rest of you stay put and be ready to jump in if things don't go to plan' He called out, waiting for the tech guru to join him before they both strolled out into the bright sunlight of a new day to greet the black-market suppliers they'd contacted to procure the necessary equipment for their trip up to Mount Hua.

'Morning gentlemen, I trust you managed to find everything we requested.' Chris said shaking hands with the man who was clearly in charge.

'I think you will find everything you asked for.' The man replied.

'Excellent, I believe fifty was the agreed amount.' Chris replied half expecting the man to suddenly jack the price up.

'It was and we're throwing in the jeep, we thought you and your friends may find it useful.' The man replied with an amicable smile.

'Very generous of you, thank you. I'm sure if it is as reliable as your reputation then we've got just the job for it. If I can just make a quick inspection to check everything is up to scratch then I think we'll be able to conclude our business.' Chris said giving a nod to Juan to go and get the briefcase with payment while he glanced over the merchandise.

'Everything looks in order.' Chris said glancing up to see Juan returning with a metallic case. Flipping it open on the bonnet of the lead jeep he turned it towards the men.

'Fifty thousand as agreed, plus an extra twenty bonus as we understand one of the items was a little more difficult than expected to get hold of.'

'Most generous, it's been a pleasure doing business with you. Oh and gentlemen, don't hesitate to reach out if you need anything else.' The man replied, swirling his index finger in the air to indicate that it was time to wrap things up.

'Of course, nice to finally put a face to the name.' Chris replied as the man jumped into the second jeep and left. 'Right people I think it's time we get moving too. Grab your kit and let's get going.' Chris said eager to hit the road for the long journey up into the Qin mountains.

The dusk was fast approaching by the time they reached the base of the mountains. The peaks high up above bathed in the warm tranquil glow of the evening sun kept watch over the sacred valley. As much as Chris wanted to set out up the slopes he thought it would be wiser to make camp and set out at first light, nothing worse than hiking up unknown treacherous paths in the dark, one foot in the wrong place on unstable ground and a deep crevice could swallow you whole.

Gaz and Ollie found a secluded copse away from the main road and set about erecting a couple of tents which had been supplied by the Chinese dealers. There was an electric sense of anticipation akin to the feeling of thunder in the air rippling through the camp for what was about to take place, and yet there was also an air of dread. A sluggish heaviness, a lingering feeling that not all was as it seemed. There was little banter that night, everybody seemed to be wrapped up in their own thoughts. And yet all had a singular goal, come what may.

As the first rays of the new day sun brushed the fringes of the tents they woke and set about packing up. Throwing the sleeping gear back into the jeep ready for when they hoped to return later that night. The smell of burning meths from the Trangia stove Ollie had set up wafted through the air around where their camp had been.

'Long time since we've had sausages out of a can, hey boss.' He remarked to Chris as he tipped the lard covered sausages out of the tin, onto the hot frying pan.

'Yeah, now that takes me back.' Replied Chris suddenly being transported back to the wet wintry days of training up in the Brecon Beacons, waking up and hoping that in the ration pack lottery, he'd hit the jackpot. Always amazed him how some you could eat all day long whilst others even a starving dog might think twice about it.

'Which route were you planning on taking?' Devan inquired looking up from her phone with a google image of the routes up to the southern peak of Mount Hua.

'Via the West Gate, it's too early for the cable car and three thousand nine hundred and ninety-nine steps just does sound like fun.' Chris replied through a mouthful of his sausage sandwich.

'Argh boss, can't we just wait for it to start running? Ollie asked knowing full well what the reply would be.

'No, I didn't beast you through all those survival courses so you could just sit on your arse and float up a mountain. You're not here to take photos for your Tinder.' Chris snapped tossing him a custom Angstadt AR-9 from the cache in the jeep.

'Ah nice, if you got the Glock extended thirty three round mags as well, I'll run up that mountain.' Ollie exclaimed as he turned over the slick 9mm carbine in his hands inspecting the expert detailing and craftsmanship.

'Better get your running shoes out then.' Chris sarcastically replied throwing him a bundle of five extended mags before passing out its sisters to the others, he almost handed one to Devan but the glare on her face told him that he'd find better odds on the sun freezing solid before the archaeologist would start brandishing an assault rifle.

'Guessing this is definitely out of the question then.' He retorted lifting a H&K M320 out of a separate box.

'Now you're just showing off. I'd zip that away before it gets crushed if I was you.' She replied with the hint of a smile.

'Just no pleasing some people.' He said. 'Right lets get moving we've got a lot of ground to cover and I want to be at the base of that precipice before midday.' Chris said pointing up towards the lower part of a sheer cliff face, majestically rising out of the mountainside and vanishing into the eternal mist above.

Moving off they entered the mountain park via the West Gate above the Yuquan Temple crossing the aptly named Five Dragon Bridge and began to wind their way along the snake like trail through the richly populated forests until they reached the pavilion on the Shaluo Terrace.

'Looks as good as anywhere for a break.' Chris said as he unslung his rucksack and sitting down on the side of a large boulder shaped and smoothed by the unrelenting meteorological cycles over the millennia he stared out contemplating the serenity of such a place that had held firm in spite of the thousands of footsteps, from simple farmers to emperors, following the one true path in search of spirituality.

'Some tea here for you, boss.' Juan said passing him a small mug from his thermos filled with hot sweet tea.

'Cheers, here's to good friends and the path.' He said before adding 'Just another one of our age old traditions when out and about on the hills, hey boys.' He said taking a sip of the sugary liquid.

'For sure, can't have a good day on the hill without a brew.' Gaz replied grinning from ear to ear.

'Wouldn't have picked you lot as the superstitious type.' Devan commented.

'Hey considering some of the spots we've found ourselves in over the years we'll take all the help we can get won't we boys?' Chris replied.

'Never failed us yet has it, boss.' Ollie added.

'Careful, there's always a first time.' Chris replied with a lightness in his tone. 'Right I suppose we better crack on if we are to make our next waypoint.'

'Ah, just when I was starting to get comfy.' Ollie replied as he stretched out his arms, rolling his shoulders back before slinging his rucksack across his back and falling in behind the rest of the group that had already begun to re-establish their hiking rhythm.

The trail slunk its way ever steeper as they approached the next terrace bending off to the east before reaching the stairs hugging the mountainside that pushed ever skywards. Ollie had to crane his neck way back just to see any hint of the sky above. The stairs they found themselves on were so timeworn that they sloped towards the drop with only enough room for half a footstep and the only support were the chains running along either side of the vertical staircase, chiselled so high into the mountain that the top was still veiled in the mist.

'I told you we should have taken the cablecar.' Ollie stated as he weighed up the hazardous scene in front of them. One false step would send them tumbling off the cliff.

'Well we're not going back now. Onwards and upwards is the only option.' Chris replied glancing back down the path before grasping one of the chains and giving it a firm tug.

'Seems solid enough.' He said, not mentioning just how slippery and cold they felt between his fingers. There was no doubt in his mind that this was going to be a gruelling climb. 'Come on, you won't even notice the exposure once we get going.' He added reassuringly.

Maintaining their metronomic tempo they kept ploughing on step after step, hand after hand on the heels of the retreating mists, torturously the passage of time was prolonged by the icy burning from the chains biting deep into the bones of their fingers. Slowly, through the murkiness, two stone pillars flanking the route came into view. But where they expected to find the summit of this infernal staircase they found nothing but more steps climbing ever higher. They steeled themselves once more, matching their previous pace, their only comfort was the solidness of the stone walls enclosing the stairs, not enough to prevent a fall but just enough to offer the faintest of hope.

Juan momentarily made the mistake of looking back down the perilous precipice, teetering on a step's edge as he felt a wave of vertigo, only regaining his balance by firmly fixing his gaze back on the stairs ahead, suppressing his tension with a nervous laugh.

'Easy bud, I ain't going back down after you.' Ollie joked giving him a reassuring tap on his arm.

'Don't worry, my hands are so cold I don't think they'll come off this chain.' Juan replied through gritted teeth just as the final few steps at last came into view.

'Can I suggest we take the gondola on the way back.' Ollie puffed, as he rolled himself out onto an area of flat ground five or six paces away from the edge to catch his breath, only for his heart to sink once more as he realised that the granite monolith of Huashan stretching across the horizon, and towering several times above that seemingly endless staircase lay before him.

'Oh fuck that for a game of soldiers. Seriously boss, you trying to give me a heart attack. Tell you what, how about I watch our six from here and see you guys when you get back.' He groaned.

'It's not that bad, we've done the majority.' Devan said. 'Not like anybody's asking you to walk a plank, or anything. It's 3 or 4k max.'

'Well ,I don't know looks like a bitch to me. No offence, you know what I mean.' He replied.

'None taken, can quite clearly see who's the blouse around here. And I thought I was in the company of the elite, clearly I was mistaken.' She jokingly shot back.

'Hey boss, you gonna let her talk about us like that.' Ollie objected.

'Ha, you're on your own there mate, you dug it, you can fill it in. Here get this down ya.' Chris laughed, chucking Ollie a banana from his pack.

'Ah food, good point. I've got some sausages left over from breakfast in my bag somewhere.' Ollie suddenly remembered. 'That puts a far more positive spin on things.' He added nodding to himself as he ripped open the banana and settled down to munching his food as if the last few minutes had never happened.

'Is he always like that?' Devan softly asked Chris.

'Who, Ollie. Yeah it's kind of his thing. He has a gripe every now and again but he'll always be there, I think it's his kind of motivation. At the end of the day it works for him, so I'm not gonna start exploring the psyche behind it.' He replied as he tried to calculate how long he thought it would take to get up to the Southern peak.

He wouldn't say it in public but privately he shared part of Ollie's concern over the arduous terrain. Not it's difficulty but the time it would take, if they couldn't find a way to up the pace then they could well be coming back down in the dark.

'What are you thinking about?' Devan asked snapping Chris back from his thoughts. 'You've got that look.'

'What look?' He asked.

'That serious look, a look that there might be an immovable object on the horizon.' Devan replied.

'It's nothing, just wondering how many sausages that boy can eat before he bursts.' He replied steering the subject away from his concerns, as Ollie crammed his sixth into his mouth.

'Yeah, he must have hollow legs for sure.' Devan laughed.

'Ol, you have anymore and you'll be rolling up that mountain.' Chris said taking another sip of tea.

'I wonder what that man Norwood and his cronies are up to.' Devan said as she admired the mountain.

'Nothing good I suspect, they may well be around here somewhere. After all if they were after the scroll in the Vatican then one can only assume that they were on the trail of the same piece.'

'But how would they know where to find it without the professor's clues?' She asked.

'Well one does wonder how the professor discovered it in the first place? It's only logical that there were other shreds of information that led the Prof here all those years ago. One can only hope that he did a good job of covering up his trail.' Chris replied. 'Right I think we better get moving again.' He added as he rose and began packing away the remnants of his lunch before they set out for the Southern peak.

Chapter Thirty: The Professor's Assistant

Dr Dillon Hart sat at the bar of the Dongfeng Hotel, sipping a tall glass of bourbon. He couldn't believe that it had been almost five months since those disastrous events at the Vatican had pretty much destroyed his career and turned his life upside down. And all over woman, a woman that never seeing again was already too late.

It hadn't been long after he'd returned home from the papal seat, that the rumours started to circulate and one by one colleagues and historical societies stopped calling, even his London club blackballed him. By mid February he'd found himself staring at a bottle of pills, but something held him back from tipping the whole lot down his throat. The faintest of notions that if he could just find the *Black Dragon Seal Scroll* and prove his innocence, all would be forgiven and he could move on with his life. He'd spent weeks after that trawling the internet, as he'd been banned from most archives by that point, looking for anything to do with the scroll, but he found nothing. In the end he gave up and began picking back through all the notes he'd ever made on it, he remembered that during his research he had found a myth about the Prince of Gui and the scroll, something about an artefact belong to the Yellow Emperor, hidden in the mountains somewhere. At the time it had all sounded like something out of the wuxia genre of films than tangible fact and he'd quickly discarded it to focus on the Vatican connection. But maybe there had been something to it, by this point his reputation was already in tatters, so what more could he lose by chasing fairytales. Finally he made the connection between Mount Hua and the Yellow Emperor last week and without another thought he was on a flight out to China and now sat within a kilometre or two of what he hoped would be his salvation.

'Well hello handsome, fancy meeting you here.' Said a voice behind him. A voice he'd hoped he would never hear again. He flushed a murderous crimson as he turned to face her.

'You! What did I ever do to deserve you. You ruined my life, my work! Everything!' He bellowed at her.

'Oh come now babe, that's no way to greet a lover.' Carla replied with such tenderness that her honeyed words almost ensnared him once more.

'Harpie!' He cried. 'I'm not falling for you again. You'll return what you stole. You have no idea what you've put me through, how long I was in the Vatican being integrated by the Swiss Guard over that scroll. I want it returned. Give it to me. Now.'

'Shhh babe, you're disturbing the other guests.' She replied. 'You can have your precious scroll, for all the good it will do. I did you a favour. It was a fake, if I hadn't have taken it, you'd still be chasing your tail amongst all the other historical trash in the Vatican.'

'What do you mean it's a fake. It can't be. God, you really are something, aren't you. Even now after all that you did, you can't be honest. You'll say anything to save your skin.' He said raising his voice again.

'I promise you it's the truth.' She said throwing what remained of the parchment at him. 'It was stolen weeks before we were there, by Professor Middleton, no less. Ha, look at you a fool so blinded by misplaced reverence that they can't see the man for what he truly was, a sham. I pity you.' She replied finally dropping her sweet facade.

The accusation that a man he held in such high esteem was in fact a thief rocked Dillon, momentarily lost for words as he tripped over a myriad of questions. He just sat there stunned.

'The only thing you can do now is help us find the temple visited by the Prince of Gui.' She said taking advantage of his bewilderment.

'Us?' He questioned, looking her straight in the face.

'Yes, my friends and I. We've learnt that he visited a temple on the mountain but we don't know exactly where it is. But I bet you do, you wouldn't be here if you didn't. I bet that beautifully inquiring mind of yours worked it out.' She said gently massaging his bruised ego.

'Ha nice try, you've got a nerve asking me that. I wouldn't help you or your friends for all the tea in China.' He replied spitting on the ground by her feet.

'Oh honey, you're so cute. But I wasn't really asking.' She calmly replied slipping a thin knife from her sleeve and digging it in between his ribs just enough that he got the point.

'Well, I see I don't really have a choice do I? Very well Milady, but if you think things are over between us you are very much mistaken.' She could see in his face that his resolve was firm, and knew that she would have to dispose of him as soon as he'd outlived his usefulness.

'Ah darling.' She said as Lord Norwood arrived in the bar. 'This is the professor from Rome I was telling you about, such a lovely coincidence bumping into him here. Really is a small world isn't it? And he's kindly offered to take us to the temple.' Carla said casually introducing Dillon as if they were old friends.

'Well, I wouldn't go that far…' Dillon started to say before he felt the tip of the blade press a little harder against his flesh. '…But how could I say no, she can be very convincing when she wants to be.' He added gritting his teeth.

'Yes, it's one of her most attractive qualities. Pleasure to finally put a face to the name, professor. I'd always hoped I would get a chance to meet the man that had kept her so entertained and thank him for being so attentive. Now darling, as long as you and the professor here have settled everything I think we really ought to be making tracks, don't you?' Norwood said glancing at his watch.

'I think we've come to an understanding.' She smiled as she replied, taking hold of Dillon's elbow with her free hand and escorting him out of the bar to join the rest of Norwood's men waiting just outside the lobby.

'Hey can I at least get my boots and a jacket before we set off. These aren't exactly designed for rough terrain.' Dillon protested pointing at his leather soled brogues in an attempt to delay their departure.

'No, I've wasted enough time here already.' Norwood sternly replied. 'Leach, give him your jacket.' He added completely ignoring the look of grievance spreading across Mr Leach's face. Nevertheless the man didn't voice his objection, he knew better than to air his feelings in public and begrudgingly removed the down jacket handing it to Dillon.

Closely flanked on either side by two muscular forms Dillon led them away from the hotel, taking the path towards the Sunshine Welcoming Cave leaving one of the twin towers of Yanggong to disappear into the swirling mist behind them. Dillon was thankful that at least they hadn't encountered him at the West Gate, there was no way in his grip-less shoes he would have managed to safely navigate the infamous Thousand Foot Precipice let alone the scaliness of the Black Dragon Ridge. *Two Kilometres*, he kept reminding himself, *it's only two kilometres, you've got this*. It was all he could do to keep his mind focused while he tried to work out where he might be able to give them the slip. That was the other problem of not having decent boots, he was just as likely to trip and screw himself over in a hasty bid for freedom as he was just doing what he was told. *Talk about being stuck between a rock and a hard place*. He thought to himself as he continued leading them, slipping and sliding on the loose stony ground with almost every other step he took towards the Southern peak.

Chapter Thirty-One: The Battle for Heaven's Gate

The Thousand Foot Precipice and the jagged ridge along Canglong's steep back had certainly proved challenging but they paled into insignificance compared to the severity of the *Sky-plank Walk* facing Devan and her companions. Constructed from narrow beams laid end to end that looked like they'd been stripped from the Ark, precariously stapled and lashed to metal piles sunk deep into the cliff. A hand line, part chain, part rope was the only guide to help them traverse across the hundred and thirty meter gantry that majestically jutted out into the open air seven thousand feet above the ground.

'Boss, you sure this is the right way?' Ollie enquired leaning out over the first plank and peering down at the ant like tourists in the valley far below that had it not been for their number would have been indistinguishable from the earth around them. A gust of wind caught him and he clung onto the chain as hard as he could.

'Yeah, we'll be fine once we get passed the toe holds.' Chris replied.

'What, what do you mean toe holds? Are you telling me this matchstick doesn't go all the way? That's just gnarly. Those ancient Chinese must've been on some serious poppy when they came up with this one.' Ollie replied psyching himself up for what was sure to be a massive rush of adrenaline. 'Can I suggest if we're going to do this, we better get cracking. Looks like there's a bit of a blow headed our way.' He remarked pointing to the patchy clouds on the eastern horizon racing towards them. 'I don't know about you lot but I don't fancy finding out how long it takes to hit the ground.' He added as another large gust buffeted him as he pulled himself back towards the rock face.

Chris was right, they hardly noticed the drop on the first section once they got moving, sidling inch by inch along the boards. It was only when they reached the end, where they were faced with a sheer descent down a tight ten meter crevice, that the feeling of being totally exposed hit them, with only the chains and a few so-called stairs, constructed out of rusty iron bars to support them.

The wind was increasing with every second, and by the time they reached the more familiar planks it was gusting force five, not just making the final stretch more challenging than the first but also difficult to communicate above the sound of the roaring wind.

Juan reached the far side first, he paused momentarily, stretching out a blind hand to feel out a safe route for the last few metres. Scrambling around an awkward boulder protruding from the crag and wedging himself tight into the crack, he turned.

'Here, grab my hand.' He shouted above the din, offering his outstretched arm first to Ollie then Devan and so on until at last they were all safely off the rickety wooden planks. Their destination, the Taoist temple nestled into a high outcrop, was at last in sight above them. Only one more flight of time worn steps lay between them and the golden Xie Shan roof capping the three storey temple resplendently shimmering in the last of the noonday sun.

'Well now I know how the Kung Fu panda felt. Fuck me that was a lot of steps.' Ollie jokingly said.

'Good thing you ran out of sausages, otherwise you'd look like him too.' Gaz retorted.

'Pfft, you're lucky this mountain's had the best of me otherwise your face'd look like a panda's.' Ollie responded to which they both couldn't contain their amusement any longer, laughing so hard that tears almost ran down their cheeks.

Two figures could just be made out standing guard at the doorway atop the temple steps, each dressed in deep blue silk robes embroidered with golden tigers and chrysanthemums, a Yan Yue Dao with a golden tassel at their sides.

'I hope they're for decoration. You could have someone's eye out with one of them if you're not careful.' Gaz jokingly said to one of the bearers just as he was about to pass, the stone faced figure didn't even crack a smile. But as Gaz took the step the two spears slammed down into a cross blocking his path.

'Well that's not very welcoming. So much for peace and harmony.' He said.

'Gaz, I don't think they'll let you in with your boots on. It's seen as a sign of disrespect.' Devan said nodding her head to a bench on the terrace with a neat row of shoes, accompanied by a bowl of water to wash their feet.

'Oh, sorry. My deepest apologies, I didn't mean to cause offence.' Gaz said to the guards, stepping back and walking over to the bench to remove his foot ware. 'They don't talk much do they.' He commented as he and the others unlaced their boots.

'They probably don't understand what you're saying.' Ollie replied standing up and making his own attempt to enter the temple. But once again the spears were slammed down barring the entrance.

'Now what?' He asked putting his face right up to one of the figures. 'Do you want the clothes off my back too?' But the stone faced figure just stared straight through him as if he wasn't even there.

Chris was about to ask one of them in Mandarin what was required of them to gain entry, when he heard a female voice in his head.

'This world has no need for weapons, only peace and tranquility have the highest value. Set aside those tools of fear and the path of serenity will be laid clear. *The Order of Pepin* has always been welcome here. This is the way.' He looked around to see who the words had come from but there was no one there, apart from the two figures who had remained silent.

'Leave the bags.' He commanded, deciding that the voice, whomever it had been was probably right.

'Boss, are you sure?' Ollie asked hesitantly glancing at the razor sharp blades at the ends of those long wooden staves.

'Yeah, I don't think we're in any danger here. Taoists don't believe in any form of violence and will only use weapons as an absolute last resort.' Chris replied, setting his pack down next to his boots.

'Okay, I'll take your word for it.' Ollie replied, doing the same.

This time the two silent sentries did not block their way, allowing the group to enter the temple. The large open space of the ground floor was broken only by the huge pillars, carved from sturdy Dawn Redwood trunks, supporting the floors above. From what Chris could see the temple had been hacked at least fifty feet into the rock as it was far larger on the inside than it appeared from the out. To the right there were a number of doorways, all closed except for one which appeared to lead down into a sunken garden at the side of the temple. They stood facing a wide staircase extending up to the next level, taking in the marvels of the sacred space.

'Wow these murals are truly amazing.' Devan remarked as the ornate artwork covering all the walls caught her eye. 'Such colour and depth, so captivating.'

'It is beautiful, isn't it? It is the story of the Yellow Emperor Gongsun Xuanyuan, that particular scene is of his death and final voyage across the

Bohai Sea to join the *Ba Xian.*' Said the voice of a woman descending the stairs accompanied by three other women. 'I am Chao-Xing. My sisters and I welcome you to the Temple of Huanglong.'

'The *Ba Xian* are the eight immortals in Chinese mythology that supposedly lived on the three mystical islands, Penglai, Fangzhang and Yingzhou in the Bohai Sea.' Devan explained catching the quizzical look on Ollie's face.

'We thank you, but how did you know of *The Order*?' Chris replied to the woman, who's voice he had heeded earlier.

'We are aware of all that happens here on the mountain, and it has long since been prophesied that sometime after the power of the emperors waned the greatest knight protectors of kings would one day return with the medallion to reclaim that which they bestowed to us.' Chao-Xing replied.

'Medallion? What medallion? The professor never mentioned a medallion.' Chris asked, his heart sinking at the revelation that after such a long journey they may not be able to retrieve the third part of the codex.

'The medallion of the Dragon Emperor. It was passed down from one emperor to the next until the fall of Zhu Youlang, the Prince of Gui and the Yongli Emperor of the Southern Ming Dynasty in 1662, after that only tales. There have always been two stories that intrigued us about what happened to it, the first that Zhu Youlang sent it to part of your *Order* around the time that his mother sent a request to the Vatican for aid in return for converting to Christianity. The other, that it was lost when his body parts were ripped apart and spread across the country by the Qing after his execution. Until thirty years ago we had always favoured that it had been sent directly to your *Order*, but then we were visited by a scholarly man wearing much the same ring as you now do, intent on reclaiming the text but he did not possess the medallion. He returned to whence he came in order to seek out that which was lost.

Only in the last few days has word reached us of a rumour that it had been seen in Dandong. We assumed that he had finally succeeded in his quest to rediscover the key of the Dragon Emperor and you were now here to take back that which has remained untouched. Without the medallion the text cannot leave this place. So if you do not have it, who does?' She asked.

'I cannot say for sure, although I fear that it may be in the possession of a very wicked man called Norwood. He and his brotherhood have been hellbent on reuniting all the pieces of the codex know to us as the *Liber Veritatis*. I assume you were aware that the text entrusted to you was part of something larger and that the whole is infinitely more dangerous than the sum of its parts.' Chris replied.

'The ancient travellers who arrived from the West with the text all those years ago, never mentioned that it belonged to something greater. But over the centuries it had been perceived that this was the case. All that the travellers conveyed was that they were no longer able to prevent it from falling into the hands of those that would use it to bring about great pain and suffering, and they felt that the emperor at the time was in a position to do this. Many of our Celestial Mistresses, including myself, have spent time in deep thought and meditation to gain further insight into the text but we always found the path was unclear; much uncertainty exists around what the text will bring and where the balance of the universe's scales will tip. The only thing that was not veiled in mist was that the text is destined to be given to whomever presents the medallion.' The Celestial Mistress replied.

'For the sake of all that you hold dear, I beg you not to give it to that man, if indeed he arrives with the medallion. Only death and destruction will follow. By all means keep it here but that man must not have it. If he takes it then all you and your sisterhood have done for centuries will have been for nought.' Chris pleaded urging her to choose another path.

'I cannot, that was never our fate. We are only the watchers and the keepers, the medallion chooses its own path and it is not for us to interfere.' There was no emotion in her words, just the cold logic that it was not for them to meddle with the balance of the universe.

Chris never had the opportunity to take the decision out of her hands and force the issue as a commotion outside tore the mistress's attention away from him.

Try as he might Dillon was unable to wrestle himself free of the two guards on the temple steps. His shirt was torn and a large gash on his forearm was angrily burning where he had shredded the skin when he'd taken advantage of Mr Leach's lapse in concentration. Upon reaching Heaven's Gate he'd made a dash for the narrow boards of the *Sky-plank Walk* realising that his kidnappers would be forced to pursue in a single file.

He'd made some gains until a lapse of his own had almost put an end to his bid for freedom. In his haste to put as much distance between himself and that of his captors those flat soled shoes had been on the brink of becoming far more expensive than he had anticipated. Their hard leather slipped like ice on the rough edge of a toe hold, with his heart in his mouth he'd grasped at anything to arrest his unintended downward demise until his outstretched forearm seared with a crushing pain having firmly wedged itself into a crack; abruptly breaking his oneway travel. How he'd managed not to lose more than a bit of skin was not worth thinking about as he scrambled up the last few steps only to be set upon by the temple guardians.

'Please I beg you, let me go. Please help me. Men, guns, come this way. Please they'll kill me!' Dillon screamed still trying to wriggle his way out of the women's firm grip.

'Release him.' The Celestial Mistress commanded as she surveyed the scene below the temple steps. 'Who are you? And what is your business here?' She asked turning her attention to Dillon who was now gathering himself up from the floor after the guards had dropped him.

'There's no time to explain. There are men with guns coming here to force you to hand over a scared artefact. They kidnapped me and forced me to lead them to the temple. Please they are not far behind. Sanctuary, that is all I ask for. They are sure to kill me for crossing them if they catch me.'

'Take him inside and secure the temple. And we shall see what these men want.' She said as Dillon was helped inside. 'Where are you going?' She asked as Chris passed her in the doorway.

'To do what must be done. You will neither stand in this man's way, nor will you allow us into the temple with arms. You may have the luxury to abstain, but I do not. Therefore I must forge my own path and settle this outside. This is my way.' He bluntly replied.

'As you wish.' Chao-Xing replied.

'Devan, stay with the Mistress. I think it may prove to be more beneficial for you to stay in the temple.' Chris suggested catching Devan by the hand as she made her way back to her boots.

'Nonsense, if I've leant anything by now, the safest place is wherever you are. Besides if they get past you, I don't think we'll be around for that much longer.' She replied.

'Your safety, although obviously a concern, is not why I think you'd be better inside. I was hoping you might be able to persuade her to change tack and get off the fence.' He replied as he slammed a magazine into his AR-9.

'Well I doubt that there's much I can say to shift centuries of stubbornness, but I'll see what I can think of. You just make sure you come back in one piece.' She replied squeezing his hand. Chris didn't reply he just winked at her with the hint of a boyish grin and darted off the terrace followed by the other three men, spreading out amongst the boulders and trees overlooking the uneven stairs which Norwood would surely have to climb to reach the temple.

Chris was just settling himself into a kneeling position using a large rock for cover, when he caught sight of the first man, soon followed by another, appearing round the awkward boulder at the end of the rickety planks. As easy as it would have been to pick the two off and then take out any more as they came around the corner, he was certain that as soon as the first fell whoever was still on the walkway would realise that they'd have to find another way. No, this time he'd make damn sure that Norwood wouldn't get the chance to survive another day.

Lord Norwood pulled himself round the last boulder, triumphantly surveying the scene. His final destination of the temple was in sight and even though Dillon had managed to escape, it no longer mattered. He would soon have the next part of the text and be one step closer to glory. Norwood was so entranced in his own self righteousness that he was blissfully unaware that he was about to walk straight into Chris's sights.

A wave of practiced calm flowed over Chris as he lined Norwood up, even with so much at stake, there wasn't a tense muscle in his body as he meticulously prepared his shot, blanking out everything else around him.

As he lightly squeezed the trigger a woman stepped in front of Norwood; the abrupt appearance of Carla in his sight caused him to flinch and at the very last moment he pulled his shot wide, the bullet slamming into the rock face a few inches to the left of his target. Everybody scattered, and what could have been the end was now just the beginning.

Immediately Chris swivelled and pealed off, from the rock he'd been using, to find a new position as Ollie laid down some cover fire. They had the advantage of higher ground although Chris knew that the numbers were stacked in Norwood's favour, this would be a battle of attrition. The less ground they gave up for every one of Norwood's men they downed the better the scales would become. Still it wasn't going to be easy he thought as he caught sight of two men trying to scramble round a ridge to the left of him, Juan got one before Chris had even brought his gun to bear, and the other made a hasty retreat. Norwood was nowhere to be seen, most likely hiding in a corner somewhere biding his time until he was assured he had the upper hand. Gaz and Ollie continued to take potshots every time one of Norwood's men poked their heads up with the idea of moving, it kept some of them at bay but there were just too many of them to prevent all of them from gradually reducing the distance. But for every meter they gained the clock ticked and with it the darkness grew.

This was what Chris had been waiting for, as the last of the daylight faded into night he quietly slipped into the gloom like a nocturnal predator and had soon dispatched three of his foe. Yet still they pressed forwards and he was forced to circle back towards the temple. He could hear their heavy breath behind him as he closed the last few yards of darkness between him and the temple steps, turning sharply he fired a burst across the area where he felt they were coming from. He must have clipped one judging on the wail of pain shattering the dark, not that he planned to find out, spinning back round and diving for cover behind the boulder Ollie was using as his sniper position.

'How we doing?' Ollie asked popping up to let off a three round burst, ducking back down as bullets ricocheted off the stone around them.

'We've been in tighter spots. Four down by my count, but there's a good number left. How much ammo you got?'

'Not enough, clip and a half at most. You?' Ollie replied hoping that Chris had an end game.

'Just over two, here take this one. Think it's time to bring out the big gun.' Chris replied drawing the M320 over his shoulder. 'Ready?' Not waiting for an answer as he fired a starburst high into the night sky, it was as if night had just become day and in the sudden brightness and pinpoint accurate fire from Juan, Ollie and Gaz, Norwood's men were sent scuttling back down the mountainside towards the safety of the shadows.

'That's bought us some time, but not a lot else. They'll regroup and no doubt be back.' Chris said as he began to weigh up their options. Now that the element of surprise had long since passed, the odds of success looked very bleak indeed.

Repositioning Gaz and Ollie high up behind himself and Juan to snipe any flanking manoeuvre that Norwood might attempt, they braced themselves for the onslaught. They could hear Norwood's forces moving about in the darkness beneath them but for now it wasn't clear what their plan was.

And then they came, rushing forwards up the mountain. Chris fired a low velocity grenade towards the group coming straight up the middle and as the round exploded he could clearly see what was about to unfold.

'The sneaky fucker's gonna flank us on both sides. We need to move now! Go, I've got you covered.' He shouted to Juan as a group reared up in front of him on the left. And his worst fears were realised, he down another man, dropping the M320 and plunging his combat knife deep into the man's chest. The man dropped as another engaged him. Sweeping the man's leg out from underneath him, Chris was on top of him before the man even knew what'd hit him and was soon lifelessly lying next to his comrade. Snatching up the M320 Chris retreated from his position as bullets streaked passed him from Ollie.

Devan stood on the balcony of the first floor with the Celestial Mistress and watched the events unfold. 'You must help them. Surely you can see they'll be killed without your help.' She pleaded in vain with the woman, the despair at the thought she might lose Chris clearly visible across her face.

'We cannot interfere, I'm sorry but whatever fate is woven into the universe must be allowed to happen.' Chao-Xing bluntly replied, there was no malice in her voice just the conviction that whatever happened was just part of the fabric.

Devan defiantly stared at her. 'How can think this is right, can you not see they are trying to protect you as much as that bloody book?' She screamed at her, knowing that as things stood without the intervention of the sisterhood her companions were unlikely to survive and she racked her brains for anything she could say that would turn the tide.

The flicker of an idea came to mind and she turned back to face the mistress. 'You know you're standing at the flood gates. For centuries you've all been treading water just going with the flow. And while this must have been a pleasant journey thus far without any big storms, you have been able to float on by, but you're now faced with a downpour. If you don't change course there won't be a Way left to follow and all that you've worked for will be destroyed. Didn't one of your great philosophers once say: *We may be floating on Tao, but there is nothing wrong with steering. If Tao is like a river, it is certainly good to know where the rocks are.*'

The Mistress didn't respond immediately but Devan could see that her wheels had begun to turn. Down below the shouts of the guys were clearly audible as they tried to reorganise themselves to tackle Norwood's flanking manoeuvre on the right that had forced Ollie and Gaz from their positions. Suddenly the mistress broke her silence, barking out a string of commands and a handful of the female warriors leapt from their positions on the balcony down onto the open ground below to join the fray.

'Give them cover.' Chris shouted watching one fall as she raced to join the fight. He knew that out in the open the spear wielding maidens would be no match for the automatic weapons of their foe, but if he could give them a change to get close enough those sharp blades of the Yan Yue Daos would be devastatingly effective.

Finally he spotted Norwood and Carla making their way up the steps surrounded by half a dozen men. He fired another grenade high up into the air, but it fell short, exploding a safe distance away from his quarry.

'I'm out.' Ollie shouted as Chris was about to make his way to intercept Norwood, his friend's need was greater and he wheeled away to resupply Ollie with whatever he had left.

'Here take these.' He said tossing Ollie the M320 and the last clip from his Angstadt. 'Light'em up, it's time to take a leaf out of the highlanders' book: hit, run, hide and hit again. No way I'm gonna be the Lucius Paullus to his fucking Hannibal. He can't flank something that keeps moving. I'm after Norwood. You know what to do if it comes to it.' He said with a pensive glance towards the temple.

'Yeah boss, I'll get it done.' Ollie replied watching his friend slip back into the cimmerian shade.

Norwood had been taken by surprise that the Celestial Mistress had chosen a side but it was of little consequence they would die like barren queens along with the rest of them. Even though he had the stronger force he knew that he was pitted against a man who'd conducted successful guerrilla campaigns against forces much larger than his. But after surviving the man's attempt on his life, he now knew his weakness. Flack wouldn't be able to resist another chance to kill him and so he set his trap to draw him out. Using the explosion of the wayward grenade as cover his men had dispersed and the ambush was now ready for the foolhardy man to blindly stumble in.

Sure enough out of the trees to the west the man came and yet to Norwood's great dismay he moved with such speed that he evaded the ambush crashing into Norwood like a thunderbolt. Over and over they tumbled down the mountainside almost reaching the cliff edge as the moonlight burst through the clouds.

High up above Ollie could clearly see Norwood's men racing down towards the two grappling figures through the silvery light, firing everything he had until the flow of bullets dried out. He was about to resort to using his one remaining M320 shell when he heard it. That unmistakable sound of a missile on a collision course streaking through the sky. Only it wasn't a missile, he couldn't quite make out exactly what it was as it burst through the remaining low clouds smashing into part of Norwood's relief force. And then he saw it, just for the briefest of moments. A dark shadowy wing descending through the night's sky blocking out the moonlight between the crossfire, as if the angel of death, Azrael himself had been released to vanquish all those that dared to disturb the serenity of the sacred mountain, before disappearing from view behind the flames of the Switchblade's wreckage that had uncontrollably come to their aid. The only question on his mind now was were they friend or foe? Had the battle that had been raging for most of the evening alerted Chinese forces to their presence or had Norwood in some cruel twist of fate managed to bring in fresh legs?

Striding out of the flames as if it was just another walk in the park came his answer; a tall dark ghostly figure with a familiar gate. The man snapped the neck of one of Norwood's men between his powerful arms in such a fluid manner that he didn't even appear to break his stride. Before drawing a Wakizashi from the scabbard strapped to his back and continued to cleave men's flesh from bone.

'God help them.' Ollie muttered under his breath as he turned away. He'd seen that kind of ferocity only once before from James and he didn't need to be reminded of it.

Both men were heavily bloodied by the time their spill down the slope halted close to a sheer drop and Chris was favouring his right side. He was pretty sure he'd felt a rib or two break on the way down, the adrenaline pumping through his veins was the only thing keeping the pain at bay. Somehow he'd worked Norwood into a choke hold and was gradually crushing the life out of him, but the man slammed his elbow with such force into Chris's already damaged ribs that if they hadn't been broken before they certainly were now and the surge of pain forced him to loose go. He stumbled closer to the edge as the pain subsided only to receive another blow and collapsed to the ground fighting for air. Managing to suck in a lungful he drove upwards wrapping his arms tightly around his opponent and the two continued to tussle against each other scattering stony debris down over the precipice onto the toothlike rocks below. Chris grabbed hold of the medallion around Norwood's neck as the man forced him ever closer to the edge, if he was going over he was gonna make damn sure Norwood was coming too. His foot slipped as he ran out of ground and he tightened his grip preparing to push off, heaving both of them into the abyss with the last of his strength.

The tip of the spinning Wakizashi crashed into Norwood's back, he stared at Chris in disbelief and as he slid across Chris's shoulder he uttered his last words. 'This is just the beginning, my brothers will hunt you down for eternity.' For a second he hung there with only the strength of the medallion's necklace supporting him, and then it snapped and his limp body slipped from view down onto the jagged rocks below.

The blurry sight of the reaper like figure walking towards him, was the last thing Chris saw before he passed out, and he hoped that his fate would come even quicker than Norwood's.

Chapter Thirty-Two: Reunion of Five Clouds

Chris awoke to the bright afternoon sunlight streaming through the hexagonal windows of the temple and raucous laughter echoing through the building. He found that someone had tended to his wounds, now wrapped tight with a linen dressing. Pushing himself up from the bed he gingerly rose and dressed himself as best he could, hindered by the pain and stiffness of his chest and midriff, before seeking out the location of so much merriment.

The stairs leading down to the cool shade in the great hall were the hardest as with every downward step he couldn't help but jolt his tender side, and he was forced to rest halfway to catch his breath. Crossing the room he followed the sounds through the door leading to the terrace of the sunken garden stepping out into the warmth of a late springtime breeze.

'Ah good to see the walking wounded up and about.' Said a familiar voice as James jumped up from a trestle table quickly making his way up the steps to embrace his friend.

'Argh!' Chris exclaimed as he felt the full force of James's warm embrace. 'You're a prick you know that.'

'Sorry bud, apparently pricks are still useful. Well at least her majesty's intelligence service seems to think so anyway.' James replied smiling as he released his grip.

'Maybe next time just don't leave your friends out in the cold for quite so long.' Chris replied.

'If there'd been any other way, you know I would. But you know the drill. Come on let's get you fed, we've got a parchment to unlock.' James said helping Chris down the last few steps to the table where the others were waiting for him.

'What about Norwood?' Chris asked vaguely recalling the events before he passed out the night before.

'He's dead along with the rest of them.' Chris replied.

'And Carla?' Chris asked recalling the moment the sight of her in his scope had caught him by surprise.

'She's gone, she took one look at me and ran. No doubt our paths will cross again. But I'm not going to waste time on a witch hunt.' There was a bittersweetness in James's reply betraying the complexity of his feelings towards the woman he'd once called family. 'Anyway enough about her, she made her bed a long time ago. You remember Josh don't you?' James added as they reached the table.

'Ah so that's who dropped in with you. Hi Josh, nice to see they had the good sense not to let this one run riot by himself at least. Hope he wasn't too much of burden.' Chris said shaking Josh's hand.

'Not at all, he kept me entertained and out of trouble. How are the ribs?' Josh replied.

'Like they were introduced to the All Black's pack, but I'll get over it. You all right fellas.' Chris said turning his attention to the rest of his motley crew. 'I see last night's antics haven't dampened your appetite.' He remarked eyeing the mountain of food on Ollie's plate.

'Nah, you know me boss.' Ollie replied with a grin.

'Where's Devan?' Chris asked suddenly noting her absence.

'Oh she's fine. She's off chatting to the Celestial Mistress somewhere. You know the breed.'

'What women.' Ollie blurted out.

'No, archaeologists fool, put them in an ancient building littered with artefacts and it'll be the last you ever see of them.' James replied laughing. 'I'm surprised you didn't join them professor.'

'I would've but I don't think my nerves have quite recover from yesterday.' Dillon replied.

'Don't worry professor, you'll be right as rain in a few days. This one was a wreck the first time he saw combat.' James said nodding at Gaz. 'Soon passes, we'll get you back to England in due time. And I'm sure these events will turn your book on that scroll into a best seller. Just don't go into too much detail.' James said amicably.

'Don't worry, I own you a great debt, my life in fact. I won't mention any names. To be honest I'm still trying to comprehend everything from yesterday.' Dillon replied. 'Speaking of scrolls I should very much like to be there when you unlock that codex you have all been talking about, if I may?' He added, ever since Lord Norwood had mentioned it he had been intrigued to see it for himself. It seemed almost unfathomable to him that an artefact of such great significance had been lost for such a long time.

'Of course, it would be my pleasure. Although it may not be quite as impressive as you imagine. We would have done it earlier but I didn't think this one would appreciate, after almost falling off a cliff, waking up and discovering we'd already collected it. Not that we can do it without our host anyway.' James replied. 'Ah speak of the devil.' He added as Chao-Xing and Devan returned from their walk around the temple. Devan let out a cry of relieved excitement as she saw Chris was finally up and about and rushed down the steps to embrace him.

'Chao-Xing, I don't want to trouble you but now that everybody is here I'd very much like to call upon you to release the codex.' James said pulling the ornate mother of pearl medallion from his pocket and presenting it to her.

'It is no trouble, we are bound by our oath to the Yellow Emperor that the codex must be freely given to the bearer of the medallion and to assist them with any request that they may make.' She reverently replied.

'Apart from the return of the codex and safe passage back to England or as far as you are able to take us I have but one. That the medallion be delivered to Mr Li at this address, he will ensure it is returned to the Chinese people and given its proper place in your country's rich history.' James replied handing Chao-Xing a piece of paper.

'May I enquire why you do not wish to keep it? After all the medallion chose you.' She asked.

'It has served its purpose, and Mr Li and I came to an understanding. He would use his pull within the party to keep the authorities away from the mountain for a few days and in return an artefact of cultural significance would be reunited with its people. I think it's safe to assume he's upheld his end, so now it's time for me to uphold mine.' He replied.

'Very well, it shall be done.' She said smiling at him. 'If you would all follow me I shall take you to that which you seek.'

At the far end of the great hall they were faced with a large golden Ouroboros surrounding what looked like a pearl without its centre. The Celestial Mistress raised the medallion up placing it into the hole and rotated it a quarter of a turn clockwise. As she did so the tail chasing dragon split in two as the rock face parted sliding back to reveal a sacred chamber inside the mountain.

The room not much larger than a shipping container was much less understated than the rest of the temple, quite simple in fact. Two of the sister's stepped forward into the gloomy room carrying flaming torches placing them into brackets mounted on the rock. And there in a corner of the room was a plain wooden desk covered in a fine layer of centuries of dust. A small key hung above the desk's one and only drawer.

Chao-Xing stepped forward into the room bowing low in respect of the most sacred part of the temple before she rose and unlocked the drawer. Delicately lifting the third part of the codex from it's humble resting place. Although similar in many respects to the other pieces this one was different, there was writing or at least some form of symbolic language on the pages and unlike the others which had just been stitched vellum with no cover to protect it this one had a thick leather cover, well half of one across its back, with an intricately gilded geometric design.

'May the reunion of yin and yang under the five clouds protect and guide you.' She said as she handed the ancient text to James.

'And may this single step be the first in your new journey of a thousand miles. If you are ever in need, you have only to ask.' He replied as he carefully wrapped the piece of the *Liber Veritatis* in a cloth and handed it to Chris.

'I suppose it's time to work our way off this mountain and get back on track before Bradbury starts dispatching the fleet to search for us.' Josh said.

'What, you're not returning home with us?' Chris asked. 'I thought you were done.'

'He's right unfortunately. My agreement with Tom is far from over. I'm sorry but everything has a price.' James replied with a sigh as the mention of home brought back the memories of both his father and Rachel.

'And what am I meant to tell my cousin?' Chris demanded.

'Tell her the truth and that I'm sorry, I'll return as soon as I can. But are you fit to climb back down this mountain?' James asked, noting that Chris's injuries were still giving him grief.

'I think we can help with that.' Chao-Xing interrupted. 'We have a way off this mountain that doesn't require climbing. Can't say that it will be less painful but will be certainly be a lot quicker. Our twins Meifeng and Xifeng will take you and escort you safely out of China.

'We'll take it.' Chris said without even a second thought as to how exactly one could get off the mountain quickly. In his mind anything would be better than hobbling with broken ribs for hours down a mountainside if he didn't absolutely have to.

'You two look strong, come with us. Oh and you can leave your shirts on if you like. We will meet the rest of you outside.' Meifeng said to Ollie and Juan. Ollie turned a deep shade of red not only taken aback by her fluent use of English as it was the first time since they had arrived that they'd heard any of the sisterhood apart from the Celestial Mistress speak in anything other than their native tongue but also because it suddenly dawned on him that they were the two women who'd barred his entrance into the temple the previous evening.

'Yes ma'am, lead the way.' He replied in an attempt to salvage his faux pas as the two young women set off in the direction of one of the closed doors adjacent to the great hall.

While Chris and the others were waiting outside in the fading sun of the evening for Ollie and Juan to appear with whatever the two women had taken them off to fetch Chris received a text from Louis.

Good news, have found the lead I was looking for. Will update you tomorrow. Hope all is well. Louis.

'Sounds like Louis' onto something. Had wondered how he was getting on, been a while since he was in contact but then we've been so caught up with stuff here I rather forgot to keep a tab on him.' Chris said to James showing him the text.

'That sounds promising. Better tell him we're just leaving China and to stay in touch.' James replied.

'You want me to tell him about your resurrection?' Chris asked.

'Probably best not too, it'll only complicate matters. Better to leave things as they are and let him get on with the task at hand.' James replied, knowing it was a bit harsh but in the long run would pay off.

Chris was just sending his reply to Louis as the four appeared outside each laden with black packs. Meifeng dropped hers down in front of Chris, giggling slightly as she did so, as if to say: *well you wanted a quicker way off the mountain.* He just laughed which he immediately regretted as pain surged across his side, the laughter turning into a cough which was even worse.

'They're not what I think they are? Are they?' Devan asked.

'Hell yeah, you didn't think we'd take you on another trip without a parachute jump did you?' Ollie exclaimed. 'Come on, I know you secretly enjoyed the last one.'

'Really…? Just give it here.' She replied grabbing the first one out of his hands.

They were just saying their final farewells to Chao-Xing when one of the youngest ran up.

'Wait!' She shouted. 'I'm coming too.'

'No Chang, you cannot. I forbid it.' Chao-Xing sternly replied.

'Please sister.' She replied before switching into Mandarin to continue the argument with her elder.

'Very well.' Chao-Xing eventually and reluctantly said after what to everybody else had been a rather awkward moment between siblings. 'It appears that my younger sister Chang wishes to aid you in your quest. She has seen something in you that she believes Tao cannot offer her and she wishes to see the world beyond this mountain. I can vouch that she is one of our best warriors, loyal and true. If at times very much a free spirit.' She added with a disapproving sisterly glare at her younger sibling.

'If she changed your mind, I'm sure there is nothing I can say that would deter her. The world is as full of dangers as it has wonders, but so long as she is with us I can promise that we'll look after her and make sure she returns safely when she's ready. Thank you again for all you have done Chao-Xing. I hope our *Ways* will cross again one day.' James replied and without a second glance back he darted forwards and leapt off the cliff into the light swirling mist.

There were tears in her eyes as Chao-Xing watched her baby sister's spiralling paraglider disappear into the mist with the others. 'Farewell little sister, may Tao always find you.' She sighed with one last look out across the valley far below.

Chapter Thirty-Three: The Valley of Lost Souls

Since abandoning Chris and Devan in London, Louis had been on a monumental journey starting with the British museum and the Geological Society, from there he'd travelled to Greece where he'd discovered that although similar stone artefacts had been uncovered in Pella they were not thought to have originated from the kingdom but rather had been sent back to Macedon by Alexander the Great during his campaign into the Indus Valley. So he'd left Greece and flown to Delhi. There he'd met with an old friend from school working for the British High Commission who warned him about the dangers of going in to the area because tensions ran high on the border between India and Pakistan often boiling over into violent skirmishes, nevertheless he had put him in touch with a local guide who could take him up there.

Louis sat in the growing heat of the morning sun outside a small cafe in one of the many bustling streets of New Delhi with a chilled creamy glass of lassi while he waited for his guide to appear. He could certainly see why the yogurt drink was far preferable to coffee in that part of the world. It was only ten o'clock in the morning but the temperature was already edging up towards thirty degrees and he really hoped whatever vehicle they were going to travel in had a robust air con system.

'Good Morning, Sir.' Said a slender woman who had appeared from out of the crowded street.

'Good Morning, Chakrika is it?' Louis replied.

'Yes sir, or Rika for short. I understand from your call that you are looking for a guide to take you up into the Indus Valley.' She said.

'Yes, I'm looking for a Harappan site which has evidence of mining and possibly orchards. Do you know of somewhere that might fit that description?'

'There are a lot of Harappan sites and most of them haven't left a great deal of evidence behind. One would certainly find it difficult to find traces of an orchard as such but as a culture they did have sacred trees, especially the Pipal tree, what you would know as a fig tree. And these would have been grown around or nearby settlements, as for mines or quarries there are a few sites that spring to mind. Dholavira to the west but it's not that close to the Indus River or the main city of Harappa, or there is Kalibangan to the north of Delhi, it is close to the Pakistan boarder and just south of Harappa on the other side which maybe of interest but they're by no means the only two. What we could do is travel to Rakhigarhi, which is the largest Harrapan site, it's around 150 kilometres from here so not too far. And you can talk to the specialists there, they maybe able to point us in the right direction.' She replied.

'That sounds great, lets do that and hopefully they'll point us in the right direction.' He replied.

It took them a while to weave their way through the crazy congestion of Delhi's streets before hitting the open roads, driving through the awe inspiring countryside towards the ruins of Rakhigarhi. Reaching the outskirts in the searing afternoon heat. Had it not been for the prior knowledge of the ancient civilisation Louis could have easily taken the uniform brickwork of the remaining foundations to have been the early stages of modern construction.

'I knew they were a great civilisation but I never realised how advanced they were.' He said.

'Oh yes, they were very skilled, their cities were planned in great detail from covered drains for sewage to grid pattern streets and buildings for social activities, not just dwellings, they really were by our standards quite advanced.' Chakrika replied.

'For such an advanced civilisation they seem to have vanished a little bit like the Maya without a trace. What happened to bring about their downfall?'

'There have been a few theories including war and disease but the evidence now suggests that it was climate change.' She said.

'Really, I thought that was a modern problem.' Louis replied in surprise.

'Oh no, it may not have been caused by human activity like we are seeing today but that is now seen as the root cause. The climate cooled and the rains diminished so much so that the rivers dried up. They were forced to migrate south but the land was less fertile and was unable to support these great cities. And so they spread out into ever smaller communities and eventually the civilisation just disappeared.' She replied.

'That's so sad, but a great lesson for us today.' Louis replied as he admired the remains of the once great city and imagined what the vibrant city would have looked like in all its glory as one of the archaeological team approached them.'

'Its amazing isn't it?' The man said. 'To think that this was once a thriving city and only recently discovered.'

'Yes, its quite remarkable. Chakrika was just telling me about how climate change was responsible for their demise.' Louis replied.

'Yes it is amazing how these things seem to come in cycles.' The man replied. 'Would you be interested in a tour?'

'I would but I'm really here for some information. I'm in India as part of a study on ancient trade routes between the continent and early European cultures. Specifically art, precious metals and semi-precious stones. I understand that the Harappa traded in such things mined from the Indus Valley.' Louis said.

'Indeed they did, especially copper, gold and lead. The mountains such as the Aravalli were a rich source for them. But you will not find so much of that here.' The man replied.

'Yes I understood as much, but I was hoping that someone maybe able to point us in the right direction after all India and even the Indus Valley are not small areas. So local expertise would be much appreciated.'

'I'm certain I can be of assistance, we have maps showing various sites where this type of evidence has been found. But they are still spread out over quite a large area. Are there any other specifics you have that might narrow it further?' The man asked.

Louis paused for a moment unsure how much he really wanted the man to know. In the end he decided that if his search was to be successful he would have to show him the orb. 'Well specifically I'm looking for mining activity for this type of stone.' He said as he took the linen wrapped orb out of his backpack uncovering it to reveal the spherical blue artefact.

'Wow is that blue carnelian, if I'm not mistaken. That's is truly something. Where did you come by it, if you don't mind me asking?' He enquired as he examined the stone.

'It's from a British collection, I managed to trace it to Pella in Greece and from there to the Indus Valley but my knowledge here is vague to say the least.' Louis replied.

'Interesting, carnelian is rare and blue even more so, but there is one place that it might be found. In fact the archaeology has only very recently begun to uncover such finds. It's at a place called Khanak. A team from the university recently discovered beads of carnelian amongst other artefacts underneath a school there. But nothing quite so large as this.'

'That's great, we'll have to go. How far is it from here?' Louis excitedly asked at the news of the recent finds.

'Oh not far, an hour and a half maybe by car. But you may well find that the mines themselves are further north into the Aravalli range themselves, if they can be found.' The man replied.

'Well it's a start and a dam sight closer than we were this morning.' Louis said. 'Thank you so much and I'll make sure I give credit to the team here when I finally publish the paper.' He added hoping that the gesture might avert the man from digging too deeply into his story.

The afternoon was drawing to a close by the time Louis and Chakrika reached Khanak and checked into a hotel for the night, having spent a couple of hours indulging the Indian archaeologist's enthusiasm to give them an in depth tour of Rakhigarhi. They spent a few hours making arrangements to see the site at Khanak the next day and looking at some local maps to see where might be the logical places in the nearby Aravalli mountains to direct their search.

'This looks like a promising area.' Chakrika said pointing at one of the maps. 'There seems to be quite a bit of mining activity there.'

'Yeah but that also means that there might not be much of a trace left of any ancient earthworks. Let's see what we find out tomorrow.' Louis said as he finished the last of his drink. 'Been a long day. I think I'm gonna go grab a wash and then I've got a bit of paperwork to catchup on, so I might not see you again until the morning.' He said.

'Yeah, that's fine. I've got to make some calls anyway, so if I don't see you again tonight, sleep well. See you here about seven for breakfast?' She replied.

'Let's make it seven thirty. I think I could do with the extra half hour.' He replied.

'Yeah okay. See you then.' She replied with a smile as Louis left her.

Louis really was tired after so much travelling and walking around under the baking Indian sun and wanted nothing more than to jump into a relaxing bath and head to bed even if the evening was only just getting started, but before the excitements of the day got the better of him he sent a quick text to Chris to say that he'd found a lead and would update him tomorrow.

Chapter Thirty-Four: Manhunt

Chamberlain was just leaving the yard as Glen continued briefing Stebbings on the case that had lead him to London.

'It's amazing really, had it not been for sheer luck and that storm changing course I doubt we would have ever found that boat. And there's no doubt in my mind it was murder, no way it was an accident. But the guy must have been massive, the bruising on the body indicates the captain was hit with tremendous force and the ligature marks around the neck were made by someone with huge hands.'

'Funny, it may just be coincidence, but I was just visited by a man that loosely fits that description, he was asking about when he would be able to retrieve items he had in that vault that was broken into.'

'What? How long ago was this.' Glen replied startled by the revelation.

'He literally just left as you arrived, I'm surprised you didn't pass him on the stairs. But surely it's just a coincidence, nobody's that brash are they.' She replied.

'I don't believe in coincidences, do you? Check the cameras, I'll see if I can catch him outside.' Glen shouted as he was half way out the door, racing along the corridor and leaping down the stairs. Bursting through the main entrance out onto the street. Catching sight of a giant of a man talking to a cabbie, Glen shouted.

'Hey you stop right there.' The man turned and as soon as their eyes met, events happened so quickly that Glen almost didn't realise what was happening. Chamberlain smashed the cabbie's door window, dragging the man out through the broken glass, reaching through to open the door from the inside and within seconds was tearing off down the street.

'Fuck.' Glen shouted as he scanned the area for anything to pursue his new suspect with. He glimpsed a police biker just about to move off on his motorcycle, immediately running towards it.

'Hey man I need your bike.' He said as he grabbed hold of the handlebar.

'Hey you can't do that.' The rider indignantly replied.

'No time to argue, in pursuit of a suspect. Give me the fucking bike and tell Stebbings to track it.' Glen called out as he shoved the rider off onto the floor, gunning straight down the road after the black cab.

The bike screeched round the corner as Glen nailed the throttle as he tried to catch up to Chamberlain. They raced down the embankment, running a red light. Chamberlain's vehicle almost took out a group of pedestrians starting to cross the road as they tore along the bank of the Thames. Glen could see a build up of traffic ahead, but Chamberlain just mounted the pavement opposite Somerset House crashing through a street stall scattering miniature Big Bens, British bulldogs and other overpriced tourist memorabilia across the road. An *I Love London* T-shirt smacked Glen in his face momentarily obscuring his view. Ripping it away he tossed it over his shoulder just in time to see the mini roundabout in front of him, with no room for manoeuvre he careered straight over the central reservation pulling level with the his quarry as he reached the far side. Chamberlain swerved attempting to knock Glen off the bike, Glen backed off dropping in behind. He couldn't risk an accident and there was no way the bike was going to be able to bring that car to a halt without seriously risking his own life.

Glen pulled back out to get a better view of the road ahead, they were fast approaching Tower Bridge where several roads intersected, if he could get passed the taxi maybe he could force him onto the bridge, hopefully Stebbings would have worked out what was going on by now. He dropped a gear and floored the bike, overtaking the stolen vehicle in a flash. Breaking hard as he reached the crossing he spun the bike to face the on coming traffic. Chamberlain ripped the wheel attempting to avoid crashing head on into the foolhardy detective, overcooking it and smashing straight into the low wall surrounding the bridge.

Glen was forced to wait for a gap in the busy city traffic as he watched the dazed man, shake himself free from the remains of the car, and run off across the bridge. Glen could hear the sirens begin to wail in the distance growing ever closer and knew that it was just a matter of time now before the strings were drawn tight and the net finally closed around the murderer. But he wasn't going to wait for backup to arrive, this man was his. A man that was not only responsible for killing in cold blood but had been indirectly responsible for the death of James Middleton. Something that Glenn too shouldered part of the blame for. At least if he brought the real killer to justice there would be some sort of redemption for him he thought as he reached the far side and dashed down the side of the bridge.

Chamberlain saw the cruiser making it's way up the Thames, realising that the bridge was to be raised he darted into the tower, taking the stairs to the upper walkway. He could hear the heavy footsteps of Glen close behind, echoing through the stairwell as they climbed ever higher. He crashed into a woman entering the top of the tower, throwing her down the flight into Glen's path.

'You okay?' Glen shouted out as he caught her falling body, sidestepping her and continued racing after Chamberlain without waiting for a response. Chamberlain was only a few yards ahead of him as Glen shot out of the tower onto the gantry.

'Hey you, stop. Police!' Glen shouted after him but the man ignored him and continued his way across. *Where's a fucking taser when you need one.* Glen thought as Chamberlain reached the tower on the other side. It had been dawning on Glen that it was one thing to chase the man but how the hell was he going to bring him down, the man was massive and surprisingly quick for his size. He'd taken down guys bigger than himself in the past, but there was bigger and then there was this Goliath of a man. As he reached the stairs leading down an idea came to him and as Chamberlain was just reaching the bottom of a flight Glen launched himself slamming straight into Chamberlain so hard that the man hit the wall with such force, cracking his head open against the hard stone. They both lay on the floor momentarily dazed by the impact, but it wasn't enough to keep the man down and as he staggered to his feet he kicked Glen hard in the ribs while he was down and continued he downward decent, passed the exit out onto the bridge and through a door marked No Entry, Authorised Personnel Only.

Picking himself up Glen followed and soon found himself in the shadow depths of the tower, working his way along the passageways, through more doors, deeper and deeper he descended, right into the very heart of it, to where the huge counterweights lived that were the vital parts for opening the bridge. Chamberlain must have been lying in wait somewhere as he suddenly loomed up from a dark corner and grabbed hold of Glen.

'Think you are gonna best me do you copper? Come on then give it your best shot.' The large man snarled at him as he and Glen tussled, colliding into machinery and walls. Glen grabbed part of Chamberlain's shirt partially tearing it open to reveal the huge man's muscular body covered with intricate geometric tattoos with a clenched gloved fist around a globe encircled by an ancient script, but the only word Glen could clearly make out was 'Vincit'. Chamberlain got a good few shots into Glen's midriff and the policeman stumbled, just about managing to cling on desperately trying to clamp the man's oaken arms to his sides. But Chamberlain was just too powerful and breaking free, hit Glen with such force he was sent sprawling across the ground into some tools left behind by the engineers. Glen grabbed hold of a large pipe wrench that had spilled from a tool box.

'Right you fucker, let's be havin' you.' He shouted baiting the massive man to come at him. Swinging the thing like a club as Chamberlain gamely obliged, he landed one hit but it was if the man was made of stone, the blow just glancing off him without even a flinch. Glen jumped up as the man gripped him again, head butting him in the face and this time Chamberlain did step back and release Glen but it didn't lay him out. He just wiped the steady stream of blood from his nose and laughed.

'That all you got copper. Come on, I'll give you a free shot if you like. In fact why not have two.' The man said taunting Glen, almost dancing on his feet such was his confidence that the detective was no match for him. And Glen knew it, he'd been such a fool why hadn't he just kept his cool and waited for backup. They could have locked down the whole bridge and then just sent in armed response. *Oh well too late for hindsight now. Just gonna have to shoot from the hip. Oh god what I would give for a .44 right about now. Fucking anti-handgun laws, would have dropped this bastard by now in The States.*

'What's the matter copper, do you want me to fetch your mama?' Chamberlain jibed at him.

That was the last straw for Glen he saw red, nobody talked about his mother. He charged at the man catching him off guard, raining a series of quick punches into the man's face. Chamberlain stumbled and dropped to one knee. This was his chance Glen thought, *just don't fucking stop until he stops breathing.*

Glen lurched, the pain was unbearable, like he'd been struck by a wrecking ball, and he fell, with the blood curdling sound of the chain links scraping against each other still ringing in his ears. Blood was pumping from a nasty gash across the side of his skull, and part of his ear had been torn open, he lay there barely conscious.

Chamberlain stood over him as the alarm bells signalling the bridge was about to be raised began blaring through the empty corridors shattering the silence. The man looked at Glen with disgust as if he was a piece of shit on the bottom of his boot. Still holding the huge length of chain in one hand, he took advantage of Glen's powerless body. Grabbing hold of him by the scruff of his neck Chamberlain dragged him towards a pit where the gigantic concrete counterweights dropped into when the bridge was raised. Throwing him down into its base and pinning Glen with the heavy chain.

Glen looked up in desperation for anything he could use to pull himself free but there was nothing, all he could do was watch as the man headed for the exit. Cruellest of all was the last sight of the man before he disappeared from view. As he was about to close the door Chamberlain turned and sneered at him spitting a mouthful of blood onto floor; his lip curled and as the door swung shut entombing Glen in the darkness he caught the man's last words and his hope began to waver. 'Goodbye Detective.'

To be continued…

www.ingramcontent.com/pod-product-compliance
Lightning Source LLC
Chambersburg PA
CBHW032358310726
48973CB00007B/2072

* 9 7 8 1 9 9 9 7 3 8 1 3 6 *